The **Last Overseer**

For more information visit- www.antontroia.com

This book is dedicated to my Uncle Salvatore, my mentor. May he continue to shine on in the afterlife.

Acknowledgements

Thanks to my Pomeranians and Chihuahuas, Lupo, Conan, Sandy and Chewy. They kept me company through the many nights I spent alone writing this book.

Thanks to my family, for their patience and support and inspiring me to continue writing.

And a special thanks to Michelle, my editor, for being as tenacious as a bulldog, never missing a thing, and catching all my brain hiccups.

Keep your eyes on the stars and your feet on the ground.
– Theodore Roosevelt

Table of Contents

1: The Summoning

Nothing could have prepared Major Brennan for such an alarming wake up call, and a phobic look of horror remained etched on his face long after he had hung up the phone. His captain's orders included a terrestrial mission to a planet no one ever wanted to step foot on—and that planet was Earth. The captain gave him very little information on the matter and after some thinking, Brennan concluded that he would probably tend to affairs that local law enforcement was not qualified to handle.

Under normal circumstances, Brennan would have welcomed a return to his home-planet, but the words *"Planet Earth"* were two words that itched the very fabric of his mind. It had been so long since Brennan permitted himself to fear anything that he unwittingly gave it power over him. All the vague, horrific memories of post-apocalyptic Earth morphed into imminent ones, and the many personal horrors he had faced on Earth during the Global Catastrophes of 2033 began to assault his mind—mostly memories of the earthquakes, the radiation sickness, and the sinkhole that claimed the life of his dear wife.

After shaking off his distress, Brennan circumspectly snuck back into his bedroom to grab his uniform and was extra careful not to wake up his twenty- three-year-old daughter Elena who slept on the sofa in the living room. The reality of actually going back to Earth sunk in more and more with each minute that passed and Brennan questioned whether or not he was emotionally stable and mentally equipped for such a mission.

After checking the time, Brennan realized he had almost an hour to report to the briefing room and so he decided to prepare a quick breakfast to help take his mind off the mission. He sifted through all the pre-packaged stuff in his refrigerator, tossing aside all the boxes of In-Vitro meat, including packages of the Trans-ham Petri-sausages, test-tube tuna, tank-steak, laboratory lamb-chops and beaker-bacon. He then reached for a small carton of Sirian chicken eggs and took out three of them. As he prepared his bowl and skillet, Brennan forced himself to whistle a tune as he turned on the steam, that hissed quietly out of the stovetop.

He almost cracked one of the eggs too hard due to his overwrought nerves and he dumped more than a handful of grated goat cheese into the egg mixture due to a lack of attention. He then poured the egg mixture into a skillet and began to cook it but almost left them on the stove too long after drifting off in thought. Luckily, the loud sizzling snapped him out of his daydream. When the egg yolks were firm, he put a dab of sour cream and chives over them, and a sprinkle of cayenne pepper imported from Titan, one of Saturn's moons. He was so preoccupied with his new mission that he failed to notice how pleasing the dish looked.

Instead of digging into his breakfast, Brennan collapsed himself on a posh moon-cow leather recliner in his living room and peered out of the view port window into the void of dark space, losing himself in the infinite mass of cold, vigilant stars. As he stared out into the black void of space, the cold, watchful stars lulled Brennan into daydreaming again. After a little while, he daydreamed for so long that his eggs stiffened up cold and his beer lost most of its carbonation. For many minutes, Brennan tittered nervously in his chair as he continued to daydream and was oblivious to the sight of the gorgeous Eagle Nebula before him. Brennan failed to notice it's beautiful crimson patches billowing in his peripheral vision because mental images took up his sight for the most part. He could not stop thinking about his last day on Earth, when the visitors came to Earth in their gleaming ships. Brennan was one of the lucky survivors chosen to work in the deeper reaches of space for the galactic mining company known as Orion Corporation—and he was grateful for his new life amongst the stars.

Like most of the Earth survivors, he resided in the V.I.P section of the starship Niagra with his daughter Elena for the better part of the last ten Earth years. They were both weighed down by busy work schedules ever since they were scooped up from Earth and cured of their radiation sicknesses and rarely had time to decorate the place. There were just a few sticks of furniture in the entire apartment, not much. The place looked cared for but not owned or lived in. The jurisprudence for working on a starship was demanding, and both of them were hardly ever home at the same time. Brennan and his daughter visited their quarters to sleep, and that was it. The walls in the apartment were bare too, because most of the family photos washed away over a decade ago, when the Atlantic Ocean swallowed up Brennan's home just off the southern edge of Brooklyn, New York. There was nothing in the place to remind him of his old life on Earth, except for the several portraits of his deceased wife in the living room.

After shaking off the tension that came about due to all of his gloomy forebodings, his eyes widened after gazing up at his clock. He had a half hour to report to the meeting and a half hour on the star-ship Niagra is more like twenty minutes of what he used to know as Earth time. Brennan hurried into his bathroom; he turned the hot water knob in his shower and hopped in before the water was even warm. The water moistened his dry lips, and he bathed the drool off the side of his mouth as fast as he could, taking no more than two minutes to wash his entire body.

After the quick shower, Brennan thought it would be a good idea to shave. He didn't want to face his captain looking all scruffy and so he wiped his hand on the steamy mirror so he could stare back and examine his face. He thought his eyes looked glassy and dull. The wars had taken the vitality out of them long ago. Brennan's height was around six feet and despite the general evidence of age on his shoulders, Brennan was still very stout and powerful in proportion. He would be considered handsome if he checked his stubbly beard and trimmed his hair a bit, but he didn't care to do those things anymore. Nevertheless, he was going back to Earth and Brennan felt he should look halfway decent. He grabbed his laser razor to clear his peppered stubble off his tight, gnarled, and battle-worn face. He shaved as quick as he could, causing him to miss a few spots of stubble on his leathery and rosy cheeks.

He noticed the progression of his trembles when the toothbrush tottered in his hand, and even though he had been subjected to trembles after he lost his wife, he realized that they weren't getting any better. After brushing, he plucked some hairs sticking out of his arched nostrils and threw a dab of gel over the few loose fringes of thinning white hair, brushing them over his high forehead. After topping himself off with a splash of tangy aftershave; he rushed to get dressed.

Brennan was so absorbed in thought that he sloppily buttoned his shirt and even forgot to tuck it in his trousers. Before he managed to finish tying his tie, he had already begun to put on his scarlet blazer. It looked like his old Army suit, double breasted, and complete with a white sash. Just as he set himself to leave, his twenty-three-year-old daughter Elena spoke up as she groggily got up from the sofa.

"Where are you going at this hour?" she said in a sleepy voice.

Brennan trotted over to kiss his daughter goodbye, cupping her chin and lifting it so he could kiss her forehead. Elena smiled; her laughing lines were deep; her cheeks were pudgy and they rounded her face even more whenever she smiled.

"I just have a meeting with the Captain," Brennan replied.

Elena's smile did not last long. She sensed the anguish in her father, whenever he had it welled up in his chest, even though his anguish barely ever registered on his face.

"I heard the intercom. It startled me awake, but then you switched over to the portable. So let me guess...another emergency job to disintegrate an asteroid heading for an inhabited planet?"

"Sweetie, look..." Brennan began hotly, "I only know that I'm assigned on a terrestrial mission, and—"

"Oh well that might work for you," Elena interrupted.

Brennan waved her off. His mouth hardened, his face stiffened, and Elena knew something was wrong. No longer smiling, Elena collapsed onto the sofa, parted her disheveled blonde strands of hair away from her eyes, and fixed her father with a curious expression.

"Where are they sending you Dad?" "Earth!" Brennan deplored.

Elena's look of confusion immediately morphed into a horrified look. Her rubicund face had become edgy, and her jaw went slack. The pain of what was lost on Earth seemed to have passed, but after hearing what Brennan had said, she began to double over in her seat as she put a palm over her mouth.

"Going back to Earth?"

Brennan just shook his head; his forehead had become lined and grooved after thinking about the hell he and Elena had endured for almost two whole years: sick from radiation, and calling a FEMA camp home, that is until the first of Orion's gleaming ships hovered over their city. Elena found it hard to find words. Her voice dropped to match her troubled expression.

"Don't worry, I'll be fine." Brennan began in a consoling voice. "The planet is still plagued by radiation, but the people have been cured for a while now, just like us. My implants will keep my DNA from mutating."

"It's not the radiation I'm concerned about dad! I know we're all engineered to withstand it. All space travelers are. It's just...it's just that I wanted us to be done with that planet..."

"I know how much you blame Earth for killing Mom, but, that's Mother Nature for you."

"I can't believe that they are making you...go back to basic detective work again!"

"Oh Elena honey, I can assure you that this mission will not include basic detective work," Brennan said, deadpan. "Besides, I am obliged to help Orion Corp's RAPDA agents whenever possible. Now I don't want to go back, but Earth is still our home and we agreed to help the Orion people after they saved us and took us into their ships."

Without any care for a reply, Brennan moved towards his door with high anticipation and waved his palm over the black biometric scanner so he could leave. However, as soon as the door hissed open, Elena called out to him, and Brennan stopped in the middle of the doorway.

"You don't owe them you know," she said. "You're a former army major and they treat you like some kid out of boot camp for God's sake! You and I; we don't owe these people anything, even though they plucked us from that unstable excuse for a planet!"

Brennan tried to reply but the words died in his mouth because Elena darted off into the bathroom. He knew she was right; his new life in space came with a price. He wasn't anything more than Orion Corp's lickspittle and it began to have repercussions on his family life. Brennan shook off the thought and looked at his watch. After realizing the seriousness of the situation, the tight ball in his stomach loosened up a bit, and he suddenly felt a painful craving to get to that meeting as quickly as possible.

2: The Meeting

The Niagra's corridors felt longer that morning, and Brennan had no idea that rush hour could get so hectic so early in the day. Brennan knifed his way through the crowd of crew members that blocked a good portion of the Niagra's busiest section on Deck 29, where most of the recreational activity took place. He moved along at a fast pace, ignoring the crew members that saluted him, and he occasionally ran into coffles of artificial gravity engineers on his way to the elevator, causing him to take detours. Brennan had become anxious to escape the ubiquitous crowd of the morning rush and could not help jostling his way through the corridors, careful not to knock anyone over.

As he walked towards the far end of the deck's forked corridor, all sounds began to dissolve the closer he moved toward the turbo-lift; a special elevator that is usually reserved for the ship's senior staff members. When he finally arrived, Brennan was elated to find that it was unoccupied. He heard a chirp after a laser shined into his eye. He skipped through a biometric scanner and entered the lift as the two steel doors hissed shut in front of him.

Holding his breath, he counted the floors in his mind as the elevator descended. His eyes continuously flicked upwards to the number above the door every few seconds, counting the decks, and his foot tapped the floor from anxiety. However, counting along did not help his patience one bit; it just made it worse.

When the elevator finally stopped at Deck 9, the doors hissed open to show an empty hall. The silence of Deck 9 eased the throb of his headache a bit, and the stillness was a most welcoming contrast to the busier Deck 29. There was nothing but one room on Deck 9 and that was the consultation room, where most of the Niagra senior staff would meet and discuss their agendas for planetary mining.

When Brennan entered, he was surprised to see only two people in the room. The briefing room was large and rectangular and mostly dominated by a long wooden table, as well as the dozens of chairs placed around its edges. The walls were basic white sheet rock, painted a pastel green and yellow, and the decor was all corporately neat.

One of the people in the room was Captain Bailey himself who was slumped in his chair while staring at playing cards. He sat across Brennan's closest friend, Lieutenant Graham, a fellow Earth human that Brennan had known since his days in the North American Union Army. Graham's superbly muscled Neanderthal of a body looked smaller than usual because he was slouched in his seat, and his concrete slab of a face was as stiff as usual.

They are playing cards? So much for the urgency...

Brennan approached his shipmates slowly, surprised at the lackadaisical behavior being displayed by the captain. Brennan figured that poker should have been the furthest thing from Captain Bailey's mind. After all, he was the one who called for this emergency meeting, and he didn't seem so eager to get it started..

"I'll let you two get to business," Bailey said to Graham as he dropped his cards.

"And that's a bottle of Alpha Centaurian Rye that you owe me," Graham replied in jest, prompting the Captain to give him the finger before turning his head towards Brennan.

"Good morning Major, sorry to bother you at this hour but my alarm went off when the transmission came in and was asked to summon you two agents in particular," Bailey said sullenly, pointing to the phone. Bailey was a stout, bushy eye-browed old man with a slightly curved spine and dark skin and nothing about his job excited him anymore.

"Is that THE phone?" Brennan asked with a furrowed brow. The Captain smiled but his teeth were not showing; the look in his eyes said it all, and he stared at Brennan with a pitying glance.

"Yes, it's that phone, the secure line."

After the confirmation, Brennan knew the mission was serious. Only members of the galactic Table of Twelve call in on the secure line. The Table of Twelve was mostly made up of military men, as well as a few scientists and CEO's who represented some of the largest corporations in the galaxy.

"What's it about?" Brennan asked brusquely, but Captain Bailey shrugged. "All I know is what General Clarkson told me. And that both of you are going back to RAPDA Headquarters back on Earth; the New York City branch to be specific," Bailey replied.

"Why would the General need us there?"

Bailey shrugged. "Apparently you two are supposed to investigate three murders, and that was all the old man told me. The old man seemed rather concerned, and he's been on hold now for ten minutes."

What does General Clarkson want with two measly Earthling engineers and why do we have to investigate any murders, Brennan asked himself.

Bailey then raised his brow. "Well...if you'll excuse me Gentlemen, I have some asteroids to shoot down before we make the trip to Earth." And with that, Bailey turned on his heels and scooted out of the room.

"Should I get the phone?" Graham asked.

"No, it's fine," Brennan said stubbornly. "I'll get it"

Graham didn't seem to mind at all. His thick neck stood craned forward, deep into his game of solitaire.

Brennan immediately focused on the crystal display monitor hovering above the hard black plastic communication console built right into the wall. Brennan activated the call on the console by sliding his fingers over several digital buttons on the thin, clear, crystal pane monitor. A small window then appeared and the console speakers crackled. Brennan anticipated a sharp, cultured voice on the other end of the line, and perhaps even the familiar face of General Clarkson that he saw so many times on the television, but no one seemed to appear on the monitor, and no one seemed to speak.

Brennan cleared his throat, "Brennan speaking."

It took a while for someone to speak; there was nothing but crackling and static coming out of the speaker on the wall. And after thirty seconds he finally heard that familiar sharp cultured voice—

"Major Brennan, this is General Clarkson, Chief of Military Operations for Orion Corp."

Brennan saw no video feed—only audio—and its lack of quality indicated that Clarkson was broadcasting from outside the solar system. He sensed that beneath his benign introduction, there was a warning.

"Good morning, sir," Brennan answered as evenly as possible.

"I'm sorry that I had to drag you out of bed so early in your morning Major and I would have come there myself, but I got my hands full at the moment guarding our freighter ships for the Sirius B run. Now, I'd love to sit here and catch up, but in case you haven't heard, we seem to have a problem on your home planet Earth. I take it that you heard about refugees escaping the FEMA camps who are now pouring into the abandoned red districts?"

Brennan exhaled. "Yes sir, I have heard that there are more people living in the red districts now that the flood water is receding along the coastlines"

"And you heard about the increasing violence taking place in those zones, as well as the recent triple homicide that took place?"

"Yes sir, I have."

"You know that it's the first homicide to take place on Earth since Orion Corporation's starships landed over ten years ago?" Clarkson said with more alacrity.

"Yes sir, I was informed by Captain Bailey."

"Major, I'm not sending you and your lieutenant to Earth just to help find a killer on the loose."

"I had figured that out already sir," Brennan answered, and trying not to sound churlish.

Clarkson then spoke faster, but his voice grew tighter, "Major, our head overseer of planet Earth, Colonel Jasso, will fully debrief you over at RAPDA Headquarters, but I'll give you a concise summary for the time being: the New York police departments were alarmed after discovering the three bodies from that triple homicide. They immediately contacted the chief overseer at our RAPDA agency after they noticed that the victims were more than just mutilated."

"What was wrong with the bodies?"

"The police department initially thought the victims had been dead for at least a week, judging by their appearances. However, after forensics they had learned that the victims died only eight hours prior to discovery. So we sent some of our scientists down to inspect the corpses and they discovered that the victims were severely mutated with stage five radiation sickness."

"How could this be, General?" Brennan answered back readily, no longer containing his emotions. "Weren't the inoculations mandatory for all citizens to protect them from the coronal mass ejections and the radioactive fallout?"

"Yes Major, that became our goal as soon as we detected your unstable sun and magnetosphere. It is the main reason why we landed on your planet after all. We just couldn't watch billions of people die after the earthquakes shifted your poles, hampered your magnetosphere and left you all naked against the sun's solar flares. We implanted *everyone* who survived for protection against solar radiation, including those we took up into space. You and I, along with all space travelers, were treated with DNA stabilizing nanobots in order to protect us from the radiation in space. We treated the Earth people the same way, and so we initially thought a few people might have slipped past us ten years ago."

"But they would have been dead a long time ago, right?" Brennan asked. "Yes, yes," Clarkson chortled. "It's obvious that these victims didn't survive a whole decade without protection. Why—that would be impossible. If you ask me, I'd say that these victims were indeed connected to our network with fully functioning nanobots—and they did show up on our census registry after all.

Therefore, we can only conclude that their cybernetic implants had malfunctioned and have been disconnected for a short amount of time—

probably for well over a year; judging by the nature of the victims' mutations."

Brennan held his gasp in his lungs. "So you mean to tell me that all of their DNA stabilizing nano implants have totally disconnected?"

"Indeed, Major, forensic reports state that every one of those DNA stabilizing nanobots in their blood simply stopped working. Without them, they would have nothing in them to help prevent cellular necrosis, as well as prevent their DNA from mutating from the radioactive fallout. To make matters worse, it was not only the cell repairing implants that have deactivated, but all of them in fact!"

"The GPS implants too?"

"Yes, the GPS implants too, as well as the implants that provide us with important information, such as those that provide us with a citizen profile ID."

"The information bots?"

"Yes, all of them! When the NYPD scanned those bodies, nothing came up—no name, no age, nothing! And so we assume every

bot in their blood has malfunctioned...even the implants that give us each citizen's health information have disconnected, including the bots that relay a citizen's vital signs, impending illnesses, endocrine and hormone levels, states of consciousness, past medical history, criminal records—all of them. It took an old fashioned DNA test for us to ID the murder victims—"

"What caused the implants to deactivate?" Brennan interrupted.

"Not sure, but if anything, the nanobots we administered to Earth survivors are a bit older, that's all. They just might not be next-gen enough. Nevertheless, they should have had longer life spans."

"I hope there aren't others out there..."

"Oh there are many others who are deactivating from our grid," Clarkson began gravely, his cultured voice was deeper and vibrated the speakers. "According to the Overseer's population scan this morning, there are almost two billion people living on Earth. Ninety percent are accounted for. Now—there are 890,223 registered civilians in New York

City. 13,666 of those civilians are no longer showing on our registry. All are completely untraceable and without working implants. Now, one my associates, a man named Doctor Baal who happens to be my fellow colleague on the Table of Twelve, is already on it and he informed me that his neuroscience company will deliver some highly advanced, next generation DNA stabilizing nanobots by week's end. That should give you enough time to round up all thirteen thousand of the disconnected mutated civilians roaming the red districts so we can upgrade them at once; and it will be your primary duty on Earth to get them all before they become rabid and violent."

The announcement sent a shudder down Brennan's spine and tightened his throat. The thoughts of all those poisoned people that died before him attacked his psyche. He too, along with his daughter were sick with radiation poisoning and knew first hand at how horrible it can be. The radiation ate at his nerves, making him edgy and aggressive at times, and the increasing violence taking place in New York City was surely due to the increasing amount of mutations.

"So...that's over thirteen thousand citizens in New York City alone— and I assume that's not counting those who will continue to disconnect each day?" Brennan then asked, trying his best to contain emotion.

"Yes, we expect more people to disconnect all over the world, but hopefully not that many if we act fast and upgrade the people of Earth with better nanobots. You two men are very familiar with Earth's recon satellites, and you know your hometown of New York City better then the Overseer. And so—since we will primarily be looking for disconnected civilians —we're going back to old fashioned eavesdropping using old satellites. The Overseer figured out a way to track people even though they don't have functioning GPS implants inside them. You can go with voice-tracking algorithms for digital spying, as well as resorting to their online footprints, but that is time consuming. According to the Overseer, well...he claims his method is not futile. And it's the only way too."

"Any details on the upgrade process?" Brennan asked.

"It's simple, every citizen of Earth must go for their upgrade by week's end. The vaccines that contain the next generation nanobots will be delivered on the space elevator by the end of the week and will immediately be shipped out to every transgenic clinic in the city as well as every FEMA camp. These implants have been tested in the most radioactive environments, and we must get these people upgraded as fast as possible to prevent more disconnections!"

Clarkson was beginning to sound as if he was rushing his speech, and Brennan could sense the General had more on his mind, and had more to say. There was a long pause after some static. Brennan swallowed his guts after sensing the doubt in the General's words and wondered if there was something else that he wasn't telling him because he sounded way too concerned for a man who seemed to have the problem all solved already.

The speaker on the wall then rattled with a metallic rasp. "Major? Are you there?"

"Yes— sir," Brennan stammered, trying to grope for more words, "What are the rates of civilian disconnections in other parts of the globe?"

"Our people reported the same in other countries but only a handful of cases. Nevertheless, our European ambassadors are also preparing for mass disconnections. However, things are getting out of control in New York—and as I said, there are over 13,000 citizens without functioning nanobots already. Anyway—measures are being taken by the TSA at all airports to prevent any difficulties in tracking people. And so every person that leaves New York City by air will be subjected to the closest scrutiny. And Orion National Guards are placed all along highways to ensure that no disconnected civilian crosses any borders."

Brennan cleared his throat. "I must ask General, the Overseer didn't see this coming? Isn't he supposed to run population scans every month?"

"Oh...who knows with that man!" Clarkson began hotly, "I'm just worried that he might have gotten a little bit of the cabin fever...you know, he's all alone in that building."

"All alone?"

"Yes, alone. He is the only one left in his building and the only one left in charge on the entire planet. As you already may know, he is no longer one of five overseers on your planet. He is the last of the overseers in charge, and other than himself, Orion Corp. has a dozen or so agents stationed throughout Europe that serve as our liaisons. Nevertheless, they all answer to the Overseer, and most of his RAPDA agents had left the company for off world positions several years ago after Orion had successfully refurbished and reactivated your planet's old SDI space defense platform. After the system was setup, the Overseer thought he could handle the job by himself but I am beginning to think he was wrong. The Overseer spent the last six years as the only man behind the curtain, keeping an eye on the population and of course running the planet in general with our supercomputer, Pandora."

"Sounds very automated, but is his job really that difficult?" Brennan scorned.

"I guess he's only got two hands and so many buttons to push," Clarkson began in thought, still trying to convince himself that the Overseer could handle his job. "Other than his eavesdropping on the population, his other tasks include Strategic Space Defense initiatives. He spends most of his time using satellites to knock out any deorbiting space junk re-entering and potentially crashing on Earth. Ever since the magnetosphere weakened, the tiniest meteor could get through it, and so as I said, he has many buttons to push. And on top of all that, his other job pertains to our mining enterprises over at Orion Corp. The Overseer's been using the satellites on the geography, and our modified satellites can send short-pulsed lasers to image beneath the Earth's surface, helping to search for anything like minerals, crude oil reservoirs, and hidden quarries."

"Now that I think about it, I imagine his job is most difficult!" Brennan said, as if provoking Clarkson to disagree in order to get more on his view of the Overseer.

"Difficult only because he makes it difficult," Clarkson replied gallingly. "The real reason he got rid of the other overseers was because he liked the idea of being in full control of everything. And besides that, he's been really distant lately and I fear I have lost him to his bottles of liquor! But I'm more than confident that you and your Lieutenant will help the Overseer fix things over there before word gets out of a zombie apocalypse taking place on Earth again. Orion Corp. stocks would plummet overnight if that were the case. Earth is our most prized possession and we would hate to see Earth civilization fall to antediluvian barbarism again. However, I have plenty of confidence in you two. I know how much you care for your planet Major Brennan, and am aware of your expertise in satellite recon. You and your Lieutenant Graham were war heroes and are both respectable of my guess. I wish you two the best of luck, and I will soon inform your captain to make the jump to Earth in six hours."

"Thanks for the kind words—"

"Oh and one last thing, Major," Clarkson interrupted. "You may find this to be a queer order, but I wanted to let you know that I'd appreciate it if you got in touch with me from time to time regarding the Overseer and his mental faculty."

Brennan stammered, "Why... of course sir." He was taken aback by Clarkson's strange order.

"Let me know about the Overseer's resolve and drinking habits, and keep me posted from time to time of his behavior. He's been ignoring most of my phone calls and he's probably always off to some tavern most of the time, continuing his ill-repute."

"Will do sir," Brennan replied, wanting to ask why, but refrained from doing so.

"That will be all then...good luck and keep in touch!" Clarkson said, and then the line went dead. Brennan turned to face his partner after the call ended. He and Graham looked at each other with expressions of incredulous amazement and both were unable to say anything to anyone for the rest of the morning.

3: The Jump to Earth

The Niagra's bridge was a sharply angled and spacious room, lined up with computing terminals that stood parallel to each other along the deck's entire perimeter. An angular catwalk skirted the second level of the bridge where many silent and busy crewmembers sat behind more terminals. All of them logged in a continuous amount of statistics, production figures, mineral deposit returns, and all the bookkeeping of planetary economic systems. One of the people behind a computing terminal was Captain Bailey himself, who logged in his final report for the day. It was mostly a catalog of stats, as well as several reports regarding the mineral content of the numerous moons the Niagra had scanned along an asteroid belt near planet Gliese.

Then, Bailey tapped a finger on the Comm. panel on his desk and spoke into a microphone—

"Ladies and Gentlemen of the Niagra. This is your Captain speaking. We will be making the jump to Planet Earth in one hour. I want all information techs to hand in your reports in ten minutes! And if you need to get off the ship, make sure you catch a shuttle off of the ship within the next hour; thank you— Captain Bailey out."

Brennan only heard his voice from the loud speakers despite standing so close to Bailey. Captain Bailey then turned to Brennan and gave a curtly nod, "You have an hour of free time to pack your things before we make the jump to Earth. And after I drop you and Graham off, I am to dock with the space elevator port station until some freighter ships arrive with supplies."

"I see..." Brennan trailed off, pausing to think. "But why are we waiting for the supplies?" Brennan asked.

"We're waiting for the upgrades and the Overseer himself ordered me to deliver them as quickly as possible. He said that we have the largest cargo hold in the fleet and there's a lot of medicine being delivered. And so it would save Orion Corp. a lot of time as opposed to waiting for each freighter ship to dock one at a time with the space elevator. It's quicker that way." Bailey shrugged.

Brennan was happy to hear that the Niagra would stay docked with the Central Park space elevator. It made his job a lot easier to know that his daughter would remain within Earth orbit as he embarked on his mission.

Brennan saluted his captain and without further word, Brennan turned on his heels and darted off the bridge, immediately making a beeline towards the part of the ship where the classrooms were located so he could say goodbye to his daughter Elena. Nevertheless, when he got to her classroom, he was surprised to learn that she had left class early. One of the professors in the classroom said that she had a bad stomachache and left class, but when Brennan got to his apartment, it too, was empty. Brennan figured she might have been visiting the ship's nurse, but he had little time to get to the other side of the ship so he decided to call her. After numerous attempts to get in touch with her, he gave up in disgust. Brennan knew that Elena was ducking him because she declined the calls never letting the phone ring more than twice. *Damn stubborn girl. It is not my fault I have to leave her alone all the time. I owe these people my life! And my services!* Brennan thought to himself.

After noticing that his time was short, Brennan decided to leave without saying goodbye and headed straight for the shuttle bay. When he got there, Brennan trained his eyes along the myriad of light channels that snaked along the shuttle hangar, and panned his gaze up and around the shuttle parking platforms to see if Lieutenant Graham had already arrived. There were no signs of Lieutenant Graham anywhere and Brennan figured he was being his tardy old self again. He could smell the hint of ozone in the air, and a thick haze filled the hangar that obscured some of the shuttles parked at the far end of the bay, making it difficult to see anyone in the far distance.

Before checking out at the departure desk, Brennan's mind and body had become paralyzed after seeing the massive star gate just outside one of large windows gracing the edges of the hangar, and after regaining control of his senses, Brennan craned his neck to watch the docking progress unfold.

Quite overcome, Brennan stared out with interest at the sight of the huge circular set of steel girders, and his eyes suddenly became bright with excitement. The large circular gate had two docking pylons on the sides and middle of each side of the circle. In addition to the docks, a port station the size of a large trailer was attached to one of the steel, circular girders, which served as a way station for the ironworkers and engineers. Several of the engineers floated out of a procession of manholes that were located on the roof of the station. Some were already performing space walks, and they looked so small that the sparks from their welding tools made them look like mere fireflies.

The Niagra banked a little bit as it gracefully hovered into the star gate's docking pylons; Brennan could feel the artificial gravity intensify as it always did during a time jump. He felt like he had just gotten out of a swimming pool. He felt heavy. He then felt a faint vibration and a quick jolt from the ship's altitude thrusters that ensured proper heading. He increasingly peered outside, inching up to the window to see how the docking procedure ensued.

He watched the outer wing-like flap of hull bank with grace, as it followed the pulsing lights beaming along the steel docking port. The Niagra slowly drifted into the docking conduits that would secure the ship into place. After hearing a loud echoing clank, Brennan knew the ship was locked into the gate.

Brennan then glanced at a monitor that was perched just above him. It showed a feed from several cameras perched all around the gate and thought it would be cool to see the ship from the outside. He watched the beautiful ship from the camera's perspective and marveled at its beauty, since he rarely got the chance to see the outside of his ship outside of photographs. The Niagra was a huge boomerang-shaped aerial craft and in the "bent" front area, he counted the separate levels, or floors, as you might look at a high-tech, thirty-story hotel.

The levels narrowed back along the trailing ends of the boomerang to what looked like gigantic quartz-crystal shaped tips where the particle accelerators operated. They weren't exactly powerful enough to be weapons. The Niagra was a scout ship and only used the particle accelerators to clear away small asteroids.

Suddenly, Captain Bailey was heard on the PA system—

"Ladies and Gentlemen of the Niagra, we are about to make the jump, please take proper measures to accommodate for any of the lag you might feel."

Brennan didn't bother to sit down. He just hoped the jump was successful on the first try. If so, then the transportation would be instantaneous. In fact, the ship would hardly move at all. Most people would never be conscious that the time jump had ensued. And the nausea that usually followed did not ensue because of a bumpy ride or because of velocity either; nausea usually followed because of a shift in energy.

The only way Brennan would tell if the jump was successful or not would be from the change of scenery that would appear outside one of the ship's windows. Therefore, he kept staring out into space and still didn't feel the nausea and saw nothing change outside. However, he knew the jump was imminent because several of the spacewalkers outside were floating into shuttles and being taken away from the gate. In less than a minute, all the astronauts were in the shuttles and were soon out of sight.

All of a sudden, Brennan saw the view outside get hazy in the corners and he then felt dizzy, as if he had experienced a bout of vertigo. The sensation lasted three seconds or so, and as expected, the view of space outside the window had changed. He was completely unaware of the multi-dimensional folds, which rippled behind the craft just seconds ago and had propelled the Niagra from one solar system to another in the blink of an eye.

Brennan immediately skipped over to the other smaller windows near the ship's coffee stand where the crowds were smaller, and so he could see a bit better. The sight of that familiar blue rock caused more nausea. The acid in his gut spurted up his esophagus after fixing eyes on the European side of Earth. Not all looked right with it he thought, and even from space, he could tell the planet was sick. The coastal regions of the continents were inundated by water and the continental shapes were hardly recognizable to him anymore.

"Shuttle's awl ready for ya Mayjah," said a man in a thick New York accent, snapping Brennan out of his daze. As Brennan walked towards shuttle bay number thirteen, he ignored the few Earth-born engineers that saluted him along the way.

"Ain't nothing like home sweet home," said a well-muscled atmospheric density tester with a southern American accent.

Brennan had no time for conversation. The remote control brick of a shuttle stood in front of him and he could see that someone was inside it from the back window port. The shuttle was a cute little ship, no bigger then an ambulance. It was just as boxy but had a beaky nose and large windshield. When Brennan stepped in, he saw Lieutenant Graham already seated in the captain's chair. His bushy eyebrows were low on his head and immediately flailed his brawny arms after noticing his friend. "About time, where the hell you been, you shacked up?" Graham chortled.

"Nah...far from it..." Brennan waved him off as he set down his small luggage. "I tried getting in touch with my daughter Elena with no result."

"She still hates your guts huh!"

Brennan gave him a crooked stare."Be nice man, I'm stressing over it"

Graham laughed, "I don't blame her for ducking your ass. When was the last time you spent time with her?"

Brennan didn't answer because of the guilt— the guilt of being such a workaholic and having no choice on the matter. He put his two suitcases into one of the several compartments above him and nestled himself into one of the shuttle's large leather recliners next to the main console.

"Now you know why I never got married. People like us shouldn't be family men."

Brennan just ignored him. He would have gotten angry if it were anybody else that said something like that, but Graham was his voice of reason, his friend and confidant, and he was right in a way.

I should have been retired by now, Brennan told himself.

"So, we're going manual, huh? Alright!" Graham said with jollity. Brennan didn't share his enthusiasm, especially after seeing the shuttle's main console.

Multitudes of plastic buttons were completely encrusted in dust due to many months of misuse. Most shuttles flew on autopilot most of the time.

"You just love the high you get from danger," Brennan scowled as he wiped some dust off the console in front of him.

Graham shrugged his broad shoulders. "Yeah, it's no big deal. We trained for weeks in the simulators after all. It is just time consuming. We're going to have to wait for an opening in the shifty ionosphere where it's less dense. It might take us a few hours to get there, or it might take ten minutes."

Brennan then gave Graham a hard stare. "You think Clarkson rushed us into this mission?"

Graham just gave him a quizzical look at first and put his feet up on the chair in front of him to think it over. After noticing Brennan's sudden change of emotion, Graham's nervous eyes began to squirm in his sockets again.

"Rushed?"

Brennan blathered on, "Yeah, I mean, Orion seemed quick to order Captain Bailey to kick all the guests off of the ship when they were due to leave tomorrow anyway."

"Oh, I think Clarkson was right to get us there quickly. There's a few thousand disconnected folk in our old hometown, and I would imagine it would take a week or more to track them down— depending on the rate of disconnections of course."

"I guess," Brennan said meekly, before raising his tone, "But the new upgrades won't be delivered for another three days anyway."

"I guess it might take us some time to round up over 13,000 disconnected mutant citizens. If you ask me, I think you are thinking too much," Graham said reassuringly, patting Brennan on the back with one of his brawny arms.

Brennan shook his head and sat slumped in his seat as he waited for the traffic controller to open the hangar doors. There was a touch of uncertainty in

Brennan's eyes, and after a moment of silence, Brennan couldn't help but persist.

"Lieutenant," Brennan began with grand strictness, "I think there's something else going on; we weren't given the entire picture here."

Graham knew to keep this conversation hushed because Brennan referred to him as Lieutenant. "What do you think it is?" Graham asked.

"Not sure...but General Clarkson was worried about something, I just don't know why."

"So if you're not sure, then don't bother fretting about anything."

"It's as if they are rushing to get everyone upgraded as soon as possible. Radiation sickness doesn't kill you in a day, a week, or a month for that matter. And they're making us fly manual too; why not let us wait a few days until the ionization dissipates?"

"Just relax, we're going back home and it's got you rattled," Graham said reassuringly.

"I saw the bodies Lieutenant!" Brennan snapped back. Graham stopped buckling his seatbelt and froze in his seat after being taken aback by Brennan's weighty words. Brennan's face reddened more with each word, "You know those three murders that just took place? Well, I saw the bodies Lieutenant; I saw them in a newspaper article. They were murdered deep into the red districts. Nobody in their right mind would choose to live in the red districts unless they were sick, mutating castaways. And that means that their murder or murderers must have been mutants as well. Now—if you ask me—no one with radiation sickness would be capable of mauling someone like that.

There was no murder weapon!"

Brennan's tension increased as he powered up his tablet and showed Graham the photos of the crime scene. "Have you read the details?"

Graham shook his head as he craned his neck over the passenger seat that stood between himself and Brennan's pilot chair. "They look pretty messed up," Graham began gravely. "Are you sure Clarkson told you that the killer was unarmed?"

Brennan replied with a nod and then pointed to the headline of a New York City tabloid's website—

"Three armed men with knives, killed by an unarmed man"

The bodies all looked as if a wild animal had attacked them—the throat was ripped out on one body, and the others had caved in faces.

"This is why we need to round up the mutants as soon as possible," Brennan said as he jabbed his finger at his tablet. "I'm beginning to think that there's more to these mutants that we don't know about!"

Graham laughed. "You're spending way too much time watching Earth films in the ship's theater, Major!"

Brennan just looked at him crookedly, shook his head and chewed back his retort.

All of a sudden, the shuttle jerked forward as it rode on the large conveyer belt below that delivered it past the airlock section of the hangar. When it stopped, two large steel airlock doors slid closed behind them, and in turn, the two doors in front of them began to slide open slowly. Sunlight spilled through the doors and onto the deck that reminded the men to put on their sunglasses. When the doors fully opened, the shuttle prepared for its descent onto Earth, which was in full view. At first, there was a dull clank, followed by a series of scratching noises as the clamps released the shuttle from its locking points.

Brennan activated the autopilot and the shuttle's plasma engines hissed instantly. The shuttle hovered upwards and out of the bay in a slow, graceful manner, and Brennan didn't even bother staring at the Earth's African/European side, which was in full view just outside the shuttle's passenger window. Even as the shuttle headed towards Earth, Brennan's eyes remained fixed on the shuttle's controls, eyeing down the odometers, fuel gauges, and telemetry graphs. After fifteen minutes of floating within Earth's orbit, the shuttle's sensors found an opening in the atmosphere that was safe enough to travel through in manual mode. If the autopilot shorted out due to the ionic soup that was everywhere, then the shuttle would have no coordinates to display. Therefore, it was best to go manual right away.

The sensors gave Brennan the coordinates and displayed a path on the central HUD display located in the corner of the shuttle's windshield and all Brennan had to do was move the throttle and follow a digital flying-line on the windshield, all while maintaining a certain speed. Brennan gripped the throttle tightly with one hand, slid his other hand over the console, and hit just one button. "Here we go!" Brennan breathlessly said as the shuttle jerked forward during the de-orbit burn.

The tiny cabin vibrated with power as the shuttle fell slowly from the empty heights of the stratosphere. The descent was turbulent, and the shuttle quivered and rattled when it entered the Earth's atmosphere. The men could hear the nitrogen oxide shooting through the pipes beneath the shuttles panels, cooling the shuttle as it sank through the fiery atmosphere. Brennan cringed after catching a whiff of ozone seeping into the shuttle and so he held his breath. He sensed the temperature in the cockpit rise a bit allowing for a bit of condensation to haze the windows, but Brennan could still see his digital flying line on the HUD display.

Soon enough, the clouds dissipated quickly in front of him, and the shuttle scooted safely under the atmosphere. It was after another twenty minutes of slow descent that Brennan finally decided it was safe enough to hit the autopilot button. The shuttle jerked down like an old elevator and continued to drop like a remote controlled brick. The turbulence began to subside as it headed below cloud level and soon enough the cityscape of New York appeared through the shuttle's front window.

Brennan gasped at the sight before him and at first he smiled at the sight of his old home. From up there it looked like an achievement to him. His hometown was one of the first metropolises of Earth and seeing it again caused the corners of his mouth to pull into a smile. However, as the shuttle flew closer, the smile on his face faded, and the city no longer appeared as marvelous as it did from afar. Many of the buildings were engulfed in lichen and ivy, and the windows in most of the buildings were cracked and broken. Judging by the piles of rubble, the city looked just as it did when he left it a decade ago.

They never cleaned up this mess! Brennan fretted in his mind.

Brennan continued to crane his neck, scratching his head in confusion in order to maintain a view of the cityscape of Manhattan. It reminded him of the total sum of all that he lost, and it was no small thing. What was once a bustling city, rich with gleaming skyscrapers, became reduced to mostly decrepit and neglected real estate. The further he flew east, and towards Long Island, the worse things began to look. Cross sections of streets were indistinguishable and disproportioned concrete valleys. The high view gave Brennan a good perspective of the coastlines as well, and as he stared out towards the horizon, he could see where the Green districts ended and where the red districts began. The scene made him miserable and his heart sank within him, but what he just saw was only but a glimpse of the hell that awaited him.

4: Charlie

The young horse was a spirited little devil, Charlie thought, and it hardly whined at all for eight whole miles. Until recently, the resilient beast had obeyed all of Charlie's commands without any trouble. However, Charlie didn't think the horse would take him past the six mile mark because of the heat. A noticeable amount of languor had possessed the horse's limbs right after the day advanced past noon, and it had become evident to Charlie that this horse had become way too tired to risk pushing further, and so Charlie tugged the horse back to a walk.

Charlie hoped that the thick layer of clouds would continue blotting the sunlight but noticed a few bruises in the overcast sky. He hoped the sun wouldn't burst through them, and not only the horse's sake, but for his. The sun has not been his best friend lately—not since the magnetosphere weakened, but Charlie was well aware that his implants supposedly started malfunctioning.

Charlie had the physique of a pro athlete, standing at 6' 2" and weighing in at a lean 185lbs. He had very little body fat and he worked out daily, but all his strength was sucked out of him the minute the sunlight hit his body.

Charlie was beginning to think he was foolish to forage the red districts for supplies in the daytime; he knew how sensitive he had become to the sun ever since the day he collapsed at his job while working the docks. Nevertheless, he had no choice but to come out in the day because the mutants slept during the day in order to escape the reach of the torturous sunlight. After he was forced to kill three mutant muggers the other night, Charlie realized he would have no choice but to forage in the daytime in order to avoid conflict in what was becoming a very populated red district.

The red districts were becoming a haven for escaped FEMA camp refugees, who like Charlie, had chosen to dwell amidst the concrete canyons rather than living in a FEMA camp. Most of the canyon dwellers were also mutants who could no longer work and keep their worker-class benefits such as an apartment and an automobile that only workers received.

Luckily for Charlie, and the canyon dwellers, animal game had become more abundant in the red districts in recent years, especially healthy animals, which helped entice more and more mutants to escape the FEMA camps and live amongst the dilapidated landscape.

Charlie was one of the first who denied FEMA aid. He enjoyed the freedom of the wasteland but hated the rising crime rates that came with the rising population. Cloudy days were gold to Charlie, but even the cloudiest of days were still hot. Too hot for a disconnected person or even a genetically engineered horse to travel in for more than an hour at the most, and Charlie and his horse have been on the move for six hours.

As he trotted his mare up an inclined street, the horse began to get stubborn. Charlie realized he would have to park his horse somewhere or the poor thing might have a heatstroke just as Charlie did over a year ago. After turning on a main road, he ended up on an avenue that had a gas station on its corner. A huge line of abandoned cars stemmed from it, and stretched all the way down the avenue for what seemed like miles. Charlie thought about taking one of the cars that had keys hanging from its ignition. It was an old 2020 Jeep Wrangler, the last of the electric cars that were banned for reasons unknown.

However, most of the cars were not in running order. Many of them had flat tires or had damaged electrical systems due to the solar storms of 2033. Most of the cars were gasless too, because those who did manage to get their hands on a car over the last decade mainly got their gas from other cars, and so many of the abandoned cars throughout the red districts had empty gas tanks. Besides, Charlie figured cars made too much noise and attracted too much attention for his surreptitious endeavor.

After clacking his way to the old gas station, he was happy to discover that it stood near a withered but enormous garage just past where the main road curved sharply. To Charlie's surprise, he learned that the gas station had since been modified into a horse stop, since no traffic ever came around the area anymore.

It is our lucky day, girl! Charlie shouted in his mind as he patted his horse's neck. Most people in the red districts stole genetically modified horses after using their monthly horse-rental ticket, a benefit for workers and unemployed alike. So many people were stealing and using horses that someone must have used the place as a way station for their travels The station looked desolate and empty, and the gas pumps looked unused for many years, mostly engulfed in shrub and bramble. However, Charlie noticed several fresh horse droppings near a gravelly footpath that headed to what looked like piles of hay, and that indicated that people were close by. Charlie craned his neck a bit to make sure the splintered tub of wood bolted on the garage door was equipped with both rainwater and hay—and they were indeed full of golden wiry hay, and the tub next to it was filled with water.

"Hello?" he called out. "Anyone here?"

No one answered. The place was unoccupied. Nothing but the wind could be heard as it whistled through the broken windows of all the cars.

Charlie dismounted from the horse with his head on a swivel and groped through his duffel bag for his last apple. Instead of eating it himself, he gave the apple to his horse as he tied its reigns to a wooden rail next to the tubs of hay and water. The horse ate the apple greedily and nuzzled Charlie's hand for more before snorting.

"That's the last apple friend, the hay will have to do for now."

Charlie wondered if he would ever see her again. He planned on coming back for her but the horse would surely be stolen by the time he got back. "I'll miss you girl," Charlie told his horse, patting it on the cheek. He then gave the garage shutter a tug and lifted it slowly, trying not to make too much noise. He escorted his good friend into the garage where she would rest in the welcoming shade, and tears began pooling on

Charlie's eyelids. The thought of never seeing her again finally hit him. His affinity for animals had grown ever since he began mutating, especially for his horse, who had served him so well in the last few months while foraging the tortured streets of south Brooklyn, New York.

She was a good mare and a pretty one too. Her coat was a chestnut color and her mane was long and rich. It had the muscular tone of a thoroughbred, although not as massive in scope. Quite a bit of flesh melted off her bones since

Charlie began foraging on a daily basis, but she held up well. Just like the two billion of Earth's surviving citizens, Orion Corp. made sure to put DNA stabilizing implants in the horses as well, horses that they had gathered during the "Great Horse Round-Up" campaign. There were few cars in running order after the catastrophes hit, and the automobile manufacturing economy died along with humanity. It didn't matter though. Many people didn't need cars because the abundance of abandoned real estate made it possible for people to live close to their jobs.

Charlie's horse helped him a great deal, and if it wasn't for her, he would have never have found most of the tools he needed to fix his home, and more importantly, to finish the secret weapon he was working on.

After leaving the gas station, Charlie headed south on an obstinate road that was full of abandoned cars and overgrown thistle. After a mile of walking along that road, Charlie tensed at the sight of sunlight. It began to bathe the street in a blinding white light that glistened off the rusty cars and Charlie cringed after seeing that. The clouds broke even more over time, and Charlie immediately felt its presence as a ray of sun seeped through a bruise in the clouds. Once Charlie felt the sun hit his skin, Charlie knew he was in grave peril.

"Another inaccurate weather forecast!" Charlie boomed aloud, and until now, he plodded along the endless urban desert of crud with ease. Charlie had noticed that the scorching sunlight was not the usual tinge of amber but instead blindingly bright white.

Charlie burrowed frantically in his red duffel bag for his water and he immediately splashed some over his head hoping it would help; it did not.

"Perhaps the clouds will blot it out again," Charlie slurred to himself, flushed and exhausted. "This whole trip is mad."

Nevertheless, he knew that had to do it. The building of his weapon was crucial to his plan. If the hardware store didn't have what he was looking for, his hopes and dreams of finishing his weapon would go down the drain; there were no more hardware stores left to ransack anymore and he needed more tools.

Charlie felt as if he was failing to meet the situation ahead of him and after his knees began buckling, he began to think the risk of encountering muggers was less threatening than traveling during the day. Sometimes his strange, newfound telepathic powers warned him of danger in ample time, but sometimes his powers would wane if he got too tired. Just like the other day when he was mugged. The hot urban desert winds picked up considerably, and the wind felt like the hot breath of a monster that stalked Charlie for hours on end. The sunlight proved to be too torturous for Charlie despite being so low in the sky. It was almost evening, yet the sun was strong. The sun not only zapped him of vitality, but also burned his skin considerably. The back of his neck suffered the most, and he could feel his blood bubbling and boiling in his veins.

To make the trip even more difficult, the sweat poured into his eyes, burning them constantly, and so he clung to a few strands of his long wet hair and tucked them behind his ears before wrapping a white towel over his drenched black hair. He constantly poured water over his stark face, and the water practically steamed off as it trickled down his strong beak of a nose, only to be absorbed by his fierce, unkempt beard.

Charlie gasped a sigh of relief after finding a rather shady block that outlined the sides of several six-story apartment buildings, and so he took his time trudging along Koch Avenue. The buildings were tall enough to block some of the rays emitted by the high sun; Koch Avenue was also the clearest road he'd traveled on thus far, except for the occasional succulent portions where some rare dandelions sprouted in masses through the cracked concrete. Other than weeds, the only obstacles on the road were the charred and rusty carcasses of old abandoned cars and some half-dead, dilapidated, leafless trees, which had fallen down many years ago and were now engulfed by thorny vines. Even the maple trees lined up along the avenue were appalling—sick from the radiation and their leaves looked dry and unhealthy.

As he ventured deep into the red district and closer to the coast, the perished property and decay had become more prominent. The putrid homes that surrounded him stiffened his face into a phobic look of horror, and his lips even quivered as the bad memories battered his mind with horrific images of the past. He thought of the times when his neighbors sifted through the floodwater, waiting for the FEMA helicopters to come. Many people starved to death on the roofs of their homes long before the radiation levels came in substantial increments.

Every structure that survived the quakes and remained standing was now a rotten configuration of its former shape, and he could hardly recognize his old neighborhood anymore. The homes and buildings were indistinguishable from one another, no longer tenanted by people but instead ravens and gulls, in which Charlie could hear cawing loudly from behind many broken windows and abandoned cars. Most of the street signs had toppled over and had been washed away a long time ago. The few street signs that remained standing were chipped and withered and they mostly served as resting places for the birds; Charlie relied on them because he could hardly recognize his old neighborhood anymore. The deeper Charlie traveled towards the outskirts, the more lost he became despite growing up in the neighborhood.

I need a damn compass, Charlie reminded himself.

Lucky for him, one particular rectangle shaped building in the distance caught his attention as it glistened from the hot sun, but it was mostly silhouetted in the sun's glare. Still, its shape was proverbial enough to distinguish from the silhouette alone. The building used to be a hospital, the same hospital he once attended during his senior year in high school when he had broken a wrist in gym class. Charlie then knew he was getting closer to his destination because the hardware store stood on the same street the hospital stood on, and so seeing it invigorated him a bit and put some spring in his steps.

Still, navigating the decrepit landscape was difficult and confusing. The many detours he would take along the way hampered his progress. Every neighborhood Charlie had passed so far was mostly abandoned. There were no people, and only the occasional feral dog, cat, rabbit, or even deer would pop up. Rabbits, raccoons, and squirrels dominated the red districts for the most part, and deer were growing in numbers too. They not only lived in the patches of woodland throughout the suburb but also in many of the homes and abandoned cars. The red districts had become a hunter's playground since Mother Nature swallowed the city, but Charlie spent so much time working on his weapon that he never thought about constructing a bow and arrow. He never considered hunting either. After all, he had no reason to hunt anything until he stopped going back to the FEMA camps for ration boxes. The occasional fishing trip was never included in Charlie's plans and only served as a last resort since the waters were filthy and radioactive.

"If I only had teeth like that guy," Charlie thought, after witnessing a coyote's silhouette scuttling along a ridge near an old firehouse. The streets teemed with plump coyotes the color of ginger and they all seemed to thrive in the city that had morphed into raw nature.

After managing to maintain a steady trot down a shady street, he came across a flatland of scattered rubble, and nothing was around to provide shade. Charlie rolled his shoulder a bit in order to keep the straps of his backpack from sliding off him. The heat made the scuba diving gear in his backpack feel three times heavier than it did moments ago, before the sun came out.

Charlie tried his best to hug the shadowy parts of the streets, and his head was on a swivel for the entire trip. The paranoia and thoughts about being followed by a gang of cannibals had stiffened Charlie's already ascetic face, and he didn't feel like killing anyone again. Charlie's eyes were always wide and nervous, and at times, his eyes looked more like those of a wild animal, instead of a human being. The degree of adrenaline he felt in his blood made his hands tremble a bit, ready to snap at anyone who crossed his path.

Suddenly, the sound of a large branch cracking in the wind caused Charlie to fight a reflex again, but it was only a bird. It was a harmless robin with unusual bright orange feathers on its torso. The bird was one of the healthiest birds Charlie had seen in years; it had a worm in its mouth and after it took notice of Charlie's approach, the robin took off into a tree to sup on his prize. Charlie hit himself for being so fitful, and it was not because he was a coward—oh no, Charlie was no coward. As disgusting as those muggers were the other day, never once did he panic. Charlie stared at their ugly faces with those usual, wolfish eyes of his and never became repelled by their proximity.

The only thing Charlie feared was the Overseer. According to him, the Overseer and his extraterrestrial corporate cronies were invading Earth under the guise of salvation. No one thought of these things except Charlie, and even he didn't know why. All he knew was that the Overseer made his life difficult, difficult for all mutants like Charlie, and Charlie just wanted his apartment back. He was sick of being stuffed into a FEMA camp like a dog, and this very fact filled him with rage and hatred for the Overseer whom he thought was abandoning the Earth humans who were unable to work for his mining corporation. What angered Charlie the most was the fact that the Overseer has ignored the media for years and ignored Charlie's letters as well. And so, Charlie figured that the only way to get the Overseer's attention was to finish the secret weapon he had been working on for the better part of the last year.

Charlie looked at his list for the last time and threw it away. He didn't need the list to remind him of what he needed. He had stared at that list for far too long.

-Allen keys
-Soldering iron

-Nuts/bolts
-Plumber's putty
-AA batteries
-Needle-nose pliers

"This is a task long overdue in its completion and the weapon could only help me thrive in this world made poisonous!" Charlie bawled out, slapping his palm on his thigh

"The Overseer's words are honeyed but false!" he continued to shout aloud, his voice echoed through the concrete canyons. After hearing the echo, Charlie took a deep breath and came to his senses.

I must remember to keep quiet, don't want to kill anybody again. I just don't understand how I killed those men...

Charlie wandered off in his head after thinking of the manner in which he disposed of those muggers the other day. The way he moved was inhuman, he thought.

"What is happening to me," he said under his breath, the words poured from his mouth in a garbled manner. He was too weak to move his lips and speak. He had prided himself on his physical ability for most of his life, but he never would have thought he could kill those muggers with his bare hands. He never thought he could muster the ability to take out three armed men, but whenever his adrenaline leapt in his veins, his strength and rage increased ten-fold.

After a while, Charlie figured that the radiation seemed to unlock something primitive in him. He checked his mirror every minute of the day, hoping his flesh would not decay like most of the refugees who choose to lurk the red districts—and for the most part, it didn't. Besides his pallor and light sensitivity, he didn't feel or look sick at all.

Charlie not only transformed physically but even his personality changed, and he scared himself at times. His calm demeanor and easygoing attitude morphed into a brash, volatile and opinionated one, and his cordial smile was never to be seen again. He even became incapable of small talk.

What am I becoming! Charlie told himself, while holding up his two hands, and rotating them around his eyes. The skin on his hands was blotchy, cracked, and flaking mainly because they were dried out from the UV rays; he prayed that he didn't have the skin cancer like most mutants had.

Even though his body was holding up better than most disconnected mutants' were, he had no idea that he was transforming into something much more monstrous.

5: The Overseer's Greet

Brennan felt a surge of heat enter the shuttle after the gull wing door opened, and the first thing he saw was the spaceport tourist center just several hundred feet away from the landing pad. Brennan took some time to look up and stare at the surroundings and then turned to the expansive dome to his left, which served as the spaceport's main terminal. Neon lights graced every inch of its framework; the entire place was mirror paned and reflective and a beautiful contrast to the rest of the city.

The dome was surrounded by attractively landscaped areas of perfect grass and neatly trimmed sycamores— all planted equidistantly and along the dome's edge. The dome-shaped building wasn't enough to dispel the gloom that lay upon his face after witnessing the decaying New York City skyline, but after he took his first step outside, Brennan became smitten by the several trees surrounding the port. Even though the leaves were sun-scorched and dry, they looked nevertheless pretty. Anything organic seemed pretty to him again.

Brennan didn't remember the space port looking like that before. The port went undamaged during the catastrophes, but Orion Corp. renovated the place anyway.

"*Space Operations*" was inscribed on a neon sign above two large glass doors.

Brennan stretched his whole body and took in a lungful of oxygen-deprived air. As he lifted his luggage and took a step away from the shuttle, a wave of giddiness washed over him for a second or two and he noticed his breaths were a bit labored. The air had thinned so much in the last decade and he had to take longer breaths to compensate. Nevertheless, the natural breezy air was still sweet, and the sound of singing birds was refreshing to Brennan's ears. There seemed to be a gladness all around him, and Brennan took off his shades to get a better glimpse of it all. After taking them off, his eyes stung and watered up instantly, so he put the sunglasses back on immediately. The sunlight was unusually bright white in tinge rather than golden amber, and at first, Brennan thought it was because he just wasn't used to seeing a star with his own eyes anymore, at least not without a tinted window in front of his face all the time.

After steadying his legs, Brennan began to take notice of how heavy he felt. It brought him to contemplate whether the artificial gravity on the Niagra might have been a tad off, and he then remembered that must not be the case because he weighed 195 pounds on the Niagra and that had been his weight since his college years.

"The gravity changed," Brennan shouted out towards Graham, who was still removing all of his luggage inside the shuttle. "Get out here and let me know if the gravity on the planet is off or it's just me," Brennan said.

Graham poked his goofy head out of the shuttle's gull-wing door and groaned, "I got to get my luggage first."

Brennan rolled his eyes. "I told you to travel light!"

Brennan traveled light to convince himself that the mission would end in a week at the most. Graham did the opposite.

"Let's get the party started!" Graham shouted through a smile while stacking his luggage like dominos. Brennan ignored him. He was too busy studying the environment and had become enervated by his surroundings— speechless even. The last time he was on a planet was a year ago, but that was a waterless desert moon.

*I forgot what clouds look like...*Brennan realized.

Brennan had little time to enjoy the bright blue sky because some light footsteps were heard coming from one of the old runways that circumvented the landing pad. A grim and callous looking escort with dark shades and a black suit approached and greeted them.

"Good day, gentlemen," the escort said with a sharp but cultured voice, his grin was brief and looked out of place amongst his craggy features.

"Good afternoon," Brennan and Graham both replied as they snapped their gazes towards his direction.

"And welcome to Earth," said the escort. He looked younger than he was, his hair was clearly dyed black, as was his mustache, and his wrinkles suggested he was over sixty years old.

"The Overseer just informed me that you may choose to head to your hotel first to freshen up a bit," the escort said through a corporate smile.

Brennan considered a moment. "No, that's okay," he replied.

The escort gave a curtly nod. "Very well sir," he replied through a modest smile and motioned the men to follow with a wave of his arm. "Just this way, gentlemen, your car will arrive shortly."

"Shouldn't we be expecting a helicopter?" Graham asked the escort with a grin. Brennan nudged Graham on the shoulder and gave him a crooked look because he was asking for too much.

The escort looked startled from the question. "Impossible," he said in a thick Liverpool accent, shaking his head in disgust. "It seems as if the solar flares are increasing in intensity—and the occasional EMP disturbances are shorting out the jet engines. We just lost another 747 yesterday after it fell into the unpopulated city of Barcelona, Spain."

"Oh thank heavens it fell in one of the unpopulated cities," Graham was quick to reply.

Brennan fixed the escort with a troubled stare. "Is the Overseer taking measures to fix the problem?"

"I hope so, but he rarely makes any public appearances anymore and so I don't know what he's going to do about it. All I know is that it was the third 747 that went down this week, and the Overseer told me that he was thinking about canceling air travel all together. After all, only the corporate bigwigs and space visitors use airliners anymore."

"That's not really a solution," Brennan started with squinted eyes. "There goes the economy," Graham chimed in.

"Or what's left of it," the escort began under his breath. "What's really hurting the economy is the fact that the people are getting sick again and the government channel just broke the news yesterday. However, there still hasn't been any word from the Overseer ..." The escort trailed off and changed the subject after noticing the limousine making its way from one of the runways behind the dome. "Ahh...there's your car now."

It was blurry looking from the vapor distortion rising from the road, and it left a trail of gravel dust behind it. When the car pulled up to them, Brennan and Graham were surprised to hear the escort say goodbye. "Well that will be all gentlemen. Good luck on your mission," he said as he began walking back towards the landing pad.

"Who will be driving us?" Brennan asked.

"It's automated," the escort said without even turning to face them.

They both knew then that the ride would be longer than it should have been if a human was driving and it only added to their heightened anticipation.

When they got into the car, Brennan thought about napping a bit, but he couldn't resist soaking in some of the sights. The auto-drive gunned the limo onto the Brooklyn/Queens expressway and maintained a speed limit of fifty-five mph. Brennan became enthralled by the urban decay all around him. He was quite annoyed at the fact that very little rubble was cleaned up—and he felt as if he never left his city despite being gone for a decade.

Other than the high tide, the city looked just as Brennan left it, except that there was more foliage growing in and around all of the various factories in downtown Brooklyn. Even the Brooklyn Bridge looked dilapidated and engulfed in lichen, since no one used it anymore. The Brooklyn Bridge was damaged during the very first earthquake that took place during those awful first few months when the earthquakes came in threes. It was structurally unsound and too damaged to travel on and the new bridge beside it was the only good thing the Overseer had done for the city since he arrived, but it was defunct of any architectural charm. The new bridge looked more like a long stretch of straight highway that crossed the East River than a real bridge.

"Damn Overseer still didn't fix the Brooklyn Bridge?" Brennan muttered.

Graham shook his head. Both of them never took their eyes off it and panned their gazes out of the window as the car drove past the bridge.

After getting off the one exit at the end of the bridge, the tires scrunched over some rugged gravelly streets for about three miles, where the most neglected real estate stood. The only traffic in the streets came from the line of abandoned cars still stuck in the gridlock of ten years ago, and the occasional cluster of horses would gallop past every now and then topped with evening commuters.

The limo zigzagged through a tangle of rusted cars until it crossed Lexington Avenue, and then they finally came across some moving traffic. The traffic consisted of several flatbed trucks, which hauled hoards of dead bodies to makeshift crematoriums.

"Damn, a lot of people are dying," Brennan said in a hushed whisper. After the limo turned onto East 33rd street, it moved towards the middle of

Manhattan Island and away from the damaged coastlines. The tarmac smoothed out, pedestrians grew in number, and the buildings had less of a slovenly appearance. After a quick turn on Broadway, the RAPDA building was seen glistening between some other skyscrapers. The building was the only one on the entire block without any ivy budding all over it, and all of its windows were intact.

However, before the car managed to get as close as two blocks away from headquarters, the limo began to slow after it had sensed a laser nearby, which relayed a signal to the limo's engine and it shut it down. The car automatically slowed to a halt just before a military checkpoint. Two squarely built Earthmen in urban camouflage approached the limo, holding what seemed to be National Guard standard-issue disruptor rifles. The passenger side window rolled down automatically and one of the soldiers hunched over to peek inside.

"G'day Major, g'day Lieutenant..." the squarely built soldier saluted them. "We've been expecting you—and it's a pleasure to serve with you both."

"Likewise," Brennan saluted back.

"The Overseer is waiting for you in the parking garage just ahead," said the soldier and gave a salute again. "Remember to call him Colonel Jasso; he hates being called the Overseer."

Brennan smirked and nodded.

The limo automatically sped away before gracefully turning into an underground parking garage just under the building and coming to a halt after pulling into one of the white-striped parking squares on the floor. The limo's radio sputtered and popped. "We have arrived," said a mechanical female voice.

After emerging from the car, Brennan noticed a burly man with a billowing cape was standing alone near the elevators at the far end of the garage. There were no cars around them except their limo and one other minivan, and so there were probably no other people in the building except for the Overseer.

Brennan leaned into Graham's face, "Is that Colonel Jasso, the Overseer?" Graham just shrugged his shoulders.

That has to be the Overseer, Brennan figured. It was the cigar that gave him away; Colonel Jasso always had a thick cigar stood tucked in the corner of his mouth, even if unlit. He liked chewing on them and it was rather vulgar for a Draconian human to smoke, but Jasso lived on Earth for so long that he was as American as anyone.

Jasso's thick arm waved at them to hurry up, as he was beckoning them from afar but didn't say anything. As Brennan inched closer, he could tell that Jasso put on a few pounds despite being so elaborately wrapped in his scarlet Draconian military suit. His wrought leather trappings were ingeniously set in and around his ribbons and medals. His short scarlet cape was made with silk, and it flowed and snapped taut in the winds. Jasso had the most intense close- set, icy blue eyes and they stood deep under his Olympian brow. Like most Draconians, he had an aquiline nose that was set low on his face, and pallid, strained cheeks. His glossy silver thinning hair was parted on the right side of his scalp, and a full beard covered the knobby chin that completed his oval face.

"Welcome to hell," Jasso said petulantly, his voice was a rich baritone. His jaw gnawed continuously at his unlit cigar and he seemed overly cheery.

"It's so nice to see you again, Mr. Overseer," Brennan said.

"And nice to see you!" Jasso replied, while awkwardly hugging them both. A rank stench of alcohol breath seeped out of Jasso's mouth, "Please, call me

Colonel, or better yet, Jasso will do! After all, we're all soldiers fighting the same battle now; I don't want you men sounding like such proper courtiers!" Jasso grinned with the cigar still sloshing in his mouth. "Last thing I want is people kneeling in front of me! You know, we Draconians are treated like Gods sometimes, it's all too obsequious and uncomforting!"

Brennan forced a laugh.

"So let us get onto business shall we?" Jasso beckoned the men to follow him into the parking garage elevator with a wave of his arm.

Jasso always had this twitchiness about him, but Brennan just thought his overall appearance was far too unkempt for a Draconian soldier. His hair was whiter than Brennan had remembered it, and the unchecked beard stood fierce and bushy on his gnarled face. What was strange to Brennan was that all Draconians remember to shave, even those not in the military.

I now understand now why Clarkson was worried, Brennan realized.

6: Orientation

Brennan hardly recognized the building's lobby anymore. The same enormous marble pillars that graced the lobby were no longer shiny, and the painted mosaics that lined the ceilings were also robbed of their gloss. There seemed to be nothing but the manifold signs of immemorial years written all over the place. What depressed Brennan even more was the smell. The lobby was filled with the miasmic stench of Jasso's cigar smoke mixed with murky air.

Both Brennan and Graham had little time to scan the place because Jasso walked with hurried steps, and a rustle of anticipation gave Brennan hot flashes as he walked away from the elevator doors and through the spacious lobby.

"We got a planet to save gentlemen!" Jasso said through a closed mouth, continuously gnawing at his cigar. "Would a couple of soldiers like yourselves ever think you'd be in charge of saving the world?" Jasso continued.

"Well...we fought in the drone wars thinking we were doing exactly that," Brennan replied.

Graham followed with a curt nod.

Jasso lapsed into a sort of psychopathic giggle. "Oh there's a place for you both in heaven my dear boys. You are both very good boys."

Brennan and Graham exchanged bamboozled glances as they trailed the Overseer, and Graham twirled his index finger next to his temple to indicate that Jasso was a bit off kilter. Both of them began wondering if Jasso hadn't developed a case of cabin fever due to his overly queer and sanguine temperament—which was very unsettling. Brennan felt things were far too serious to deal with the small, inane banter that had come out of Jasso's mouth for the past ten minutes so he changed the subject and spoke what was on his mind.

"Colonel, if I may—why are only some disconnecting and not all people at once?"

"Oh we expect this to affect everyone if we don't get the new technology in them soon, but I guess my answer to your question would be that some people are just more conductive than others."

"Do you know why the implants are failing in so many people?" Graham chimed in.

"Well—to make a long story short, the shifting of the North and South Poles are not only affecting Earth, but affecting the consciousness of mankind. And now whenever there is a shift in consciousness, the body begins to change as well. The waves of geomagnetic flux are essentially changing the vibratory nature of a person—therefore, mutating their DNA too quickly for the DNA protection to commence. The nanobots simply can't keep up and compensate correctly because the cellular necrosis just happens so fast," Jasso paused, and then he continued with downcast eyes and a bit more fire in his voice, "those murders were a wake up call! I should have realized people were disconnecting when unemployment statistics began rising. I should have known! I should have known!" Jasso scowled shamefully, with his head down.

Then without warning, Jasso came to a halt and faced one of the marble walls in the lobby before touching it.

"I deduce that you both remember our secret elevator?"

"Of course," Brennan and Graham replied in unison. The men walked several inches in front of a wall. Jasso pressed a hand on the huge slab of marble and a beam seemed to scan downwards from a sensor on the ceiling. A tiny chirp was heard, and a rectangular section of the marble began sliding inwards, and eventually to the right revealing a small void inside. Jasso ducked and vanished into the chasm and towards the secret elevator lift inside the wall. Brennan and Graham followed him with mounting astonishment, stepping onto a shaky steel platform once they got inside. Jasso hit one of two buttons and the lift thrummed to life, immediately jerking downwards, slowly descending down into cavernous bowels of the building.

The cagey turbo lift took a slanted direction, and Jasso hardly spoke for an entire minute, which happened to be his longest bout of silence since he met the men. Brennan studied Jasso carefully and noticed that whenever he did speak, he sounded sanguineous—and when he was quiet, he always looked unusually taciturn and always preoccupied by some absorbing thought.

The ride was slow, and the silence only made Brennan and Graham even more nervous. Brennan forgot how deep RAPDA's basement was. He knew the place well; after all, he worked in the building when it was being run by the NSA—way before it became an alien-controlled RAPDA agency. Brennan swiped a thin tuft of hair away from his eyes as he stared down into the abyss. There was nothing but darkness below, and only the tiny neon lights gracing the bare rock all around them gave off light. The rocky walls on both of their sides were jagged and stunk of dank Earth, and it wasn't until the chasm got a bit wider that a brilliant light began to stream upwards from the abyss. However, their destination was still far beyond what the eyes could see.

During the three-minute ride, the men exchanged basic political gossip but Jasso never mentioned anything regarding the mission to cure New York's mutant citizens. When they finally reached the bottom, Brennan's nerves reset and cooled after recognizing the familiar cave.

A sign near the lift said—*"Satellite control center ahead"*

Jasso yanked the gate to the turbo lift open and scampered out.

"This way," Jasso said blankly as he stepped off the turbo lift and into a long rocky corridor. Jasso felt very much the emperor of all he surveyed; he regarded his setting with an imperial eye and moved ahead dutifully.

Brennan noticed some dusty doors lined up alongside the corridor that looked like they hadn't been opened in years. The long neglect had made the air stagnant and fetid, and Brennan fought the urge to hold his nose. He was a hard man, Brennan was, but when it came to mold and thick air, he had a hard time with it. The whole corridor was deep with dust, almost inches deep in some spots.

When the men arrived at a door at the end of the corridor, Brennan knew that the room on the other side of it was traversed frequently because there was no dust around the doorknob. After they proceeded through the clean door, Brennan soon found himself in a huge room surrounded by nothing but jagged limestone walls. The expansiveness of the room astounded Brennan, and he realized that RAPDA had gotten a significant amount of funding and renovation since he left for the Niagra. The primitive look of the cave mixed with the technological advances made the entire place look like one big mechanistic nightmare.

Brennan gave Graham a sideways glance. "Looks like they tricked the place out since we left it," Brennan whispered. Graham almost seemed deaf to his words. His head just swiveled around, and his jaw was so loose Brennan could see his tonsils. Brennan pulled himself up and straightened his posture as he panned his gaze along the room, and he was baffled by how much the place changed. Stainless steel shelves lined the walls—all the way up to the ceiling. The lights fell on all sorts of odd-looking forms that were on the shelves and Brennan couldn't tell what the inexplicable gadgetry was.

In other spots of the cave, it was damp and hollow and there was nothing but signs of decrepitude all over the entire span of the large cavernous room.

Besides, a thin haze everywhere robbed even the nearest objects in the room of perspicuity. The volume of Brennan's anxiety rose a few notches because it was hard to believe such an alien place existed under a New York City street. As they walked closer to the satellite control center, the lighting increased and the shabbiness diminished. The bare-rock walls were covered and beautifully garlanded with mosaic tiles and large mural paintings of the Hedonic type; Brennan only wished he had time to stare at the artwork. However, Jasso kept trudging on and he had to keep up with him.

"This way, gentlemen," Jasso said in a solid tone, glaring at Brennan resolutely. Jasso led the men to another door. It was normal sized, like any you would see at the entrance of any apartment. Jasso walked through the first; his shape vanished instantly into the darkened room causing Brennan and Graham to stammer before entering. They figured that they would wait for Jasso to put on the lights because the men did not recognize the place anymore to walk in; it was too dark. When the lights flicked on, Brennan and Graham entered and looked nervously around the room.

The room was absolutely jaw dropping in size and scope, and Brennan knew the architects who built and designed such a wondrous room were definitely alien, having nothing in common with the Earth folk who had originally used the underground facility when it served as an underground base for the NSA.

Jasso walked ahead with the most ostentatious steps, and he chuckled whenever staring at the faces of the men. The walls around them were clad with mosaic tiles like the previous room, and the occasional feeble lighting that emanated from iridescent light bulbs glinted off the tarnished brass pipes that snaked along the walls. Brennan could tell that Jasso spent quite a bit of time in that room even though spider webs hung from everything and every corner.

There were a dozen slimy, sludgy cigar butts all over the steel plated floors, and along with the cigar butts, there were torn up paper coffee cups, plastic forks, and napkins littered over the ground. Brennan wondered why Jasso didn't use garbage receptacles, but after staring at one, he knew why. He figured that the cleaning people didn't visit the place as often as they used to because the thing was full to the brim. The science stations were covered in spider webs, the desks and computers were all covered in dusty tarp wrapping, and fetid fluids dripped onto them from the pipes above leaving circles of sludgy dust in many areas.

"This was where the scientists initially studied the sick," Brennan whispered over to Graham, who nodded vigorously. "I remember all the scientists that wriggled about this place, engineering the molecular medicine, working sixteen hour shifts with the tridithalifane for the nanobot's microprocessors," Graham recalled.

Jasso didn't hear them; he was a few steps ahead, walking in vast, flying strides, occasionally playing his fingers across his silver hair in half-conscious, nervous swipes. Jasso's boots made an endless scraping whisper on the rocky floor, sporadically crushing a paper cup or smashing a cigar butt flat, and he walked as if he was in a rush.

"This way, gentlemen," Jasso said without even turning around. He violently pulled at his cigar, and the fiery tobacco helped light the way as they walked through the darker parts of the place. After climbing a steep spiral staircase that led to a catwalk, Brennan felt a sharp pain coming from his left hip joint again. He ascended more steps then he cared to climb, and for a war-scarred major with a replaced hip, the climb was an ordeal. After a minute of climbing, he found himself on a catwalk where large spiders dominated the spaces between the metal. Brennan had no idea where he was going; it was dark and the scattered lamps that lined the catwalk weren't strong enough to cut through the darkness that ensued whenever the three men walked away from each bulb s individual radius.

In the silence that followed, Brennan couldn't help but ask the question, "Colonel, how do you maintain decorum while working in this entire skyscraper alone?" The way he stared at Jasso suggested he left a maddening impression in him.

Jasso took a violent drag from his cigar. "It was tough at first, but after the first whole year alone, I've become inured to the peculiar effects of solitude," he said haughtily and paused to take another puff of tobacco.

"I'm sure it could be maddening at times," Graham said, as he trailed behind not only Jasso but Brennan too.

Jasso snorted his disdain. "The job is tedious and exasperating, but I have indiscernibly grown to grasp it. My patience has grown to meet the job's limitations, and I think I did a pretty damn good job on this planet!"

The men were taken aback by the sharpness in his tone.

"I did not mean to imply that you weren't," Brennan began. "It's just that being alone everyday could do something to a man."

Jasso chuckled, his cheerful attitude returned, and Brennan thought he might have been trying best to hide his true feelings. "I love the peace and quiet," Jasso bellowed, stroking his wooly beard. "Unfortunately, it only takes one man to helm our supercomputer and someone's got to be the guy to sit in this cave all day long, by himself, doing what's necessary to keep Earth from falling into barbaric degeneracy..." Jasso trailed off, seemingly aggrieved.

"So do you get out much Colonel?" Brennan asked, but Jasso didn't reply right away.

Instead, he relapsed into those psychopathic giggles of his. "No way would you ever see me out there in that concrete jungle," Jasso began under his own breath with a grudging voice. "It's been a while since I been to a restaurant or a ballgame. Whenever I used to go, I'd find myself eating radioactive food and watching ballplayers play without the skill that the old players used to have.

Besides—you haven't seen a football game unless you've seen one in my hometown of Thurnax, on planet Alpha-Draconis B... now those Draconians could really run."

Brennan thought it was best not to ask any more questions after hearing such demoralizing frankness, which was very irritating to the ears of the two Earthmen. Also Jasso acted in a way that suggested he didn't feel like talking much and seemed to be more interested in his own thoughts.

"I'd love to catch up and chit chat, but let's turn our thoughts to more pressing matters," Jasso said with solemnity in his voice. The sense of urgency had suddenly become clear and so he quickened his pace down the catwalk, towards another door. However, this door was different. It was a thick, glistening slab of solid steel with a rotating handle like a bank vault.

Jasso put his hand over a slab of plastic near a biometric scanner that was mounted the side of the door and the huge door lock clunked open. A sudden wind rushed past Brennan as soon as he entered the room, causing him to gag. The odor inside the room smelled worse than in any of the rooms he smelled before, including the lobby and where the science stations were. It was a faint but malodorous air, musky and earthly, and it made Brennan cough repeatedly.

Jasso laughed madly. "The air circulators went out a few weeks ago and so the oxygen levels might still be a tad low in here." He laughed harder whenever Brennan coughed. Brennan eyed him with a resentful stare and the thick miasma became worse as he walked towards the computer on the far end of the room.

The repulsive smell was a mix between the acrid fumes of heated plastic and the scent of alcohol and tobacco. Every breath exhaled by the slobbering Overseer seemed to cling to every wall and both Brennan and Graham tucked their noses in their palms, trying not to breathe.

Loud ceiling exhaust fans whooshed above on the rocky, twenty-foot ceiling but hardly did much to circulate the air; there wasn't any air to circulate. A dim glow came from the hundreds of LED's that graced the many RAM stations lined up along both sides of the room, but none of them gave off much light.

Pandora, the supercomputer thrummed quietly on one side of the room. It was massive; its servers were almost as large as the main console itself.

Lieutenant Graham stood wide-eyed at the computer's sheer scope and size.

He instantly skipped over to one of the chairs near the supercomputer's main console and plopped into the seat, rubbing his two flat palms together. He stood hunched in front of a huge screen's phosphorescent glow and erupted in a chuckle as he spun his rotating chair like a little boy with a new toy.

Brennan, however, didn't share his excitement. He walked around the place in a profound and lethargic reluctance, not so much because of an aching hip joint but because he was sick from the odor and wanted to get on with the orientation already.

Brennan tried to breathe as lightly as possible. "This computer's design must have revolutionized satellite based weaponry!"

"In a sense—yes," Jasso laughed. "We could now control up to three dozen satellites at the same time, as well as all 2,300 spy drones currently in service— including the drones and satellites from the old Russian and Chinese militaries."

Graham swiveled his chair around and had to stop himself from doing a 360. "What kind of processor does she have?" .

"It's nothing too powerful really," Jasso began unfeelingly, waving him off. "The differences between our computers and your old Earth NSA supercomputers are minor," Jasso ended nonchalantly.

"I hear you Draconians have learned how to rearrange the atoms in the crystals, creating a new type of computer memory," Brennan said with wonder.

Jasso succumbed to his pride and he could not help but get into the details. "You heard right. Information can be rewritten into the molecular structure of glass, creating whirlpools of polarized light that can then be read in the same way as data in optical fibers. My guys simply combined Plasmonics and

Nanophotonics, and it led to the emergence of new *quantum DNA information systems* which are far more powerful than today's super computers. The relation between Plasmonics and Nanophotonics could guarantee the use of light to overcome limitations in the operational speed of conventional integrated circuits."

Jasso then walked over to where Graham was seated and slid open a drawer beside him. He reached into it and revealed what looked like a small jewelry box and a small shiny power cell. He handed both things over to Brennan who stared at his new gifts with narrow eyes. Jasso seemed to grow speechless as he stood over him, implacable and grim, almost in regret to have handed Brennan his favorite toy. When Brennan opened the jewelry box, he took out what appeared to him as contact lenses.

"These got shipped in from the space elevator just a few months ago," Jasso said.

"What are they?" Brennan asked with squinted eyes.

"We call it the *Eye-Net Lenses;* they are contact lenses for the eyes. They are connected to our private internet and help us communicate better and faster on the field. These micro lenses shoot out pixels of light directly into your retina and will have access to our private internet on the fly at any time, any place. You can access your emails, files, and even the civilian internet anywhere and at anytime with just the touch of a button."

Jasso then demonstrated how to turn them on. He pressed a button on the shiny battery he called a quantum capacitor.

"I've seen people wear these on the ship. Mostly logistics personnel," Brennan said as he twirled the lenses in front of his eyes in astonishment. Brennan marveled at the cute little device and carefully inserted the lenses, blinking a few times to make sure they were in place.

"Where are my fancy toys?" Graham asked.

"There's an extra pair in there for you Lieutenant!" Jasso said pointedly. Graham slowly inched his hand into the drawer and stared at his jewelry box like he'd just seen fire for the first time.

"Now these lenses…you'll find that they are quite comfortable and no different from ordinary internet browsing contact lenses in shape and appearance. You see, Major, these lenses could do much more than browse the internet. As you walk around searching for disconnected folks, you can automatically find out who is connected and who is not by staring at them through these lenses and switching to detective mode. They are configured to detect the nanobots inside everyone. Anyone with working nanobots are in accord with these lenses, and you'll be able to see people's vital signs, states of consciousness, emotional state, DNA integrity, and endocrine functions. You can even use them to see the property lines of real estate, and the names of people living in homes and apartments will appear in front of each home's door. In addition, of course, the lenses can display everything our satellites can scan a person for like the different classes of each citizen and whether that pedestrian is a sex offender or an ex-con. It can scan the crime rate of areas you visit, the destinations of over-flying airliners, and even a person's blood-alcohol levels."

"I'm surprised they can't detect a person's thoughts," Brennan said in astonishment.

"Not yet at least," Jasso said in a sardonic snicker.

Without further word, Jasso trotted over to the far end of the northern section of the room and attempted to open up what looked like a P.O. Box. He finally succeeded in opening it after a few tries.

"Damn Earthly medieval locks," he muttered. Brennan followed him towards the safe deposit boxes, walking slowly because of his mounting curiosity. When he got there, Jasso took the entire safe deposit box out of the wall and handed it to Brennan like a quarterback hands off a football to a running back. It caught Brennan off guard, and he almost dropped it.

"That is my present to you both," Jasso said before taking a violent tug off his cigar.

Brennan opened the box and it revealed two disruptor phaser pistols. They looked like a bunch of fancy remote controls, slightly curved and made of what looked like titanium steel. There were several buttons on them but not as many as the phasers the security officers usually carried back on the Niagra. Brennan handed one over to Graham and both marveled at the weapons before holstering them.

Then, Jasso's face seemed to shape-shift in just seconds. Gone was the cheerfulness that he had displayed all day; his face had stiffened considerably and his eyes grew dark as a serious situation just dawned on him. "Now...let us get to business, shall we? We need to get Pandora, our super-computer, fired up because we have little time before all hell breaks loose."

"What do you mean by hell?" Brennan asked.

"Once we upgrade them all everything will be fine...right?" Graham added rather strangely, but his inquiry went unrequited. Jasso's face seemed to set to stone, as if he was just reminded of how grim the situation was. He tapped on Graham' shoulder and flicked his flat palm upwards, motioning for Graham to get up from Pandora's main console chair. Graham stumbled after he got up from the seat. Before Jasso even sat down, he punched in a few commands, and a few numbers were displayed on the main monitor. It showed the network's status.

"Let's see, there are now 14,009 disconnected civilians left in the city, still unaccounted for. Most disconnected are in the FEMA camp, but many refugees have escaped lately and they are likely to be roaming the abandoned red districts. We have to find each and every one of them. It won't be easy to find them with the Eye-Net lenses I just gave you" Jasso sighed.

Brennan's face turned to steel after soaking in Jasso's pessimism. "But—we'll find them!" Jasso barked out.

Brennan and Graham actually flinched at Jasso's sudden outburst. Brennan wondered if Jasso had a personal vendetta against people with radiation poisoning. Jasso scratched his head, digging his fingers into his stiff, hair- sprayed hair and then running them down through his beard in frustration.

"I originally thought we could only resort to putting more National Guard on the streets— in order to help eavesdrop on the population and look for signs of mutation...but—"

"That would be time consuming," Brennan interrupted.

"Yes it would," Jasso began, nodding sharply. "We then figured the police could go door to door as well, but we realized that we would still miss a few people."

"How so?" Brennan asked curiously.

"Because if someone's implants disconnect, they don't begin to mutate right away, and any recent disconnected civilians would slip unnoticed."

Jasso roughly hit a few buttons on the console and then used the sensors on his glove to scroll in a new window on the crystal pane monitor. A city map suddenly popped up on the screen that showed an overhead view of a random city block in Harlem, New York. The block was full of moving pedestrians and cars with blips over them, and each blip over a figure's head contained each citizen's biography. As Jasso went over to each blip with the cursor, a comic- book style bubble would pop up, describing a citizen's personal information. "This is how I gather info about a citizen's vital signs, state of consciousness, hormone levels, emotional state, impending illnesses, criminal records and so forth."

"Fascinating," Graham said torpidly.

"Your software never gets old," Brennan said, raising his eyebrows.

"It's changed a bit. So I'll give you a brief demonstration of how to use it to find disconnected folks," Jasso said with more alacrity. He then typed in the name *"Michael Jones"* into a search bar at the very top of a window. Jasso hit a button on the console to initiate the search and within seconds, the words *"No Results"* appeared in big black letters on the large monitor.

"Disconnected!" Jasso growled. "Michael Jones?" Brennan asked.

"Yes..." Jasso began slyly. "I randomly chose a name that no longer shows on our registry; you see—this Michael Jones fellow was a janitor who used to come visit this building. Michael and twenty of his men were hired to clean the building every once in a while—you know, to throw out the trash mostly. As you can see, I no longer have him, nor can I find him. He's gone, completely gone, and I can no longer track him because his GPS bots malfunctioned as well as all of his I.D. bots."

Jasso then switched to a feed over the Coney Island section of Brooklyn. It was part of a red district and deemed uninhabitable.

"So without the bots, we're going to do it like the old NSA used to. Take a look at this neighborhood here; we're just bound to find a few canyon dwellers in these parts because it's a red district." Jasso clicked a button and zoomed in to a section of the old Astroland amusement park, which had since become somewhat inundated by the sea. Jasso clacked his fingers over an old-fashioned keyboard and the view switched to a satellite overhead view at about three hundred feet above street level. Jasso then slid a cursor over the heads of several civilians walking along the beach.

Brennan and Graham stared at the tiny people walking the streets just off the edge of the water. "No pop-up boxes, no GPS info, nothing...they appear to be disconnected, of course," Brennan said.

"Yes, however, not all disconnected civilians are dwelling in the broken urban canyons of the red districts. Many disconnected people are living amongst the common connected folk in the green districts and so trying to find them would be a most arduous task if we were to click on each person one at a time. But...no reason to fret," Jasso paused, and wiped the window away from the screen, only to reveal another section of the city. Suddenly, Jasso's angry tone turned to one of ribald jest. "Now watch when I turn the spectrum over to infrared," Jasso smiled as he pressed a button.

Brennan watched in awe as the spectrum changed and the people suddenly turned blue.

"They are cold, cold, cold, cold!" Jasso beamed. "The body heat is lower in disconnected folks; there is no reason to roll the cursor over each and every citizen spotted on our satellite feeds. This is an easy way to spot and track dozens of civilians at a time."

"But Colonel!" Brennan began quickly. "The infrared could only scan through transmissive material! Depending on the way the camera is calibrated, cooler surfaces will show up brighter and warmer surfaces will appear darker, but the cameras can't see through windows and anything that blocks heat for that matter!"

"You mean the old NSA thermal imaging satellites cannot," Jasso replied in an ostentatious tone. "The satellites have undergone significant upgrades since you left. Our cameras are different because of our unique laser rangefinder, and most importantly, a highly advanced thermal imaging sensor that is not bound by the constraints of ordinary thermal imaging cameras—like the ones that your CIA and NSA used to use on Earth citizens."

Brennan just poured on the questions like a rookie out of training. "But what about if someone is in a basement, no thermal camera could ever detect them," he said with doubt.

Jasso laughed but didn't reply right away. He took out a tin flask from inside his jacket and took a swig of bourbon. "Did I mention that you can also switch the feed to the X-ray spectrums? This way, you can detect anyone inside a house or building or a basement," Jasso stopped himself short because he belched between his words. "We'll get these degenerate bastards..." Jasso said between burps, moving the tip of his tongue across his lip and almost salivating as he spoke.

Graham and Brennan matched puzzled glances.

"I'll get you degenerates!" Jasso continued slyly, chewing back his irritation.

What's he angry about? Brennan asked himself. *What's the Colonel have against sick people?*

"Every single one these gutter rats will soon be civilized!" Jasso shouted in a heedless tone, and then slapped a flat hand on the hard plastic of the console's hull. Jasso was so strung up that a few strands of his thick white hair broke free from the bind of his hairspray and fell to his collar. Jasso's odd behavior did nothing to disarm Brennan's suspicions, and Jasso's quaint remarks a moment ago only pushed the suspicions to the forefront of Brennan's mind.

Jasso realized that he might have gotten too dramatic for the men after noticing their body language and so he took a deep breath. He fixed his tie and repositioned his hair before speaking softer than before. "Pardon me gentlemen, I'm not the best company when I'm stressed and drunk," he snickered.

Suddenly, a chirping sound came from inside Jasso's coat pocket. Jasso's face seemed to darken all at once after hearing it. He reached into his coat and took out a small tablet. Jasso's face immediately jerked away from the screen after reading his text message. He then turned to face the men and spoke out in a maddening, deadpan voice, "I'm sorry gentlemen, but I must insist that you both excuse me for a while."

"Now?" both Brennan and Graham asked in unison.

"Yes, it seems that I have an urgent message in my inbox from one of my superiors. It pertains to the mission; I must make a phone call right away."

Brennan and Graham exchanged matched glances of uncertainty. Jasso seemed taken aback by whatever was on his mind and was acting quirky.

"Very well, Colonel," Brennan said.

"I will be with you both shortly, and I'll finish showing you around. Keep in mind that the biometric scanners throughout the building have been reconfigured to recognize both of your irises and fingerprints so you are both free to roam about the headquarters. You two men are now my official agents—RAPDA agents at that, the very best, and my personal guards. But— before I go, I wanted to let you know that your offices are on the thirteenth floor, just beside our briefing room. You won't spend much time in there except when you feel the need to wind down and communicate with your families back on the ship. You'll see your names engraved on the doors there, and so your offices will be very easy to find…oh…in case you get hungry, the cafeteria is on the thirty-third floor. There, you will find a few vending machines and a water cooler, but that is about it. Remember to page me if you need me."

Without further word, Jasso fixedly headed for the door to leave, but before Jasso took two steps, Brennan readily spoke up, "If I may, sir?"

Jasso stopped dead in his tracks, and turned around like he was caught stealing something.

Brennan cocked his head to the side and spoke pryingly, "Colonel, if your phone call pertains to the mission, should it matter whether or not we are present while you make the call?"

"No, it's best I speak to my superiors in private," Jasso said resolutely. "You are my personal guard, but even RAPDA agents don't have a high enough clearance for certain information."

Jasso ignored Brennan's bewildered expression and spoke faster to change the subject. "Come to think of it, I may be a while. You can stick around here if you wish, or you can go check into your hotel down the street. There's no telling how long I'll be," Jasso said as he walked towards the door.

Brennan considered for a moment and thought it would be best to get a meal in at his hotel.

"Very well, Colonel," Brennan sighed. "I'll freshen up at the hotel and await your call."

"You two know the way out," Jasso said with a grin.

And without further word or warning, Jasso darted out of the room. Brennan and Graham exchanged puzzled glances as they watched Jasso head down the catwalk, and eventually, vanish into the darkness of the cave.

For the first time, Brennan knew why General Clarkson was so worried about the Overseer after all. It wasn't the incompetence, his sloppy countenance, or the drinking problem. It was his secretiveness—and Brennan suddenly found that his uniform no longer rested easily on his shoulders.

7: The Search

There was an uncanny bitterness in the air at night, and the temperature was inclined to drop fifty degrees once the sun dipped below the horizon. Charlie didn't mind the cold at all, and it helped slow down his overwrought and fiery nerves. The darkness of the night would obstruct his search for the hardware store but he didn't care. The sun was beneath the horizon and that's all that mattered to him. Besides, Charlie had realized that his ability to see in pitch darkness improved dramatically in the last year since his heat stroke and transformation.

So far, Charlie had encountered nothing and no one, and he hoped it stayed that way. Only the wind spoke to him as it sighed through the leafless branches of the trees and the occasional howling of rabid coyotes in the distance sent a woeful presage through the night.

By the time Charlie got to the coast, the moon brightened up by the minute, and it hung bright against the starry sky. The moon always seemed to look down on Charlie and it spoke to him lately. He felt different at night ever since his alien nanobots disconnected. For some odd reason, the night made him happier, and he thought the night did something to his pineal gland because the surging energies from the moon seemed to moan to him, startling his ears and heightening all of his senses.

Such a fitting canopy for the task ahead, Charlie thought

Charlie enjoyed the view of the moon so much that he took slow steps towards the new coastline and he occasionally lifted his head to fill his lungs with the pure, invigorating night air. The crisp night air acted as an immediate tonic for his nerves and he practically leapt from avenue to avenue, inching closer to the coast. He could smell the salt in the air and that was the only reason he knew he was near the coast line and the hardware store.

Charlie moved as furtively as he could through the dark, deserted streets, hugging the shadows of buildings, having no desire to arrest the attention of any rabid canyon dwellers lurking about now that he was so close to his destination.

The street ahead of him sickened him because he remembered the place all too well. Memories of what happened on that street had surfaced again. They were memories of the events that happened just several days after the first earthquake and tsunami, when the tide receded on the very spot he walked on, leaving a fresh crop of water-logged corpses all over the streets.

What horror.

The memories marked his mind with stains that could not be removed. His brother washed up on the third day after the tsunami hit. He found him just a block over to his right on Pine Street, and he could still see that crumpled white face and wrinkled body of his laying on the cruddy and mud-choked street.

Charlie took a deep breath and shook off his grim thoughts, trudging ahead in a semi-trot and closing his eyes to his surroundings. He had to travel on that road even though he didn't want to; he just had to make sure that he was heading down the right path. The faint sounds of water and waves were heard near Pine Street, where few homes still stood untarnished by the disasters of ten years ago. Many of the undamaged homes were semi-attached two family style homes and almost all of them displayed some mark of mourning. Graves replaced their front lawns since so many cemeteries became overcrowded. Those who survived the catastrophes and the solar radiation had no choice but to bury their relatives under their front lawns.

As he approached the coastline at the end of Pine Street, the homes began to stretch out into the new Atlantic Ocean—made deeper by the rapidly melting icecaps. The water looked far from invigorating, and it was so starved of oxygen that it almost looked rusty. The coastline lined up perfectly with the sidewalk on Pine Street, and an occasional tiny wave would slam into the side of the houses just on the edge of the coast, taking small chunks of wood, glass, and plastic siding along into the ocean.

The sight of that warm, rusty, and murky broth made Charlie think twice about jumping in but it was no time to fret over the conditions of the sea—it was now or never. He had to find a way into the submerged hardware store or he would never finish his weapon.

As he leaned down to grope through his duffel bag, he noticed a couple of small crabs scuttling along the stony tarmac. They were typical blue crabs, and Charlie immediately picked up a rock after spotting them, and proceeded to smash one with it before it got the chance to scamper off into the dark water. He hefted it in his hand by its claw before he greedily sucked out the meat.

He wiped his mouth with the back of his hand and thanked the crab for giving him the energy he would need for his search. After his quick meal, he fumbled through his bag for his snorkel and prepared to dive into the murky waters. First, he would have to plan a path to the hardware store, which was just up ahead, a few hundred feet up Manor Road. A quick glance through his binoculars showed nothing but putrid looking rooftops popping through the sea, as well as dozens of cars. Some of the cars in the deeper waters bobbed like apples, and some of the cars in the shallower waters lay still as the water poured in and out of their broken frames.

The bright moon commanded the water silent and still, making it appear as if it were a flat sheet of shimmering iron that seemed to stretch into infinity.

Even though the buildings were no longer completely inundated, he still found it difficult to locate the hardware store. There was nothing in sight but chimneys and thatched roofs poking out of the sea, and a procession of dead trees.

"Damn big oil," Charlie hushed to himself in a half-whisper.

Charlie had a grudge against oil companies and the ways they scavenged for oil. Even though the media claimed that the damaged magnetosphere and chronic polar shifts caused the Artic areas of the Earth to heat up, Charlie realized that was a lie. He knew that the oceans have been rising way before the earthquakes shifted the Earth's poles and hampered the magnetosphere. He knew the real reason for the rising ocean levels was all of the X-raying performed by oil companies in order to scan the Earth's crust for previously untapped oil reservoirs located around the Artic areas. Oil companies became so greedy that they eventually moved into the Artic. They melted so much ice that the oceans rose several meters in just over a decade.

Charlie broke out of his daze when he noticed a boat on someone's front lawn just off to his right. The boat was parked in the middle of it, overturned, but after walking up to it in the ankle deep water, he had seen that the boat's bottom was painstakingly rotted out.

Charlie lugged his duffel bag up to his waist and took out his mask and snorkel. He slipped off his boots and dipped a bare foot into the water. He took a few steps, careful not to splash or make noise. The foamy salt water splashed up to his plump lips, tasting like death and he almost gagged up the crab he ate.

Charlie then perched himself on an old abandoned automobile stranded along the sidewalk so he could finally put on his scuba flippers. The car was all rusty and white after having been attacked by salt water for the last ten years.

After tightening the flippers to his sock-less feet, he clutched his flashlight before taking his first steps through the two or three feet of water. Charlie obstinately hopped through the shallow water and all the seaweed, and then came to a halt when he inadvertently stubbed his toe on a sidewalk curb that had since become part of the sea floor.

Charlie gritted his teeth to fight the pain and moved on, taking tentative steps before the water became waist deep—deep enough to swim. It stood that deep for another sixty yards, and by the time he reached the public school on Koch Avenue, he was already chest deep under water. He dipped his head into the soapy, oxygen starved water to see if he could see underneath, and some crud latched onto his scuba mask in the process. Water seeped around the seal of his snorkel and lips, and it made Charlie gag, almost vomiting into the snorkel, but he swallowed the vomit down after it climbed to the middle of his throat.

Charlie once again dipped his head into the water to test the field of vision with the flashlight this time.

Hope no canyon dwellers see this...

Charlie pointed the wavering beam under the water and dipped his head under. He pushed his body along with one arm until it eventually became deep enough to swim. The flashlight was barely strong enough to pierce through the opaque waters, and when he swung the wavering beam to the sea floor, the cloudy water obscured his vision until he swam right in front of the eroded concrete and tarmac. Some of the stripes were still painted on the street but it was mostly as gravelly as a normal sandy beach's seafloor. The land in that particular neighborhood fell away in a marked declivity and would forever be inundated by the rising sea levels.

As he swam, a school of terrifying fish cut in front of the wavering beam of the flashlight. They looked like small barracudas, but were unlike anything he'd ever seen before because they seemed to glow. Until then, most of the unfamiliar animals Charlie had encountered were usually mutated and deformed, but the fish in front of him looked far from sickly. Charlie even thought they looked extraordinary for that matter and unlike any other fish he had seen before.

Charlie would have loved to observe the fish some more, but he had to get moving. He continued to kick and slosh his way through the soup of death until he saw a street sign poking up out of the water just ahead of him. It said Clove Road, the street where the hardware store should be. He pointed the flashlight ahead and down the street with a fully stretched arm, and after a hundred feet of swimming, the beam of his flashlight confirmed the location of the store's façade.

"Harry's Hardware" was written on top of the front double doors. "Thank god the shutters aren't down," Charlie exhaled. Getting in the

building would have been much more difficult if the owners of the store managed to close before the initial storm surge that turned the neighborhood into a coastline.

The bottom third of building was submerged in the water, and it was a ramshackle of a place. A shard or two covered every one of its windows and its wood was mold-ridden, water-logged, and splintered. He floated to the building and headed for one of cracked front windows to inspect it. The windows would be the only way to gain access, and they were mostly broken. Charlie knocked some of the glass off the front window with the butt of his flashlight. He poked his light through the window and was happy to see many shelves still packed with merchandise. At least the top shelves were. The ones on the bottom were water-damaged and submerged all together.

He began to think he was unprepared to venture into the utterly black interior, which might topple in on him if he knocked over something as small as a plank of wood. Alternatively, the place could be so dark and cluttered inside that Charlie might never extricate himself from the place if his flashlight decided to crap out on him. The strength of the beam was dimming by the minute and Charlie had to find batteries as soon as possible. Nevertheless, he swam through a window, careful not to cut himself. Charlie pumped his arms, flailing through the opaque water, kicking his legs hard through each and every aisle. His eyes remained bright, expectant and hopeful and he had to get close to see anything at all. His beam wavered down one of the aisles, labeled aisle #5, revealing shelves stacked with all sorts of paint cans and brushes. Even though they were not damaged at all and were untouched by water, Charlie refused to take some of them. Charlie could not afford to lug anything he didn't need.

All he needed was what he needed for his weapon, but there were no signs of any of the supplies he needed in aisle #5. More worry and doubt festered inside him, but on the bright side, Charlie noticed that the shelves were still full in aisle

#4 too; he spun around in the water and swiveled his wavering beam towards both sides of the aisle. He might as well have struck gold. A morning's worth of difficulties were wiped off his face, and his journey would pay off.

In the post apocalyptic jungle, a packed hardware store was a gold mine. He immediately began filling his duffel bag with random, but useful things— wrenches, Allen key sets, nuts, bolts, screws, soldering metals, some needle nose pliers, a few tubs of plumbers putty and most importantly—double A batteries for his walkman.

Charlie pumped a fist through the water and let out a gleeful "Yes!" He got everything he needed to finish his weapon and begin his plan to ensure that the people of Earth would no longer languish under the boots of the Overseer.

8: Elena

Elena was not only single, but she hardly interacted with anyone. She was a loner and happy to be in her own company most of the time. After her twenty- third year of age, the isolation began to catch up to her. She didn't know it, but she was longing for a friend or for a man just to call her pretty. She was a bit on the plain side, not ugly, not gorgeous, but attractive. Her plain and innocent doe- like face was enveloped by an uninspired hairstyle. Her long blonde locks were a bit wavy and rested lazily on her shoulders in idle ringlets. Brennan always told his daughter Elena that she looked like her mother—with that plain beauty of hers, and despite the compliments she'd gotten throughout her life, she didn't act confident.

"A hopeless dream," she said in her mind over and over as she began to prepare her breakfast. However before she got the chance to mix her pancake batter, her phone rang.

"Go away, I'm taken!"

She didn't need to read her caller ID to know that it was Thomas Claymore calling as usual, a former Earthman from Toronto. He called her before class every single day of the week to discuss what they learned on the previous day, and Elena was in no mood for him today. Elena had had enough of him. And it wasn't because he was a pain, or a nuisance in any way whatsoever. She hated him because she liked him.

Deep down inside Elena knew a relationship with him couldn't possibly last due to her self-involvement so she never bothered trying to pursue one with him. Elena figured that the only way to forget him was to ignore him as much as possible and so she never picked up the phone. Elena hoped she would find the courage to actually tell him to bug off someday, but she couldn't do it because she was actually lying to herself.

Subconsciously, Elena didn't want him to bug off and she kind of looked at him as something she wanted but couldn't possibly have. The truth was that she was afraid and had no experience standing up for what she wanted. She couldn't deny that Thomas was a decent looking guy, not really her type, but he was kind and dedicated to his studies. He didn't act with an impertinence or lack propriety in anyway, nevertheless, he was a man and all men were evil; according to her dad that is. Brennan was a bit too overprotective over her, and she began to hate him for it. Of course, Brennan's scathing advice stemmed from a particular trauma Elena had suffered after the disasters when several male looters tried to rape her.

From that day on, her dad taught her to stay away from men and that they were no good anymore. He drilled the same information into her skull repeatedly as a kid—men were no good, society was crumbling, and she should stay single for her own sake. Her father's strict upbringing had bounded Elena's heart in chains.

When she went back to the kitchen to make pancakes, she found herself still trembling a little bit, not because of Thomas but mostly due to Earth that had spun graciously outside her window all day long, prompting Elena to become assaulted with more memories of her ill-fated past. The spoon shook as she mixed the sludgy pancake batter, and she could not keep her eyes away from the window all day.

Elena proceeded to pour batter into her skillet, trying not to focus on Earth or think about Thomas. She hated her weakness and didn't like the hole she crawled into whenever a man came into her life. She was negative about the repercussions of a relationship, and life in space was too complicated for a relationship, she thought. Everyone was in their own little bubble, preoccupied with their careers and the duty of keeping a ship running. Life had gotten too complex to get into a relationship on a large scout-class star ship— forever on the move, and rarely ever stopping near a planet for more than a day at a time.

Elena thought that if she ever had any kids they would probably wind up being raised by a nanny, or stuck in some daycare center for six or seven years. Jobs came first on the Niagra, not family.

Why bother getting into a relationship, she often thought.

Focusing on her task, she took a deep breath and concentrated on her meal. She created several four-inch pancakes consisting of Sirian eggs, breadcrumbs, Alpha-Centurion parsley, grated-parmesan style cheese, and ricotta cheese from Sirian moon-cow milk. She plopped a few globs of the mixture over the Plaideian coconut oil on the skillet and turned on the steam.

She daydreamed about Thomas for the entire time as she prepared her pancakes, and then her phone rang again.

"Get the damn hint already!" she shouted, and her fiery nerves caused her to break one of the half-cooked pancakes as she tried to flip it. Elena wondered what a fool this guy must have been to be interested in such an antisocial stiff such as her. "Why can't I just tell him that I'm taken!" she blurted aloud.

Somewhere in her mind, lurked all of the stuff her father drilled into her skull since she was a kid.

"Life just sucks, and people suck even more," she mumbled to herself.

Elena was a cynic who snarled more than smiled. It was a shame too. Her laughing lines were deep, and when she did manage to muster a rare smile, she would light up a room with it, just like the beaming smile of a child. However, when she frowned, she could suck the life out of a party from her mere presence alone. Therefore, she figured she would skip the parties for everyone else's sake. Her speech was usually conveyed as flat, and uninspired, and so she didn't like being around people much— and people did not want to be around her either.

When the pancakes were done, she topped them with chopped chives from planet Lyra and a few gobs of sour cream, but before she could even take a bite, she stopped the fork midway to her mouth after catching a glimpse of Earth from outside her view-port window on the observation deck. The thought of Earth stirred some pent up emotions inside her and the food wasn't going down at all, so she decided to retreat into her bedroom to get lost in one of her daydreams. First, she needed something to quash her nerves. She reached into her fridge, grabbed a cold bottle of brown honey nut ale, and poured its contents into a tall beer glass.

After slugging half of it down in three gulps, she headed to her viewport window in her living room area and stared at her home planet, Earth. She lingered over the window for a while, pacing recklessly at times. Elena decided she had enough with Earth; in a sense, she blamed the Earth for killing her mother and so she brutally tugged the thick cotton drapes over her the window. She then figured she would tidy up the place.

Her quarters were small and plain, and it really reflected on her character.

Her apartment was extremely funereal and without a hint of personality anywhere. As clean as it was, she was always hesitant about making the place her own, so she kept the place unadorned. Ever since the earthquakes destroyed her home on Earth, she never thought it was worth fixing up a place ever again. Besides, she still felt alienated out in space, almost like a permanent tourist.

There were but a few sticks of furniture in the place and nothing but the essentials. Her bedroom's vanity set featured a dusty mirror, and she never bothered looking into it anymore.

After realizing that she could no longer concentrate on her chores, Elena leapt across her bedroom and flung the drapes away from her window with a swift swipe of the arms. She stared at the culprit of her mother's death; Earth, and the G-class star known as the sun, in all its glory, bathing her apartment in a golden richness. The sunlight did nothing to displace the gloom that was stuck to every inch the place. The thought of making a connection to Earth again caused a pang of adrenaline to flow through her. She only wished she had answered her father's call before he left. In a sense, she wanted to see some photos of the place. Undercurrents of curiosity melded with the begrudging anger she felt for her old home.

When Brennan called her earlier that morning, Elena thought her father just wanted to interrogate her, just like usual, so she never bothered to take the call. She figured that he probably wanted to know how her schooling was going or seek details about her internship on the ship's cargo bay. Never in a million years would Elena have thought that she wanted to see Earth again—a planet she so hated.

The Niagra would usually visit Earth and its solar system once every three years because Orion was in charge of scanning the Earth's moon for helium 3 deposits. As much as she was reminded of all the horrors she experienced on her home planet, she could not help but miss the place, and miss the lifestyle. Elena routinely caught up on Earth's current events from time to time through the galactic web. The same thoughts played in her mind every time she read Earth news websites—

I miss home—life in the suburb, the malls, the spot by the beach or in the country by the lake...

Elena just plopped herself down on her bed and put on her music media player's headphones. She tried to relax and clear her mind and hoped to get lost in the music, but she could not. If anything, the music made her more anxious. All she ever listened to was old, classic Earth music, which only added to the nostalgia. Elena forcibly jerked her feet to the music and she tooted to herself— the music was fueling her desire to live the Earth life again. The guttural vocals from her favorite singer brought back memories of her young teenage years, and whatever coming-of-age moments she might have had before her teenage childhood was stilted by the global catastrophes. The familiar melody and the heavy guitars crashed through her headphones and chased away her reflective mood a bit due to the adrenaline-thumping vibe. Even though the songs became played out after a while, she continued to listen to the same playlist every day and every night. Elena just couldn't let go of her childhood and wished she could relive it again—without the catastrophes, of course.

After the song had finished, Elena tossed her headphones aside and sprang up out of bed. Once again, she fixed her eyes at her view-port window and obsessively parted the silk drapes. She stared at Earth for one whole hour, standing sulkily and with hands on her hips. The reflection of her face on the window got in the way so she dimmed the lights and continued to stare. To Elena, the Earth had since become a place that only existed in fairy tales, and it was hard to imagine all the horrors etched in her memory cells actually did occur on that blue ball outside. It was only a decade ago, but felt like it might as well had been a lifetime.

Elena recalled what happened when she first left the planet, and she could never forget the images all the people left on the ground as the ship rose into the heavens; such a memory was forever engrained in her mind. So many people wished to be in her shoes, and yet, Elena now wished for the opposite.

After thinking about what she left behind, Elena sighed deeply, leaving vapor on her window.

The stars are pretty, the nebulas are wonderful, but I'd do anything to feel the wind blow against my face on a cool spring day by the lake, or witness a flock of birds bathing in a puddle on the side of the road.

She rarely got the chance to do any of those things because shore leave was once a year. Even so, no planet had the bio-diversity that Earth had, and no planet could match Earth's mountains, waterfalls, forests, canyons, and many other rural wonders. All she had come to know for the last decade were the sand- less beaches of planet Gliese, the monotonous sunrise on planet Lyra, the mechanistic metropolises of Alpha Draconias, the cratered flatlands of planet Sirius B, and the thirty-three decks of the starship Niagra.

Aggravation routinely set in by the ongoing jurisprudence on the ship; she felt like she was caged. Time even seemed to lose all of its multidimensional scope out in space, altering her perception of it and even aging her much quicker. Depending on the Niagra's speed, time would sometimes be perceived quicker, or slower, than usual. On the ship, she suffered from the desolation of her four walls and found herself weeping whole days with misery and despair. The heavy work of the ship were filled with nothing but the most hateful duties and she spent most of her time learning about interplanetary telecommunication circuits, operating airlocks, and calculating approach maneuvers for the autopiloted shuttles. Such a job barely motivated her to slip out of bed each morning.

The more she stared out towards Earth, the more regret she began to feel for not answering Brennan's phone call. She sometimes wished she had died back on Earth along with all the rest of her family and friends. *What use is it to go on living?* she asked herself in a grief-thickened voice. *I'm dead anyways.*

Her jaw wobbled as she stared out to Earth, and tears began to seep through her closed eyelids. When she first boarded the starship Niagra over ten years ago, she was grateful to be alive and glad that the aliens gave her and her father a new life. Space was new to her and it mesmerized her at first. The stars looked amazing and flying through an asteroid belt captivated her every time.

Still, most of the time, there was darkness and Elena would soon learn that space was a violent place. As pretty as space could be, it could be equally as treacherous, and she never forgot the day the ship was stuck in the gravitational pull of a star for weeks and weeks during her second year on the ship. The members of the star ship Niagra didn't know if they would be freed from the large sun's grip and it was a nightmarish two weeks full of uncertainty and doubt. Nothing compared to it, not even Elena's month long experience during the catastrophes of 2033.

At least the earthquakes had hit quickly: roofs crash fast and the crushing death is imminent. The same goes for the tsunamis: the waves come without warning and it takes less than a minute to drown. As for the radiation fallout that followed, no one knew they were dying of radiation until the aliens landed and told them so. Most people thought they were sick from drinking dirty water.

What occurred on the ship for those two weeks topped the list. It was horrible knowing that you were being pulled slowly into a sun and about to be cooked slowly. Each day was just treacherous as they waited for help. Eventually, they got through it with help from several other towing ships that made it all the way from the Alpha-Centurion sector of the Milky Way, which was over ten parsecs away from the Niagra. A few parsecs more, and they would have never made it in time. Elena and the rest of the eight hundred people on board would have roasted to death, and not even their genetic enhancements would be enough to stave off the rotting effects of the sun's radiation when in such close proximity.

From that day forward, Elena always wondered if mankind was even meant to traverse the sea of stars in the first place because after all, all humans had to be genetically engineered in order to survive out there, because the radiation was very high. Elena always figured that relocating to another celestial body would only become necessary if overpopulation hindered a planet's infrastructure.

Moreover, that space travel was a need—not a want.

Suddenly, a crazy idea swiftly permeated in her mind. The idea made Elena question her sanity after thinking it, but after some pondering, she came to realization that it might not be a crazy idea after all.

What am I doing here? What kind of life is this? Earth may not be the paradise it once was, but perhaps one day, I'll get to see it return to its former glory!

Elena scampered over to her bedroom and kneeled down on her rough carpeting. She immediately grabbed the backpack under her bed.

I am a lunatic for doing this! she thought.

If she was really going to see Earth again, now was her chance. It was now or never. And so she went with it. Even though she knew taking a shuttle was out of the question due to the ionic interference, she figured that the only way to get down there was to sneak into the Space Elevator airlock and take the eight hour plunge down on the cable car.

Elena dragged some basic clothes out of her dresser and stuffed them into a backpack. She was traveling light. After grabbing a few pairs of jeans and some sundresses, she stopped for a moment and surveyed her drawers for anything else she might need. She hopped around the room as she dressed, and opted for a sundress, because she knew how hot Earth had become, even during winter.

Elena slipped her dress on quickly and slipped on a pair of sandals. It was a demure outfit, but after looking in the dusty mirror, she thought she looked good in it.

I'm going to Earth for good, I'm out of this hellhole and I'm actually going to do something with my life!

Elena then stuffed her tiny camera in her luggage and tucked her universal credit stick in her purse. It was good for only about five hundred Sol credits, but it would sustain her until she found a job. Elena was about to embark on a journey of self-liberation. Today, the young and delicate flower that was Elena had grown thorns.

9: A Conflict of Interests

Charlie and his father's long time friend, John Lancaster, lived in a small ranch-styled home at the furthest end of the red districts in Gravesend, Brooklyn. They picked the area as part of a strategy for its seclusion, since most of the area was partially flooded for years. Therefore, few mutants resided in the neighborhood full of damp, mold-ridden homes.

Their home was habitable compared to most of the homes in the area but was still the most ghastly of things. The walls were bare and the wallpaper peeled in the corners where it was black with mold and mildew. The few sticks of furniture in the place were very old and brittle. To make matters worse, they had no plumbing or electricity.

Charlie and John toiled endlessly for over a year to get their devices finished, and now that Charlie had found the supplies they both needed, they could finish what they started. John Lancaster was one of the few electronic engineers left on the planet and one of the few skilled survivors on Earth that were left behind by the Orion corporation. Initially, Charlie and John planned to build a generator, in hopes of powering up their home. With John's limited experience in magnetic engineering and Charlie's education, the task would have become almost impossible if it wasn't for Charlie's freaky experiences with astral projection.

Just four months after Charlie's implants deactivated, Charlie began building the generator off the top of his head. What puzzled John the most was that Charlie not only succeeded in pioneering secret formulas, but also exceeded their limitations. Charlie was no longer an innocent after that day and began experiencing para-psychological events that would forever mystify him. At first, Charlie was consciously unacquainted with the reasons as to how he managed to understand science ever so suddenly—and after some time, he realized it was due to the succession of epiphanies he had every night while he slept.

Before the dreams, life had been an unproductive and dismal trial; what scared Charlie the most were not the vivid dreams, but what resulted after he woke up. Charlie always felt changed afterwards. Suggestions and ideas throbbed in his mind, and it was as if something downloaded into his mind after each dream. It was as if he absorbed the souls of his relatives and ancestors while he slept, and with it came memories and knowledge... including the knowledge that his late father had, knowledge that he patented just before his death—knowledge that Charlie needed to build his dad's pioneering free energy device.

Charlie and John never cared about starting such a project until the Overseer denied John's pitch to help restore the city's electrical transformers to full capacity. From that day on, Charlie decided that the generator he began building could be used for other purposes besides electric current generation, so he decided to weaponize his invention without John's behest.

After Charlie started weaponizing his invention, the two began speaking less and less. John didn't have the complicated personality Charlie had. He was reasonable and not as thick-headed as Charlie, who was too puritanical and very difficult to maintain a conversation with. He and John differed when it came to the technology's primary purpose and they began to argue more than talk after a while, so they figured they were better off not speaking to each other about anything any longer. John went about his business and continued to build the generator and Charlie focused on the weaponized version of it. That angered John to the point of ignoring Charlie for good, and even though they lived together, Charlie and John avoided each other as much as possible except when they ate dinner.

Every now and then Charlie and John would engage in brief political gossip over their lunch or while out hunting for raccoons. Of course, they sometimes spoke about the weather but it was mostly small talk. When they did talk, they behaved with an exaggerated politeness as if each was striving to be perfectly normal, but both inexplicably failed.

Just before Charlie's father died from his radiation-induced brain tumor, he knew death was imminent after his sudden weight loss, so he entrusted his friend John with not just his patents, but all of the contents in several storage containers he had tucked away that would help complete his pioneering inventions. John was an electronic engineer for most of his life, but his realistic conciseness was nowhere near the level of Charlie's father's skills.

Besides the blueprints, there was a substantial amount of equipment in the storage sheds, ranging from hardware to high-powered magnets and some biofuels made from wood. However, Charlie's inexperience and John's lack of practical brevity caused them to use up all of the resources Charlie's dad had left them.

Finding that hardware store was the best thing that happened to them in a long time, and yet, only John seemed jovial about it. Charlie was as hard as he ever was, and unlike his friend John, Charlie was forever consumed by his hatred for the extraterrestrial visitors.

The day after Charlie raided the hardware store, he had experienced more brain fog and had to halt working. He looked so bad that John actually spoke to him for the first time in weeks.

"You feeling okay?" John asked.

Charlie ignored him. He walked away from his workstation near the dining room table and walked into the bathroom to wash the sleep off his face. The look on his face said it all. His complexion indicated that he was ailing from not only radiation sickness but also from malnourishment. Three days without food was usually long enough to remove all decorum from even the most civilized men, and three days without food would surely remove most of the subtle differences between a civilized man and a savage.

After washing his face, Charlie headed back into the living room looking as dour as ever; he was sick, sore and disgusted. John fixed his deep-set, puppy dog eyes on Charlie all day, scrutinizing him and wondering if he had gone mad from all that ultraviolet radiation he absorbed yesterday during his hunt for the hardware store.

John Lancaster was about the same age as Charlie's dad, approaching sixty years— and he looked good for a canyon dweller. He was lean and squat, his woolly short hair was white, but his wrinkles were few. His usual dark brown skin was pewter in color, and looked as pale as a black man could ever get without looking white. John wore a look of grief that was forever imprinted on his face; his eyes indicated that they had seen a lot in his fifty-eight years, especially in the last ten.

"You look like crap," John told him as he stared at Charlie's pockmarked, splotchy, and flaky skin.

Charlie's voice whined due to incomprehension. "You think?" Charlie looked into a mirror that hung near the front door; his skin was dry and pale and he looked as pallid as ever. His features were still nothing like those of the rabid canyon dwellers, but he was afraid he would soon become one. His good looks were debased by his animalistic passions and the increased hormonal activity that resulted when the implants began malfunctioning. There simply was not a mark of happiness or pride upon his bestial countenance anymore, but he was in denial about it.

"I'm okay," Charlie replied, staring at the mirror with consternation and dismay.

"You look sick, my friend," John began, sounding concerned. "I'm afraid you might be turning into one of those things."

Charlie tried to catch his breath after listening to John's decrees and gazed upon his mirror with dilated eyes. He sighed and clenched his teeth, and it brought roguish dimples to the corners of his mouth. He turned away from the mirror, and just shook his head. Charlie didn't tell John was that his insomnia was caused by the muscle twitches that had plagued him the past few days; he experiencing the early stages of multiple sclerosis.

"Have you looked in the mirror yourself lately?" Charlie then asked.

"I have," John began mournfully. "I noticed the rashes on my skin as well, but you...you have those darkened eyes, and you lost so much weight this past week."

Charlie just shrugged. John could sense his fear. Both of them were very empathic and could sense each other's emotions.

"I know what you're going through Charlie, I know," John started sympathetically, pausing for the sorrow to set in. "It's the sun...it's the heat...it makes us so weak, and cranky, and the funny thing is—that it began to happen to me during the same time it happened to you."

"The bots in our blood, they don't work anymore," Charlie said, rubbing his fingers into his temples.

John nodded with downcast eyes and spoke as he screwed a bolt at the hunk of steel before him. "Why us? Why don't the bots work in us as they do in other people? Why isn't everyone else getting sick?"

"Perhaps in time, all will get sick again."

"I guess not all of the implants in us are build the same.'

"Or people aren't built the same," Charlie began with confusion. "I saw some positive results in the animals John, the animals are getting healthier...and it's as if they're evolving somehow."

"Yes, I noticed," John nodded quickly. "I noticed a lot of healthy deer and rabbit populations...some of those rabbits have the strangest ears..."

Charlie drifted off into a brief daydream and hazarded a wild guess as to why he was mutating slower than most. What worried him the most was the fact that he felt inhuman lately: especially since he murdered three canyon dwellers in the past few days with his bare hands—and especially since he began making contact with dead people as he slept each night.

Charlie then turned to John and put his hands on his shoulder, "John, it's getting worse," he began acutely.

"Your skin?" John asked.

"No, not my health, at least it's not if I stay out of the sun!" "Then what's getting worse?"

Charlie stammered, "The powers, the dreams, the nightmares…"

John looked away from him after he said that. He did not like to think about such things. Charlie just stared at the ground and decided to change the subject, focusing his physical abilities. He spoke dazedly as he began recollecting what he did to those muggers the other day. "I ripped a man's head off with my bare hands. I don't know how I did it…it just…it happened so fast! And besides my physical changes, well…this thing I'm building—this weapon, it's all made possible because of the dreams and visions I've been having—dreams of marvelous cities, full of wonderful technology! One peculiar dream is reoccurring—and it always features a vast, high-tech city located on a huge island, unlike any Earth metro, and far more futuristic. Blending with this display of magnificence are always glimpses of large airships occasionally docking on the buildings themselves, which extended high into the sky, stabbing through the clouds. The peaks of their spires were just impossible to behold John! It is so beautiful!"

John wanted to add something but Charlie kept rambling on.

"And it's impossible to determine how high they went. Some of those structures kept growing and growing into the heavens in an indescribable splendor, and the buildings seemed to grow before my eyes, like trees and plants do. The civilians…well…the civilians are usually human looking, but they are much hairier—even the women. They were all stumpy, yet wiry old things, short of neck but not of limb. Almost all of them dressed alike. The men wore long white beards, and they were all strangely robed. Every night, in the dream, I would gather in a particular plaza to speak to several of the hairy people who spoke in sharp cultured voices, and always with high enthusiasm and alacrity.

They spoke often, the bearded men did, and with their words came holographic forms and images that floated above their heads. They were forms of splendid things usually, mostly images of ancient technology! Including the machines that we're building today! The city was called Atlantis, I have seen Atlantis!"

John raised a crooked brow upon hearing Charlie's claims, but did not dispute him. After all, he had witnessed an uneducated man such as Charlie build two pioneering contraptions by simply imagining them into fruition. Sure, Charlie studied his dad's blueprints and patents religiously, studying them intently, up into the wee hours every night but it was almost a waste of time. All that Charlie had were a few sketches, more or less. Charlie did it all himself.

Even though he had his father's blueprints, Charlie couldn't possibly find any use for them given his educational background.

Later in the afternoon, Charlie realized working would be impossible unless he ate and so he succumbed to the idea of preparing a meal. He had to fill his famished gut or he feared that he might collapse from the brain fog and dizziness he was experiencing. Charlie dropped his wrench and headed to the geodesic greenhouse in the backyard, hoping to find something growing.

When he got there, all he saw was three tomatoes and a few tufts of radishes. Most of the vegetation looked far from edible and Charlie knew the soil was to blame. It was too acidic. The tomatoes hung limp and dry, and the bell peppers never ripened all together. Charlie's stomach growled even more due to his anxiety.

The greenhouse was a small thing made of wood and hard plastic and even though its circumference was no bigger than a normal backyard pool, it served its purpose well. It was substantial enough to provide at least a month's worth of potatoes, leeks, peppers, shallots, and tomatoes that would contribute to a good soup or a ratatouille every now and then. However, the soil had to be treated constantly, and John was neglecting his farming duties lately because hunting was easier.

Charlie paced about inspecting the starved soil and decided he should treat it because the crops were not growing as fast as they should. After heading back inside, the tumult and clank of John's wrenches and hammers echoed through the vacant rooms. His calls for John went unanswered due to the clanking, and after peeking into the dining room, he saw John hunched close to his device, deep into his work.

"Any nitrates left?" Charlie asked.

"No, I used the last of them a month ago!" Charlie shook his head. *There goes our little farm.*

Charlie took angry steps to his cupboard hoping to find a can of corn in the back of the cabinets somewhere—but there were none left. The only thing inside the kitchen cupboards besides the dust were some strips of the salted Rabbit and Venison jerky that John had prepared, but Charlie didn't want to dip into John's private stash anymore. Charlie spent so much time searching for tools in the past week that he did not have time for finding food. John would gladly give up some of his jerky strips Charlie thought, he was sure of it. However, Charlie just did not want to rely on anyone, and he hated asking for favors.

After weighing his options, Charlie figured he would have to head to the FEMA camp so he could fetch his allotted ration box but first, he had to tidy himself up a bit. He walked very heavily up the stairs to his bedroom, dragging his feet. He changed his socks and put on his usual pair of blue jeans and surveyed his pile of clothes for the freshest shirt—a plain black one in decent shape, although frayed at the neck.

Charlie made sure to take his anti-drone cloak; made of metalized fabric—a special fabric that attenuated infrared light. The metalized fabric of the cloak held his body heat in check, body heat that would otherwise burn bright for all the infrared cameras mounted on the Overseer's recon drones, making him harder to pinpoint.

Before heading out, he thought John should know he would be gone for the day.

"John, I'm going to the camp for a ration box, it's cloudy out, and I need to take advantage," Charlie said.

John turned to him and his big eyes looked bigger through his magnified bifocals. He then shook his head in protest. "The hell with that place, take some of that salted rabbit—"

"No, no, you've done enough my friend," Charlie protested, waving his index finger.

"Rations wouldn't keep a house fly alive!"

"I might as well take advantage and fetch me one…besides, I need some of the radiation pills they give out."

John stopped working, set his screwdriver down and got up to face Charlie. "The pills don't work Charlie, I mean, look at us!" John cried.

Charlie ignored him. He grabbed his baseball cap on the coat rack and was about to head out before John ran over to the door to block his path.

"Charlie you might find it difficult getting back! I hear there's more security at the camp lately, ever since the Overseer found out that people were escaping the camps in droves."

Charlie did not seem worried. "Hopefully the camp still extends to the adjoining streets, it should be really easy to get back into the camp by accessing the city of tents. Besides, they still let people out to go on job interviews and I still have my FEMA camp resident ID."

John sighed, and he threw his hands into the air in disbelief. "Why are you so thick headed?"

"Look John, it's not just the food that I need—or the radiation pills—or the bus passes they give out to job seekers. The real reason why I'm going to get a ration box is for the prepaid cellular phone."

John scratched his chin. "I thought you said you didn't like using those prepaid cell phones because they have GPS trackers in them," John said uncomprehendingly.

"I know, but I'm not taking it back home. I only need it for a few minutes so I could access the internet. It has been a while since I surfed the web and need to keep up with the times. I mean—we live in the damn dark ages here, toiling day in and day out, without a hint of what's going on in the world; and most importantly, there's some rumors going on John! I heard some canyon dwellers mumbling about these rallies that are beginning to take place near the Central Park space elevator— something about a movement that is spreading, and the organizers of this movement have a website I want to take a peek at."

A heavy weight seemed to come over John's shoulders after hearing that. He knew about the recent rallies lately and they could only end in violence he thought. John asked himself, *What would Charlie do if the police instigated something? What if one of the protestors got out of hand?* John did not trust Charlie; he was too hot-tempered lately and too overconfident in his physical ability.

"You want to come with me?" Charlie asked.

John just stared at him in dismay. John had no interests in protests; he only wanted to finish his electromagnetic generator; he wanted to help all the refugees rebuild their lives again, and to give them the electricity they would need to store and cook food; he wanted to give all the jobless refugees the chance to charge their laptops again so they could watch their home videos and access the social media sites that would link them to friends and family scattered all over the planet; most of all, John wanted to reduce the dependence on the Overseer and his worker benefits. John felt the Overseer shouldn't matter, and John wanted to give free, sustainable energy to the masses so society could get the boost that it needed to rebuild again.

John approached Charlie, wiped his brow, took a deep breath, and spoke with a consoling tone. "Look Charlie, I know you're angry with the visitors and their Overseer, but these protests will only end up in violence. And that weapon you're building, well...if you ask me...the whole thing is too mad! I don't know what you plan on doing with that thing!" John shouted while pointing to Charlie's shiny metal antigravity scaler-wave cannon sitting on the dining room table. "I don't know how you managed to conjure up such a monstrous thing like that and I don't know what kind of dreams and epiphanies you may be having, but I do know one thing..." John paused to catch his breath, "your father would have been disappointed in you!"

Charlie cocked his head to the side, his frown deepened. "Look John, I know that machine of yours means a lot, and it's what my father's legacy was built upon, but it's only one generator. If we build it and power up several homes, what good will it do? If the Overseer shot down our plans to rebuild the transformers, then he'll surely shoot down our plans to mass produce my E. M. generators because to be quite frank, the

Overseer cares little about handing over free, sustainable, zero point energy to the people. Think about what it would do to his work force. No company of his would need to drill for oil anymore. No one would rely on the Overseer anymore for electricity and gas! Now... I really want to finish that thing tonight," Charlie continued hotly, pointing to the device on the other end of the table, under a bed sheet. "I'm just itching to demonstrate it!"

John's cool face stiffened after hearing that. His face leaned downwards and showed a stony look in his eyes. He nervously scratched his head, rubbed the bridge of his nose, and slid his hands down his long sideburns that went halfway down his cheeks. John just stared at him with pitiful eyes and Charlie didn't need to see his expression to know he was thwarted. Charlie could sense the pent up anger inside his friend.

"Charlie, look," John snorted, pausing to fight the urge to call him an idiot. "The generator is all you should be thinking about building! It is a huge breakthrough and it would surely get the attention of the masses. More and more people will inquire about our invention and perhaps only then will we gain the attention of some extraterrestrial sponsors that we'll need to begin mass production."

Charlie only returned and matched his steely gaze and said nothing in return.

Charlie knew what John was feeling and thinking. He knew that John was worried that he had lost his ability to reason, and he feared that Charlie was solely driven by his anger and rage just like anyone with advanced radiation sickness.

Charlie sucked in a gulp of stale air. His breaths became shallow and labored. He was the angrier one of the two because unlike John, Charlie knew something he did not. He knew something about Orion that only he thought to be true—and if John knew what he knew, he'd probably hate the Overseer and his corporation as much as Charlie did.

Charlie was always an authoritative man, but he never threatened John until now.

"John, I swear, I will go as far as ripping up the blueprints I gave you if I must," Charlie barked out fiercely. "I want you to cease all work on the generator and continue to work on the weapon in exact accordance with my instructions. And remember—we're just smiting the wicked!"

John could not look him in the eye after that. And Charlie could not either. After regretting his outburst, Charlie calmed himself down.

"I'm sorry for ordering you around all the time. Why—I don't even know why you stuck around for this long. But I think it's because deep down inside—you know John. I know you know! You know this was an invasion in disguise and the Overseer's goal is to create the perfect prison planet of slaves!"

"This act you plan on carrying out will stain you forever!" John shouted gutturally, his doughy face betokened his disapproval.

Charlie felt the strength of John's rejoinder and did not bother countering with any retort of his own. Charlie immediately wrapped his thoughts around the terrible conspiracy theories he had regarding the visitors. Ever since Charlie had conjured up his these theories, he couldn't stop gloating over them. His interest in helping the community with his father's scientific zeal degenerated into an unhealthy mania, and he became quite the extremist ever since his string of epiphanies led him to alter his father's blueprints and create a weapon out of them.

Charlie exhaled a lungful of tension and pointed to the weapon on the table, jabbing his index finger at it. "That thing I'm building—it's the only way John! You know why they refused our proposal to help rebuild the transformers! You know why they failed to alkalize the soil in order to create domed community farms! And do you know why they won't reopen the universities? Dependence!" Charlie finished in a snarl.

John did not bother to offer any retort of his own, and in a way, he was as cynical as Charlie was, but surely did not side with his cause which was to cause destruction and mayhem and to join a cult of disconnected civilians .

Charlie continued in a wide-eyed tirade. "They offer food, bread, jobs, and medicine during catastrophic times and you must very well know that the man who offers food and shelter in hell is crowned king! And if things go back to normal then we won't need them anymore!"

John shrank backwards after noticing Charlie's eyes begin to glow from the mania that seized him. Charlie didn't let up and continued his maniacal discourse. "If the rallies don't help and the masses don't awaken to the fact that they are being enslaved under the guise of salvation then I must send them a message with that weapon there on the table. I swear to you John—and I swear on my father's grave—that if I get that cannon to work, I will not hesitate to oscillate that RAPDA building with it! And if the Overseer does not come out, well—I'll use that scaler cannon to manipulate the molecules of his RAPDA building and melt its steel like ice cream! I will shake that Overseer out of his building! Only then will the visitors feel the wind of our displeasure! Only then will we release their corporate stranglehold that has gripped our government! And only then will we have the opportunity to ask the Overseer what nanobot implant's' true purpose is!"

John did not reply. He figured it was useless to try to reason with a man so consumed with paranoid delusions—and so he quietly walked back to his bench, put on his bifocals, and began working on the generator's semi-conductors.

Charlie grunted and waved a flat palm in the air after being ignored. He walked out of the door and towards the bus stop on the edge of the green district, which was just six miles down McDonald Avenue. He dismissed John's logic as the logic that comes from a man that is uninformed and naïve, and most of all— a man that was scared. According to Charlie, the weapon he was building was a necessary contraption that was long overdue in its completion.

10: Hunting For Canyon Dwellers

Brennan spent a whole day cruising through a red district in South Brooklyn, following Lieutenant Graham's drones, and he and his crew were averaging six arrests per hour. A grand police cavalry bracketed Brennan's vehicle all day long as they searched the streets; they were dressed in typical black SWAT setups with external bulletproof vests, black helmets, and full faced visors. Sometimes they spotted mutants before Graham did with his satellites and drones, and surprisingly, Brennan's team found more success just by going door to door. Occasionally they checked parked cars, and every once in awhile a mutant would be found sleeping in a bush or in a home. Most of the time, Brennan played paramedic more than policeman, because so many people the police had arrested were sick.

The NYPD had collected over three thousand mutated people in the last two days since the mission began. Most mutants happily agreed to be taken back to the camp where they would await their upgrade. They were so sick that they welcomed Brennan's task force with open arms after learning that their implants were malfunctioning, and most were glad that they were being detained so they could be upgraded with the promise of good health again.

Some, however, did not welcome the police presence in the red districts— and some refused to be detained, or "arrested" as some civilians had put it.

Brennan was surprised at how many people did not want to be cured; some just wanted to die. One mutant had to be shot and killed earlier that morning after she resisted detainment and tried stabbing one of Brennan's police officers with a sharp toothbrush.

As the evening sun dipped lower beneath the jagged horizon, Brennan wondered why Jasso was taking so long to give the order to call it a day. He was about to phone the Overseer but just before he reached for his hand-held, a digital envelope flicked in the corner of his contact lens. It had a number "1" next to it. Brennan blinked three times in order to open his inbox and found the message was sent by Colonel Jasso. On his contact lens, he saw-- *One Message:*

URGENT Still at the meeting, no time to talk. I want you to work a few more hours because they tend to come out at night

-Colonel Jasso

Brennan sighed at the notion and gave all the police officers in his van a doubtful look before grabbing the car's PA radio. "Our day isn't over boys," Brennan said sluggishly. "Looks like we're being mandated and need to continue our search."

The police on horseback sprang down the road in an instant. Their horses clacked carefully through the cracked streets and hugged the sidewalks to search the parked cars, which proved to be the more favorable of resting places in the concrete desert of crud.

Sergeant White, a superbly muscled veteran of the NYFD for thirty years, was driving Brennan's van. He was in charge of using the P. A. speaker on the vehicle, and spoke the same words all day long—

"Citizens, hear this; living in the red districts is no longer permitted by the chief Overseer. Many of you are sick and need immediate treatment. Please come out of your structurally unsound homes and allow us to deliver you back to the nearest transgenic clinic where you will receive an upgrade to your bio- modifications.

"I repeat; living in the red districts is now prohibited by the Overseer.

Besides the dangers posed from the increasing amounts of exploding gas mains and uncontrollable fires—you are all sick and I am sure you all know this by now. We only seek to help cure you all, and if you refuse to come with us to the nearest FEMA camp, you will be charged with refusing a mandatory upgrade and held on suspicion for harboring an infectious retro-viral disease. All citizens are to receive an upgrade by the end of this week. There have been an alarming amount of malfunctioning implants that have been taking place lately and some of you must already know that you've been getting sick. Now we know why. The Overseer has informed me that many of the clinics could be understaffed, and so you may get your upgrades at any FEMA tent or kiosk located in and around the green zones. Keep in mind that this is mandatory, and those who stall or refuse the upgrade will not be able to work, henceforth, losing all privileges. If you are homeless and do not reside in a FEMA camp, then please leave and visit your local FEMA camp immediately so we can appoint you to a transgenic clinic. Living in the red districts is now prohibited by the Overseer and against the law. Take notice of any National Guard or police patrolling the abandoned red districts. They will escort you to a nearby FEMA camp or transgenic clinic for your upgrade."

"Oh nobody is going to care," Brennan said to Sergeant White. "They all know they're sick, but no one is going to approach us. I just don't understand why no one seems to want any damn help!"

Sergeant White nodded. "We're going to have to go and fetch them then," he said.

"They're animals," shouted a police officer in the back of the van.

"They like living like animals," said a cop who sat behind Sergeant White. Brennan snorted. "Then we're going to hunt them down like animals!"

Brennan twitched his nose as he poked his head out of the car window. "I smell barbequed meat," he said inquisitively as he got out of the van. "Someone is cooking nearby; I'm going to go door to door to see if I find anyone. Besides, my legs could use a stretch anyway. I'll radio in when I'm done," Brennan ordered Sergeant White who grumbled, "yes sir" through his bushy mustache.

Brennan's real reason for leaving the van was not that he needed to stretch his legs, but that he wanted to call Elena one more time. He dragged a hand over his tired eyes as he dialed her number with his tablet, but the call was immediately disconnected. The ionic interference had made interstellar communication impossible, and he was flabbergasted at the fact that the interstellar communications were still down after three whole days. He then thought about General Clarkson and how he wanted to keep in touch with Brennan as the mission went on—and most of all, he wanted to be kept up to date with Jasso's strange behavior.

General Clarkson, I can't call you. I hope you get the hint and come down here already! Brennan thought.

Brennan rubbed his hands over his limp, grey hair and began to think about Colonel Jasso as he walked down a muddy sidewalk that was missing all of its concrete. He had trouble trusting the man, for all his courtesies. Something seemed to be bothering Jasso, despite Jasso's sleek flamboyant smiles and sanguine tone. Jasso's forced joy only made Brennan even more suspicious. Nevertheless, he swallowed his concerns and trudged on through the mud, peeking into the sun-washed cars that lined the gravelly road. Brennan was so taken aback by his surroundings that he didn't make too much of Jasso's queerness even though he would have liked to. All of Brennan's doubts and surmises about his boss became prominent in his mind only when he had time to spare. After all, he was being paid to do his job and follow orders. That's all Brennan had ever done in his career and that's all he could ever do.

After catching up to his cavalry at the end of the road, a gust of wind sent dry, brown leaves swirling around the hooves of the horses, and the smell of rain cut through Brennan's nostrils. It wasn't long after the wind picked up that a crackle of thunder was heard in the southwestern sky. Brennan looked up through the gray blanket of cloud and noticed how they were darker in that part of the southern sky. It looked like it was about to pour any second.

"Where do you think the smell of that meat is coming from?" One of the squarely built police officers asked.

"Let's try Victory Boulevard; seems like there's plenty of good homes left on that street. Let's go get this cook before he himself cooks to death."

The cops on horseback clacked down the perpendicular street and when the horses were out of his hearing range, Brennan took in the silence of the red districts; his ear twitched to the sounds of shouting in the distance but it only lasted for a few seconds. Following the audio trail, Brennan trudged across a nearby weedy mall parking lot and thought he saw something move in his peripheral vision. He stopped in his tracks after seeing something ruffle through the tall corn grass, but before he could make it through the waist-high weeds, the shapes were gone.

Brennan grabbed his walkie-talkie and hit up Graham who was back in Pandora's room, playing eye in the sky. "Lieutenant Graham, are you picking up anything just ahead of me?"

Within seconds, Graham's reedy voice popped over the radio. "Negative, Major. Just a pair of coyotes."

Brennan slapped his palm on his thigh in frustration and continued to scour the area for mutants until Jasso finally decided to give him the order to stop for the day. After scouting the neighborhood of Gravesend for an hour on foot, Brennan came across nothing but wild dogs and the occasional deer. What came across as strange about the wildlife was that they no longer had any of the tumors they used to have. And in fact, many of the wild deer were some of the strangest deer he had ever seen. Some of the younger deer seemed to glow when the sun hit them at the right angle. And it was not just the deer. Even the younger coyotes seemed to be born without any physical mutation.

At the intersections, mounds of concrete and steel were pushed aside, almost like snow banks, and the terrain was so full of nooks and crannies that Brennan did not know where to look first. In just one hour, he covered so much ground that he found himself standing a block away from his grandmother's old home, a place he really tried hard to avoid.

Brennan's tears pooled up at the bottom lid after witnessing his old neighborhood again. It was in such a sordid state that it made him too upset, and he had to wish the sadness away quickly because he couldn't possibly be seen crying in front of the other police officers who were all around him on their horses. Brennan took a deep breath to retune his nerves, and just as he was about to order his men to turn around and head back inland, the sight of a man with long black hair and a fierce beard appeared just up the block on Montauk Avenue. He was at least four hundred feet away and just a mere silhouette.

Lieutenant Graham's voice immediately rustled over the walkie-talkie. "I located a stray just ahead of you!"

"I see him!" Brennan blurted back into the radio.

Graham sounded worried through the static. "I can't see him anymore! Why —he seems to have disappeared entirely after putting on what appeared to be a cloak. But my Landsat satellites could only zoom in so close, so I couldn't really tell."

"Roger that, I still see him," Brennan said evenly and routinely. "But why do you think he disappeared?"

"Not sure," Graham said apprehensively. "But it may have something to do with a cloak he put on. I saw him put on a sweater or a hooded parka or something. It could be the material it is made out of that is shielding his heat signature from my satellites. Probably made out of some attenuating materials."

"Roger that, I'm moving in to engage," Brennan shouted out readily.

Graham then continued in a more jaded voice. "Not so fast, Major, I think you'd be interested in the larger group that I just picked up close by. I am picking up a crew of about five, located three hundred yards down Armstrong Avenue to your right."

"Mutants?"

"Yes Major, they're all mutants. I got them on the infrared and they all seem pretty cold compared to normal humans. They seem to be waddling about aimlessly, and one of them is wheeling a cart full of provisions. If I were you, I would focus on the larger group. We'll get the lone wolf with the fancy sweater later."

"Good idea; I'm on it!" Brennan blurted.

Brennan hefted his radio to his mouth and switched the VOIP channel so he could speak to his squad.

"Gentlemen, we have bogeys, I repeat, we have bogeys! Twelve o'clock. Corner of Armstrong Avenue and Montauk street!"

In just a half minute, all the men on horseback seemed to huddle together and galloped right past him, sending a gush of wind and a flurry of dry leaves into his backside.

"The sooner we get them all the quicker I get out of this hell," Brennan mumbled under his breath incoherently. As the police officers stampeded towards the mutants and commenced to arrest them, a distant rumble of thunder shook the ground beneath him and heavy rain began to come down in sheets.

Brennan's cavalry moved in towards Brennan's position and commenced towards Armstrong Avenue where the larger group of mutants were spotted, and when he got there, a crew of about five female mutants slowed down to a crawling speed after noticing Brennan and his cavalry. One of them was wheeling a shopping cart full of dead rabbits just like Graham had seen from the satellite vision.

Brennan clicked his Eye-Net lenses, and he immediately switched to the infrared spectrum. Sure enough, he noticed that the people ahead were indeed very cold, and their body heat gave off very little white light.

"They're mutants alright," Brennan relayed to his men rather dryly and routinely.

As his cavalry apprehended the paltry lot of people ahead, Brennan couldn't help but think of that lone wolf with the fancy cloak.

Should have gone after him instead, Brennan told himself. *A man who prepares to shield himself from the extensive gaze of the RAPDA agency must have something to hide.*

11: Back to the FEMA Camp

After hearing the tinny words coming from the police car's P. A. speakers, Charlie asked himself, *I'm not only plagued by radiation, but by retroviruses? Why don't they just let us die?*

Charlie furtively skipped through more mud soaked streets for miles, and was fortunate enough not to come across any authorities. After about an hour's worth of walking, he had reached the green zones unscathed and only a ten-foot chain link separated him from the green zone. He climbed the fence with the agility of a cat and when he peeked over his shoulder, Charlie became wowed by the contrasting images of the encroaching suburbs ahead. Behind him, the abandoned rec districts seemed like worlds of their own, reduced to nothing but desolate deserts of wreckage that seemed to span thousands of miles across and far away from civilization. To Charlie, the six-mile trek to the green district was like landing on another planet, so far from civilization yet, so close. Charlie walked to the nearest bus stop on Elmont Street; he was about to enter public life for the first time in months and it made him nervous. He tightened the buttons on his cloak and prayed that he would continue to remain indefinable for the entire journey ahead.

Oh no, I am not being implanted with anything anymore! Charlie told himself. He knew how dead he felt inside after being implanted and was keen enough to realize that his newfound psychic and physical powers were the result of some freak mutation that he didn't want corrected.

A pang of fear then rippled through him as he began to wonder if his GPS implant in his body was still active. He prayed that it disconnected a long time ago with his other nanobot implants—and after some thought, Charlie realized that it must not have been working anymore or the policemen in the van would have tried to apprehend him earlier when he saw them just down his street.

Even though Charlie entered the green district and was out of the prohibited red districts, Charlie's head was still nervously moving like it was on a swivel until the bus finally came. The bus was a bouncy old tub of bolts and Charlie's attempt to nap for the twenty-minute ride into Manhattan was pointless. The bus was such a rattlebox that he kept hitting his head against the window and the turbulent ride gave him a headache. Therefore, Charlie decided to get off a few blocks before his usual stop after realizing that something did not seem right with the surrounding skyscrapers. Something was definitely wrong because the tickers in Times Square were turned off. The billboards were all taken down years ago but not the lights, and even though it was still bright outside, Charlie found the whole of Times Square to be mysteriously darker than usual.

He crawled through Broadway with a furrowed brow the whole time, insensible to the torrential rain that soaked him to his bones. He was too preoccupied with his incisive search for any signs of electricity and by the time he got to 44th Street, he came to realize that there must have been another citywide blackout because there were no signs of any working electricity coming from any of the buildings that surrounded him.

Charlie feared the worst. *Another power outage!*

Charlie gritted his teeth and kept walking. The wind sighed between the tall buildings, delivering more rainwater into Charlie's face every so often. He walked with shorter strides because the puddles in the street began to thicken due to the onslaught of rain, and besides the rain, the streets also swelled with the commuters of the evening rush. Workers in street cleaner uniforms gradually gave way to workers in suits and business outfits. There were children coming out of the Internet schools on 45th Street and none seemed to say anything about a blackout taking place. The kids seemed unenthused, walking stiffly, and conversing plainly. They all spoke in monotone and were dressed in their identical uniforms: the boys in grey blazers with the Orion red trim, and the girls wore the same.

Charlie noticed a group of middle school children talking evenly under their umbrellas about job placement within the waste management system. Their schooling was more about job training than real education.

These kids are too young to be working such jobs!

They were barely eighteen years of age and Charlie thought they should be studying for skilled careers, not for mandatory waste management positions.

When he finally arrived at the edges of the FEMA camp, he gasped at the size of the fence that separated the camp from Central Park.

"Hoover City 2" was written on a shredded banner made of vinyl. It hung from the center of a chain link fence that enveloped a good chunk of Central Park, where the camp stood. He could see the refugees moving about from within, and Charlie could not believe how packed it had gotten. It grew three times larger since Charlie had seen it last, which was only four months ago.

As more and more people began to get sick and disconnect, the camp grew larger. Colonel Jasso knew the park had to be expanded somehow, and so he often thought about dedicating the entire park to FEMA's needs, however, he could not do such a thing because of the space elevator port located on the Great Lawn. The camp has since evolved into all the unoccupied, neighboring movie theaters, condemned apartments, and hospitals. However, the adjoining real estate ran out eventually, and so FEMA had no choice but set up a city tents around the edges of the park that began spilling into the streets and sidewalks. Hence the name, "Hoover City 2" which was named after the original Hoover City in Central Park back in 1929, when the depression forced the homeless into tented communities all around Central Park.

Charlie approached the opening in the chain link fence where a cone-shaped man stood inside a kiosk.

"Returning?" the FEMA employee said rather dryly.

Charlie nodded and groped in his pocket for his ID and handed it over to the man who took it carelessly. The FEMA man in the kiosk looked bored with his job, and he looked like a man who has not had a day off in months. He had long blonde hair that fell to his shoulders and his beard was unchecked. Hard work removed all the softness from his face and the FEMA worker made little eye contact with Charlie as he unflappably scanned the ID card on a small computer latched to his forearm. After swiping Charlie's card, a holographic image of Charlie's head emitted from the contraption on his wrist. The FEMA worker held out his arm and a laser shone into Charlie's eye. After the computer on his forearm had beeped, the FEMA employee nodded and allowed Charlie to walk through.

The large city of tents stretched deep down Broadway, and Charlie had to peer through squinty eyes to see how far the tents went. The exact size of "Hoover City 2" was hard to determine because of the lack of light. Shadows pooled and crept down the tall skyscrapers and onto the streets, grazing the masses of light-sensitive mutants with a welcomed shade.

Charlie's attention diverted towards many directions because of all the activity going on. All sorts of people were swarming in and out of their tents, and the ambient uproar from the masses had already given him a headache shortly after arriving. Charlie's head spun to his left when he noticed a few mud- specked men escorting a sheep inside a small storage container. The shutter was halfway open and a gang of children disgorged from it, carrying bottles of milk. Ragged and malnourished people poured from many of Hoover City's surrounding buildings; some held job applications and some walked aimlessly with their heads down, their cloudy looking eyes fixed on the ground. Charlie then focused on an old, thin, and toothless man that encircled his tent and shouted, "For the kids! For the kids!"

He was holding a basket full of withered looking apples and before he set the basket down, a crowd of skinny children greeted him. They pushed and jostled each other for a chance at getting their hands on an apple, and those who were lucky enough get their hands on an apple ate it greedily.

The sound of crying babies was deafening, and Charlie shook his head at the thought of all those newborns. No couple should bring a child into this world, Charlie so often thought. Processions of women were lined up near a small tent with a Red Cross symbol on it. They were all carrying newborn babies who drank from their dried up and wrinkled breasts. Some of the women were definitely pretty once, but not anymore. They had gaunt and hollow-eyed faces, and their hair looked brittle and dry.

Charlie had figured they had lined up for the inoculations, or perhaps the new upgrades Charlie thought. *They are not upgrading me! I'll kill anyone who makes me do so against my will...*

Charlie began to have doubts and began to think John was right about the risks involved with returning to the FEMA camp. *What if they won't let me out of this place unless I am upgraded?* Charlie thought. *Over my dead body! I'll kill again if it means not being stuck with another needle.*

Suddenly, Charlie saw a mother emerge from the Red Cross tent who cried over an infant girl that had apparently perished in her arms. The mother's grief- stricken wailing lasted for what seemed to be an eternity, and Charlie put a flat palm over each ear until it stopped because he didn't want any part of witnessing such a tragedy.

He eventually walked away from there but everybody around him depressed him. Charlie just shook his head in abhorrence whenever he stared into their dejected eyes. Charlie wished away the hackles on the back of his neck. At first, Charlie attached no special significance to the common sight of lumbering people, but after some thought, he realized how unnaturally sick most of them appeared. Almost every person in the camp was homeless because they were too sick to work, and like him, they were the terrestrial castaways and obsolete citizens of the new world order.

Charlie forced himself to pay no attention to the madness that enveloped him and then shifted his focus to the reason of his visit—the ration box. *The sooner I get this ration box the sooner I'm out of here,* he thought.

Charlie fixedly headed down a gravelly bike path that led to a patchy grove where the FEMA kiosks were. The closer he got to them, the more people he encountered. Charlie loped behind them, careful not to get too close to anyone because the stink coming off some of them was choking. Charlie eventually got tired of clamping his nose, so he just quickened his pace and decided to get off the bike path all together. He began to regret coming to such a ghastly place.

You were right John...for once, you were right...

He dashed across brown wet weeds in order to get a jump on the crowd and came out of the foliage with wet, dead leaves stuck to his jeans. When he arrived at the grove, he saw nothing but a procession of ragged people lined up in front of the many tents and kiosks set up by FEMA. All sorts of people scampered away from the kiosks with their boxes, opening them tightfistedly and immediately consuming its contents. Some people however, were too sick to eat and vomited right there on the line. Some spat up blobs of mucus and blood, and those who were in bad shape were escorted to Red Cross tents by FEMA personnel where they would be upgraded at once. For some it was too late.

Some people were just dead on the ground, yet to be discovered by the many paramedics who routinely marched about the place.

Charlie shook his head in disgust. *If there were a God or a group of Gods, then they would not have spared us.*

On the bright side, Charlie did notice that some people did not look sick at all. Just like him. One particular woman stood a few spots in front of him in line, and she seemed to have the healthiest of teeth, although she still looked a bit pale. Another young woman behind him was slender, but still had meat on her bones compared to most people. She had a cute heart shaped face and had glossy chestnut hair, and Charlie could see her humanity still left in her eyes.

Oddly enough, Charlie had fancied the quaintest of ideas after spending time around the people. He noticed that whenever he walked by one of the healthier looking mutants, he could almost sense a different energy from them—an odd connection of some sort. Charlie could only guess that it might have been an empathic response, but he shook it off as a misapprehension. However, he did acknowledge the fact that he felt the same energy emanating from his friend John, who also wasn't as sick as most disconnected people. He originally thought he and John lived together for so long that they sensed each other well. However, he was beginning to think it had something to do with certain mutants— the ones who still had human eyes.

Charlie shook of the thought, blew out a few bursts of tense air in his lungs, and trudged ahead through the crowd until he got to a line of people. Charlie then noticed that a healthy looking mutant male with long stringy blond hair turned around to face him, and the mutant stared him down.

What's his problem? Charlie asked himself.

The truth was that Charlie's presence had distracted the blonde man, who like Charlie, was one of the healthier mutants in the crowd—and capable of empathic responses. The blonde man was pale and his eyes were red-rimmed, but he did not look like a zombie by far. The man locked eyes with Charlie and never shifted his gaze from him.

Charlie sensed that the blonde man was sad and filled with anguish. He also sensed that his sadness mingled with rage too. There was still a soul behind those eyes of his. Suddenly, the man approached him with determined steps as he swiped at his sallow cheeks in order to wipe away tears. He never freed his eyes from Charlie's the entire time he approached, his face was only clean where the tears streamed down to his chin, and when he got close enough, he handed Charlie a flyer. Without much ado, the man changed direction and gave Charlie a reassuring nod before disappearing into the crowd behind him.

Charlie immediately read the flyer with wide eyes; it was more like a parchment than a professional computer printout—

"Where is the Overseer? We will draw him out from behind the curtain and inform the masses about the depths of his failures. Join the movement.

Tomorrow, Central Park Great Lawn, 12pm. Weather permitting of course."

- A Patriot

12: Civil Unrest

Charlie hated that term—"third world." After all, it wasn't until the aliens landed that Charlie had realized what third-world living conditions meant.

The third world term is from the alien perspective! In reference to the simple and primal way in which Earthlings used to live in the past, before the extra-terrestrial intrusion on Earth—and the way native Earth Indians chose to live on Earth, which we all know is the third world from the sun. Therefore the term—"third world living conditions" was born. It was obvious to Charlie that the alien intrusion on Earth had occurred a long, long time ago. Way before the term "third world" was invented for sure, he thought.

Charlie shook off his thoughts after the line began to move a bit. Charlie's frustration subsided as the line suddenly inched forward shortly after another FEMA employee joined to help at the kiosk.

"Food for all" was written in a digital sign bolted above the kiosk.

There were just three people ahead of Charlie in the line, and as he inched up, Charlie approached the kiosk with curiosity, observing his environment with the eyes of a cat, watching several FEMA workers unload the boxes from the military cargo trucks parked just behind the kiosks. The FEMA director that handed out boxes was a heavyset man with a fleshy nose that seemed disfigured with red boils. Charlie watched him for a better part of a whole minute, and judging by his body language, Charlie knew the man surely must have hated his job—and he surely hated all the scummy people that surrounded him.

"Good day to you," Charlie said to the director when it was his turn in line. The director only acknowledged him in silence. He scanned Charlie's iris with a shiny metallic rod, punched his name into the computer and then handed Charlie an eight-by-eight square inch cardboard ration box before muttering the words, "You are disconnected."

Charlie swallowed his stomach back down after hearing that.

"You must report to a Red Cross tent for your upgrade in order to continue to receive your benefits every month," the director said. He said it in a manner that indicated he didn't feel like talking. Charlie gave him a dirty look as he trailed away from the kiosk with his ration kit. "Thanks for the tip," he said. But what he really meant to say was, *over my dead body*.

Charlie stood well clear of the Red Cross tents and he suddenly felt he should get out of the camp as soon as possible. However, he was so languid from the hunger, that he decided to hang around for a while and eat right then and there. He found a nice clean spot on the ground, courted himself on his clean towel, and opened his ration box. Charlie furiously rummaged through all of its contents. In it were a few dried foods, some dried soup, chicken paste, veggie powder, dried milk, a packet of crackers, a rainwater filter, a bottle of water pills, anti-radiation pills, and a bottle of what was labeled, "Happy Pills." Charlie tossed the pills aside on the ground. He figured some poor soul in his last few days of life could use them.

Charlie quickly took out a tube of hydrolyzed chicken paste and squeezed the contents into his mouth. It tasted like salty butter, but it would do. Before he swallowed it, he stuffed a few crackers into his mouth and hardly chewed for more than a second before swallowing it down. He cared little for the taste; he ate quickly and boisterously. He had just a few sips of water left and gulped it down before opening up his new bottle. He then reached for the powdered vegetables, poured the powder into the fresh bottle of water, and sipped most of it before taking a final chug. Charlie topped his meal off with a water pill to keep him hydrated. Last, but not least, Charlie burrowed through the box for what he originally came for, the pre-paid cell phone, and he wasted no time flicking it to life.

Good afternoon Charlie Beasley, said the font on the cell phone's small LCD screen. He then tried logging onto the Internet but he had no service.

All of a sudden, a FEMA employee began to speak to a crew of National Guards. "Guards!" he shouted out to the several guards patrolling the lines. "We are short on boxes so don't let anyone else get on the line!" the heavyset FEMA employee said to a square-built soldier who replied with a nod. Several people in the crowd gasped at once after hearing it. Within seconds, several National Guard hopped off their horses to guard the back of the line, making sure no one else got on the line.

Ration boxes were never short of supply, Charlie thought. *They were never short on food before!*

The heavyset FEMA director grabbed a bullhorn. "Ladies and gentlemen, we regret to inform all of you that we have just handed out our last ration box for the day; those who did not receive their box will get one by Friday morning at the latest," he said rather indifferently.

"Not again," Charlie whispered to himself. People immediately began hurling insults towards the FEMA personnel inside the kiosks and tents. Charlie had a flashback to the time when an Orion Corp. official announced to the remaining ambassadors of the United Nations that there was no more room on the starship for people. There were many riots in the streets those days; they continued for weeks on end, and Charlie had figured they were about to start all over again.

The heavyset FEMA director continued to bawl into the bullhorn in a most indifferent way. "Ladies and gentlemen, please stay calm, we have received word that our backup generators will bring power to this facility shortly."

"I'm starving, damn you!" said a skinny man towards the director who remained unfazed at all the riposte coming from the masses. He was, after all, very accustomed to the quarrels and tribulations that came with his job.

"We are very sorry for this inconvenience," the FEMA director said blankly. "Unfortunately our re-inventory systems are all electronically controlled—and as you all may have come to know by now, we are experiencing a citywide blackout and a shutdown of wireless communications. Our ration orders are digitally tied to the freighter ship's computers that are responsible for our deliveries, and so many of our freighter ships never made the trip to Earth in time due to the lack of computer access. Therefore, you see, ladies and gentlemen, we didn't receive all of our shipments this morning due to the power outage and so our trucks are a bit short. Like I said, we have made efforts to get some emergency shipments here by tomorrow morning at best, but apparently even wireless communication is not available to us due to an X-class solar flare that hit Earth yesterday."

The FEMA director's explanation was not enough to calm the crowd. Some of the more mutated looking people began hurling foul language at the man and so he walked back to his cargo truck parked behind the kiosks and found safety inside.

"We need more food now, my family is starving!" said one frail, old craggy- looking man wearing what looked like a homemade tunic.

A couple of superbly muscled National Guardsmen with standard urban camouflage uniforms approached the crowd with their hands on their pepper spray. One of the soldiers shouted, "Now! Calm down or you'll be forced to feast on mud and rock in one of our prison cells!"

"Aren't we already in one?" screamed out a stony-looking feeble woman wearing nothing but a sash, all while busting out in curses. "Damn you, Orion puppets! You are all being used by the visitors!"

The soldiers just smirked and gave out chuckles of amusement. Charlie had little cause for fear, but he backed away a bit after witnessing several National Guardsmen draw pepper spray canisters. Charlie stiffened for a moment before scampering off towards the bike paths that skirted the park fence. He wanted no part in the skirmish.

After a while, the crowd snapped. The rocks flew, and the soldiers had no choice but to drench the crowd with yellow clouds of pepper spray. The crowd of people who were angry just minutes ago collapsed to the pavement in agony, clutching their faces, bellowing in pain. Those who weren't in the mist's path had given up and most of them had their heads down in disappointment, hopelessly walking back towards the tents and storage containers with empty hands and empty stomachs.

The act made Charlie sick, seeing the masses reducing themselves to barbarism, and seeing how incompetent the government had become. Charlie could not understand why they had to throw rocks just because they didn't receive their concentrated rations and water pills. After all, all of the new, evolved animals that are roaming about in the red districts could support an entire city for years on end; no one should starve if they had any hunting skills. After bearing in mind the hateful disposition of several citizens, Charlie began to feel pity for them in a way, despite seeing them fall to barbarism.

Charlie continued to back-trot away from the chaos so he could see the riot's outcome. In just seconds, the crowd dispersed and all that remained were those who were sprayed—left on the ground blinded and incapacitated. After the turmoil had ceased, there was a tense silence amongst the crowd; no one and nothing in the crowd seemed to speak or move—except for the great muscles in Charlie's face, which were worked with passion due to the revulsion he had just witnessed. Charlie's face turned red and he frothed from his mouth as he felt his hot blood leap around his veins. After calming himself, he realized that he was glad he made the decision to come to the camp. What he saw all day was enough to motivate him into doing something and after reading that flyer, Charlie looked forward to grasping that opportunity to enlist the masses to resist the alien oppression.

13: The Rally

It was a perfect morning for a rally, and the organizers made sure the day would be cloudy. The rally began during the latter part of a warm and sunny morning, but once Orion's cloud-seeding planes made a few rounds over the city, a thick blanket of engineered clouds blanketed the morning sky, providing the sickly civilians with a friendly shade.

Over two thousand people filled the Great Lawn in Central park, mostly "Hoover City 2" residents, and the surrounding avenues and plazas were buzzing with all sorts of people who were making their way towards the Great Lawn—workers and refugees alike.

Most commercial businesses had ceased operation due to the power outages and the rally gave some of the worker class something to do. Charlie noticed all types of workers: factory workers, waste management personnel, internet teachers, restaurant cooks, bus drivers, teachers, elevator port workers, HAM radio operators, sanitation workers, office clerks, landscapers, and even some police officers stood in the crowd.

Charlie noticed there was an unhealthy glitter in most of the eyes of the refugees, but the healthier people scared him even more. They seemed to have a swarthy and sinister look in their eyes as if they were saying, *Who is this degenerate with the bullhorn?*

Most of them were laughing, but the poor folk stared intently. Especially a peculiar group with designer T-shirts that spelled, "Visitors, help or get out."

Charlie's energy was good, as good as it has been in quite some time, especially since John decided to show up. John's appearance only gave Charlie more confidence. What Charlie didn't know was that John thought the rally was a waste of time; he only showed up to make sure Charlie didn't lose that irrepressible temper of his.

Charlie walked towards the center of the Central Park lawn and stood in front of the crowd with his bullhorn, waiting for his cohorts to finish handing out pamphlets. The protesters were kind enough to let Charlie use the bullhorn for an hour after hearing what Charlie had to say and so Charlie wanted to make the most of that hour. He felt butterflies fluttering in his belly but wished them away rather easily after taking a good look at all the blank apathetic faces in the crowd. Charlie peered over to get a glimpse of his friend John for some confidence. John never had a thing for crowds, and so he sat patiently on a park bench over by the bike paths, where he was close enough to hear. When Charlie made eye contact with him, John gave him a military salute and nodded reassuringly.

The crowd was impressive; it reached all the way down to the edges of the space elevator port, as well as down to the park's East side where all the leafless trees stood. Charlie then heard whistling from the stringy looking blonde man that initially handed him the flyer over at the FEMA camp. The man nodded, indicating that every one of the organizers were finished handing out their pamphlets.

"You may start your speech now," said the blonde man.

Right before Charlie was about to speak, he noticed something that would make for a suitable stage. What was once a satellite that orbited the Earth was now a pile of charred, space-junk around the size of a school bus. It went down a year ago after an X-class coronal mass ejection fried its navigation system and it landed right in the park and was never cleaned up.

Charlie found a few divots on the charred steel and used them to climb the eight-foot high hunk of metal until he found some flat, steel paneling that would support his weight. When he got to the top, he stood erect upon his platform before the masses and then stared at the crowd. All one thousand plus stood broadside into each other, staring at him at once, causing Charlie to swallow a lump. An icy firmness had taken over his body, and he could feel his pulse pounding in his fingertips as he grabbed his bullhorn. His mouth turned as dry as sand, words were hard to come by at first, so he took a deep breath, cleared his throat and then spoke in his usual silky smooth voice.

"Thank you for showing up, ladies and gentlemen; I'm happy to say that this Inhabit Central Park movement is larger than I had foreseen it to be. And I come here before you all today in hopes to lead us back to the ways of kindliness and fellowship so we can regenerate our dying planet together!"

As loud as his voice sounded through the bullhorn, some did not seem to pay attention. Charlie stalled after noticing some of the healthy working class people not listening, instead, talking amongst themselves. Some broke out in peals of laughter and some never even cared to pay Charlie any mind at all, and it irked Charlie. Therefore, he took a deeper breath, and he spoke into the bullhorn with more gusto—

"People, people, quiet down," Charlie began in an unmoved tone that suggested he was not used to commanding a crowd of people still. "I'm here before you all today because I demand a reckoning from you all, and I want to express my feelings towards this hard and pitiless existence on our dying planet that has been worsened by the visitors who had so ruthlessly and wantonly ravaged us."

Charlie was surprised to hear a mad gasp erupt from the startled crowd. Charlie could not hear exactly who was shouting back at him, because all he heard were muffled voices— ranging from the back to the front of the crowd.

"The visitors have saved us!" a shrill voice was heard in the distance. "They are our benefactors!"

"How could you blame them for anything?" another voice said.

Charlie cleared his throat, and even though the adversity stung his pride a bit, he figured he would reply in a reserved tone, suppressing his nerves as best he could. He told himself it was the ignorance amongst the masses that made them think such things, so it didn't arouse his fierce nature. Getting angry with the people would solve nothing and would most likely diminish his reputation as an upright leader.

Charlie took in a lungful of air and pressed the bullhorn closer to his lips. "People, people, just sit back and think for a moment. Do none of you see that the visitors have curtailed our liberties with social and economical barriers to ensure them that their slave labor force remains intact? Our natural resources are being sucked dry and taken up into space, and I do not speak of just the minerals and the crude oil, no, the resources I also speak of is the people. They took the best people and our most educated survivors! They literally have left us commoners here to toil for their corporation. Yet, none of us share Orion's prosperity, and none of us receive the proper education that would potentially lead us out of this mess we're in!"

The crowd began to cheer, causing Charlie to pause. Charlie felt a surge of vitality flow through him from a couple of cheers that emerged here and there. The words that passed through his lips had engrossed over a thousand people, and it was a good feeling. During his pause, he noticed a meek and ambient gossip arise from the crowd, and many of the people turned and muttered to each other—some nodded, and a few shook their heads. The full import of Charlie's declaration sunk in upon the crowd and a great cry arose from them. The cheering made Charlie shudder with confidence. It was good to know that there were indeed some people out there beside himself that had common sense as well as the human instincts of a civilized order. However, he noticed a few jeers again, mostly from healthy looking people.

"To all of you who haven't received your monthly ration box...do not fret," Charlie blurted into the bullhorn and paused for a more dramatic effect. "There is plenty of animal game in the red districts—squirrels, pigeons, and even fish. And to all of you who still live in the FEMA camp there," Charlie continued pointedly. "There is plenty of good real-estate in the red districts!"

Then, a voice that came from the middle of the crowd arrested Charlie's attention. "Who needs a home in the green zone anymore nowadays!" a grim woman in the crowd began to shout. She was attractive, and had a finely chiseled face and exquisite eyes, yet her face was red and splotchy. She then shouted, "This gentleman speaks the truth. There's plenty of real estate out there for us that we could fix very easily if we had electricity for our tools and if we could power all the cars and trucks with anything other than their gasoline!" she then bawled out as she turned to face all parts of the crowd. Charlie smiled.

Seeing such flecked beauty diminished all the weight upon his back and released all the shy reserve previously ensnared in Charlie's throat. Moreover, his pained expression on his face slowly formed back into place.

"Yeah!" Charlie began. "We don't need their gasoline!" Charlie boldly barked. The crowd's noise died down after he said that and after a pause of silence, some people burst out in laughter.

Suddenly, a burly man in a business suit spoke up. "What do you expect us to do, walk to work? Sure, many of us take horses to work, but what about me? I'm a guy who works twenty miles away from my house! Do you expect me to take a horse to work?"

Charlie stammered after most of the crowd began to laugh and snicker amongst themselves. He thought about a device he planned on working on that could turn water into combustible gasses, but he did not dare tell the crowd about his inventions. He was afraid someone would follow him and steal it, or perhaps the Overseer would confiscate it and deem it a weapon of mass destruction.

Charlie then figured he'd tell the people about the ability to turn water into fuel and gave Orion the credit for knowing how.

"People, people, people," Charlie shouted. The entire snickering in the crowd stopped. "Orion knows of ways to separate the oxygen and hydrogen molecules in water; I read up on how they extract water from asteroids, and this water could be processed into fuel by breaking apart the oxygen and hydrogen molecules."

"Yeah!" All the disconnected mutants shouted in unison. On the other hand, the healthier people began to laugh and snicker again.

"This guy's a dreamer," said a voice from afar. "This guy's a quack," said another.

Many of the people in the crowd began arguing amongst each other.

"Let the man speak, let the man speak!" an older woman demanded—she was thin as rails and had bloody feet. Most of the crowd listened. She then began cupping her hands to her face and shouted, "Where's that oxygen manufacturing plant they promised for the terra-forming project?"

Charlie continued eagerly. "They promised us technology but didn't deliver.

They promised us that they would reduce our ocean levels by refreezing the polar ice caps with a process they called ice-denucleation—but they didn't. The problem here is that we are forced to depend on them in order to rebuild our society because they took away our most skilled workers and shut down our factors and universities. To make matters worse, they continue to suppress pioneering technology in geomagnetic free energy...and do you know why?" Charlie asked before pausing.

"Because they fear geomagnetic power would lead to advanced space travel. And the alien Orion Corporation doesn't want us out amongst the stars!"

Many of the mutants cheered—but more of the healthy people in their uniforms laughed. The laughter was heard as far as the space elevator dock, where most of the loaders had stopped unloading the cargo because they were distracted by Charlie's speech. It was discouraging to Charlie.

On the other hand, Charlie also noticed some people taking videos with their cameras and it sparked even more life in him. If the videos went viral on the web, then he might not only be talking to a thousand people standing on a lawn, but potentially tens of thousands, or even more, Charlie thought. Charlie then jumped down from the satellite and walked amongst the crowd, hunched over his bullhorn and shouted, "We belong in space! We belong in space!" Charlie yelled the phrase repeatedly until a well-groomed man with glossy hair approached him.

"Why would Orion not want us in space? I'm sure Orion would be proud to see us build ourselves up into getting out there. This takes time!"

Charlie lost it. The veins in his neck became corrugated and thick; his face flushed. "Time?" he snarled, and then climbed back on top of the satellite. "If we ever made it up there, they would lose another slice of the pie that is their mining monopoly. We would wind up exploring space and discovering celestial bodies and Orion wants every planet's resources for themselves! They want nobody else invading their real estate! That is why the visitors have been suppressing technology on this planet for years and ensuring that our economy revolved around crude oil!"

Then a deep voice from within the crowd rang through the mob after they had lapsed into a silence. "Why do you think we never went back to the moon after 1969? Even with 2020 tech, it couldn't be more dangerous than space shuttle missions!"

Another voice then chimed its way through the silent park. "They were already on the moon and didn't want us taking their Helium 3!"

Voices came from all directions, and Charlie could only filter out a few of them. A sickly looking black woman then squirmed herself in front of the crowd so she could speak. She looked haggard, skinny, and had melanomas on her face.

"Mister, mister," the women cracked. "Why— why don't we just hop on these space-elevator cars?" she choked out and continued with a note of hysteria in her voice. "The elevators are scattered all over the world, and we should board them one day and sneak into the ships that are docked above it!"

Charlie waved her off. "That was already tried years ago when they announced that there was no more room on their ships for us poor folk to live. I remember a group of folks planned on doing exactly what you just said—they hopped into the space elevator cars out in Moscow somewhere, but the car never rose up the wire. They kept it grounded. The only way to get their attention is to stop buying gasoline and speak out! Let them hear our voices, and let them know that the Earth will no longer continue to be raped and deflowered of its resources!"

A wild howl of jubilation arose from the crowd; some cheered in approval, while some grudgingly jeered again.

"We want the Overseer to show himself and to come out from his building there...there." Charlie pointed to the RAPDA building in the far distance, looming high in the north, shining between several slits and cracks in the cityscape. "We want him to let us through the road blocks and military checkpoints that lead to the building already! We want him to let us in there so we can set up a government! Run by us, the people of Earth!" Charlie snarled on the bullhorn, his cheeks burned, and his eyes intensified to the size of golf balls. "And most of all—we want the Overseer to grant us access to the Vatican Archives, which they continue to keep guarded in fear that we will learn of the ancient knowledge stored there. Knowledge that can lead to solving our energy crisis!"

The crowd froze again; the entire mass of people seemed to draw in a collective breath all at once, and the cheers and jeers that followed seemed to balance out. Most of the jeers came from the space elevator port workers, who suddenly began approaching the crowd from the dock port. A taut, stocky looking worker in an Orion uniform suddenly shouted from afar, "Oh just put a cork in it mister, why do you complain about gasoline and oil?" The crowd became silent after the stocky man spoke up louder. "You have food, a phone, a FEMA camp to live in, free horse rentals, you are lucky to be alive! These aliens landed and saved us! They gave us jobs and so what if they took whatever was left of Earth's greatest minds? We have cars to get to our jobs, and that's all that matters. We all have solid roofs over our heads and most of all—we all have good health! And it's all because of the visitors!"

Then, a paunchy man jostled in the crowd to get to the front so he could speak. He wore a collared shirt, tie, and an Orion ID dangled from his shirt pocket. He was a clerical cataloger for Orion's hydrofracking mining operations. Charlie sighed because he knew he was about to be assaulted with more words from this man judging by his unyielding frown and his rigid eyes.

"I've seen your kind before," said the man, jabbing a finger towards Charlie. "I know a mutated savage when I see one, you're not sick physically, but mentally! I have nothing but repugnance for your kind, for that hideous, lonely, and loveless life you must live! You deny Orion's upgrades and their medicine. You're must be so ashamed of yourself that you cannot bring yourself to live amongst us because of what you may have done in the past, and the demons that prowl within you tell you that you don't even deserve to live amongst society! You feel as if you don't deserve anything good so you just lurk around the edges of town, never accomplishing anything in life. You figure that it's best to bring others down with you, hoping they will help you burn the world some more by telling us to quit our jobs and live as barbarians, just like you do!" The man quickly turned around on his heels and headed away from the crowd.

Some people cheered the man, and some booed him.

Charlie stammered as he attempted to reply—the man's words seemed to stir something primitive in him and he had to refrain from lashing back. The man had assumed him for some misfit based on his vagabond appearance, and that was all the worker class citizens needed to see that would lead them to dismiss Charlie as a lunatic.

Charlie reminded himself to stop pressing his lips as he stood atop the satellite groping for words. Even though some of the unemployed mutants cheered, all Charlie could hear were the boos. Charlie tried hard to block the onslaught of adrenaline that leapt in his veins and fought hard to refrain from losing decorum. If he did, the people would deem him unstable and a savage for sure, Charlie thought, and if the people got a glimpse of Charlie in his angriest form, no one would take him as seriously. Why—he would probably scare everyone off the lawn, both mutants and workers alike.

Charlie tried to forget the storm of denunciation he heard moments ago and took a deep breath. He then wiped the anguished look clean off his face and proceeded to speak calmly. "I've said enough," Charlie began in an unmoved tone. "I see that most people in the crowd agree with me and some do not. Now, some of you won't boycott gasoline and some of you will continue to work for Orion Corp. It doesn't matter what I say, you will dismiss me as a lunatic and go on. However, to those who stood by me today and supported my dictum—I say this—" Charlie paused to take a deep breath and then roared into his bullhorn, "Do not give into Orion's mandatory upgrades!"

This time the entire crowd sighed and gasped at once. Most of the workers booed him.

"You're out of your mind " hundreds of voices shouted at once. "He's right, he's right," screamed another hundred voices.

Charlie lost all control of his emotions and began growling into the bullhorn this time. "To all of you there, in the Hoover City FEMA camp!" Charlie turned towards the outlying camp to his right. "Stay away from those Red Cross tents!"

Even though the fenced encampment was a hundred yards away, Charlie could see some of the refugees rushing towards the enveloping fence.

"The nanobots they are putting into us are not what they say they are! Sure, they keep our bodies from decaying, but I have a feeling that they are doing something to our minds! We just don't know what they're putting into our bodies and until we do, please, I beg you all, don't visit your local transgenic clinic this week. Don't get that upgrade!"

"But what if we get sicker?" an old man with a hunched back asked with doubtful words.

"Yeah, I can't afford to refuse those upgrades," said a skinny man with a red, swollen face. "Have you seen my face? I have radiation poisoning!"

Charlie replied with good grace. "We will demand an investigation of their molecular medicine, which shouldn't take long once we get some blood results, and if the visitors do not comply, then they will surely feel the wind of our discontentment!"

The crowd gasped itself still. Most of the worker class citizen even began leaving the lawn and fixedly headed towards the park's main gate.

"I had it with this quack," said a voice. "He's a real loon, that guy," said another.

Charlie glanced over to his friend John who sat in the distance near the bike paths. He was shaking his head. In less than a minute, the workers all began making their way off the lawn, towards the footpaths and out onto the streets. Most of the mutants seemed to cheer after they began to leave and they all applauded with wide grins, some pumping their fists, and many of them shouted reassurances at Charlie.

The majority of the crowd rang with applause and that was good enough for him. Even the refugees could be heard cheering from behind, where the fenced in Hoover City FEMA camp stood. Unfortunately, some of the working class citizens did not agree with him and they all stormed away. It was unfortunate too, because after all, they were the ones who had all the power— the power to change things. Charlie thought that the implants in their bodies must have taken away their ability to reason and took away their souls all together.

Nevertheless, a surge of poise ran through Charlie's spirit after realizing that some people had supported him. The cheering helped to thin out the sorrow that had gnawed at Charlie's heart for many years before.

14: Charlie's Arrest

Elena was so intrigued about what the peculiar man on the bullhorn had to say that she decided to stay at Central Park until she saw the rally through. She didn't hear Charlie introduce himself at first because she arrived late, and Elena didn't get close enough to hear him until the working class citizens stormed off the lawn, giving Elena some well-needed elbow room to move in close enough so she could catch the end of Charlie's speech.

Elena didn't hear the part when Charlie begged the crowd to refuse the upgrades, so she didn't know what all the booing and cheering was about. By the time she got there, Charlie was wrapping up his day and getting ready to go home with John. Charlie spoke less and less ever since the worker class citizens left. Instead, he began making rounds through the crowd, shaking people's hands and only occasionally shouting something out through his bullhorn. Elena spent the entire day listening to people who recounted segments of Charlie's speech, and she found that Charlie shared the same enthusiasm that she had when it came to fixing Earth. Therefore, she tried hard to get closer to Charlie, who seemed to be making many friends as he sifted through the crowd.

Before she knew it, the day advanced past five p.m., and Elena found herself yawning so hard that her jaw muscles began to lock. It' had been twelve hours since she left the Niagra and arrived on Earth via the space elevator cargo car, which she had to sneak into. She was hungry and tired, and even though she still needed to find a hotel room, Elena could not bring herself to leave after several people in the crowd began chanting Charlie's full name in one massive, jubilant cheer. After hearing Charlie's name, Elena pulled out her tablet.

Her adroit fingers slid over the glass in a hurry, and she wasted no time browsing the one and only social network site on the internet. After typing in Charlie's name, Elena learned that there was no profile with the name Charlie Beasley. Besides a few blogs here and there, Charlie had very few online footprints all together.

Elena found him to be a full-spirited man, and she admired him for what he said, even though she had missed what he said earlier about the upgrades. Elena found Charlie's speech enlightening to say the least. She had no idea how neglected Earth really was until she heard the latter half of his speech and she wanted to hear more. After some jostling, she finally made it close enough to see Charlie a bit better but not well enough. She squirmed through a crack between two bodies and craned her neck over the looming crowd to get a glimpse of him, but he was barely visible through the dozens of picket signs in front of her. All she could discern from where she stood was that he seemed to be a decent looking man, despite his haggardness. Elena thought that Charlie was very singular in appearance, and an almost ideal example of manhood. He had a lofty frame she thought; and showed the carriage and posture of a king whenever he spoke.

It took some time to knife her way through the sea of bodies, and after a few minutes of jostling, she got close enough to see him even better. His face was attractive but almost completely hidden by his ruddy beard. His dark eyes were bloodshot but they seemed to be full of life. He would have come off as impressive if it wasn't for his unkemptness—and of course, his stark, pale complexion.

Suddenly, the majority of the crowd began to boo all at once.

What is going on? Elena wondered. All she could see was an army of helmets bouncing their way through the crowd, heading straight towards Charlie. The sea of people parted to let them through, and Elena saw that the men were indeed law enforcement personnel. The majority of them were local riot police and there was one other soldier in a scarlet uniform trailing them.

Dad? Elena wondered.

She couldn't be sure from her vantage point because all she saw was the RAPDA logo on the cap. It was the cap of an Orion Corp. military man, like her dad's. As the crowd dispersed, the police approached the satellite that Charlie stood on but didn't do anything at first. .

A couple of squarely built police officers seemed to be muttering under their breath, and whatever it was that they were saying, Elena knew it took everyone who heard it by surprise because people began to boo.

"Come on! What's the big idea here!" a voice screamed. "We're holding a peaceful protest!"

Elena pushed through the crowd and inched closer to the front so she could listen in on the RADPA agent's discussion with the police. When she got close enough to make out the details, Elena learned that the RAPDA agent was not her dad after all, but a younger man that she did not recognize due to the large dark shades that covered half his face.

Suddenly, one of the police officers motioned for Charlie to give him something, and he was curling his palm towards his body. Charlie shook his head in protest and his refusal to cooperate seemed to anger the RAPDA agent with the extra large sunglasses.

"Take it from him," the RAPDA agent whined.

Without hesitation, several superbly muscled police officers lunged at the bullhorn and ripped it away from Charlie's hands.

Charlie looked bewildered. "What's wrong, this is a peaceful protest, isn't it?" Charlie asked.

The officer rolled his heavy-lidded eyes and rubbed his beaky nose before speaking insipidly, "Yes, the protest is legit, but you can't use a bullhorn out in public—you are disturbing the workers in the space elevator port."

"Okay, well you have the bullhorn now. Let me go about my business," Charlie spat back before turning his back on the police officer and walking away.

All of a sudden, the RAPDA agent began signaling to the beaky-nosed policeman with feeble gestures.

"We must take a more prudent measure," said the RAPDA agent with the large, dark shades. "The Overseer just contacted me and told me that he wants this Beasley guy to stop spreading that filth that comes out of his mouth and has issued an edict!"

The police officer with the big nose immediately trotted up to Charlie's backside. He put both hands on his shoulders and spun him around to face him. "I regret to inform you that this rally is over sir!" cried the big-nosed cop, all while brandishing a scuffed wooden club and tapping it in his loose hand.

Charlie furrowed his brow, and a demoniac fury spread over his face after seeing the cop brandish his club. Elena could see his veins throbbing in his forehead and neck, but Charlie didn't say anything. He didn't have to.

The beaky-nosed police officer then spoke in a sterner voice, "I regret to inform you that I must give you a summons...disturbing the peace and noise pollution requires you to do ten hours of community service," the cop said dutifully.

"You're taking orders from him!" Charlie snarled while pointing to the RAPDA agent.

"Now, now, we're all working together," the RAPDA agent chortled. His voice did not go with his hulking frame and after hearing it better, Elena almost recognized the voice but could not place it. She still had no idea it was Lieutenant Graham.

Charlie continued angrily, "This city used to be protected by the NYPD. Now you're all reduced to sheer puppets by the overseer's personal guard!"

The officer did not take that remark too lightly probably because it was true.

More boos ensued, and Elena could hear Charlie muttering some obscenities under his breath. He waved a flat palm and flailed his elbow, waving the cop off, before turning on his heels and walking away across the weedy grass field.

The crowd loped behind Charlie, all the way towards the edge of the Great Lawn where tangles of brush lined the bike paths. Elena had no choice to follow along or she'd be trampled. She didn't like the idea of being nestled between all those vagabonds but her curiosity fueled her to move along with crowd. The occasional breeze blew into the park, bringing in the rich smell of pine from the trees, helping to dilute the whiffs of body odor coming from everywhere.

The whole thing looked almost tribal or militaristic to her. Hundreds of people trailed behind one man, and Elena wondered if this one man could essentially take over the city with the army he had amassed. Suddenly, the agent with the dark shades and familiar voice began running so he could keep up with Charlie, and his men followed with their nightsticks out.

Graham began shouting into his radio, and his typically reedy voice deepened considerably. "Send in back up!" Graham blurted into his radio.

Within seconds, a set of alien-looking soldiers unexpectedly charged in from the streets and immediately approached Charlie. They were Draconians for sure, Elena thought. They were the most elite law enforcement around, and Elena cringed after seeing them. She knew they were Draconian Ashtar forces because of their striped pants, knee-high leather boots, long capes and exquisite leather trappings. For them to get involved meant that Charlie was a serious threat, Elena figured.

They marched ahead in vast flying strides and almost all of them were indistinguishable from each other. When they got to the meat of the crowd, they aligned with the police officers and marched ahead of the crowd. They quickly flanked Charlie and the crowd and stood perpendicular to them, henceforth, blocking them from marching towards the street.

One of the Draconians, a towering man with thick neck and square jaw, began shouting at Charlie before facing off with him. "Any man heard speaking nonsensical things about Orion Corporation will have their mouths taped shut!"

More boos ensued from the crowd. Charlie stood still in confusion and was unable to progress any further because the Ashtar guards and police lined up and blocked his path. He just stood there, eyeing down the dozens of law enforcement personnel, feeling helpless and trapped. Some of the police officers were equipped with riot shields and stood straight as arrows, stony faced and with pepper spray in their hands.

Elena cringed after seeing the pepper spray, but before she could think about leaving, Graham took off his sunglasses and Elena's feet turned to glue after seeing his face. From that moment on, Elena stopped pushing her way to the front of the crowd, and became greatly concerned that he would meet her gaze— so she retreated backwards to avoid him, but was sure to remain close enough so she could hear what was going on.

"We need to scan you," Graham insisted.

Elena watched Charlie carefully for his reaction.

"A scan?" Charlie replied, while backing away from the soldiers. One of Draconian guards intercepted his line of passage before several other Draconian soldiers grabbed him by the arms. Charlie squirmed, but the four splendidly built Draconians were quite a match for him because one single Draconian had the strength of three men alone.

The crowd booed as loud as ever. "Leave him alone," someone said.

Then, several of the vagabonds got closer to Charlie, forcing the police officers to jab them away with their riot shields. Most of the people were so undernourished and flimsy that they bounced off the shields; some fell on their faces.

Charlie stopped resisting when a Draconian Ashtar guard shined a flashlight into his face. Part of him welcomed the check up because deep down, he knew he was sick so he calmed down a bit, hoping he might get an answer or two regarding his health status.

The soldiers prodded and pried at Charlie like some wild animal, checking his face and folding down the bottoms of both his eyelids. Another soldier then told him to open his mouth so he could get a look at Charlie's tongue. Lieutenant Graham activated his Eye-Net lenses and examined Charlie with them.

"Yep, he's disconnected alright," Graham said as he held a finger to his earpiece's comm. link. "No nanobots active!" he continued to whoever was at the other end of the line.

*Probably the Overseer or maybe even my dad...*Elena figured. *The implants are malfunctioning; no wonder everyone looks so sick!*

Elena then seemed to notice that Charlie's eyes turned red like burning flames, but a second and third look dispelled the illusion. It seemed as if Graham might have noticed it, but like Elena, he wasn't sure of what he saw. It happened so quickly. Lieutenant Graham then began walking around Charlie in circles, scrutinizing every inch of his body. His hand rubbed his knobby chin before speaking out in a low but superior tone. "Mr. Beasley, the Overseer has ordered me to take you back to a transgenic clinic so you can receive your upgrade, and so I'm afraid to say that you have no other choice but to come with us," Graham demanded.

Charlie's entire forehead puckered up in wrinkles and he began squirming, however, the Draconians had no trouble maintaining their grip on Charlie's arms. Suddenly, a lubberly, regular police officer approached with handcuffs. The site of those shiny steel cuffs made Charlie's squirming much more tenacious.

Elena noticed that the two Draconian soldiers that seized his arms were having trouble maintaining a grip on Charlie despite their superhuman strength. Charlie soon came face to face with a few riot shields that the police officers poked at him.

"Stay still and let us help you!" Graham demanded.

"I don't want to be upgraded, just give me my damn summons and let me go back to the camp!" Charlie snarled as he continued to squirm. The two Draconians were holding on, but were beginning to struggle, and Elena wondered if they could hold on to him any longer. The Draconians grimaced more and more as Charlie resisted, and one of them stammered so hard that he almost fell. Eventually, the fascist behavior displayed by the law enforcement personnel did not sit well with the crowd and some people were as brave as to get right into the faces of the police.

"You can't force anyone to receive medical treatment!" a man with bloodied feet shouted out.

Soon enough, the crowd began to scream and shout all at once, "Leave him alone! Leave him alone!"

When the front lines of the crowd got too close to the line of police officers, a Draconian Ashtar guard sprayed wisps pepper spray. Dozens of people dropped to the ground after catching the mist. Many people retreated towards the park's main gate after that, but many people decided to stand their ground and only became angrier—including Elena, who gritted her teeth in frustration and stood her ground.

Charlie continued to resist, making it difficult for even the beefy looking Draconian soldiers to get their cuffs on him. "Keep in mind, it should only take a few hours and then you are free to go," Graham then told him, his reedy voice thicker that time, but Charlie wasn't having any of it. He began to resist again and tried to pry his arms loose from the soldiers.

"I want to know what's in those upgrades!" Charlie shouted, and the adrenaline in his body deepened his voice considerably. He almost sounded inhuman. Elena wondered why Charlie wasn't taking his health into consideration and instead was questioning the nature of the medicine. She continued to stare at the confrontation intently and she hardly blinked her eyes.

"Those upgrades are unregulated!" Charlie screamed. "I know what you guys are doing to us!"

Elena scratched her head. *What is in the upgrades?* Elena thought to herself. "I don't feel sick!" Charlie bawled repeatedly as the Draconians finally

managed to wrestle his arms close enough so they could latch the cuffs on his wrists, and even though they had succeeded in handcuffing him, Charlie still needed to be restrained.

"Since when does my body belong to Orion Corp.?" Charlie growled. Several voices rang out from the circumventing crowd, "Yeah, since when?

We're not your property!"

"It's for your own good sir!" Graham snapped. His cordial tone was gone. "The radiation could be giving you Chernobyl AIDS, do you know what Chernobyl AIDS is?" Graham asked.

"Yes, I know what it is..." Charlie replied.

"Your body still seems healthy so it's not too late," Graham warned. "The fact is that you are indeed disconnected and it's a grave danger to you. Besides the Chernobyl AIDS, your junk DNA could be mutating to the point of awakening dormant endogenous retroviruses. If you continue to resist arrest, I must sedate you and forcefully arrest you on suspicion of harboring a dangerous retrovirus," Graham ended very grimly.

Elena almost sensed a bit of sorrow and pity in Graham's voice. But before the two hefty Draconians managed to lug Charlie off the lawn and towards the street where their squad cars were parked, Charlie's chest started heaving, and once again, Elena saw his eyes seemed to glow red with a look of contempt, causing some of the surrounding witnesses to let out a couple of gasps.

Elena could feel a chill come over her after watching Charlie's calm poker face morph into a face of a complete maniac. A flash of Charlie's red, glowing eyes once again made her squint in disbelief, and this time Elena knew what she saw. Elena watched in awe as Charlie faced the sky and growled, and then broke the chains on his handcuffs.

15: Riot

Lactic acid burned in Elena's leg muscles, her heart thudded through her ribs, but she continued to run anyway. The curiosity about the implants made the adrenaline shoot through her veins and gave her more determination to continue to run along with the city's most unwanted citizens.

The crowd wended their way towards the streets, stretching out like thin fingers along the great lawn, with law enforcement flanking the mass of mutants on both sides. Elena ducked under some elbows, using every bit of her stamina to scramble through gaps in the crowd in hopes of getting a glimpse of Charlie who was still obscured by the mass of mutants. The front of the crowd thickened around him and Charlie remained out of Elena's sight until she noticed him scaling a small wall just off the great lawn and towards the outlying streets— however, after that, his location became hard to confirm.

He occasionally appeared between apertures in the crowd, but he moved too fast for Elena— too fast for almost everyone else for that matter—except for a handful of healthy looking mutants that seemed to keep up with him. The Draconian Ashtar soldiers had no trouble keeping up, but it didn't matter because the crowd of mutants seemed to protect Charlie and none of the law enforcement could penetrate the mob. The wall of mutants outran the yellow, pepper spray clouds as well as the reach of the police officers' nightsticks and stun batons.

Elena then noticed that a another group of riot police had approached from the street in front of her and stormed through the park's main gate just before the bike paths. The police rattled their the way to the edge of the lawn, their shields and armor clunked and bounced as they clumsily marched ahead with their thick transparent shields held in front of them.

However, Charlie did not stop. Instead, he ran straight towards them. Several husky Draconians in Kevlar doublets groped at him as he ran, like football or rugby players trying to arm-tackle runners. However, there were too many people around him and very few soldiers could get close to Charlie at all. One soldier took advantage when some of the protesters fell, and Elena watched him as he slipped through a gap in the crowd and began wrapping both arms around Charlie's hip—only to find himself being dragged for dozens of feet as he clung to Charlie's jeans.

My goodness, that Charlie is strong! Elena thought.

Charlie shed the Draconian soldier off eventually, and the crowd mercilessly trampled the soldier as he tumbled on the grass. Elena had no idea what happened to the soldier until she gained some ground and noticed him lying motionless on the ground. By that time, he was reduced to a bloody pulp, and Elena just hopped over him, unaware of whether or not he was dead or alive.

Elena gasped and slowed her pace when parts of the crowd clashed with police. She did not want to get too brave after all. Many fell victim to the riot shields, bouncing off them like the frail sticks that they were— but some of the stronger mutants seemed to be putting up a good fight as they rammed themselves into the wall of shields, even knocking some cops onto their backs.

Several of the bigger Draconian soldiers joined the fray and blocked the path to the park's main gate. Elena didn't think Charlie would ever get past those guys. The hefty Draconian soldiers strafed Charlie as he tried to reroute his path, but it was like trying to catch a chicken. Charlie cut on a dime like an all-star running back as he evaded his assailants, ducking under nightsticks and evading tacklers in the most unnatural and swiftest speeds. One Draconian with thick shoulders and huge hands stepped up to Charlie and took full-fisted swings at him. Charlie seemed to evade their haymakers like a skilled boxer would and he then countered with some punches of his own.

The force of Charlie's punches were so hard that one of his hooks propelled a soldier backward, right into another soldier, making them both fall to the grass like one big domino effect. Charlie swiveled to his left and right, holding up bloody fists, and after realizing there was no opposition left, he instantly hewed a pathway towards the streets.

The uncanny thing to Elena was how Charlie managed to absorb stray shots from several nightsticks here and there that some police officers managed to land as they chased him. By the time Charlie got to the park's chain link fence and gate, Charlie managed to distance himself from any of the remaining law enforcement personnel still hot on his heels. He was just too fast for them. Many of the police officers seemed to give up after witnessing Charlie's terrific onslaught.

Elena gawked when she saw Charlie scale a ten-foot-high chain link fence with the agility of a cat. Never before had she seen anyone move as he did, not even in a world-class gymnasium. Most of the crowd— including the officers and Ashtar guardsmen—had to climb the fence slowly. However, some other mutants scaled it just as Charlie did—in one single bound.

When Elena reached the park's encompassing fence, she essayed the task for just a moment, and realized she should just wait and fall back a bit until most of the crowd had climbed over. She tried not to let her curiosity propel her to the thick of the fray.

All of a sudden, the ground began to tremble and a platoon of Draconian Ashtar cavalry stampeded past Elena, leaving a trailing gush of air that blew her golden hair across her face. Dozens of hooves thudded the soft grass, knocking many people over, but some people were smart enough to move out of the way. The mountains of muscled horses had no trouble hewing a clear path towards the main gate and out onto the streets.

Elena tried best not to trail too far behind and not to get too close either. She gathered her nerve and continued to march ahead in long strides, holding her dress down as she ran, and cursing herself for not wearing sneakers. She took advantage of the clear space that the cavalry created, but by the time she got the fence, the crowd huddled together again, and the mass of stampeding mutants had blocked the small opening in the fence, which was bottle-necked by the weaker and slower mutants.

Elena had no choice but to climb the fence, and the task was more demanding than it should have been because of her backpack, which weighed her down. By the time she climbed it and stepped onto the street, most of the faster mutants were already well past Columbus Circle, with the cavalry just behind them. The horses that galloped in front of her had blocked Charlie from her line of sight, but Elena continued to follow the concourse of law enforcement personnel making a beeline towards their assailant. Elena kept churning her legs, digging for more stamina, and dodging the oncoming traffic as best as she could. Her impulses of curiosity always got the best of her, but this was surely the craziest goose-chase she had ever embarked upon.

I want to speak to this man and ask him about the implants. I want to know what is going on! Elena told herself as she ran.

The exhilaration was something she never felt before, so she decided to hazard everything on a straightaway course towards the mass of people heading towards Times Square. Elena still could still not locate Charlie through the occasional apertures opening up between all the bodies and horses, and after running down the avenue for what seemed like an eternity, the eeriness of a dark Times Square ahead of her made the dangerous ordeal even more frightening.

Still, nothing would alarm her more than what she was about to hear. The sporadic sound of gunshots made Elena falter a bit, and the closer she got to the crowd the more guarded she became, pausing frequently whenever hearing the haunting pop of a gunshot.

Are those from the police? Do they want to kill him?

Elena could not possibly think they would shoot an unarmed civilian for refusing medical attention. A flush overspread Elena's cheeks and her short- lived sense of home she had felt ever since landing on Earth had completely vanished. The sounds of gunshots eventually stopped, but another sound echoed

from the distance, and this time the sound was hard to define. It was a whiny sound, a sound that Elena had never heard before, and it only lasted for about five seconds before it stopped.

After the sound ceased, most of the crowd dispersed and some of the crowd began to slow down. Eventually all of the people stopped running in front of her and she had finally caught up with the mob, which pooled at the intersection ahead of her just off the edge of Times Square.

"They got Charlie! He's down!" a voice screamed from afar, which made its way to Elena's ears. All of the tumult from seconds ago immediately ceased to stillness.

16: John's Strike

Most of the police had their helmets off and were red in the face, as if with fierce implementation. Even some of the mutants joined in and fixed their eyes on the ground before them to see what had become of Charlie. Elena jostled through the mob of mutants for a better look, and when Elena finally knifed her way to the front of the astonished assemblage of civilians and police, she found Charlie laying down in the gutter, motionless, and semiconscious. His eyes fluttered open and shut, and Elena knew he wasn't dead because his chest was moving ever so slightly.

"Did they shoot him?" Elena asked at random towards the direction of a barefooted and malnourished looking man standing next to her.

"They was using rubber bullets," the man began in a cracked voice. "But them things just bounced off of him." The man shook his head before pointing to a military grade Humvee parked on the corner of 43rd Street. "It was the thing on top of that truck there is what brought him down," the man cracked out in wonderment as he pointed. "Luckily the beam that shot out of it was focused only on him and not the entire crowd or we'd all be laying on the floor with him," the man finished gravely.

Elena noticed what looked like a satellite dish on top of the truck but nothing more. She had no idea what it was and figured it was probably some sound weapon—the same weapon that must have made that horrible droning sound seconds ago. Her attention darted towards several broad and squat looking police officers that continued to threaten the mob of people. They promised to rain all the penalties of the law on the mutants if they did not disperse, but the crowd didn't seem to listen. Some of the people who initially fled came back to join the crowd, and most of them growled out their curses, prompting a group of Draconian Ashtar soldiers to approach with bullhorns of their own.

Most of the law enforcement personnel were quick to inform the masses that they would meet the same fate as Charlie if any decided to resist scans for potential disconnections or if they opposed the mandatory upgrade.

Some police threats however were mingled with apologies, and one particular apology came from Lieutenant Graham himself, who Elena found pacing around Charlie's incapacitated body.

"Sorry it had to come to this people, we don't want this to turn...any...more violent," Graham said and seemed to find it difficult to find words.

"Keep your alien fingers out of our human affairs!" shouted a voice from the crowd.

"I'm only looking out for...you...all," Graham shouted back. Graham looked like he was choking on his words. Elena had known Lieutenant Graham for her whole life and long enough to know his body language. Judging by the look on his face, Elena figured he was bothered by something; he looked shaken by guilt. She thought about approaching him so she could ask for Brennan, but she changed her mind. She thought it was better to remain incognito for the time being.

Elena decided to fade into the back of the mob to escape Graham's gaze once again, but stood close enough to hear his words. She then craned her neck to listen in on the lengthy exchange between Graham and whomever he was speaking to on the other end of his phone.

"The pariah is down. I repeat—the pariah is down," Graham bellowed into his comm. device. "It is unfortunate that we had to bombard him with all those microwaves to take him down but the bastard took down about twelve of us. He even took all of our rubber bullets and some jolts from our cattle prods!"

Suddenly, the crowd became restless again. Elena couldn't hear Graham's conversation anymore so she turned towards Charlie's body. She saw Charlie's lips move and it appeared as if he was trying to speak, but Elena could not make out what he was saying because of the cacophony of conversation taking place all around her. However, Elena noticed that Charlie seemed to be talking in the direction of a dark-skinned man with wooly white hair and droopy puppy-dog eyes.

"Step back!" a soldier said to the dark-skinned man while pressing a riot shield to his chest. A police officer nudged the dark-skinned man away with his riot shield, but when he walked away from him, the man inched closer to Charlie again. Elena came face to face with a riot shield herself, forcing her away from the Plaza and towards the main sidewalk. Of course, Elena waited until the police officer left so she could get back into the fray. There were so many people to control and so little police that the crowd began getting the upper hand on them.

Then, a rowdy chatter came from the quaint looking dark-skinned man and Elena scrutinized him for a bit. She wondered what he and Charlie were communicating. Of course, she was unaware of his friendship with John, and hoped that their sign language would offer hints. It was then when Charlie and Elena locked eyes, and he kept his eyes transfixed on hers for a few moments. Elena looked behind her to see if there was anyone there, but there wasn't.

Charlie was indeed staring at her and she wondered why Charlie chose to stare at her during such a time, while being in such a vulnerable position. He stared at her for almost twenty seconds before shifting his gaze towards John, who stood twenty feet beside her.

Charlie waved it back and forth, as if he were telling the man, *No, no, no.*

Charlie could not keep his arm up for too long however, he was too weak. There seemed to be a weight infused in his body, and he looked glued to the street. His arms lifted shortly, only to plunk back down to the ground, but he was strong enough to get some words out to John.

"Don't John, don't!" Charlie croaked, as a paramedic began to take his vitals. It was getting so dark that Elena would not muster the ability to see

Charlie's face if it were not for the flashlights fixed on his body that caused his lugubrious eyes to glow red.

Elena turned keenly at the black man known as John who proceeded to slip something shiny out of his pocket. It looked like a small remote for an automobile lock. John then pressed a few buttons. Ten seconds later, a distant cawing sound distracted Elena, arresting her attention towards the southern sky.

A flock of seagulls came swarming in from the high sky. There seemed to be over a thousand of them dotting the evening sky, and they were all flying so close to one another that they appeared as a cloud of black smoke. John then began to gesticulate with his arms in a manner that mimicked Tai Chi, and he continued to do it repeatedly despite being incessantly nudged by a police officer's riot shield.

"Come on man, off to the sidewalk," the police officer shouted at him but John never listened and continued to gesticulate his arms in the queerest of ways.

What is wrong with all those birds up there? Elena asked herself.

Then Elena noticed that John made a sudden movement with his arms and seemed to toss that shiny object up into the sky, and when it fell back to him, he caught it. In an instant, the cloud of birds began to disperse and came swooping down 45th Street at stoplight level—heading straight towards her.

Alarmed, Elena bolted down the street because the birds seemed as if they were about to converge on the very spot where the masses of people stood. In just seconds, hundreds of gulls reigned down from the sky in an unyielding white blur and attacked the crowd as if they were one solid organism. The flurry of the birds sent a deafening flapping sound through the street and the horses were the first to flee. The horses buckled and fled without notice, shedding their mounts ever so suddenly, injuring the police officers in some cases.

The gulls attacked ferociously, mostly picking at the faces of the officers in relentless fashion. Many of the civilians fled and scampered off in all directions but oddly enough, the birds seemed to attack only law enforcement personnel. Elena became seized with terror after witnessing such a freakish episode and she stopped herself from running away after realizing that the birds were selectively attacking only the law enforcement personnel. Nevertheless, thousands of people were running in all directions and she was still at risk for being trampled to death.

She used the corner light post on 43rd Street as a shield against stampeding civilians. Everyone ran around her as she watched the attack. The officers however, couldn't run away. The birds swarmed and blinded most of them, poking at their eyes, nibbling on their flesh, and even clawing at their faces with their talons.

Oh...my...God, Elena said to herself in a voice tinged with fear and awe. One officer ran away after finally being able to get up from the ground. He appeared to be missing an eye, and rivers of blood streamed from his face. Another officer tried swiping at the birds with his nightstick, but there were too many of them. If a police officer even took so much as a second to uncover his eyes, they were instantly plucked out.

Through the chaos, Elena spotted John through the blur of white birds and his gesticulations had ceased. She could have sworn she had seen his eyes roll to the back of his head, but he was coming out of his trance and after he did, he turned around to face the scene and jumped from the shock of what he saw. Elena noticed that John immediately put a palm over his mouth and it was then when the attacks began to subside. Still, there were twice as many birds whooshing over the masses than people. Elena found it difficult to see anything but blurry feathers, and after a minute or so, the birds began acting normally. Many of the birds flapped harmlessly up to the lampposts and street signs and perched themselves. Some of the birds began to fly away all together. Some police and Ashtar guardsmen managed to get into cars, and they fled the scene, including Lieutenant Graham, who was lucky enough to get into his squad car during the attack. Nevertheless, dozens of law enforcement staff were sprawled on the ground writhing in agony as they rolled around in bloody puddles.

The first thing Elena thought about after the birds flew away was Charlie. She felt as if it was an opportunity to help him escape, since all the police were incapacitated. Elena realized that this was her only chance to ask him what he thought of the new upgrades. If she didn't ask him then, she would never know the truth about them, and so she turned her focus towards the corner of 43rd Street, where Charlie remained sprawled on the ground. She hopped over some of the bodies on the street, trying hard not to stare at the screaming police officers because gore was not her thing. Instead, she focused on Charlie and stared at him intently. He was untouched by the gulls, and he appeared to be shaking his head in disappointment.

When she got closer to Charlie, Elena had noticed that he began muttering unintelligible words towards John. "John, most of these cops are just innocent men following orders; they are Earth men John, they may work for the visitors but are not the visitors," Charlie said hollowly.

John shook his head and buried his face in his hands. "I didn't mean to do it," he said.

It had become clear to Elena that this creepy looking man named John was indeed controlling the birds and that was exactly what Charlie begged him not to do moments ago. The thought of it all made Elena stammer and stop in her tracks. After a sigh and a huff of exasperation, Elena figured that she should forget getting involved with such people. Until recently, she thought of them only as mutants but never thought of them as non-humans. The supernatural displays she witnessed from both Charlie and John were enough to throw her off. Elena hastened away from the plaza with her stomach stuck in her throat.

It was tough fleeing the scene because of the rubbernecking people everywhere, blocking the street. Scores of rush hour commuters watched the fiasco take place from their cars, traffic was at a standstill, and she wasn't the only one running away from the plaza either. What made it tougher for her was the fact that she may never see Charlie again, and may never find out what he knew about the upgrades. She figured she would have to rely on some other source of information, or perhaps she figured she could tell her dad about the upgrades and convince him to bring about an investigation.

Elena continued down the crowded street in vast flying strides and never looked back. Before she had the chance to get to the corner on 45th and Broadway, she came to a direct halt after witnessing an entire mass of infantry marching around the corner—and they were heading straight towards her and the plaza behind her.

Local SWAT and Draconian Ashtar guards marched ahead dutifully; some were on horses and some on foot. A procession of police vans whipped the corner at high speeds, melting the rubber off of their tires and skidding to a halt because of the traffic blocking the way. The police cavalry had no trouble making their way through on the sidewalks, encroaching on the mob of people from both sides of the avenue. Before Elena could take another step, she became taken aback after the side doors on all the vans slid open, spilling uniformed officers out onto the streets like roaches out of a hole.

With no regard for the civilians or even their downed comrades, the police fired tear gas canisters into the plaza, right towards the crowd of civilians and fallen police officers. Billowing fumes wisped out of the canisters as they rolled down the street. Seeing a tear gas container scuttle past made Elena swallow her stomach, and she had no choice but to run back from whence she came. She quickened her strides while evading a trail of the smoke that vectored from a tumbling canister, and more uncertainties crowded upon Elena's rattled psyche as she ran scared, surrounded by smoke and carnage, and it all looked and smelled like hell.

For the first time since arriving, Elena regretted embarking on such an inhospitable adventure but little did she know how much worse it would get. When she got to the corner of 44th, something told her to turn around, and a pang of concern shot through her after being smitten by a most deafening noise. The droning sound was so loud that Elena had to slow down to cover her ears. She heard the same sound before Charlie was incapacitated. Suddenly, immense pains flooded her whole body and she found it difficult to run. Just three seconds after the noise was heard, the wind was completely knocked out of her. She dropped to her knees in the middle of her stride, scuffing her bare knees, and when she tried to get up, Elena realized that she could no longer control her muscles. The pains were followed by vast nausea and she vomited all over the street before continuing to scream in agony due to the sharp stabbing pains that rippled through her.

Elena was frightened because nothing seemed to be touching her. All she heard was that deafening purring noise as she rolled on the pavement, unable to see what was causing the rigorous pain. All around her, people rolled around on the street and many appeared to be in the same pain as she was. Soon enough, everything turned hazy in the corners of her vision and then everything went black.

17: Finding Elena

After John whisked him away from the radius of the riot control beams, Charlie needed a few minutes to regain strength in his legs. Luckily, the chaos that ensued gave Charlie and John the opportunity to find refuge in an abandoned McDonald's restaurant just a block away. Twenty minutes was all he would need to regain his bearing, and when Charlie felt strong enough to walk, he headed back towards the plaza instead of retreating.

"I have to find that girl!" Charlie shouted at John, who continued to pull Charlie by the arm. However, Charlie didn't budge. "I locked onto her brain signature while I was down, and I sensed her in the vicinity right up until the microwave beam attack by RAPDA. I fear she was incapacitated and she deserves my help."

That was all Charlie would tell John, and he scampered back into the plaza where over a hundred people lay on the ground unconscious. John didn't bother helping him, and he left after Charlie told him that he couldn't go back home anyway because after all, he would be a fool to use his bus pass. After the police had his name, Charlie had figured that all of his digital footprints were being monitored now, specifically the bus pass, which was his only ticket back home.

Of course, Charlie could never visit the FEMA camp again, so John figured that he might be able to trade some of Charlie's rations for a bus pass; otherwise, Charlie would never make it back home to Brooklyn on foot. A hungry soul would surely be willing to make the trade, Charlie and John thought, especially since so many people were shortchanged of their ration boxes today. John thought Charlie had lost his mind for sticking around just so he could find a girl: a girl he did not know, but a girl Charlie needed to find. Before John left for Hoover City, both of them made it clear to one another that they were to meet at the corner of Lexington and 6th in three hours, which should be enough time for John to make the trade. It also should be enough time for Charlie to find the girl that took a hold of his senses.

When Charlie came across the first blonde female laying on the street, he stooped down to inspect her face, but then a police officer ran past him, causing Charlie's throat to tighten.

I have to be quick! he told himself as he scanned the street for that lovely blonde girl he had locked eyes with a short time ago before the bird attack. Charlie hoped that his hooded, lead cloak and dark shades were enough to conceal his face because after all, the entire police force was present on the scene, and he was the most wanted man in the city.

His newfound empathic ability gave him an impression that this was a woman who cared about what he had to say—and cared about making things right. Charlie had sensed her affinity for him while he lay on the ground almost a half hour ago and was determined to seek her out despite John's protests.

When Charlie had locked eyes with Elena, he sensed something in her that he only sensed in the disconnected mutants. He felt compelled to find her for various reasons, reasons he himself did not know for sure.

Lucky for him, most of the police were talking to the various paramedics scuttling up and down the street, tending to all of the law enforcement officials who had their faces clawed apart. The police and emergency workers cared little to inspect the bodies of anyone without a police or Ashtar uniform, so Charlie figured he had some time to search. Strobe lighting came from the many ambulances parked along 43rd, drenching the scene in rich red and blue hues. It helped Charlie see better too. The sun was gone for the night and Charlie's sunglasses only hindered his ability to cut through the dark and powerless Times Square. Charlie searched the long avenue and plaza as inconspicuously as possible, praying no one would see his pallid face.

Charlie scanned the street with desperate eyes. Every person near and around the plaza at the time of the attack were sprawled all over the street, and some still were hunched over the steering wheels inside their automobiles— unconscious. Even the motorists were affected by the RAPDA microwave attack as they sat in traffic. Charlie was lucky he had

John's help because he would have been zapped again if John hadn't whisked him away from the microwave beam path.

Charlie sniffed through the hot, sooty air hoping that a stray breeze would bring the scent of her shampoo to his nose. Charlie could never forget the pleasant smell he sensed while incapacitated on the ground. He could see her face imprinted in his mind; her face was oval and beautiful in the utmost, her every facet was finely chiseled and delicate. Her eyes were large and gleaming, and a glowing throng of golden blonde hair surmounted her head. It has been quite sometime since a woman had lifted his heart just from physical beauty alone but it was different this time. Until now, Charlie had never gotten an empathic response from anyone other than a fellow mutant and Elena—a clean- cut person of the working class— gave him that feeling. It was rare for Charlie to sense the emotions of a connected citizen. In fact, he could not recall if he ever did sense any emotion from any of them at all. After a half hour of searching, Charlie began to get patchy after seeing more and more police officers driving up to the scene.

Fearing to be caught, Charlie decided to forget the girl and stop for the day, but just before he was about to leave the scene, the lovely smell of the lavender shampoo scent cut through his nostrils. Charlie felt a weight lift from his back immediately and felt a great lightening of his heart again. *That's her scent,* Charlie was sure.

The scent led his flaring nostrils straight to her body, which lay sprawled out next to a garbage receptacle near the corner gutter of 44th Street. She was lying in the prone position and hardly moved. Charlie scanned the scene before attempting to roll her over; a thin line of blood trickled down her calf and appeared to be coming from a minor abrasion on her knee. Her sundress billowed in the slight breeze and Charlie stooped down to make sure it did not flutter enough to reveal her upper thighs. After removing her backpack from her shoulders, Charlie turned her over. Her glowing face affirmed his search was successful.

That's her alright.

He checked Elena's pulse; it was strong. She was unconscious from the sudden heightened blood pressure, which was normal. When Charlie cradled her head, he figured all she needed was a light tap on the cheek, so he gently tapped her sweaty cheek three times until her eyes fluttered open a crack. Elena struggled to keep them open, but in seconds, she opened her eyes wider after feeling Charlie's fingers pressed upon her carotid artery. Her eyes looked up at the hooded Charlie with a pitiless appeal for protection but after seeing his unkempt appearance, she became spooked.

Elena immediately snaked and wiggled away from him as she dragged her weakened legs on the street, staring back at Charlie as if something was about to pop out of him.

"What do you want? Who...who are you?" Elena asked without a care for an answer. She was barely able to see and therefore, unable to recognize Charlie through his shades.

"I'm just trying to help,' Charlie said in his friendliest voice.

"Why...why can't I feel my legs?" Elena yelped as she regained her senses.

Charlie looked around, putting his index finger to his lip, hoping that her shouting didn't alarm any of the police officers in the plaza.

"They used an ESW on you," Charlie hushed. "A what...?" Elena asked.

"It was an Endocrine Suppression Weapon," Charlie whispered to her. "An endocrine what?" Elena asked.

"Suppression weapon—it came from that van there—do you see that satellite dish on it?" Charlie told her as he pointed to a patty wagon parked alongside the ambulances. "RAPDA calls it the Active Denial riot-control weapon. What it does is send out frequencies that target the neurotransmitters of the limbic system in the brain, suppressing the adrenaline of rioting civilians, rendering them unconscious and making their muscles useless."

Hearing Charlie's explanation made Elena stiffen with fear and the thought of being attacked like that made her tremble as she struggled to get up. Charlie scanned the scene for any potential scrutiny placed upon him but he had arrested no one's attention thus far. Most of the police were still huddled with their fallen colleagues near the ambulances across the street.

"Your legs will be wobbly for a while, but in time, you will gain control of your muscles," Charlie said. He was hit with the weapon less than a half hour ago and he knew its side effects. It took him ten minutes to regain his bearing after John dragged him away from the gutter just before the second microwave attack.

Elena gave up standing for a while; she took a knee and took some deep breaths. Elena stared at Charlie with grim fascination after finding some familiarity in his voice but still could not place it because he had whispered to her all this time. She could not see his eyes through his dark glasses, and his hood covered those black locks of his—even covering the sides of his fierce beard. Of course, it did not help that her vision was not fully restored either. She took a lungful of painful air, and in time, the nausea subsided, her gait returned, and she got back on her feet, but her knees buckled with each step.

"Here let me help you," Charlie said, offering his hand. Elena cautiously accepted. Charlie clasped an arm around the small of her back, and draped her arm across his shoulders, holding her up as she regained her way of walking. She sagged like a rag doll, and Charlie was surprised how heavy she felt since she was so thin.

Must be the dead weight, he thought.

Elena never took her eyes off of Charlie as he helped her. *Who is this man?*

Elena thought. *Why is he helping me?*

She stared at him for a whole minute and still could not recognize Charlie with the hooded cloak and sunglasses on. Elena could barely hear him when he spoke, his voice sounded hollow and feeble without a bullhorn to amplify it.

As she took her steadiest steps, she noticed that her hobble was lessening, and her muscles were more coordinated than before.

"We should leave," Charlie said in a tone of imperious command, and his voice was louder that time. Suddenly, it all then came to her. The voice— although strained, became familiar to her.

Charlie Beasley?

She noticed the same long, grey cloak and the beard, but it was the bloody manacles on his wrists that gave him away.

"What happened before?" Elena began through a twisted mouth, but Charlie didn't reply.

"The birds!" she cried.

"Quiet!" Charlie snapped. "We've got to get out of here because everyone is looking for me. This way," Charlie escorted her along, her arm still draped over his shoulder. They both knifed through the crowd of rubbernecking schoolchildren and skipped across the street towards the corner of 43rd Street, only to come to a halt in order to allow a coffle of emergency medical workers to hobble past them. When they turned the corner, they were mostly out of sight, and so Charlie removed his hood and sunglasses. Elena took a deep breath.

"You...you are that guy on the bullhorn!"

Charlie put out his cold hand. "Name's Charlie Beasley, pleasure to meet you," Charlie said in a courtly manner.

Elena was glad to see him and found it ironic that he helped her up when she thought about doing the same to him less than a half hour ago so she could finally ask him about the upgrades.

"I appreciated your help back there, but why did you bother to help me? And why are you telling me to run with you?"

Charlie did not answer; he did not know what to tell her at first. He was so confused about it himself and had simply acted on impulse thus far. However, he sensed her affinity for him, and so he was confident enough to make demands. "This way," he said, ignoring her inquiry. He grabbed her arm with a grip of steel that made her wince. She knew he had prodigious strength and had just experienced some of it herself. Both of them dashed through an alleyway of broken concrete; their steps rang heavily on the crumbled and gravelly ground. Even through her thick sandals, Elena could feel the sharp shards of broken concrete beneath her feet, preventing her from running too fast between abandoned skyscrapers. Besides, the shrubs and weeds were up to their necks as was some unattended garbage and litter piled along the alleyway.

By the time they reached the end of the alley both were full of pollen and smelled like waste.

Elena sighed deeply. "Look mister—"

"I know this seems strange," Charlie spat back readily. "But I need someone to take over for me."

"Take over?" Elena asked, bewildered.

Charlie replied in a broken sentence. "Yeah, you know..." Charlie stammered. "Take over...to give pep rallies...to...help inspire and inform the masses about the Overseer's misdoings…"

Elena scratched her chin, maintaining eye contact with him. Elena remembered when they locked eyes. She shuddered from thinking of his red eyes and what his friend had done with the birds. It all made her more interested, but also more petrified.

Elena hesitated before saying, "I'm not sure I want to—no," Elena told him, standing stiffly at attention. "Do you tell all strangers to do things for you?"

"I can't do it anymore. Now that the whole city is on my ass," Charlie flushed.

Elena didn't reply right away. She just stared at him, shocked and overwhelmed by the sudden responsibility that came over her shoulders. After receiving no retort from her, Charlie's gaze shifted away from Elena and thought about what to tell her. He sensed her will to act and he knew she was fit for the task. Besides, if the working class had someone pretty to listen to instead of someone like him, then perhaps the connected civilians might snap out of their endless torpor. At least Elena did not have to wait for cloudy days to make a speech either.

"Forget that I asked," Charlie then said rather squarely. He angrily put his sunglasses back on and tugged the hood over his black frizzy hair.

Elena's eyes squinted in confusion. "What makes you think I want to protest anything, I'm just a tourist here and until yesterday, I thought Orion Corp. and the Overseer were the best things that ever happened to the people here—not to mention the fact that I do work for Orion Corp."

Charlie sighed deeply. He knew she was playing dumb. She was just scared, but what he didn't know was that the fear he had sensed in Elena was not just a fear that came about because she was micro-waved but because Elena was scared of him.

Memories of the fiasco that took place earlier had beaten her memory cells.

What were those red eyes? The man with the birds? The other people who scaled that wall? The super speed and strength of this man before me? It is not normal! Elena thought.

This witnessing of such supernatural behavior niggled at her mind for too long, so she decided to ask him the question that lingered on the forefront of her mind.

Elena stuttered before blurting out her question. "Why did… you refuse… to be upgraded?"

Charlie's gaze dropped to meet the ground. "I thought you heard my speech?" He said.

"Not the beginning of it, no."

Charlie sighed again and realized it was best not to tell her why. After all, he had no proof and he didn't know her well enough to tell her about his outlandish theories. Besides, it was a long story. Charlie began to regret getting involved with a girl during such a turbulent time in his life. He then thought about walking away from her.

"I think it's best that I be going now," Charlie said, avoiding eye contact with Elena who looked confused from Charlie's abrupt behavior.

The words he spoke came off as a suggestion to her, and she didn't believe he wanted to part ways. She wondered why he didn't answer her questions.

Elena tried as hard as she could to take the stones out of her throat, stifling the shyness. "You're going? I thought you wanted me to help you?" She asked.

Charlie clenched up. "It's okay, it's a burden that is best left off of your back," Charlie said in the friendliest voice he could muster at that moment. He put out his hand but Elena did not shake it.

Finally, after a long deep breath, Elena felt a hot flash ripple through her in fear as she fought her insecurity. She pushed herself to ask him out. It was the least she could do for a stranger that helped her, and as creepy as he was, he had nice eyes, she thought. Charlie's eyes were not always icy; they were soulful at times. She grew so lonely in the dark of space for the ten years that she hungered for another human voice to share interests with whether it would be with a mutant or a normal person. However, Elena really wanted to know about the implants and why Charlie refused them.

"Why don't I buy you a coffee for helping me back there?" Elena said through a tight throat, her warm smile was far too convivial for Charlie at this point. A part of Charlie told himself that it would be unwise to accept her gracious offer. He would have agreed if he were not so scared of being spotted and arrested by the authorities.

"I must politely decline," Charlie began in a sorrowful tone. "I'm supposed to meet my friend at a bus stop in two hours."

"We have some time," Elena differed.

"I know, but besides—I can't risk being caught, and it's best that I go meet my friend and get to my safe house."

Elena shook her head and sighed.

"What are you going to do?" she began hotly. "Hide in a hole for the rest of your life because you punched a few cops?"

Charlie thought she had a point, but what he really feared were the upgrades —more than being arrested.

"Let's start by shaving that beard of yours," Elena then said between chuckles of amusement. "It will help deter prying eyes."

Charlie stroked the bristly beard slowly and thought it was a great idea. *It couldn't hurt,* he thought. Besides, his anti-drone cloak gave him some confidence to remain out in public.

"Why not?" Charlie shrugged. "I would have shaved it myself a long time ago if FEMA included a damn razor in those boxes they give us!" Charlie beamed.

Elena settled her small backpack, took out a pair of scissors, a disposable razor, and a can of shaving cream, and dutifully set to shaving his face and trimming his unruly, dark hair.

18: Dinner Date

Elena and Charlie would sup at a cute little rustic Italian joint called La Candela, and it was one of Elena's favorites as kid. The place was gorgeous inside. The old, pre-industrial look of the place was classic in every way, and Elena thought that the old vintage style from the days of old always had a beauty of its own that mere modernity couldn't match.

Such extraordinary evidences of wealth were rare to their eyes, even before the world came to an end. The tables were made of solid gold, beautifully wrought and topped with clumps of synthetic trees and fruit blossoms. Even though the foliage was fake it still looked pretty, despite not offering any aroma.

Candles lit the place with a dim, flickering orange, but the kitchen was powered by electricity. The generator could be heard thrumming in the backyard, loud enough to blot out all the nattering that went on inside the joint. The place was packed with chatty customers, and pale blue moonlight seeped through the shuttered windows, creating a zebra like effect of shadow and light on the walls and on the tables.

Charlie forgot what it was like to dine in a restaurant...and had not done so since his days as a registered worker. At the time, Charlie's salary allowed him to shop at high-grade supermarkets, but it all ended after he mutated and was too sick to work out in the hot sun. La Candela only offered food to those with the elite Sol currency. Lucky for Charlie, his new girlfriend was from space and was an Orion Corporation employee to boot.

"Your table is ready," said a squat looking usher as he swung his arm towards their table.

When they sat down at their table, both of them wasted no time in grabbing the menus, flipping through them quickly. They both found it hard to ignore the bowl of crispy pita bread chips and yogurt dip already on the table and munched on them while they sat on the edges of their beautifully upholstered chairs.

"Sup how you please," Elena demanded. Charlie felt bad ordering an expensive plate.

"I'll just take the coffee," Charlie said pointedly.

Elena sighed and cocked her head to the side. "Order an entrée," she insisted after giving him a pitiful stare. Charlie looked all too pale and skinny, she thought. And she wanted him to eat. It was the least she could do for him after he helped her during the riot.

Deep down, Charlie knew he was famished and he wanted to gorge on everything the menu had to offer. However, he figured the pita chips would suffice and thought it was best not to accept the offer.

"I'll just fill up on these chips here," Charlie said as he stuffed a few of them into his mouth.

"No please, order anything you want!" Elena insisted.

Charlie didn't want to seem ungracious to refuse the lady who meant well, but he was too stubborn to have someone do something for him. When the waiter came, Elena had no choice but to order for him, and she ordered him a ziti marinara with sautéed eggplant and capers. She opted for the same. As they waited, both of them cleaned the bowl of pita chips of its crumbs and Charlie licked the bowl of yogurt clean. They both could not help but eat greedily after all they have been through in the last hour.

When the main dishes arrived, Charlie was so hungry that he abandoned his fork a few times, making spoons out of slices of warm, fresh bread—and even though his stomach had shrunk to the size of a chestnut in recent days due to food deprivation, he ate feverishly and greedily. It has been over a year since Charlie enjoyed a good meal, and he finished his pasta plate in less than a minute.

He was so thankful for what Elena had done for him that he could not shake the guilt. Still, Elena wasn't finished helping him even though she had already repaid the favor. After looking at Charlie's bony cheeks,

Elena felt too bad for the guy and so Elena decided to order seconds, despite Charlie's protest to stop her. Charlie thought that her offer to buy him another meal was pressed upon him with an earnestness in which he could take no denial. Charlie simply acknowledged her demand in silence.

When the second dishes arrived, Charlie was happy to see that the steak was a flank cut, his favorite. It was rolled up and stuffed with gorgonzola cheese, onions, and bacon. Both of them wasted no time digging into it; but first, Charlie generously topped it with red pepper and began cutting it in tender chunks for immediate consumption.

It was a moment of happiness for the both of them, a rather refreshing date that both Elena and Charlie needed more than they thought. Their hearts could no longer attune to mirthful things due to the gloomy lives they both had lived, and the dinner served at the restaurant brought the child out of them both.

For dessert, Elena ordered extra fresh dinner rolls made from imported grains from planet Gliese. With it came a tub of fresh rare goat cheese from Sirius B, along with some exceptional sour apples grown on planet Lyra—which had less flavor than Earth's sour apples—but they were better than nothing.

While eating, the bad memories of earlier surfaced in their minds, especially for Elena who could not stop thinking about Charlie's red eyes, his super strength, and his speed.

Her heart was hard though, and she had gone through enough during the catastrophes of 2033. The disasters she survived through had hardened her soul a great deal, so much so that the recent incident in the last couple of hours caused minor anxiety at best. However, it wasn't the riot, or the paranormal display she witnessed, or the microwave weapon attack that filled her thoughts but instead, it was the fact that Charlie refused to be upgraded. And judging by his bad skin, he needed it.

As shy as Elena was, she felt it was up to her to break the ice and spark conversation.

"Isn't the place pretty? Just look at how they slice the tomatoes!"

"Cute," Charlie replied, while stopping his forkful of food midway to his mouth. A small smile pulled at the corners of his mouth, but not for too long. He seemed to be deep in thought as well, and the tension of the day still lingered in his gut— in both of their guts.

The food didn't settle as well as Elena would have liked it to. Elena chewed the bread and goat cheese slower and slower after tensing up from the day's memories. The tension made the food turn to glue in her mouth and it took some effort to swallow it. Few words were spoken after Elena ordered coffee, and both of them hardly spoke even after they emptied their coffee mugs of every drop. Whenever Charlie would divert his attention to his surroundings, Elena took time to examine his physiognomy.

Elena thought his complexion needed work, but she liked that he had a strong face; his nose was an aquiline type nose but not too big. His forehead was rubicund and domed, complimented by a massive brow and deep-set eyes. His eyebrows were bushy but not too fierce looking. She even noticed that there was excessive hair on the back of his hands, and even though his beard was gone, it still wasn't enough to diminish his scruffy look.

However, even through his ruddy image, Elena saw a good-looking man. She thought it was too bad that he was pale, and that there was a drawn, faded look on his ascetic face. He also had offsetting, icy brown eyes that threw her off sometimes, and he would always reply to her questions in logical and forceful ways. There was nothing but a wealth of sorrow in his words regardless of what he spoke about and he seemed starved of emotion. Nevertheless, she thought that he had a calm decorum about him and a quiet strength. He always addressed her in a thin voice full of fawning respect and ingratiating hospitality and Elena found him comforting. She had figured him for a sweet heart if he would lapse into a chuckle now and then, but even his smiles were out of character. Charlie's lack of communication discouraged Elena into befriending him, and so she began to think negative thoughts again.

What am I doing with this guy? Those powers of his, what is he? What did he mutate into?

Nevertheless, even through the ghastliness, there was honesty in his eyes, Elena thought—at least, most of the time. She loved some things about him, mostly because Charlie appeared to be so innocent and new to the world. He blushed frequently, and he stuttered in embarrassment whenever he spoke for more than ten seconds. His voice was hoarse and tremulous most of the time too. Yet, years of her dad's negative advice about men were still infused in her skull and it could not be forgotten in just a few hours. Elena was just sick of being that girl who missed the party due to her father's over protectiveness.

Not anymore! she thought, and she felt that she was too old not to be wild and daring at her age. Her mind raced so much in the past few hours due to everything she had experienced that it finally began to sink in. Elena suddenly had the feeling of sensory overload, and her head pounded with a migraine.

"You okay?" Charlie asked after noticing Elena was rubbing her temples. "I'm fine, it's just that...everything kind of just sunk in; it's been a long few days," Elena replied. Her nerves were sore, and the caffeine made them worse. She took a deep breath to calm down and didn't want to cast off an impression of being weak.

"You just need some good old rest, that's all. There's a hotel up the block that should have power and electricity. I'm sure you can afford it," Charlie said with a tinge of sarcasm, and he finally let out a smile, it was a patronizing smile, but it was brief.

After Charlie loosened up, the stillness at the table began to break, and the two soon found themselves talking a bit more. Charlie ranted on with an almost vehement cordiality about his life and goals regarding the rallies and the state of politics on Earth. Elena would never have believed such a poorly groomed and pallid man would possess such peculiar mannerisms. Charlie filled her ears with details about how he quit his job because he couldn't handle the heat, and he told her that his body was breaking down due to the malfunctioning implants in his blood. However, he still didn't tell her why he didn't want the upgrade.

Elena tried to convince him to get the upgrade but Charlie would not answer her whenever she pried. He would just turn his head away from her and remain silent for a while. Elena figured Charlie didn't want to tell her the reason why so she zipped her lips about it.

It was only after she had asked him when she sensed Charlie's mood change. The cordiality in his tone would disappear. His speech became much flatter and unenthused. He eventually stopped talking and an awkward silence overcame the both of them once again. They didn't say a word for quite sometime until the waitress offered the check.

He is a moody bastard this one, Elena thought to herself.

***

Charlie's life had become an enigma. He would only wind up frightening her if he told her the truth and he didn't want to tell her about the whole situation taking place on Earth. It would terrify her. However, on the flipside, Charlie had realized that all this chiding seemed to relieve a pressure in his heart and brain, and he grew calmer after each minute they spent chatting. It actually felt good to have someone to talk to other than John, who couldn't possibly match the emotional stamina of a woman. No man could.

As much as I want to get to know her, I cannot. I must keep this relationship on a business level only! Charlie told himself repeatedly.

When they left the cafe, the two of them spoke less and less, and at times Charlie considered walking away from her all together. However, his heart wasn't cold enough to do such a thing. When they finally got to the bus stop on Lexington, Charlie checked his watch and figured he would see John there waiting for him, but he was nowhere to be found.

He is probably running late. Charlie figured. It was then when he had one of his mood swings. Reality had suddenly sunk into his brain, and his fantastic idea of having a girlfriend finally came off as ridiculous to him.

Walk away! Walk away! Charlie said to himself. Deep down, he knew it was unwise to accept her company any longer. He was no longer human, at least he wasn't in his mind, and he thought that he had no business consorting with innocent and ignorant people.

He gritted his teeth and decided to say goodbye to his friend. "It's getting late, maybe we should call it an evening."

"Yeah, I guess I'll be getting to a hotel now, the evening is bringing a chill in the air and I traveled so light that I have forgotten a sweater," Elena chuckled.

"I'm sleeping on the street tonight if my friend doesn't come with that bus pass."

"And you can't use yours because they'll track you down with it right?"

Charlie replied with a nod.

"I can get you a room somewhere," Elena offered.

Charlie exhaled a chuckle, "No, it's okay, you've done enough, and I'll be okay," Charlie insisted. "Eventually, I'll bump into my friend here. He'll find a bus pass somewhere."

Elena wasted no time digging into her purse and took out two credit sticks— one stick was good for five-hundred Sol credits and one stick was empty. She then tapped the sticks together five times.

"There," she grinned. "That's five Sol credits in that stick there. It should buy you a seat on the city bus."

Charlie stammered as Elena took his hand and stuffed the stick in his palm, closing his fingers over it. Charlie sighed not from disappointment but due to gratefulness, and he held onto her hand after she put the credit stick into his palm.

"I really owe you," Charlie said, and it took him a few seconds to let go of her hand.

"No, no...just thanking you for getting me out of that mess back there," Elena was quick to say.

"I can't tell you how much I appreciate this," Charlie said, his voice sinking more and more after each word. "I guess I'll get going now."

A brief silence overcame them both. It was an awkward moment for the both of them. Somehow, Elena thought his words and the expression on his face did not seem in accord, and the cast of his face made his smile look saturnine and phony. She sensed that he too didn't want to part without offering a phone number or an address to keep in touch, and just as she was about to offer her goodbyes, her intuition about Charlie's true desire caused her to remember an old saying she used to tell herself during times of timidity. She used to tell herself that her shyness and weakness were just the selfish things she would turn to when feeling sorry for herself.

Elena fought her doubts about the man in front of her and decided that she wasn't going to run and hide from men anymore—not this time. She had no experience standing up for what she wanted and it caused her to grope for words. Elena gritted her teeth and grew valiant enough to offer him her cell phone number. She dug through her purse for a pen and a napkin and wrote it down, handing it to him with intent.

"Here, you can call me at this number if you ever need help organizing a rally some time," she said more volubly.

Charlie smiled authentically but didn't take the napkin; he just stared at it. A sense of restiveness enervated Elena after realizing that her offer was not accepted, but she did not show it. Charlie sighed and continued to stare at the napkin. Deep down, Charlie knew that it was more than plain old business that forced him to seek her friendship. It wasn't the fact that he needed someone to speak out for him at the rallies. It was also a crush.

Before Elena withdrew her hand, Charlie reached for the napkin but pulled away at the last second after remembering that he threw his prepaid cell phone away.

"I'm sorry, but I might need to stay away from cell phones for a while now that the entire Earth military and police force might be looking for me. You see, these phones, they have GPS chips in them and each phone is tied to its recipient."

Elena raised a brow. "Oh.. I see," Elena replied, crumbling up the napkin and stuffing it in her purse.

Charlie began to stutter due to his conflicting feelings. "But hey, write my address down in your tablet if you ever want to—"

"Discuss my taking over for you at the rallies," Elena answered for him. Charlie finally let out an authentic chuckle. "223 East 33rd Street, Brooklyn

NY, 11202. But please Elena! Please do not come too late in the afternoon. Always in the daytime, you must remember to come in the day: the red districts are no place for a lady such as yourself! Especially at night!"

"I'll be sure to buy pepper spray."

"You won't have to if you come early, trust me," Charlie started laboriously. "And make sure no one follows you to my house please."

"I'll be careful!" Elena shot back. "I heard that a lot of people of the working class reenter the red districts from time to time to visit old homes and the graves of their loved ones. And so it won't be the most abnormal thing if some drone spots a connected person roaming around there. It's the disconnected folk they are looking for."

"You got a point," Charlie said, rubbing his chin. "So... I'll see you around then..." Charlie smiled again and put out his hand.

Elena logged the address into her tablet; they shook hands, said their goodbyes, turned around in opposite directions, and walked away. Charlie never thought he would be attracted to a woman ever again. His mind would not let go of the mental picture of Elena's face, the one ray of light in his life as of late and the only thing that seemed to cut away at the net of gloom that had closed in around him ever since he morphed into a monster.

19: The Advent

The novelty of being one of the most powerful people on Earth wore off by week's end, and Brennan just wanted to call it a mission already He was sick of not being able to contact his daughter and equally sick of the stench given off by all of the mutants he had arrested for the last three days.

Lucky for him, Lieutenant Graham liked getting his hands dirty, and he took to the field for the last two days while Brennan helmed the supercomputer Pandora. Nevertheless, it was an arduous task finding all of the disconnected people even from Pandora's main chair. Brennan worked all Friday long searching through every rotten edifice of the red districts, and it wasn't until seven p.m. that he finally came across a couple. After locating them, Brennan straightened in his seat and lurched forward; his hands flew to the controls on his holographic keyboard immediately. The overhead shot on his flat crystal glass monitor showed a three-square-block radius of Bensonhurst, Brooklyn, New York. The segment of the city was depicted in the infrared spectrum. Brennan focused the satellite feed on a particular set of dots located inside a large abandoned semi-attached home on Bay Parkway. Quickly, the view from the Landsat satellite zoomed in and singled out the single room in the home where its two occupants were. Both of the forms in the room gave off little body heat confirming their status as disconnected civilians.

Brennan wasted no time texting the address to Lieutenant Graham who was patrolling the area: "Two disconnected bogeys. 233 Bay Parkway. 2nd floor"

Strangely enough, Lieutenant Graham did not reply and Brennan began to worry about that because Graham usually responds to his texts right away.

That is all I need, more setbacks! Brennan sighed.

Brennan was tired and overworked and could not afford to miss an opportunity to arrest the two people he had tracked. The quicker they detained people, the quicker he would get back to his daughter. Brennan was distracted about it all, and he worked with only half his mind, thinking of Elena, the power outage, the interstellar communication outage, and most of all, his thoughts of General Clarkson and his inquiries about the Overseer. It was exhausting to think about so much at the same time, and his nerves had become so overwrought by day's end that his back muscles began to spasm.

As he waited for Graham's response, Brennan became absorbed with consecutive daydreams between his tasks and got so lost in his forebodings that he failed to notice Jasso standing over his shoulder.

"Good job, Major!" Jasso said, causing Brennan to jump in his chair after realizing he was there."

Jasso then patted Brennan on the back. "You managed to round up over eighty percent of the disconnected citizens in this city—all in just a few days."

The stink of tobacco tinged Brennan's nose, forcing him to crane his neck away. "Thanks for the vote of confidence," Brennan answered glumly, "but there's still thousands of people unaccounted for."

"Oh don't you worry, Major, we'll get them," Jasso began before pulling out a cigar from the pocket on his lapel. Jasso lit his cigar and spoke between puffs. "And so now, we shall take time to relax, recoil, and thrash out over some cigars!"

"Thank you for the kind sentiments, but I'll take a rain check on that smoke Colonel. I should go try to check in with my daughter; the ionic interference might have subsided by now."

"Oh my dear boy, I wouldn't be so quick to rule that out. I am more than sure that the atmosphere is still too dense for an attempt to communicate with anything in orbit!" Jasso said, speaking sanguinely, all while gallingly pinching Brennan's cheek. "But don't worry my dear boy, I'm sure you'll get to speak with your daughter in a few days anyway.

Once we upgrade everyone and round up the missing refugees, you will be up in that ship again in no time!"

Brennan just nodded in acceptance. What he really wanted to do was call up General Clarkson in order to inform him of Jasso's overly secretive ways. Jasso then began patting the back of Brennan's neck as though he was his pet. "Well you go and do your thing; take the rest of the day off, you look tired," Jasso said with jest in his voice.

"Before I go, you should know that I located two mutants there in that apartment," Brennan said, pointing at the monitor. "Also...for some reason, Lieutenant Graham isn't answering my email and I'm uncertain whether or not he is assailing them."

After hearing that, Jasso rubbed his hand over his short, bristly beard in confusion. "Yes, now that you mention it, Graham didn't answer my phone call ten minutes ago either," Jasso said, stuck in thought. His eyes glinted coldly as he stared at the monitor, and the surmises that set into Jasso's mind took away his sinuous temperament from before.

"He must have his hands full..." Jasso trailed off and scratched his head as he pondered over Graham's disappearance. "A lot of mutants continue to refuse our help."

"Yes, that could be it. I'm sure it's nothing he can't handle. Most of those mutants are all mouth ..and they are so weak they couldn't possibly pose a threat."

"Well—that will be all, Major," Jasso grunted. "Enjoy your night off."

Brennan gave Jasso a curtly nod, and darted out of the room.

Instead of heading to his hotel room, Brennan decided to stay at headquarters in hopes of finding out what had happened to Graham. To pass the time, Brennan spent a few hours in his office reading up on Chernobyl AIDS, nano- medicine, and most importantly of all, radiation poisoning and the effect it had on the human mind. After just ten minutes of reading, his stomach began calling out to him. He was hungry, and Brennan shut down his PC and quickly dialed the number of a local Mexican takeout.

The food came almost an hour after calling, and Brennan couldn't wait any longer for it. Brennan's stomach churned in the elevator as he treaded down to

the lobby to accept the food he had ordered. The deliveryman was a wiry looking lad that chewed gum all too noisily, and he looked nervous.

The delivery man handed Brennan a hot paper bag full of steaming food and said, "Man, oh man, it took me twenty minutes to get here because I was frisked by six different guards outside!"

"Sorry for the trouble, we just need to be cautious with who we decide to let in here," Brennan said. With a glad heart, Brennan tipped the man well after the gratifying smell of the seafood fajitas seeped into his nostrils. He tapped his Sol credit stick with the man's stick three times until he heard three beeps.

"Thank you very much sir!" the deliveryman said—his sharp and bony face made his smile more pronounced. He kept saying *thank you* repeatedly as Brennan escorted him out of the lobby. The man surely wasn't used to getting a tip in Sol credits.

When the man left, Brennan darted back into the elevator and pressed the button that would take him to the cafeteria. When the elevator doors dinged open, Brennan shot out of them and bolted for the nearest table. He was starving so badly that he tore open the brown paper bag like a ten year would open a Christmas present. The tangy aroma of roasted onion and pepper put a permanent grin on his face. However, just as he was about to take a bite, his quantum capacitor chirped in his pocket.

A tiny digital red box with a number "1" appeared over a little bright red envelope in the corner of his left contact lens. Brennan blinked three times to open his inbox and sure enough, it was an email from Colonel Jasso.

Damn it, why would you tell me to take the rest of the day off if you are only going to harass me an hour later! Brennan said to himself, tossing his fork and knife on the table in frustration.

The email said, "I finally found out why Graham didn't respond. He lost his Eye-Net contact lenses and his radio during a scuffle with some canyon dwellers a few hours ago. Apparently, rabid birds attacked him too. I need you to helm Pandora for me because I am leaving the building for a little while; there has been some sort of riot in Times Square and my presence is needed there. Hurry up and get down here so I could leave.

Signed, *Colonel Jasso, Chief Overseer of planet Earth.*

In his anger, Brennan slapped a palm on the side of his thigh and began to sift through his thoughts. *I knew there'd be a riot someday, but how serious could it be? The police could handle weak, scrawny mutants...and since when does Jasso leave the building...for a riot nonetheless...*

He left his fajita dinner steaming on the cafeteria table and shot towards the elevator without hesitation. When he arrived at Pandora's room, Jasso was curiously talking to himself while pacing the room like a maniac. After he took note of Brennan's arrival, Jasso's feet took off towards the door immediately.

Brennan shook his head. "What sort of riot happened that the police can't handle?" Brennan asked.

"Not sure," Jasso said.

"Do you want me to go instead?" "No!"

Brennan thought his replies all seemed somewhat reticent and brief and there was a swarthy look in Jasso's eyes. His forehead was lined and grooved the whole time as he loaded his firearm and strapped his holster to his shoulder. His hands were tremulous, and he violently slammed his cigar into the ashtray, leaving a trail of ashes and embers that fell to the floor.

"I'll handle this," Jasso said as he prepared his utility belt. Brennan noticed his hands were shaking and seeing that made Brennan wonder some more.

"Colonel?" Brennan began inquisitively. "You sure everything is alright?"

Jasso forced a smile. "Yes, my dear boy, everything will be okay. All I need you to do is wait here and standby for orders. I will be sending you an email shortly containing the file of a Charlie Beasley, age thirty-three, escaped resident of Hoover City 2 and reported leader of some crazy movement that is only getting bigger."

"Culprits of a movement?"

"Some waste of a grassroots movement," Jasso grunted through his gnashing teeth. "They have no ambition and only misguided zeal."

"This movement you speak of—how big is it?" Brennan asked.

"This bubble of anarchy isn't that big," Jasso said, pausing to think, while scratching his bearded chin. "On the other hand, several makers of discord are enough for me to take seriously. In the digital age, the words of one man can echo to many. And I'm going to find this Charlie Beasley tonight, just watch me!"

"What else should I do to help?" Brennan asked.

Jasso looked like he was about to pop from the rage. "I want you to send at least a dozen drones towards the midtown area in Manhattan. I want the Landsat recon satellites pointed towards every bridge and tunnel! Do not stop until you search through every rotten edifice of this city! We must find these besotted animals and put an end to their congregations!"

Brennan cocked his head to the side and furrowed his brow. "With all due to respect Colonel, you're making this sound much more serious than it sounds."

Jasso lapsed into a psychopathic giggle. "Oh, my dear boy, it's not serious I can assure you of this. I have everything under control."

Brennan didn't buy it. Jasso's rebuttals were all too firm and steadfast, and he acted as if his most prevalent qualm had suddenly become a reality.

20: Insomnia

A quick blast of wind rattled the windowpane, startling Charlie awake.

Charlie tried to open his eyes, but they could not conform to the bright sunlight seeping in from the window. The sun looked far too bright, and instead of giving him courage to start the day, the bright rays only enticed him to sleep longer.

The sun-drenched room had a malign influence over him that affected certain parts of his mind and it made him tired. He was so tired that he failed to hear his alarm clock radio that had recently gone off. All hopes of getting up early and starting the day felt unfeasible due to the repulsive vibrancy emanating from outside his window. Charlie worked so hard to fix his schedule, but he was slowly going back to living a nocturnal lifestyle again. He couldn't help it; he gravitated towards sleeping during the daytime because the sun was much too powerful for the new cells forming in his body.

It was so hot in his bedroom that he thought about taking off his anti- surveillance cloak. However, he didn't give in. As difficult as it was to sleep under the oppressive weight, he couldn't risk being tracked by the Overseer's satellites and drones. Charlie rolled over and buried his head under his pillow. He ignored the David Bowie song "Starman," which was blaring on his alarm clock radio. He figured more rest would make him more efficient at his work and sacrificing a few hours for sleep would outweigh the negatives of lost time. Eventually, the music playing on his alarm clock forced him from his semiconscious state, but he was too tired to shut the alarm clock. But then he fretted in his mind about his batteries that operated it because he did not want to waste them. And so he blindly swung a cranky, rubbery arm over the table beside his bed and groped for the clock's snooze button. He pressed his palm over it and closed his eyes again, hoping to fall back to sleep. However, after twenty minutes of tossing and turning, he realized that sleep was impossible because all of the qualms jammed in his mind, so he dragged his indolent legs off the bed and slid on his slippers. He rubbed the bridge of his nose until his dry eyes became moist enough to open, and Charlie blindly reached across his table to grab his glass of water. He kicked his head back and slugged it down in one gulp, immediately moistening his parched throat.

Outside, the sun was still blazing, and the prospect of the day was not enough to motivate him into hitting his lab in the dining room. Even if it were late in the day, all of the distractions would probably keep him from his work anyway. Besides, he needed John to help him out, and unfortunately, he never came home last night. A whole agglomeration of thoughts kept his mind busy, and he deliberately shut out any thoughts of the riot from yesterday, the possibility of having AIDS, and especially thoughts of Elena. He purportedly focused on his missing friend.

A quick search through the house confirmed that John never came home last night and he had been missing for almost twenty-four hours. Charlie couldn't call him because he threw his smartphone away, and so the suspicious demise of his friend contributed to his mounting anxiety. The thought of John missing for all that time made the air a bit fouler in the room, not because he was worried about him, but because he had just come to grips with the fact that he badly needed him in order to help build and test his weapon.

As for John's well-being, well—Charlie didn't worry too much about that. After all, it wasn't the first time John had gone missing. John loved spending days at a time hunting and camping out in various locations throughout the city, so Charlie figured he would be back. What Charlie didn't understand was why John would just leave him hanging at the bus stop. Then again, after some thought, Charlie realized that it was he who might have left John hanging. His dinner date with Elena might have taken up more time then he thought.

Why would John decide to go hunting after all that they went through? Charlie asked himself.

Charlie thought he might as well plop back onto his bed to get some more sleep until John returned. However, as soon as he closed his eyes, Charlie knew that his effort to return to sleep would bear out to be futile. It wasn't the back pain, the fatigue, the retrovirus, or even his missing friend that made it hard to sleep. It was all the thoughts and feelings he had for Elena. They were getting harder and harder to repress with each moment that passed, and he began to regret going back for her after the microwave attack.

The conflicting feelings made his cranium rattle and his heart pump faster as he slipped in and out of dozes, unable to sleep for more than twenty minutes at a time due a series of chronic hypnic jerks that had plagued him due to his overwrought nerves. His nerves were rapidly deteriorating and Charlie began to wonder if his new brain and nervous system was too powerful for the body to handle. Love, for one thing, was undeniably and excessively powerful for him right now.

As he tossed in his bed, all he thought about was Elena's gray eyes, and that icy twinkle from the few green striations in her irises. He could almost smell her glossy blonde hair and could almost see the gracious neckline she had, as well as hear the cute sounds she made when she chuckled. The sound of her voice comforted him whenever she spoke, and being around her seemed to recalibrate his fiery nerves and snap him out of his morbid reticence all together.

Charlie hated himself for not taking initiative. He had to wait for Elena to offer her number first, and he regretted his cowardice. He knew he had pushed her away with his unenthusiastic behavior, and he put no effort into his speech when they conversed during their date yesterday. Less than a day ago, his solitude seemed to be unassailable. She was one of the first women to come at him with smiles in a very long time and he felt silly for not giving her confidence. As he lay on his bed, eyes closed, Charlie remembered his mother's words, words she had told him after he broke up with his childhood sweetheart.

"we are most vulnerable when we love someone. We can be hurt very easily. However, when we're in love, what we receive is much greater than what we risk."

As positive as those words may have been, Charlie could not repress the darker thoughts that entered his mind, and his inner demons began to take over. The negative side of him began thinking again, debasing all of his optimism for establishing a friendship.

She's just another girl, same like the rest, he told himself. *She is just a lonely girl living in a turbulent time...she needs a man to lift things for her and move furniture, or help protect her in this eat or be eaten world. Women are so logical, treating men as tools, survival is all they care about.*

Charlie continued to drown himself in pessimism and the same words played over in his mind: *Forget women—Never trust anyone; it's safer to live like that*

—Loving a person makes you weak—Love makes you do stupid things just to keep the ones you love safe and happy— The world has gotten too complex to share it with someone—People will only get in my way—Work comes first.

The words played in his mind all morning as he redoubled his efforts to drift off asleep. He rolled over on his side, gripped his pillow violently, and engaged in self-psychoanalysis again. He thought about his entire life and his way with women, and throughout his life, he constantly walked away from them. He didn't care about making new friends or establishing any relationships whatsoever. Charlie feared very little. He would stand up and fight anyone if he had to, but was a coward when it came to relationships. His self-imposed isolation was proof of that, he thought.

He figured people were made into introverts as they grew from the experiences of life, however, this was not the case with Charlie. Charlie was a loner from the start, and even though he had a few friends as a kid, it was always one friend at a time. He hated groups, and the competitions kids would engage in. That is why he preferred his own company and this is why he was his own best friend. He was an introvert straight out of his mother's womb, speaking very succinctly to the girls in school, always basic conversation and only if necessary. He was too busy living inside his own head, observing, analyzing, and failing to take initiative.

Despite his shyness, it was the fear of losing someone that brought out Charlie's furtive traits. He thought about it too much and constantly worried about losing another loved one for whom he could potentially grow feelings. The deaths of Charlie's relatives marked his life with stains and only made him more of a recluse. Ten minutes after the first earthquake hit Brooklyn, his sister died tragically by falling into a sinkhole. The sinkhole swallowed her car as she waited in small parking lot for Charlie to come out of a pharmacy. They had made the trip to the pharmacy because Charlie needed hydrogen peroxide for a few small cuts he had on his head after some sheetrock fell during the earthquake. In a sense, he blamed himself for her death.

Then there was his brother who lived in the basement apartment of his family's home. He was swept away by floodwater when the storm surge brought the sea right through the door, only to return the next day when he washed up dead just a block away.

Perhaps most tragic of all was the death of his mother. She died before her husband during the first of several category-nine earthquakes. The quake made the roof cave in on her above Charlie's bedroom where she was sleeping that night because the bottom floors had flooded. Charlie felt that it should have been him in that bedroom and he should have died in his mother's place.

Then there was his dad of course. His death wasn't Charlie's fault, but he died of radiation sickness nonetheless. Therefore, Charlie asked himself, why should he lose another one? Besides, the world became excessively complex to venture into a relationship with anyone. It has become a dangerous eat or be eaten world out there and Charlie thought it was logical to be a recluse— choosing to keep relationships on a business level only—and to make acquaintances and not friends.

All of these domineering memoirs and oppressive feelings finally overcame his nerves and his pique for Elena. He finally became satisfied enough with forgetting her. It stuck in his mind enough to calm his nerves, and he actually calmed down enough to drift off to sleep with nothing but dire memories to afford the material for his dreams.

21: Searching for Supper

After sleeping through the whole morning, afternoon, and early evening, Charlie awakened to a much more pleasant view outside his boarded window— the moon. The rich moonlight that seeped between the slits in his boarded window enticed him to spring up out of bed and head straight for his ration box.

As he prepared the oatmeal and dried milk mixture, he knew John had not come home yet because Charlie didn't sense a presence in the house, so he never bothered to check. Instead, he trotted over to his living room, peeked through his boarded front window as he ate his breakfast, and surveyed the scene. The grief-stricken streets bathed in the moon's blue hue, and the rich moonlight erased whatever mystery lurked behind every dark shadow. The moon was full, the air was windless, and nothing but the howls of coyotes could be heard in the distance.

The few houses that remained on the particular avenue were empty and silent. The string of cars were parked and empty, right where they have stood for a decade—rusted, untouched, and all with flat tires. After inhaling his bowl of oatmeal, Charlie fiddled through the pockets of his anti-surveillance cloak and took out one of his five remaining cigarettes. He lit it with one of the various candles that flickered on the table and immediately took a violent drag, inhaling the smoke deeply as he stared through the boarded window, hoping John would return.

Suddenly, out of the corner of his eye, Charlie caught some movement up a street that was perpendicular to his house, directly ahead of him. A man was waddling towards his home. He wearing all white, so he really stood out.

Who could it be? Charlie thought, and at first, he dismissed the idea that it might be John because of the unusual saunter in the figure's steps.

However, Charlie wasn't quite sure. The man walked like he was injured or as if he had a spring on the bottom of one shoe. Up until recently, no one was ever spotted in the neighborhood before, and so Charlie thought it was a good chance that it might be John after all.

In a fit of curiosity, Charlie pressed his face against the wooden board on the window and squinted his eyes to help his vision cut through the darkness. As the man hobbled closer down the road and towards Charlie's house, the moonlight crept around his home, and the light fell on the sidewalk where the figure walked. Charlie sighed in disappointment. It wasn't John but some other gaunt looking swarthy fellow who was new to the neighborhood. The man walked unevenly and seemed to have the shakes because his arms twitched at times.

He must be one of those derelict ogres who resorted to cannibalism to survive, or some decrepit mutant searching for food or shelter... Charlie thought as stood there, smoking his cigarette and watching the man.

Charlie actually found amusement in his waddle, and a coughing chuckle emptied from his throat after experiencing a brief euphoria from the tobacco. He found it silly to find amusement in his walk, but there was just nothing to laugh at anymore. The figure eventually vanished as he turned a corner, and so Charlie's entertainment for the evening was over.

Charlie turned away from the window and took one last drag of his cigarette before dousing the butt in his ashtray. After the smoke, Charlie thought about getting back to work but his stomach was calling him out for food despite the fact that he had just ate.

Charlie realized his body required more calories lately and so he thought about eating something else. After sifting through the contents of the ration box, he became frustrated with all the rubbish in there. He reached for some soup powder and set it aside. He then fetched a gravity filter filled with clean rainwater and poured it into his kettle before holding it over four large candles. Of course, the water would never boil, but after ten minutes over the candles, it became warm enough for soup; and so he poured the contents of the soup powder and plunked a spoon into the kettle. He drank it so fast that a quarter of the soup never even made it to his belly and had mostly dribbled out of the corners of his mouth. Feeling unsatisfied by the meal, Charlie decided it was best to go hunting, and so he ran back up to his bedroom, quickly slipped on his boots, and threw on his darkest anti- surveillance cloak before quietly stepping out onto his porch. He locked the padlocks on his door and vanished into the dark streets in search of a meal.

I will eat anything right now, my gosh; I am so damn hungry for real food...animal flesh!

As soon as Charlie walked out, a still fog swept over the area, and a thick blanket of clouds diminished the moon's authority over the landscape. Charlie would have to rely on his other senses because it was difficult to see, and even his keen sense of night-vision could not help cut through the mist. Charlie couldn't smell or sense any life forms present in and around the area so he continued to trudge ahead down Seaver Avenue, praying that he'd stumble across anything to eat—a rabbit, an opossum, or even a deer for that matter. The street was a swampy, mud-choked street of rubble, which ran through a flat, concrete valley of death. The houses that remained stood as molded shells, and there was water-damaged desolation for miles around.

The smell of salt water still hung sharp whenever the wind blew, and only the wind seemed to move in that street. The only other sounds he heard came from the black ravens that lived in most of the abandoned automobiles and homes—calling out to the moon with guttural shrieks. Furthermore, the howls of distant coyotes tore through the dilapidated landscape like a primal fury from the gulfs of hell.

After turning the corner on Seaver Avenue, he came across another heavily pined street engulfed in weeds. There was nothing ahead of him but empty shopping malls consisting of old bagel stores, diners and pharmacies, and a wide median of corn-grass invaded much of the mall's parking lot. It was almost impossible to see anything ahead of him but he trudged on anyway.

Eventually, Charlie's keen sense of smell led him across the parking lot after detecting the scent of animal droppings. Charlie inched closer with sneaky and stealthy steps, moving almost mechanically through the mall parking lot, and as he inched closer to the abandoned diner, the presence there felt more like an attendance.

It is animal life, not human, Charlie was sure of it.

The parking lot was tough to cross because of all the tall spears of corn-grass and so it took him a few minutes to finally find a means of ingress. Parts of the dense corn-grass looked disturbed and parted in some sections so Charlie followed the path while sniffing through the air like a bloodhound on a mission. Unfortunately, the foliage wasn't the only problem. An oncoming rush of dank mist closed in on all things around him and the thick gray pall in front of him rendered his great eyesight useless. He would have to rely on his nose only.

He swiped at the tall grass in front of him, following the parted areas. The presence he felt wasn't a human brain emission, but that of an animal—several animals. Catching an animal should not be as difficult as he previously thought. He was confident enough in his ability to sprint fast enough to catch anything with four legs and he probably did not need his knife for the kill. He thought it was much more humane to choke the animal to death or directly snap its neck.

Then, the shuffling of foliage just behind him caused Charlie to swivel around, only to discover a rather healthy looking set of rabbits hopping about the brushes and wheatgrass. The rabbits were grey and fat; Charlie saw no tumors on them and they surely looked healthy enough to eat, he thought. The rabbits didn't run at first, they only stared back at Charlie, noses twitching.

The sight of the fat looking rabbits abruptly stirred something primitive in Charlie, and Charlie's nostrils flared from the pang of hunger and primal rush that overcame him. In an instant, Charlie charged the rabbits, causing them to scamper off into the deeper brush down towards the middle of the parking lot but Charlie's adrenaline increased his speed and was hot on their tails. His boots thrashed through the tall grass, and his strides morphed into to skips and hops in order to gain more ground. The shorter weeds and grass swished at his ankles, soaking his socks—and the cattails lashed at his face, leaving it damp with dew. Eventually, Charlie's cat-like agility led him within an arm's reach to the back of one of the rabbits and he lunged desperately at them after each stride, but all ten of his fingers groped nothing but empty air at first. With a final burst of speed, Charlie leapt and pounced one of the slower but fatter rabbits and the poor rodent found its ears in Charlie's grip.

Charlie licked his lips as he held the rabbit up to his face by its ears, still possessed by the thrill of the hunt. The rabbit was thrashing violently as it struggled to get free and so Charlie mercilessly snapped its neck, sparing it of pain and fear. The rabbit went limp in an instant. There was no need to think it alive; it's breathing had ceased.

On the way home, Charlie began to feel bad for the poor thing; it was full of life one second, and an empty shell the next. However, Charlie's growling stomach immediately nullified his guilt and had watered down his feelings of compassion. When Charlie got to his home, he did not even bother to enter. Instead, he sat down on a small chair that stood on the corner of his front porch and inspected his catch. He was so hungry that he thought about eating the rabbit right there and then. The primitive sensations that stirred in him were still there and he did not know why he felt compelled to eat the animal raw. After all, he was eating three small meals a day, but it was the blood that he craved more than anything.

Then, just as he set his mouth to dig his teeth into the rabbit's warm and tender flesh, a silhouette emerged from the dark, misty street and a familiar female voice called out to him.

22: A Night at Charlie's

As the woman got closer, Charlie's face softened and a burst of merriment ran through him. He made a connection with the voice even before he saw Elena's face. Her beautiful blonde hair was floating from the slight breeze that had come in with the fog and a very glad look came into Charlie's eyes but only for a moment.

"Quick, let's get inside," Charlie said as he unlocked three padlocks.

Elena's curiosity overmastered all the vague fears that had accumulated in her mind during her eight-mile trek from the edge of the green districts, and her quest for knowledge made her forget all of her doubts about entering such a grisly house. Charlie's home was festooned with patches of ivy and moss that crawled all over it, and the steps were smothered with various specks of bird droppings. Its hint of morbid habitation depressed her and she never thought Charlie would choose to live in such decrepitude. As crazy as she thought she was for pursuing this man before her; her search for truth made her almost fearless at this point in her life.

Charlie fumbled in his pocket for his keys and unlocked the last lock before opening the door that led to a pitch-dark foyer.

"Welcome to my palace," Charlie said sarcastically, but before they entered, both he and Elena heard a whirling sound up in the sky ahead of them. A small Dragonfly spy drone was hovering just above the height of the telephone polls up the street, heading towards their direction.

"Quick, get in the house!" Charlie said thickly.

He took Elena by the arm and nudged her ahead into his hallway, almost tossing her across the room. Charlie didn't know his strength and so she stumbled from the force. He then turned to her, put an index finger to his lip, and with his free hand, he locked the door. Charlie scampered over to his boarded front window and gave a startled glance out into the dark streets as if fearful that someone might have tailed Elena to his house.

"Are they looking for you specifically?" Elena asked. Charlie shrugged his shoulders.

"Probably not..." He paused to sigh. "They're looking to upgrade everyone.

It is mandatory, and that Dragonfly drone is just a scout with a couple of cameras on it. It can't see through walls like the predator drones or satellites."

Charlie then fumbled through a pile of clothes and handed Elena what looked like an ordinary hooded sweater.

"Put that on" Charlie insisted.

Elena looked at Charlie like he was crazy. "What is it...?"

"It's made of leaded fabrics," Charlie was quick to answer. "It will keep us obscured from all of Orion's eyes in the sky. I bought the cloaks many years ago on the Internet, way before the first Earthquake hit."

"But they wouldn't be interested in a connected person; like I said, a lot of connected people visit the red districts."

"Yes, they wouldn't be interested in you because you have working implants in your body. Still, it's better to play it safe and put the cloak on."

After Elena put on the hooded cloak, she immediately thought about asking him what weighed heavy on her mind—why he refused to be taken in for an upgrade back in Central Park when Lieutenant Graham tried detaining him.

Charlie's suspicions about the implants held very little credence, but the fact that the upgrades were mandatory made her suspicious enough to believe that his qualms about the upgrade held some water. First, she had to ask him about it, but a part of her was too afraid to ask.

Charlie walked into the kitchen with his rabbit in one hand and a candleholder in the other. Elena took a deep breath and looked around the place. It was dark; she could not see anything past the den until

Charlie lit a small candle in the kitchen. Its glow radiated out into the living room and that helped her see the place a little bit better. Although, she realized that it was not necessarily a good thing after considering all the decay that surrounded her.

She could not help but wonder if the roof above her head was about to collapse on her, judging from the looks of the place. Besides the putrefaction, there was clutter everywhere. All around the dining room were maddening rows of textbooks piled on the floor, and there were glasses and dishes all over the place—some droopily set on the armrests of chairs and on the stairway that led to the bedrooms upstairs.

He sure was a picturesque survivalist and seemed to have no use for ordered life anymore! she thought.

Charlie continued to rustle around the kitchen, and Elena tried to figure out what he was doing but couldn't see due to the dim lighting. Elena was about to tell Charlie about her new job as a waitress but Charlie's queer behavior made the words die in her mouth. After inching closer to the kitchen, Elena's curious glance morphed into one of suspicion after witnessing Charlie's horrific behavior. Charlie was evidently licking the dead rabbit's blood off its furry mouth like a hungry dog, emitting a blissful look on his face after each lick.

This man must be starved! Elena thought, forcing herself to understand the ravenous act, which helped reduce her nausea just a little.

Charlie noticed that Elena was staring at him so he stopped licking the blood and put the rabbit in the freezer.

Is that freezer even working? Elena asked herself. Charlie walked into the living room but did not speak.

Why is he so quiet? Elena thought. She began to feel unwelcome but that was not the case. Charlie was just distracted. After lighting the second candle, the room lit up enough to keep Elena from bumping into anything.

"I never light more than two," Charlie said.

"You don't want anyone to know you're here right?"

"The fire is too weak to be detected by the Overseer's infrared drones, but it's the luminescence that I'm worried about. Even though the windows are boarded, the light could radiate through the slits."

Elena answered with a nod and she began to regret coming to see him.

Charlie had a serious and stern expression on his stony face and the candlelight

showed it sufficiently. It was clear that something was torturing his mind; his candle tottered in his trembling hands more and more after each minute that passed. Charlie looked all too scatter-brained and quirky, and his face was alive with what looked like gnawing pain.

Charlie sat down on a dust-encrusted sofa, just staring at the wall silently, whilst drumming his fingers on dusty and splintered coffee table. He was alarmed from the fact that Elena looked so travel-weary, and her waitress uniform was far from clean. Her skirt was mud-specked, her blouse was un- tucked, and her kneecaps poked out of the holes in her black tights.

Then, all the concern welling deep inside him came out at once, "You could have gotten hurt out here you know!" Charlie snapped, sounding concerned. "There are lawless men out on these dark streets, men with the coldest of hearts, made of steel! Never come out here at night! Only in the day!"

"Thanks for your concern, but it was light outside when I got here."
"You were here before?"

"Yes, I knocked on your door for an hour and figured you were out hunting or something so I waited."

Charlie slapped his palm on his thigh. "I overslept today," Charlie said regrettably.

Elena shrugged. "It was still early at the time, so I decided to go take a look around the old neighborhood. My aunt used to live a few blocks from here and seeing her home brought back some happy memories. I got so caught up in my past that time slipped past me in an instant—and before I knew it, it was almost dusk. I really had no other choice but to go back to your house, because I didn't think I would make it back to the bus stop before sundown anyway. So, I hurried to get back here as quick as I could."

Charlie sighed. "Out here they would rape you before cooking you and eating you Elena!" Charlie's face then began to lose the rigid lines associated with his concern and his voice softened, "Well, nevertheless, I must say, that I am pleased by your company."

Elena felt a weight come off her shoulders after hearing that. Charlie got up from the sofa and headed back towards his kitchen. "Would you like some water?" he asked.

"Oh no, I would hate to use up your ration water," Elena replied.

"Oh, it's fine really, I'm not using the ration water. They only give two sixteen ounce sized bottles a week and mostly water pills. I rely on my collections of rain water."

Elena furrowed her brow. "Well okay..." She dragged her final syllable. "I guess it's okay as long as it's clean."

"Gravity distilled, crisp and cold," Charlie said as he fumbled in his fridge for a pitcher of cold water. Elena then wondered how he kept it cold. She remembered the sounds of ice cubes when Charlie put his rabbit inside the freezer.

How is he keeping that thing running? Elena asked herself.

She didn't hear a generator thrumming anywhere. She figured he must have found a way to do it and never bothered to ask because she became aware of his resourcefulness after he told her about the generator during their dinner date.

Charlie came out of the kitchen with a rusty tray, topped with two glasses of water and two candles to light his way. Elena gladly accepted the cold glass of water.

"Thank you so dearly, I haven't had anything to drink since I left the hotel this morning,"

"Photo-voltaic paint," Charlie said off-topic. "Excuse me?"

"You must be wondering how I keep my fridge running without any working electricity in the home."

Elena thought he must have read her mind. "Yes!" Elena said astounded. "I was!"

"I painted my roof with the special photo-voltaic paint, a paint I made with several metallic filings that my dad left me before his passing. I can paint anything and make a solar panel out of it. The fridge there is wired to a water based capacitor on my roof that holds in the solar energy harnessed by my painted roof tiles."

"Sounds like some exotic paint you got there!"

Charlie took a long swig of water. "Any luck finding a job?" he asked.

The question came as Elena took in a gulp of water and she rushed to swallow it because she suddenly became eager to speak. "Yes, thanks for asking! As of today, I am no longer an Orion employee," she told him gleefully. "The restaurant manager hired me, you know, the place... where we ate..." Elena trailed off when she saw Charlie raise an eyebrow.

"That's great to hear but the best you're going to get is a dorm room in some old public school that Orion converted into living space," Charlie shook his head. "You should have gone for the truck driver positions that are always open. Remember, unless you work for Orion, your chances at getting your own flat or private apartment is slim."

Elena dismissed him with a wave of the arm. "I thought you wanted everyone to quit their Orion based jobs?"

Charlie huffed more than sighed. "Yeah, I meant the mining jobs mostly, but regardless...I would hate to see you living in some dump."

"Oh, I had it with Orion Corp.," Elena snapped. "I want to work in a positive environment—like the restaurant. It's an environment that houses many of my best personal memories."

Charlie reluctantly decided to ease off. He just couldn't understand why Elena was sacrificing so much to live on such a sordid planet. All these years, Charlie had yearned to be taken up amongst the stars and yet, Elena was doing the opposite. She must have more resolve and dedication then he first had imagined.

"How did he hire you if you never went through customs? You came in on a space elevator and there are no records of your arrival," Charlie said.

Elena nodded sourly. "I realized that after the hiring process. The manager of the restaurant was kind enough to pay for a cab and it took me to the nearest spaceport in Long Island. I registered as a temporary tourist."

Charlie squirmed in his seat and stammered with concernment. "So you're basically on the New York census now...did...did they send you for a physical?"

"Yes they did," Elena said, and she paused after seeing Charlie's worrisome look. "The manager did indeed call some paramedics. They scanned me to verify if I was connected to what he called the Earth network but ceased to continue scanning once they learned I was connected to the galactic network. The manager knew I was fresh from the heavens, so he informed me that the continuation of the physical would be unnecessary."

"Thank the heavens," Charlie swallowed his water hard, no longer sipping it, but instead chugging it down to quash his nerves. Elena sensed that something off-putting had deterred him from the conversation.

"What's wrong?" Elena asked. "Why did you thank the heavens?"

Charlie shook her off. He puckered his lip and took a deep breath before deciding to search the skies again through his window. There were no signs of any drones and as Charlie continued to stare, a brief silence overcame them both. Elena sensed his doubt and surmises and studied his face as he paced from window to window, gripped by paranoia.

Elena decided to break the silence by inquiring about his friend. "Is your friend home?"

"No, he never came home," Charlie said evenly, continuing to stare outside. "Oh...I hope he's—"

"He'll be fine," Charlie interrupted. A part of him was in denial about the potential harm that may have befallen his friend. "He disappears sometimes. He's got a hell of an appetite and he loves hunting...he'll be back."

"Speaking of food, got anything to eat?" Elena asked. "The rabbit is sure to feed two," Charlie said.

"No thanks," Elena chuckled. "I'm not eating that rabbit after seeing it look all furry and cute."

"Why do so many people eat meat every day, but are quick to refuse the meat of an animal that they witnessed being hunted right before their eyes?"

Elena shrugged but agreed. She thought it was true and she tried to squelch her grin.

"I rather see the meat already breaded and garnished and wrapped in supermarket foam and plastic," Elena grinned.

Charlie stood there with his hip cocked out, shaking his head. "Anyways, if you're hungry, there might be a few cans of beans left in the kitchen cupboards. You are more than welcome to snack on what you find."

Elena grabbed one of the brass candlesticks and skipped into the kitchen, immediately opening the cupboards. Some of his cabinets had no doors to them, and there was very little food inside them except for a few cans of corn and beans and some dried strips of what appeared to be salted meat were enclosed in plastic wrap.

What intrigued her most were the impressive processions of bottles all neatly organized in one of the cabinets. She saw dozens of corked vials and another dozen jars filled with dried herbs. She recognized only one of the items in that particular cabinet—a white plastic bottle of anti-radiation pills with the label *"Potassium Iodide"* on it. She figured all the other herbs in the bottles were medicinal as well.

Elena then decided to head over to the only picture frame that hung in the entire house. She held the candle-holder by the frame and giggled. It was a collage of Charlie in various stages of his life with several relatives.

"That was you?" She chuckled, pointing to a photo of Charlie when he was twelve.

"Yep, all thirty pounds of me," Charlie attempted to joke, but the pain of losing his family had surfaced again, so he tucked it away.

"All of those people in the photo are dead," Charlie said with distaste.

"I lost many relatives too, and it takes determination and vigilance to move on," Elena replied.

Charlie stammered a bit. "It's true—but sometimes it takes forever," Charlie said with a phlegmatic voice, fighting back the memories.

"I'm sorry to hear it," Elena replied piteously, unable to repress a wealth of sympathy.

He wasn't a cold guy after all, she thought.

Charlie's mouth stiffened, "They all died due to the catastrophes, except for my dad. He and I survived but he never made it in time for his upgrade. He almost made it, but not quite—and even though his tumors weren't as bad as mine, he died. You see, it was the lottery that saved me. My name was called during the daily announcement at City Hall and so I was one of the first survivors to be upgraded in this city."

Elena shook her head; she too had plenty of odious memories, but at least she didn't lose her whole family. "I was about to be upgraded but I then learned that I was selected to be taken up into Orion's flagship scout ship, the Niagra."

"You were on the Niagra?" Charlie asked in awe.

"Yes, you've heard of the ship?"

"Yes, I remembered seeing it on the news, but only in photos—it's a pretty ship".

Elena waved him off. "It's a nice ship, on the outside that is, but it's not somewhere I want to live."

"I don't blame you."

"Besides losing your family, did you lose any friends? Or girlfriends?" she asked him.

"No, no friends or girlfriends. I never had many friends to be quite honest. My life is a sterile one Elena. My life is so full of work that I have not had much time to make friends," Charlie lamented.

Elena's heart sank within her, and she couldn't help allow Charlie to control the conversation. She didn't want to pry and get too personal.

Charlie just stood there meekly, and in a sense, Charlie had become annoyed by Elena's prying. It is as if he suddenly had a crow pecking at his open wounds. The last thing he wanted to do was dwell upon the spring of sorrows that had drowned his heart many years ago. Elena never broke eye contact with him; her jaw was too set in place to say anything. Charlie saw nothing but resolution in her bearing and so he was trying hard to give in to her inquiries. There was a motherly nature in the woman, he thought. And that made him feel liberated to express his tender side without feeling it derogatory to his manhood.

Still, Charlie was not the type to open up to anyone and so he decided to end the conversation. He headed to the window for a quick reconnoiter. He could sense Elena's eyes crawling all over him even though his back was turned. He so badly wanted to tell Elena about Orion and all of their misdoings, but he figured ignorance was the best thing for everyone. Especially since everyone was so powerless to change anything anyway.

Charlie finally turned from the window and faced Elena. He inched towards her with his head down until he stood face to face with her.

"Elena...why did you come here?"

Elena could not speak at first because the question came out of nowhere, but she gathered some air in her lungs and decided to tell him the truth. "A great solicitude for what you stand for, and for what you fight for—that's why I came here Charlie. Your endeavor to finish your dad's work is the most interesting thing I could think of right now. I shudder at the thought of you succeeding in restoring the power grids here in the red districts. It would surely help things get moving again And it would surely quell all the hostility in people, giving them a chance for a normal life again and everything..."

Elena trailed off after noticing Charlie walk away from her.

"But what really made me seek you out was the fact that you seem to be the only one to know what Orion's motives are. You're the only one that knows why they locked up our universities and with them our textbooks. I want to know why they censored our Internet. But what I want to know most of all is why you're so afraid to be upgraded!"

Charlie didn't answer right away. He continued to stare out of the window in silence and thought it would be futile to offer any answers anyway. He had no proof of anything at all and relied on gut feelings for answers. After groping for some words, he finally spoke up.

"Please sweet woman, you must forgive me if I have placed my worries upon you in the midst of your happy life and I think it's best that you just forget you ever met me, and you should just leave here in the morning when the sun comes up and forget it all."

Elena wasn't having any of it. She wanted answers.

"Tell me what's going on Charlie!" she demanded. Her foot tapped repeatedly on the hardwood floor.

Charlie continued glumly, choosing not to answer her question directly, and instead, he wandered off a bit, speaking as if he were speaking to himself. "I was a fool, thinking I could change things. I ask myself why—why do I strive to help others, why? I don't know why! I wanted to serve humanity, help humanity in these troubled times like my father before me, who sought to introduce free energy into a planet plagued by pollution. But I realized that humanity doesn't want to be helped, and in fact, it resents guidance!" Charlie paused to catch his breath. Elena thought that his attractive face seemed to be getting colder and more sensual.

"The truth is," Charlie began, "that my scientific zeal for prolonging our civilization had degenerated long before the rally the other day. The people don't want to do anything to help themselves, and all they care for is their paycheck at the end of the week. I had realized I was wasting my time months ago!"

Elena walked over to him as he stared out his window with his back to her.

Charlie turned half way when noticing her approach but didn't face her. He continued to stare through the slits of the boarded window with both hands folded behind his back. He then turned to Elena with an implacable and grim face.

"Look Elena, in your ignorance, you will only rouse up avoidable trouble," Charlie hissed, his eyebrows joined together and his eyes tapered to a slit. Elena just stared at him, expectantly. Then, Charlie could no longer defy the appeal of mystifying her, and he spoke more brightly than ever before. "Now what I have to tell you is so queer that you must not laugh. My dear, if you only knew how strange the matters are here on Earth, and if I told you, you would deem me as a lunatic!"

23: Charlie's Mania

The look on his face sobered Elena's previous feelings from being snubbed, and a form of mania seemed to have seized him as he got ready to explain it all. The purity of his features was no longer sweet and charming, and instead his face grew carnal, like some sort of devilish version of Charlie's normal face. "You still think these aliens are saviors and are willing to help?" Charlie asked with no care for an answer.

Elena shrugged.

"Do you know that they've been suppressing technology on this planet for decades? Do you want to know why they locked up our schools and censored our Internet? Well, it's not because of bureaucratic incompetence," Charlie chuckled mirthlessly. "Or lack of resources, or none of that hogwash! Orion Corp. was always here, for hundreds of years, and maybe more! They've been coming and going since forever and have been using us, watching us, molding us, all for the sake of their business enterprises—especially crude oil, their number one resource for keeping civilizations primitive and away from the stars! Orion Corp. strives to form economies that revolve on fossil fuels, purposely striving to keep man grounded and quarantined on Earth, away from the stars, away from the moon and all the planetary real estate they own, and away from all of their planetary resources in general. This is why free energy has been suppressed for so long...because it can lead to advanced propulsion systems!"

Elena raised a brow and stood dumbfounded. She couldn't speak or reply right away; her mind was clogged with thoughts after hearing Charlie's maniacal tirade. While living on the ship, Elena thought Orion cared very little for crude oil. She knew that her father rarely ran any scans for it. Orion Corp. rarely used crude oils for the purpose of energy, but instead to make plastic mostly.

Charlie noticed Elena's curious eyes crawling all over him, waiting for him to say more. Charlie thought that he might have at least gotten Elena to debate it all in her mind, and it spurred him on. "Why do you think Orion decided to

show their faces right after the disasters? Because we were about to embark on a new industrial revolution that started back in 2023 and people were waking up after realizing our planet was plagued by fossil fuels and carbon emissions. As our civilization progressed, Orion and their overseers couldn't keep up with suppressing technology. There were only so many black vans and so many lobbyists. The population on Earth began to rise, science and technology became harder to control...and so...Orion did the only thing they could do to maintain control of their planet..."

"Which is?"

"Curb the population!" Charlie shot out with clout. "And they did it so cleanly too!" Charlie paused after noticing the horror in Elena's eyes. "Orion Corp. decided to eventually destroy our planet with all their weather modifications! They caused the catastrophes! The floods, the Earthquakes, everything!"

Elena immediately put a palm to her mouth. She kept telling herself that Charlie was deluded in order to make her feel better. However, she had no time to think it over. An odd pang of repulsion came over her after noticing a shifty look came into Charlie's eyes as if he was some fanatic that had seized an idea.

"They are treating us like we're their damn cattle!" Charlie cracked. "Why do you think they would do such a thing?" Elena cried to him. "According to the N.A.U. Department of Homeland Security, there was an

increase in seismic activity before the catastrophes of 2033 that can be traced down to industrial oil drilling, as well as ionosphere research being done from the HAARP facility in Alaska. There appears to be a link between an increase in earthquakes in and around the cities where deep drilling is being done, and at first, I thought the quakes were caused by accident. They were not accidents!

Orion found a way to make the quakes more powerful and on a wider scale. It would be the perfect way to curb our overgrown population and to curb the new industrial age that we were embarking on during the time."

"How did they manage to do such a thing?" Elena coughed out through a tight throat, "You mean, the quakes were man-made?"

"Yes, and they did it by manipulating the magnetosphere with a HAARP-like facility," Charlie snapped back readily.

Elena had so much emotion pent up in her that her words tumbled out of her mouth. "But Charlie, the coronal mass ejections! That is what caused the quakes! The coronal mass ejections rippled into the Earth's core and caused wave explosions, therefore shifting the north and south poles, vibrating the Earth to hellish proportions!"

Charlie waved an index finger and lapsed into a mirthless, sardonic chuckle. "No, the coronal mass ejections would be no match for a healthy magnetosphere. They were only X-class solar flares after all. The only reason why they caused earthquakes was due to the fact that the Earth had no protection from its magnetosphere—because the Orion people basically diffused it!"

"How could they do such a thing with a HAARP facility, a basic research lab for Aurora research?"

Charlie laughed again. "The HAARP facility in Alaska is a military installation—not a scientific one. Just try asking for a tour of the place, see what they tell you! I can assure you'll be turned down. HAARP is what caused the polar shift Elena! HAARP sends controlled and tuned streams of high frequency radio energy into Earth's ionosphere. The enormous amount of energy added to the ionosphere creates a tuned vibration, which is then directed around the globe on the jet streams. Wherever this enormous vibration ends up, it creates extremely low frequency waves that travel down to the Earth's core. HAARP is capable of extremely deep earth tomography, basically "X-raying" the earth.

Orion Corp. uses this method in order to scan for oil deep under the earth's crust. But if they tune it to resonate with the geological features of a fault line, then they can really shake things up! Why...they can split the Earth in two!"

Elena sighed deeply. "Charlie, how do you know all this'?

Charlie didn't answer, he was too caught up in his tirade. "That is not the only thing HAARP can do. It has a range of applications. Wanna know how to steer a hurricane? You simply heat up the water along its path! HAARP can manipulate weather patterns by heating land, air, and sea, as well as by changing pressure levels in the upper atmosphere. Wanna shoot a giant bolt of electricity at a target... HAARP can do that too! Wanna create an EMF blast to wipe out all electronics in an area? HAARP can do that! How about an EMF blast that will kill all living creatures, but won't damage structures? Wanna put up a missle shield over your country? Wanna send down some of the extensively researched psychoactive and biophysically active frequencies, to create 'non-lethal' effects on huge areas of people, all at once? HAARP can do that!"

"All this to keep us from embarking on a new renaissance?" Elena asked.

Charlie was quick to answer. "Yes! Technology was on the rise in the early 2020s, and a lot of marvelous patents were being developed by privately funded scientific delegations—especially geomagnetic energy generators—which would prove to be a huge threat to the crude oil empire. And even worse, a threat to the aliens within our governments. Such technology would eventually lead to an advanced propulsion system and drive Earth humans towards the heavens. Like I said, Orion Corp. didn't like that idea. For years they sought to keep us Earth humans out of space and away from all their real estate in order to protect their mining monopoly in the galaxy!"

Elena was thrown off by Charlie's resolute tone. This was no theory according to him; he really believed it, and it spooked her to think she worked for such a diabolical corporation all these years.

Charlie then grabbed both of her shoulders and shook her. "Orion Corp. has guided the progress of Earth civilization for many, many years! Official disclosure happened only after the disasters, and why? Well, I will tell you why! Because it was the perfect condition for a planetary takeover! Their attack had no strings attached to it because it was under the guise of worldwide natural disasters!"

Elena nodded vigorously. "A...perfect...way to take over a planet for sure," Elena said dreamily as she stared at the ground in thought.

Charlie continued maniacally. "After the first few days of continuous earthquakes, the governments of the world had disbanded because of the power outages. Earth militaries and their nuclear weapons no longer posed a threat to the extraterrestrials and so Orion thought it was the best time to take advantage."

Elena's heart almost stopped at the thought. It would have stopped completely if she knew what he said was true, but she so wanted to believe otherwise. There is no way she could believe her dad was involved with such a fascistic enterprise. Elena's spine seemed to shrink from disappointment and a feeling of defeat replaced her former sense of value.

"And I didn't even get to your question yet," Charlie shot out coldly. "You want to know why I don't want their medicine? And why I don't want to be upgraded?"

Elena just stared at him in shock. In a sense, she didn't even want to know anymore.

"The upgrades serve two purposes...one purpose is to cure our bodies, and the second purpose is to deliberately stilt our minds and take away our free will!"

Elena just stood there with her jaw to the ground, hoping Charlie would just shut up; he did not.

"After my implants malfunctioned last year, it all dawned on me. The implants themselves shackled my mind—and everyone else's for that matter. After my implants deactivated, I began to experience all of these physical, mental, and spiritual changes and I wasn't the only one either. Humankind on Earth was awakening from its ignorant slumber and we were evolving as a species, but Orion did their best to stop it. They no longer resorted to heavy metals in the drinking water as their drugs, but highly advanced cybernetic cells known as nanobots—bots that imitate cellular function and even predetermine a person's role in society."

"So you really believe that they're not only trying to halt our evolution, but seek to control us like their toy puppets?" Elena cried out.

"Yes indeed!" Charlie began. "The radiation from the sun was the excuse they needed so they could come down with their medicine. It is causing people to walk around as empty, soulless shells!"

Elena's jaw felt as if it was glued shut and she couldn't find any words after hearing such claims. Charlie had crammed her mind with a catalog of eccentricities and her brain was fried. After taking some time and soaking it all in, she finally concluded that Charlie was just paranoid. She figured his brain was so overwrought with stress that it made him think excessively much because after all, he had no proof of anything. After a half minute, Elena finally mustered up some words.

"Apathetic, many do seem, but your mind control theories are outlandish. I too was pumped full of nanobots, they course through my veins as we speak, do I walk around in a soulless manner?"

"Oh come on, you are no longer an Earthling Elena, and your nanobots are programmed to heal your cells—but who knows what they programmed these nanobots to do down here. These upgrades are unregulated by the galactic food and drug administration!" Charlie snarled.

"But you have no evidence," Elena said.

"Not direct evidence no!" Charlie snapped. "But I have plenty of indirect evidence."

"Which is?"

"Besides my transformation, which happened after my bots malfunctioned, there are also other clues. The very first murders took place the other day for the first time in a decade, just one whole year after the implants began deactivating in people. Before that, there were no murders. Not for the ten years since we were all implanted. And during that time, there was no crime at all for that matter."

"That is a bit fishy," Elena nodded, but still, Charlie had no evidence and she could not believe him based on his sheer intuitive analysis.

"If you only knew how strong their grip on our planet really is! These people, this Overseer and his Ashtar guards—they're part of a secret society of extraterrestrials that have been hunting down scientists for years. Now, they no longer have to hide because they have established themselves on this planet after thousands and thousands of years and have finally taken over every corner of our planet's infrastructure. This suppression of our civilization is nothing more than a modern day witch hunt. They infiltrated the Catholic Church hundreds of years ago and did everything in their power to make people believe that the Earth was located at the center of the universe, and when Galileo invented the telescope, he was placed under house arrest...."

"Because such an invention would cause people to ask more questions about what is really up there in the heavens!" Elena chimed in, with a more emotionally stretched voice.

"Correct!" Charlie nodded briskly. His final word was spoken in such a superior sort of way and Elena began to think that through the muddiness of his lunacy, he might be right.

Charlie calmed down a bit after realizing that Elena was considering what he told her. A brief silence overcame them; Elena was speechless. Besides, there was no way to hazard an opinion on such wild claims anyway. Elena knew she could not muster up any data on which to bid a supposition of her own. Any opinion of hers would be looked upon with limited value anyways, she had figured.

"Let's forget we spoke of this," Charlie continued on frostily. He realized it was a waste of breath to tell her anything, because after all, no citizen was powerful enough to change anything anyway. Charlie just trotted past her, sat down on his dining room table, and began tightening some bolts on one of his devices. It was an invisibility cloak he had started working on months ago. He got the idea to build it in a series of dreams that he had a few months ago, but had since neglected it ever since he had focused all of his energy on his weapon.

Elena then took notice of the contraption and it piqued her curiosity. Her eyes shifted from the invisibility cloak that Charlie was working on, and instead, she focused on the bed sheet covering what she figured to be his prized invention. Elena didn't look at the table for too long and didn't give any indication that she was paying attention to it. She figured that if Charlie wanted her to see it, he would offer to show her.

However, as always, Elena's curiosity had gotten the best of her. She was at the point of no return, she thought, and needed to know everything—and so Elena walked over to the table and began giving the thing under the bed sheet a few side-glances as she paced around the table. She noticed Charlie's face fall whenever she got closer to it and the fierce, sidelong look in his eyes only fueled her curiosity even more. She reached for the sheet and slowly lifted it, bending her torso sideways as if to steal a peek at it.

Charlie sighed after realizing it was too late to keep the scaler-wave weapon hidden from her. He only hoped she wouldn't figure out that it was indeed a weapon, because the thing looked so alien that it would surely remain obscure to ignorant eyes.

Elena then reached for the sheet and pulled the entire sheet off the thing in one effortful tug. She eyed it down very suspiciously, as she circled the table with a slack jaw. The cannon gleamed in the candlelight in an almost sinister luminosity, and it all looked excessively alien—even to her.

24: Epiphanies

Charlie told Elena everything that night, mostly details relating to his experiences when his mind had suddenly become unhinged right after the nanobots deactivated in his body. Elena thought that Charlie was getting stranger and stranger by the minute, and the more he spoke, the more Elena lurched forward in her chair. Elena could not stop staring at him even during silent moments, and her surveillance made Charlie feel restive because everything he told her about his occult experiences were far too personal. As perplexed as Elena was, she remained open minded and demanded to hear more and more as the night progressed into the wee hours.

Charlie felt embarrassed to describe his experiences because it sometimes involved auditory and visual hallucinations. However, Elena encouraged him with convivial words after assuring him of her open-mindedness.

"Don't be shy, you can talk to me about it," Elena persisted throughout the night. Charlie would stammer often, almost embarrassed to tell Elena his secrets. "It's nothing glorious," Charlie told her. "I've become borne away to this accursed abode of sorrow and monotony ever since my nanobot implants disconnected."

Elena sensed the pain in his eyes. "Did you astral project anything before you were implanted, and before the catastrophes?" She asked.

"I think so," Charlie said readily. "I remember the premonitions I was getting just before the first earthquakes. I had feelings of impending doom and had some vivid dreams of my home being swallowed by water."

"That's deep," Elena said, astonished. "What about you?" Charlie asked.

"Now that you ask, I did feel as if everything was becoming clearer to me just before the first earthquake. I too began to have feelings of impending doom and felt like my consciousness was being expanded, right up until I was removed from Earth and taken up into ship. Then, I felt like normal old me again," she concluded.

"Yes, of course, up there, your body was removed from Earth and had no time to reshape itself according to the Earth's new bioelectric field. You were unable to resonate with its natural energy grid, and that's why it stopped. Your mind lost the link to this great energy upheaval that was, and still is taking place on Earth. As for me, well—after the disconnections last year, I began experiencing a series of epiphanies that resulted into a set of peculiar eruditions. This all led me to building these things on the table here," Charlie said, pointing at the shiny contraptions strewn on top and underneath the dining room table including his generator, his invisibility cloak, the water/power converter for automobiles, and finally—his scaler-wave gravity weapon.

"And I did it all with little or no help from my father's blueprints in fact. I got it all from a set of dreams...peculiar dreams...and the dreams did something to my subconscious residuum that influenced this work."

After Elena raised her brow, Charlie let out a nervous laugh. "Oh, you think me to be mad!" he chortled.

Elena reached for Charlie's hand and spoke in a filial tone.

"Charlie, I'm tangentially sound on subjects such as the occult and astral projection. I wrote a paper about it in school back on the Niagra during my first semester."

Charlie felt more at ease after hearing that and spoke through a looser throat. "The experience was wonderful and frightening at the same time; I'm still having a hard time accepting that it happened to me."

"Its okay, you don't have to talk about it if you don't want," Elena said, trying to cheer him up. Nevertheless, Charlie kept speaking as if he were under a spell or possessed by something ethereal.

"After my nanobot implants deactivated, it was as if my mental faculties had enlarged ever so suddenly, and I must have entered into a conscious relationship with the super physical planes of the cosmos. I could literally turn the pages of human history without the need to read what I learned in any physical book or body of text at all. Through it all, I have learned that the records of time are not personal. And they are not individual memories either; instead, they are detached albums of collective recollections that continue living outside of the physical brain, which have registered within the river of time. Many occultists used to refer to this phenomena as the Akashic Records. These records are essentially a person's compendium of genetic memories, memories of past lives lived and perhaps even future lives."

Elena looked away after hearing that and needed a moment to let it all sink in. She wanted to tell Charlie to speak English because she had no idea what he meant. However, Charlie's demeanor assumed an unwonted grace and even a noble dignity that she would have never believed him to have judging from his haggardness. And so Elena tried to tell herself simply to take his word for it because he really believed it.

"But it was all for nothing," Charlie chimed in to break the silence, and his shoulders sagged again. "I built these things for nothing. If I introduced them to the public, the Overseer would confiscate all of these things and deem them as weapons of mass destruction."

"But Charlie, the free energy generator!" Elena cried. "Especially the generator!" Charlie shot back.

There was something pathetic in his demeanor that made her realize that he needed a boost—both in morale and in his self-esteem. What she really wanted to do was help him the best way she could and she then thought about her connections in space. Elena smiled nervously before bringing up her argumentative concept.

"Charlie look," she shot out intrepidly while pointing to the contraptions on his moth-eaten dining room table. "These things are too important not to mass produce. One of your inventions can help get people out of those camps and into homes again—powered homes! It is too important to throw away because of one man. I know plenty of people who work for Orion funded science groups who are not chained to the Overseer!"

Charlie didn't answer her and all Elena felt was Charlie's hot breath hit her face. Charlie then turned away from her, plopped down on his sofa, and cracked open a textbook. He sat in silence as he flipped through the pages, seemingly uninterested at what Elena had to say.

Elena continued to persuade him.

"I will be more than glad to offer your blueprints to some people of science in hopes of recruiting some sponsors from space," Elena continued.

However, Charlie continued to read, acting as if he did not hear her. Elena sighed and tapped her foot repeatedly waiting for him to reply, but Charlie kept turning pages on his book, offering no reply.

"I'll even go to my father if I have to; he knows a lot of scientists up there who used to live on Earth and would be honored to return here in hopes of contributing!"

"Who will pay the scientists?" Charlie asked before laughing. Elena looked down to the ground and tried to answer but could not.

Charlie looked at her crookedly and spoke in a scolding manner.

"You think they are going to come down to this hell hole and work for free?

And if they do, do you think that the Overseer won't notice the scientists attempting to manufacture unregulated technology without his consent?"

Elena's optimistic face drooped.

"I'll tell them everything you told me about the Overseer and his clandestine operation! Why—I'm sure Orion will conduct an investigation after hearing my testimony," Elena countered, but Charlie laughed after sensing her disillusionment. No investigation would ever end up inside a courtroom.

Elena couldn't resist debating even further. She patted the dust off the sofa and sat down close enough to Charlie so she could get through his thick skull.

"If you think it's a hopeless world..." Elena paused for a more dramatic effect. "Then why did you continue to build them then?"

Charlie was humbled a bit by her authoritative tone and saw her disgust on her face. His anger subsided considerably. Charlie took a deep breath after hearing Elena's edification; this time he was the one who could no longer find words.

Charlie would not dare tell her that he put more effort into his cannon lately and that he planned to resort to violence in order to accomplish his goal.

However, he still managed to give John the advice he would need to put the final additions on the EM generator, and a part of Charlie's subconscious mind must have retained a sliver of hope after all. Charlie soon felt that his inability to give into her plan was foolish and all due to his unassailable cynicism. All this time, Charlie never once thought of Elena's contacts in space and only thought of her as someone to take over for him at the rallies—someone that would only help continue his rebellious crusade against Orion Corp. and the Overseer by speaking out in public and handing out flyers. Never once did Charlie think about her connections in space.

After thinking it over, Elena's comforting words of warmth and pure logic caused Charlie to find his reasoning ability, and he tried his best to cast aside all of his hate. Perhaps she could help him, he thought, and maybe she could find enough people to help loosen the Overseer's iron grip on human affairs. Just like John had wished. After all, there was nothing more to lose.

After some thought, Charlie walked over to his window again to stare out in contemplation, horrified by his thoughtlessness and ashamed because his cynicism clouded his judgment. For the first time in his life, someone offered to side with him and help him, and he was about to throw it all away because of the negative demons that took hold of his mind.

He walked over to Elena on the couch and sat next to her, even going as far as taking her hand, and then spoke in comforting tones.

"Please...please forgive me Elena; I seemed to have forgotten myself. I am so troubled in my mind that I am apt to be short-tempered, and if you only knew the problems I have, you would have mercy for me. You would probably endure and even pardon me," he said with a worn and pitiful face.

Elena countered in a low but commanding voice, "We have the chance to stop the tyranny by giving free sustaining electrical power back to the people and you must focus on attracting private sponsors. It's a battle we're going to have to face."

"Elena, perhaps your help will bear fruit, and if not, then at least we tried," Charlie began apologetically. "Anyways, the electromagnetic free energy generator is almost done, and is set for testing tonight. I don't know where John is, or if he'll ever come back for that matter, so I'd love it if you stayed and helped me finish it."

Elena's eyes brightened considerably. "Let's do it!"

25: Wake Dreams

It was almost one a.m. and Elena never once thought about getting some sleep. Charlie was about to test his generator and she sat and stared with her eyes glued to him all night long as he clanked away at it. The E.M. generator seemed as if it had no power source, but Charlie showed her that it was indeed connected to a powerful chemical battery he designed from his father's natural biofuel, made from wood. The natural power from the neodymium electromagnets provided the main source of energy.

After his first test, Elena was shocked to learn how quiet the thing was. She didn't even know it was powered on most of the time. It sputtered a bit at first, then it quickly turned to a subtle whine, and after some seconds, the sound concluded to a hum so soft that she originally thought he had turned if off.

As the night progressed, Charlie would speak less and work more as he got closer to finishing. Charlie worked at a slower pace than usual, not because of all the time it took to explain what he was doing to his curious friend, but because Elena's beauty was too reasonable not to look upon. Her eyes radiated when he stared into them and Charlie had to nerve himself back to work from time to time. Elena was so caught up in Charlie's intellectual effort that she simply lost track of time, and it wasn't until she was exhausted herself that she began thinking of getting sleep. Her heavy-lidded eyes bulged at the sight of the time displayed on a small digital alarm clock on Charlie's coffee table. It was three a.m.

She was tired—and for all of Charlie's oddities, she trusted him enough to spend the night at his place. After Charlie gave her a clean pillow, Elena wasted no time setting herself up on the dust encrusted sofa and began to drift in and out of a doze just minutes after hitting the pillow. Elena would occasionally wake up whenever she heard some of the clanking coming from Charlie's workstation, but Charlie made sure not to make too much noise.

After an hour of sleep, Elena woke from the sound of pattering rain, which smacked the roof in torrential sheets. The occasional crackling of thunder vibrated through the living room and it made her jump at times. Brown rivulets of rainwater flowed from several spots on the damaged ceiling and came close to pouring onto Elena's head causing her to toss and turn to avoid the moldy water. It was hard to sleep. Wind and rain seemed to converge on Charlie's house all at once, and the howling of the wind was sometimes confused with the cries of the coyotes heard in the distance. The weather outside did little to blot out the sound of Charlie's tools, which would awaken her now and then.

The battery operated alarm radio said 4:23 a.m.

When does this guy ever sleep? Elena asked herself.

Eventually, the sound of rain lulled Elena back to sleep again but not for long. A crash of thunder awakened her one hour later with a thumping heart. A thin film of sweat formed on her face and chest and wondered how long she had been asleep. Her vision was blurred and she knew she had been asleep for quite some time because her eyes were dry. When her vision settled, she saw that the alarm clock said 5:33 a.m.

She noticed that the rain tapered off a bit, and a chilly post-rain wind seeped in through a window, causing the candlelight to sputter. After looking through the top part of the boarded living room window, she saw the clouds aglow from the rising sun. The sun's rays began peaking over the horizon, and the red hue in the sky meant the cusp of dawn was near. Elena opened her eyes wider and looked at Charlie, who was still working and sitting in the same chair. Oddly enough, Elena noticed that he wasn't moving that much, and was staring at the wall in front of him— apparently in some sort of state of pathological withdrawal

His self-induced trance made him look extremely creepy from Elena's point of view that morning and she wondered why he wasn't even blinking. It seemed as if something in front of Charlie had detained his attention. His face was still and fixed straight towards the dining room wall, and his eyes looked ice cold and stiff.

What the hell is he staring at? There is nothing there! Elena thought.

Elena then noticed that his lips were moving slowly, and she took a deep breath and held it; it made it easier to hear Charlie's murmuring.

"Please remove your curse from me and do no longer fill my sleep for me," Charlie said in a hushed tone.

The rain had stopped and so the stillness of the night allowed Elena to hear everything he was saying as he spoke to himself.

"I give you the stale air that fills my lungs, why do you steal my sleep?" Charlie continued louder. "Must all of your spiritual guidance come to me in my sleep? You bring me nothing but terror, greater than any terror I have ever known—a terror I cannot escape. It stalks me in my dreams and I'm always bound to face it in my sleep. These things that you unleashed are hunting me now, dark things! These things want to dissolve me and devour my soul! I know how to elude them but it is not facile! Please, I beg of you, do not burn me...please, go, go away...and close my mind again...I miss my febrile mind in a way...oh yes, I know...you're right...and I do acknowledge that I am puny and weak without you...but please do no longer fill my sleep. I do fear your flame, I do admit, you burn me!"

After hearing that, Elena had gone from semi-dazed to being fully alert after hearing such enigmatical speech. Charlie's unfilled and distorted voice had appalled her.

What sort of words were these from what sort of poor soul? she asked herself. *He must be mad!* Elena told herself.

The cold stare of disdain on Charlie's face gave her gooseflesh, and a childlike fear ran through her. She tried to go back to sleep, and she hoped that the odious occurrence would all be forgotten in the morning, but she couldn't sleep while Charlie continued to talk to himself.

Charlie spoke to himself louder after each word.

"I am puny and weak without you and it is you that stirs my untutored mind. I am nothing without you, and without you, I am just a vacant container and a corroded trap. Without you I am curbed within the margins of my Earthly packet, yet, I want to escape you and the lavish brawn you carry. To be frank— you burn me. You burn me! Your presence is demanding; and it cannot escape my mind. You bring with you a fog that clings to me, and to the very edges of my mind. Your presence brings unrest and fear—fears from the darkest pits of the mind anyone could know. This anguish of the night that you bring me, it puts a heavy weight on my mind, and pain! Oh the pain! And not just physical pain or emotional pain, but spiritual pain! I cannot go on—my resolve is fading. And this is why I tried escaping you as a kid, and this is why I tried to escape you by drinking whiskey that night, the night I almost jumped. Now you know why!

The breath that you breathe into my lungs brings me to shine like a star, but you're burning me up!"

Charlie then ceased to speak for a moment when his breathing became labored and shallow.

"Just let me sleep!" he then shouted all at once.

It was as if he had no idea that Elena was in the same room with him and he was not in control of his actions.

Elena's face then warped into one with unrefined, untrained fear. Thoughts clogged her racing mind.

Charlie is just a schizophrenic, that's all.

She wondered if Charlie's claim about the Overseer and Orion Corp. was nothing more than a product of a deluded mind. However, as she tried hard to convince herself that Charlie was alright in his head, she began to recall all those tales of Moses talking to the voices he had heard—the voices of God. Elena then began to think about the philosophy of Christ and his Holy Spirit contact.

Where does one draw the line between labeling one a schizo or a psychic medium? Which spirits are holy? Oh, this is ridiculous to think about, it is all just an anathema! It is just a claptrap extrapolation of a grave notion! Elena thought.

When Charlie's lips began to move again, Elena almost felt like covering her ears. She could see his hard eyes from where she stood in the adjoining living room and his blank, blink-less stare really scared her. It was disturbing; she called for him, hoping he would stop.

"Charlie...everything okay?" Elena's voice cracked.

Charlie jumped in his seat; he was not used to having a real person next to him, and in his delirium, he must have forgotten about her as she slept. He looked shamefaced for a moment, straightened up in his chair, and an outline of a smile then stole over his whitish face, but just for a second.

"Yes...I'm...I'm fine..." He stammered before settling his nerves. "I was just going over some notes, reading out loud. Just go back to bed, don't worry about me," he told her, and his look and gesture forbade discussion.

Elena plopped her head back down but never took her eyes off him. A myriad of negative fancies filled Elena's mind, and she knew that the poor soul before her was frayed about in his mind—regardless of whether he was crazy or not. Perhaps, if he indeed was in contact with odd-worldly beings, then it had an effect on his nervous system. Charlie bore all the signs of inner struggle, and he was never able to shake off that maddening sensation of being haunted with immense truths, truths that a human being shouldn't be forced to handle.

"Why don't you get to bed, you seem tired," Elena then asked him, in a voice that was low and strained due to the fear that still rippled through her heart.

Charlie waved her off. "I'm almost finished," he replied hotly; his expression was frantic as he spoke. "I'll be quiet, I promise. I'm sorry I woke you up, and please do try to get some sleep yourself. You're the one who has to be at work in five hours," Charlie insisted.

Elena took a deep breath and shook off the feelings of doubt.

How can I ever fall asleep after that, she told herself.

After confirming that Charlie was no longer talking to himself, or whomever he was talking to for that matter, Elena buried her face into her pillow so that it almost covered her ears, and in time, Elena's sleepiness set in again. Elena slept just on the edge of consciousness for the rest of the early morning, Charlie's recent episode had condemned her to a sleepless night on his couch.

26: The Precinct

The police precinct in Redhook, Brooklyn, New York was old and appeared neglected despite the hoards of police officers wriggling about the place. As Brennan waited, he stared outside of a window that had bullet holes in it, and it looked as if it would shatter any minute judging by all the cracks that snaked across it. The place had power and electricity, and the luminosity lit up the gloomy landscape that surrounded it, but barely.

Outside, traffic was minimal. It was still dark, and only the merchants remained— peddling their carts and selling their findings to any pedestrians willing to look at their secondhand inventory. Brennan took a few moments to look towards the jagged horizon, and he felt like he was desolated from civilization by thousands of miles whenever he looked outside. Gone was the muffled roar of the great city that still operated substantially in the daytime instead replaced by the feeling that he was on the Niagra, near one of the corners of the galaxy that had few stars and nothing but the dark void of space surrounding him.

There was a thick mist out there and it was the only thing that had any vitality at all. It crept along the dark buildings with an imperceptible slowness, all across the streets, and stretched out into the horizon. A faint red hue from an obscure and early rising sun began to peek over the horizon but it was still very dark out. Brennan tried to see where the green districts ended and where the red districts began, but the lack of any working street lamps made it difficult. The sounds of some generators roared in the distance, but not many judging by the lack of any illuminated windows in the tenement buildings that surrounded him. Only the hotels had power and some of the light coming from their windows helped carve out the texture of the surrounding buildings.

Brennan peered far down towards the jagged horizon and did not see one lit up window where the red districts began. He strained his eyes to cut through the darkness, aiming them towards the semi-flooded coast to the east. He saw nothing but innumerable black summits, shadowy hunks of crumbling concrete and billows of wood and steel laying in heaps and piles. The scene only depressed him more and so he focused on the task at hand and attempted to continue reading the file on the John Lancaster, who was about to be interrogated by Colonel Jasso, who in turn was still in a meeting with a local captain discussing their plans for interrogating the prisoner.

The noise inside the place distracted his already tired brain, and so he gave up on reading the Lancaster and Beasley files. There were dozens of RAPDA agents from the European branches who had just arrived. They pullulated in and out of all the hallways and especially the conference room, where all the catering was. Brennan could have used a bite to eat, but the last thing he wanted to do was walk into a room packed with Draconians.

Brennan was left with no choice but to stare dejectedly at his coffee mug, drumming his fingers on his leg, thinking of his daughter Elena more than his job. As successful as the work day had been for the city's law enforcement, Brennan found it hard to find joy, mostly because he still could not call home and more importantly, General Clarkson, who wanted to know whether or not Jasso was acting strange. Brennan figured that Clarkson probably never knew about the interstellar communication outage or he would have definitely visited the planet by now.

The hazard of sleep was also weighing on his mind, and being inside the precinct hardly seemed to vitalize him because the entire place seemed perished. Scaled paint chipped off the walls, hunks of plaster hung by the thin paper of the sheetrock on the ceilings. There was clearly a lot of activity in the place in the past, like some sort of riot, Brennan had figured, judging from the bullet holes in so many of the walls.

There seemed to be more Draconian Ashtar guards in the place then there were RAPDA agents—and even more than local police for that matter. The Ashtar looked like football players compared to everyone else, and they were impossible to tell apart from one another because they were all swathed in their scarlet velvet suits and they even wore similar haircuts. Almost all of them were eating too, and Earth-grown foods were at the mercy of the Draconian metabolism, who found Earth-grown food to be nutritionally defunct compared to the fare they ate on Alpha Draconis. At times, several Draconians in the room had to supplement with odd, tube-like containers filled with gas that they would occasionally inhale, refreshing them with all the nourishment they need. *What the hell is in those gas containers?* Brennan asked himself. Brennan never bothered to ask any of the Draconian Ashtar guards—for all he knew it was pure concentrated oxygen.

The Ashtar guards shouted like a throng of drunken louts as they simultaneously went over Earth geographic maps on their holographic emitting wrist computers. The Draconians spoke with full mouths as they gulped their beverages in long pulls—and bit into their turkey drumsticks like ravenous wolves.

Suddenly, as Brennan peered down across the lounge area and through a doorway, Brennan witnessed Lieutenant Graham skipping over to one of the buffet tables inside. He was wide-eyed and grinning like a child after grabbing a couple apple-cinnamon donuts. Brennan shook his head after wondering how the man could be thinking about food after the riot he was involved in.

Nevertheless, Brennan could not help but savor the smell of all the food himself, and so he decided to head into the conference room and take a stab at a donut or two.

"These guys sure know how to make themselves feel at home!" Graham said after inhaling his donuts in two bites each.

"Speak for yourself," Brennan eyed him crookedly.

Graham didn't reply with his usual wisecrack; he wasn't in the mood to joke around, and Brennan noticed a bit of shock in those eyes of his. In all their years of battle together, Brennan could always tell when Graham turned his war- switch on and when he turned it off.

"You okay?" Brennan shouted over the cacophony of conversation all around him.

"Yeah, yeah," Graham said, taking a moment to wipe the powdered sugar away from the corners of his mouth. "I'm fine, it's just—I saw some freaky stuff tonight man, stuff that would make your hair stand up for days."

"What did you see?"

Graham shrugged. "I'm not even sure what I saw was what I saw."

Brennan furrowed his brow after hearing that and figured his friend needed some sleep. However, a part of him thought that whatever Graham saw, it must have been the reason why Jasso fretted earlier. Graham looked shaken, but his appetite seemed unaffected by his jitters. He proceeded to take another donut, and this time, he dipped the whole thing into his cup of coffee. Brennan finally took a sugared scone before returning to his seat by the lounge area. The sugar and caffeine invigorated him into thinking positive thoughts again. On the bright side, Brennan was sure his mission on Earth was ending, and the taste of his sweet scone helped goad a celebratory mood in him. It was only a matter of time before they traced John Lancaster's phone records and found Charlie Beasley.

Once everyone was upgraded, Brennan could get back to ordinary life again and leave the hellhole of Earth for good.

When Jasso finally came out of the police captain's office, he headed straight towards Brennan. He looked much more jovial than he had when he left Pandora's room last night; he was grinning widely and was holding a bottle of liquor.

"Come and join me!" Jasso shouted over the noise. "Year 2031 champagne from Tuscany!"

Brennan's once impatient body language softened as he walked towards Jasso.

"I could use a glass," Brennan said, rubbing his palms together.

"This bottle would fetch me a fortune in an auction on my planet!" Jasso said, chuffed as he twisted away the wiry aluminum cork cap.

The talk of toast and celebration reached Lieutenant Graham's ears and his nostrils flared like a hungry dog.

"Yeah why not—let's celebrate!" Graham said while limping on a slightly injured ankle he suffered during the bird attack.

"You deserve a drink Lieutenant!" Jasso said genially.

Graham was beaming. "I had no trouble finding Lancaster after the bird attack. He was in Hoover City consorting with some other homeless folk. He looked cleaner then most disconnected people and he matched the description of the man seen consorting with Charlie Beasley right before the bird attack. My Eye-Net lenses did the rest and I arrested him."

"You made me proud!" Jasso said as he sniffed the champagne before pouring it.

"The way that guy summoned those birds...it was just...so strange and all..." "It's over Lieutenant," Jasso interrupted, changing the subject and hoping to

keep him and Brennan ignorant to anything that could be considered supernatural.

Graham flushed. "I could have sworn those birds were fighting for John!" "Drink up," Jasso said as he poured himself a refill.

"Oh, I saw it alright," Graham began in a half-daze, "and as for Charlie Beasley, that strength...that super speed..." Graham trailed off in thought.

Jasso took a long swig of champagne.

Brennan's curiosity had piqued concerning these men who seemed to have super powers. He then coupled this thought with the other strange creatures he had seen since landing on Earth. He then thought of the glowing fish, the strange deer, and the raccoons with gills. After a while, Brennan thought that the animals weren't the only things evolving on Earth and that some people were too.

After downing his third drink in one gulp, Jasso cut himself a huge plug of tobacco and stuffed it in the insides of his two cheeks. Then, without further word, Jasso stepped towards the interrogation room. He waved his arm for the men to follow, and both were quick and obedient to his gesture.

Jasso checked his watch constantly. "Doctor Baal should be here any minute now; he arrived at his hotel over an hour ago and when he gets here he will personally inject the prisoner himself with one of his unique upgrades."

Why would Doctor Baal, the CEO of Orion Corp. and member of the Table of Twelve, come all the way to Earth just to upgrade a mutant? Couldn't any normal doctor do it? Brennan asked himself, wondering if it all pertained to John Lancaster's sorcery.

Then, Brennan heard the precinct's main doors creak open on the other side of the main hall, past the main desk. Everyone in the precinct lapsed into a

heart-freezing silence after taking notice of Doctor Baal—silhouetted against the glare of the doorway. Baal moved ahead with definite employment and in vast strides. He wore a plain black, double-breasted suit with a black collared shirt, and a scarlet tie.

A dozen Draconian Ashtar sentries bracketed Baal as he walked past the precinct's foyer; their scarlet silk capes whirled in the wind that had seeped in from the open door. They were all fully ornamented with black leather satchels and they made for an impressive lot of warriors. Disruptor pistols were holstered on one side of their hips and traditional swords swung in their scabbards on the other side.

After Baal and his men exchanged salutes with the man at the main desk, they quickly marched ahead and scooted past the conference room, heading straight for the interrogation room. As he got closer to Brennan, he looked even scarier, Brennan thought. Baal's face looked as morose as it ever did in the pictures. His face was pure Draconian, voluptuous, aquiline, and wantonly. As he got closer to Brennan, he noticed Baal's strange dead eyes and it made him uneasy. Something was clearly irritating him, Brennan thought. He had pruned, wind-damaged, sun-leathered skin and a cleanly trimmed and shaven square jaw. His cheeks were large and bony, and his mouth looked so stiff that he probably never looked good smiling, Brennan thought. Baal's haircut was a mushroom cut, shaved and faded at the base of his neck. His silver hair was parted in the middle, and two ducktail waves were laboriously styled atop each side of his forehead.

He also had a peculiar and small, square shaped blood-conditioning machine latched on the base of his neck. Brennan knew what it was because most

Draconians over a certain age were fitted with such machines. If an older Draconian should visit Earth, the machine would supply their blood cells with more oxygen. Draconians are rather anemic compared to Earth humans, and there isn't as much oxygen on Earth as there used to be. The machine injected oxygen particles into the bloodstream, and it also monitored the pulse oxygen levels. The particles are injected directly into the bloodstream, where they mingle with circulating red blood cells. The oxygen then diffuses into the cells within seconds of contact. By the time the micro particles get to the lungs, the vast majority of the oxygen is transferred to the red blood cells, and it helps older Draconians tremendously.

Conversations ceased once Baal entered the interrogation room. Baal entered with such straightforward fluidity, that it would command the attention of anyone.

"Welcome to Earth, Doctor," Jasso said.

Baal didn't say anything, he just walked past Jasso and entered the interrogation room.

Brennan saluted Baal as he walked by him in the traditional western Earth military salute, and Graham gave Baal a slow courteous nod as he passed him. Baal didn't seem to notice.

Inside the small interrogation room, every one of the law enforcement personnel stood stiffly at attention next to the prisoner John Lancaster, who was handcuffed and sitting at a table in the center of the room with his hands folded. He was surrounded by the officers on all sides, and he appeared to be wearing pain bracelets on his wrists, incase he decided to use his telekinesis.

After Doctor Baal sat down in the far corner of the room, he curled his finger at Colonel Jasso, and Jasso immediately approached him. Brennan couldn't tell what was being said because Baal spoke in a low voice.

"I don't want to stay on this rotten planet any longer than I should, so I want to begin the interrogation right away. We must find this mutant known as Charlie right away or we'll lose our planet."

Jasso took a swig from his flask. "Yes, I know what you mean." Jasso replied.

27: Interrogation

The first thing Brennan noticed about John Lancaster was that he presented no evidence of his supposed perilous disposition. His grubby look was misleading, and his overall unkemptness hid some of his noble Asiatic features. His isolation in the red districts caused him to sink into barbaric degeneracy, but underneath the grime was an honest looking man. John seemed exhausted, lifeless, and was almost a senior citizen. He hardly looked dangerous enough to warrant a fitting of pain bracelets. Nevertheless, Jasso added a pair on his wrists. The bracelets worked just like the Active Denial System, and they served as the military's primary non-lethal weapon for small, tight spaces. The bracelets were equipped with giant antennas that emit microwaves. If activated, the microwaves would cause him to reach his pain threshold in a matter of seconds by making him feel as if he were burning alive.

Brennan never broke eye contact with John, as he sat on other side of the interrogation table. Brennan became a bit scatterbrained and quirky as he thought about what to say to him—and after a brief thought, Brennan lurched forward in his seat and began to ask him the questions that he was ordered to ask him by the Overseer.

"So!" Brennan snapped. "Is there a reason why you attacked those cops?" Brennan asked, and John did not answer until a few seconds afterwards.

"I don't know what you're talking about, I was twenty meters away from those cops and I never touched anyone," Lancaster said unassumingly.

"We know you controlled those birds, someway, somehow. My colleague watched you operate some sort of fancy device that made you summon the birds."

John shrugged his shoulders. "I have no idea what you're talking about; all I carry is a wallet and a cell phone."

Brennan could hear Jasso sigh from across the room. Several Draconians muttered under their breath to each other in frustration. Brennan then cleared his throat.

"Actually, there were several witnesses that told us you used something to summon the birds; some of the witnesses are in this very room as we speak. They said that you were gesticulating very quaintly during the attack, but what was most suspicious was the shiny device in your hands that was said to have attracted the birds in the first place. And when the birds arrived, they singled out law enforcement personnel while you continued to gesticulate in a queer manner."

A police officer then shouted from behind Brennan, "That freak's eyes were rolled to the back of his head, he's lying! He's a freak!"

John began to breathe heavier; his chest was heaving and a thin film of sweat made his dark face shine from the lamplight that hovered above his head. He was scared, and not because of his arrest, but because he surprised himself about his unusual connection with animals and he began to think it might be a good idea to tell the truth. Perhaps he would get some closure on these phenomena.

"Okay look," John said, pausing to gather his thoughts. "I don't know what's happening to me. And I didn't mean to attack those cops like that; I kind of just wished the birds would distract them enough so they could stop shooting these rubber bullets at the people."

"We aren't interested in why you did it," Brennan was quick to reply. "What we would like to know is how did you do it?"

John stuttered, "The device just summons the birds, it's nothing but a simple sonic transmitter that a friend of mine had built with scrap parts. The magnetite in the brains of the birds hone in on the frequency."

"So the signal only attracts birds?" Brennan asked.

Lancaster nodded vigorously. He looked scared, and his dark face looked pale gray.

"How did you get them to focus the attack on the police and Ashtar guards?" Brennan asked inquisitively.

"My will." John's lower lip quivered. "Animals act according to my will."

The entire room of people seemed to gasp all at once. Several police officers in the room shouted, "Hang this freak!" and "Burn him at the stake!"

Jasso told everyone to calm down, and he then locked eyes with Doctor Baal, who seemed to speak to Jasso with a curtly nod. Jasso then locked eyes with Brennan, and lip-synched the word "weapon" to him to signify to him that he wanted to know its whereabouts.

Brennan cleared his throat. "Besides that sonic transmitter, what else are your friends building?" He asked John.

John raised a brow and sounded confused, "Nothing, they're not building anything at all, and I have no idea where they live now."

Brennan then continued to speak in an intimidating manner after noticing Jasso's look of conviction.

"We have traced ninety percent of the phone calls you've made in the past two months with your FEMA allotted phone. Therefore, we know everything John...everything. We know about your affiliation with the Charlie Beasley fellow who injured my colleagues. One of your phone conversations with your brother gave it away. You asked him for advice, on how to handle your friend Charlie. It was revealed that you disagreed with Charlie's plans on building a weapon...so you know what I'm talking about John."

John's face then stiffened considerably after shunning the denial regarding Charlie's conspiracy theories. He never really doubted Charlie's claims about Orion Corp. and the Overseer. It was all out of fearing to believe it and in the last 24 hours, John realized Charlie's qualms about Orion Corp. rang true because the Overseer seemed hell-bent on getting the population upgraded at all costs.

"You're such a cherry head, do you know that!" John snapped, and his lips trembled. "You're supposed to be some RAPDA agent? Do you know what's going on with the people of Earth right now? And what your employers are preventing?"

Brennan looked confused. "Of course I do, the people are becoming sick, and we're preventing a zombie apocalypse." Brennan said palpably.

John laughed, and continued to laugh.

Brennan looked at Jasso, who was grinning nervously. Doctor Baal seemed to squirm in his seat, but sat there, still, steely, and silent.

"Do you even know what's in those needles they plug into us? Of course not!" John continued hotly.

Suddenly, Baal gave one of his Draconian Ashtar guards a look, and nodded at him. The tall guard looked like death in the flesh. His eyes were like glass, his hair was white like paper, and it was all matted on his head. Then, the guard took out a small remote control and pressed a button before a pulsation was heard, and in an instant, Lancaster's pair bracelets activated with a—

Zzzzzzapp!

John toppled down to the floor and screamed.

Brennan moved back in his seat; it was so unexpected that he almost tipped his chair over backwards. John continued to scream, and Brennan almost wanted to rip the device out of the guard's hand because he did not like what was being done, and he did not sign up for torture. Brennan exchanged a brief glance with Lieutenant Graham who was nestled with the crowd on his right. He was also clearly disturbed by the torture being committed by the Draconians.

Doctor Baal then put up a palm and the tall Draconian immediately released his finger from the button. The pulsating sound dissipated and John stopped screaming. He took a moment to catch his breath and he then ascended slowly on wobbly legs, using the chair to help him. John looked angry, and spittle dripped from his bottom lip. His eyes were still glowing from his anger, his tongue still wet with hate.

"Don't worry you alien bastards," John paused, taking a second to fill his lungs with more oxygen. He then lifted his gaze towards the brutal faces of Doctor Baal and Jasso. "There are more of us out there and your little prison planet you created is coming to an end!"

Without hesitation, Jasso sprang forward and took two steps before hitting John with a haymaker that caught him right in the mouth. The force of the blow knocked John off the chair again, sending him face first onto the hard floor.

Brennan swallowed a lump as he watched John groan and drift in and out of consciousness.

The force of the blow almost knocked him unconscious, and after he gained some bearing, he muttered several indecipherable words as he got up, squinting from the pain. John took the back of his hand and wiped a trickle of blood that came from his split upper lip. As he regained his gait, he rolled his large puppy dog eyes towards Jasso and stared at him in disgust.

"Go ahead, hit me, lock me up, and throw away the key," John began stormily before spitting a mouthful of blood towards Jasso, just missing his boots. "Soon, more will begin to awaken! And only in our union will we see you Orion scum forced to your knees!"

Displeased by John's threat, Colonel Jasso started to run so he could hit him again but Baal caught him before he had gone a yard.

"He won't talk if he's knocked out cold," Baal whispered into Jasso's ear.

Displeased with the interrogation, Brennan gave Baal a searching stare, but his face gave no hint as to what he was feeling. Baal walked over to the back of the room near the door, and he began pacing with his arms and hands folded behind his back. His footsteps echoed through the silent room, and a cold look began to form on his face.

"Yeah that's right, pace the room and think about what to do with me!" John then lashed out. He then turned to Brennan and looked at him with a piteous stare. "Shame on you homeboy! You damn puppet! You VIP's think you're all that—you work for these scum and blindly follow their orders without any clue about what you're really doing!"

Brennan turned his gaze away from John and exchanged a fretful glance with Graham, who had mystification written all over his face.

"They want us disconnected folk dead because we have free will!" John flared, pointing his finger at Baal with a fully extended arm.

Baal let out a throaty chuckle and he seemed to dismiss John's words as the height of all folly. Jasso laughed too. However, Brennan scratched his head and wondered if John was telling the truth.

Who makes up this stuff? Brennan asked himself.

"This guy's brain is shot from all that solar radiation," Jasso chortled. "I wouldn't even upgrade the bastard—just throw him in a jail cell and let him sleep away his madness."

Just then, John's eyes seemed to glow red. The look of demoniac fury in his eyes caused several of the cops and Draconians in the room to reach for their disruptor pistols. Baal put up a flat palm, and every one of the law enforcement officials in the room eased off in unison.

"Easy gentlemen, we have it under control," Jasso said. However, after the tables and chairs began to rattle, most of the law enforcement personnel in the room gasped in horror. Brennan also gasped as he studied John critically. He had no idea what to think of the fiery, orange-red glow in John's eyes. Suddenly, all the tables and chairs in the room began to rattle and shake. Brennan's words were caught in his throat; he was so startled that he sprung up from his quivering chair.

Apparently, both Baal and Jasso had different feelings towards John's demonstration of power. It was as if the two Draconians were studying John and testing him to see how far he could go with his telekinesis.

What the hell are they smiling at? Brennan asked himself. Their smiles looked jovial, and he sensed no contempt behind them.

Nevertheless, as the shaking intensified and some of the chairs actually began to move across the floor, Baal and Jasso grew alarmed by John's unexpected and advanced abilities; they both figured it was time to take action and put an end to John's ineffectual stratagems. Baal pointed his index finger to the tall Draconian sentry holding the remote control. The sentry pushed a button and Lancaster instantly fell to the ground as the bracelets cooked his nerves. All of the furniture that shook a second ago became still and John rolled on the ground in agony.

Brennan looked on and felt useless. He didn't have the guts to protest the torture. He kept his lips sealed because he was of a lower rank than Jasso and that's all there was to it. That's how it always was for Brennan during his service in a militaristic hierarchy, whether on Earth or in space. You don't question your superiors.

Unless they're mad, Brennan thought.

John was writhing in pain on the ground, his wooly gray, and curly hair stuck up straight on his head. His eyes were bloodshot and strings of saliva dangled from the corners of this lips. After several seconds, Baal raised his hand again in silence, and the tall Draconian released his finger from the button immediately. John still twitched well after the bracelets were turned off, and he needed almost a minute to gather his breath. He crawled back onto his chair with diminishing vigor, coughing and gagging, and his breaths were wheezy.

It was then when Baal first spoke aloud.

"Tell me where Charlie is, and tell me where your safe house is," Baal said humbly, but superiorly, as if he was so used to getting everything he wanted out of people all the time.

"The hell with you; you're the virus that infected my planet...and I'm not telling you anything," John replied between coughs.

Tell him you fool! Brennan said in his head as he watched the prisoner's split lip ooze blood.

Baal stood over him, studying John intently. He seemed as calm as a poker player, but Brennan could sense the pent up anger inside the Doctor.

Brennan was a bit shocked and he could no longer ask any questions.

Besides, Baal and Jasso seemed to take over the interrogation process anyway. "I read one of your emails to your brother. You told him that you wanted to

stop a friend from blowing up RAPDA headquarters," Jasso said.

John didn't reply.

Baal then reached across the table and cupped John's chin, lifting his head up, and locking eyes with him.

"We know that this weapon is highly advanced and based on magnetism," Baal smiled. "We know about the details because we heard it from your mouth on the phone and in the emails to your brother. And so Mr. Lancaster—I'll ask you this once more: where is it?"

John composed himself, and spoke out in a voice sweet with malice. "We never wanted to build weapons, but you forced us to," John began, pausing to spit out blood. "We originally used our resources to build generators that run on a few simple biofuels and magnets. We sent countless queries to the Overseer about reconstituting the electrical grids. We sent him plans to rebuild the transformers in hopes of creating a zap proof grid, but our queries went largely unanswered for years causing us to lose hope. So, when we lost our implants and were too sick to work, we put our energy to use—and decided to help ourselves. Right after we built our electromagnetic generators, one of my partners snapped; he went crazy after realizing that you Draconians were enslaving us and keeping us down in the dirt purposely! We weaponized the technology in hopes of getting your attention. But we never planned on killing anyone!"

Why would the Overseer deny the chance to help rebuild? Brennan asked himself.

He looked at Baal, and he could hear a hiss from Baal as he let out as sigh. The entire room fell into a heart stopping silence. The only noise in the room came from the small portable oxygen machine that was latched on his back of Baal's neck. It chirped every once in a while, and it only added to his almost super human impression. Baal completely disregarded what John said earlier about the generators and only cared to speak of the weapon.

"What if you overvalue the power of your weapon," Baal scorned. "Do you realize what a scaler wave gravitational ray gun can do?"

John nodded readily and rapidly. "I warned him about that...please...we're not evil people," John replied, and his sentence was broken up due to his need to take deep breaths.

Baal jerked forward and leaned into John's face. "Do you realize how lenient we are being? Why...these pain bracelets are nothing compared to what I will do to you if you don't spill it! Now, I want you to tell me where your safe house is before the night is through so we can end this terrible affair at once!"

John didn't reply. He looked like he was about to die. His eyes fluttered open and shut, and he was drooling.

Brennan was reduced to a spectator as he watched, horrified. He wondered how much more microwave radiation John could stand before having a heart attack. And when Brennan fixed his eyes on Baal and Jasso, he could almost see the steam coming out of their ears.

"He won't talk," Jasso then chimed in. "Plan B!" Baal growled.

In an instant, one of the Draconian Ashtar sentries stepped forward. This Draconian sentry appeared more muscular, even beneath his uniform. He took out what looked like a medium sized handheld torch lighter which was five times bigger than a normal cigarette lighter. He also took out what looked like a metal pipe and oddly enough, began heating the tip of the pipe with the torch.

Again, Brennan looked at Graham on the other side of the room, and from the look on his face, it was evident that even his iron nerve had failed this evening. This was not customary, and never had Brennan or Graham engaged in such a maltreatment of POWs in all their years of war experience.

As the Draconian continued to heat up the rod with the flame, Baal walked over to the table and a sleazy grin stole over his wooden face.

"Mr. John Lancaster, you do not want to make me angry now do you?" Baal asked wincingly. "Why do you continue to twist the lion's tail John Lancaster? I'll hurt you!"

John turned away from his face and became alarmed from the hulking Draconian that stood over him with the hot metal rod.

Baal then nodded to the Draconian sentry and he immediately stopped heating the metal rod with the torch. The tip of the metal rod glowed red-orange, and the young, hulking Draconian approached John and grabbed him by his shirt before pinning him to one of the walls. John's eyes hardly blinked as he stared at him, his whole body trembled after seeing the hot piece of steel before his eyes.

Brennan wanted to stop the torture right that minute, but he came to realize that Jasso and Baal were both psychopaths, and they would not listen to his protest anyway.

"Tell me John Lancaster, what moves you to be certain of victory?" Baal asked in the manner of a polished gentleman, but his words were still cruel in connotation.

John temper flared. "You know the answer to that question you damn snake!"

"Speak to me with vile language again and I shall have your tongue!" Baal growled.

John looked like hell. His wooly hair was still standing straight on his head.

Brennan watched in horror. He could not believe a man was being accused of attacking the police with birds. Nevertheless, Brennan hoped John would tell Baal what he wanted to hear. Unfortunately, he did not and John continued to remain silent.

Baal then cupped John's chin and lifted his face so he could see his eyes. "If you don't tell us John, you know my sentry here will do something

terrible to you now don't you?"

Meanwhile, Jasso joined into the fray and grabbed John by his throat.

"The weapon of mass destruction Mr. Lancaster! Where is it!" Jasso barked into his face. "Tell us what we want to know and I would then abide by the course of meeting your wishes of freeing you without any indictment!" Jasso then said.

Baal put up a palm and Jasso finally released his grip on John's neck.

"Go to hell!" John countered and spit bloody saliva right into Jasso's face. Brennan's heart sank. *Fool!*

Jasso was about to take another swing at him, but Baal stopped him again by hooking his elbow with his arm. Baal then became a little more fixed in his manner. He tugged the blazer of his uniform down and set his tie. He wiped his brow and motioned to the sentry guard holding the rod to go ahead with the torture since his efforts to extract information from Lancaster was unavailing.

"Take his pants off!" Jasso and Baal both screamed, and without hesitation, the Ashtar sentry with the hot metal rod began wrestling John's belt off his cargo pants with his free hand.

John shrieked through his clinched throat.

Brennan also had his stomach in his throat, and he swallowed it. He had to intervene, he thought—he could not witness such a thing and have it on his hands. He looked at Graham in the corner of the room and read his lips.

"We got to do something," Graham said silently.

Brennan studied Jasso and Baal's idiom keenly, and after seeing the great negative in their faces, he got up from his seat so he could intervene. However, Baal began screaming again before Brennan could muster up a word.

"Shall I squeeze out your eyeballs, or should I end your ability to sit down and go to the bathroom for the rest of your life!" Baal shouted.

The hulk with the hot metal rod flashed it in front of John's eyes so he could see it well.

Brennan once again thought about taking charge and protesting the act of torment. He looked at Graham and saw his own conviction reflected in his eyes as well, but all Graham could do was give a slight shrug of the shoulders.

Brennan looked at all the guards, agents and police officers in the room. They all just stood in their places—woodenly—like the old London guards at Buckingham palace.

Brennan took a deep breath and then walked up to Jasso, who was busy choking John.

"Colonel?" Brennan called to him with a tentative voice. He was sure that he failed to speak over Joan, who was shrieking and pleading mournfully.

"Put my pants back on, you guys are sick! You Draconians are all sick, demented, and twisted!" John retched out through his narrow and squeezed throat.

Brennan moved closer and spoke louder.

"Colonel...oh Colonel!" Brennan finally got through to him. Jasso turned around and was surprised to see Brennan talking to him at such a time.

"Colonel, this won't work, he's only going to make something up just to save himself from the torture and pain!" Brennan screamed.

The Draconian man with the metal rod turned his head slowly towards Brennan and squinted.

Baal turned to him as well and gave him an austere stare.

"This is the only way Major," Jasso growled. "We're doing it our way!" "Suppose we shift the ground of our requests?" Brennan asked.

Jasso said nothing, and Brennan didn't know if Baal heard him or not, but if he did, he ignored Brennan's plea all together. It was obvious to Brennan that his rejoinder meant nothing to them, and it was obvious to Brennan that Jasso had no say over the matter anyways. For the first time, Brennan realized that Doctor Baal was the one who was in command even though he wasn't the Overseer of Earth, or even a military guy for that matter—he was a CEO of the galaxy's biggest corporation.

"You fool! You bite the hand that feeds you!" Baal yelled in John's face. "You're a delusional rabid paranoid dog—do you not see how your humanity is slipping away?"

John was too scared to speak.

Brennan was at a loss for words and he sat down, feeling useless.

The Draconian sentry continued to heat the rod as he waited for Baal's signal.

Brennan watched Lancaster's eyes show the alarm he had seen so often in prey during his battles in war. John clasped his hands together, shaking more than ever now. He was wringing his hands with gestures of a mournful plea, and then began to nod heavily.

"Wait a minute, stop!" John garbled through a mouth full of blood. The shape of John's face became animated with the deepest of emotions.

"Wait, wait, okay, okay, I'll tell you!" John cried out. And without much ado, Baal ordered his sentry to step back with the flash of a palm. The bulky Ashtar sentry backed off and dipped the rod into a pitcher of ice-cold water. Hot steam whooshed from it and dissipated into the air.

"I'll tell you—I'll tell you..." John said in a more relaxed manner after realizing the sentry retreated, and so he began putting his pants back on.

Baal and Jasso just stared at John as he got dressed both with their hands on their hips and their heads lurched forward.

"It's at a safe house... on 442 East 33rd Street...Coney Island," Lancaster said feebly. Tears were streaming from his closed eyes. Even though he felt ashamed for giving up his friend, he figured that Charlie might actually be prepared for the situation if he indeed finished his weapon, which should have been finished by now, John figured. For the first time in his life, John was glad that Charlie built the weapon.

After John gave up the address, the room erupted. All of the law enforcement personnel in the room were eager to get to the address and everyone fixed their eyes on Doctor Baal awaiting orders with itchy trigger fingers. Baal immediately stepped through the crowd of guards and made his way towards a short, wiry, and bald man who was sitting down in the corner of the room. He was dressed in a long white lab coat.

Brennan figured him for a doctor.

Baal nodded to him and spoke with haste. "Doctor Hark! Give this man his upgrade and let's make sure he rejoins society effectively and conformingly!"

Doctor Hark waddled over to John and set the briefcase on the table before taking out a long syringe. He held it to his eyes; his thick glasses made his eyes look like billiard balls as he stared at the tip of the syringe. He then let out a trickle of fluid before sticking it into the meat of John's deltoid.

Brennan noticed that John Lancaster's resisting and fearful gaze began to fade slowly after being stuck with the needle. And an ominous calm grew over John ever so suddenly, as if the fluid in the syringe contained a sedative as well as the nano-serum. All the previous intensity in his eyes had seemingly vanished, and his eyes seemed to turn into dull, bovine things made of glass.

"That is all gentlemen; lock this man up until he faces a trial, and appoint a lawyer to him," Baal said to several policemen.

John didn't resist as he was dragged out of the room from his armpits. He seemed to be nothing more then dead weight. Many of the police foolishly muttered obscenities at him, even poking fun at him as they escorted him to his cell.

While Brennan and Graham shook their heads at each other, Baal and Jasso passed nods to each other, and their eyes flamed red with devilish passion.

Brennan could have sworn he saw Baal give him a side-glance before walking out of the room.

As Brennan and Graham made their way towards the door, Jasso scurried over to the door and blocked their path.

"Lieutenant Graham, Major Brennan, I shall have words with you," Jasso snorted in resentment, with both hands on his hips.

"Yes sir," both men said with heightened anticipation.

"You won't be coming with us for the raid on the address," Jasso said with a hint of dread in his voice. Brennan and Graham stared at each other in astonishment.

"I want you both to head back to headquarters and report to Pandora's room.

I'll phone you shortly with further orders," Jasso continued. "Yes sir!" both Brennan and Graham said in agreement. "Oh and one last thing!" Jasso said bluntly.

"Sir?" Brennan asked.

Jasso approached Brennan so that their noses almost touched.

"Never, ever show me up in front of my men like that ever again!" Jasso growled. "Or you'll surely regret it."

Without further word, Jasso left the room, and Brennan pressed his lips white so he wouldn't open his mouth.

28: The Message

Elena awakened to the sounds of singing starling blackbirds, which invaded the nearby trees just outside Charlie's house. She rubbed the sleep from her eyes and saw that the alarm clock read nine a.m. Elena was awake for hardly ten seconds but the reality from last night hit her. She immediately thought about Charlie's quaint behavior and then thought about what she would say to Charlie regarding the matter. She couldn't just let it go and really wanted to disbelieve that Charlie was unstable in his head. Sure, all people talk to themselves, but not like that. Not like Charlie. The words he spit out were mind-boggling.

Elena hoped he was still awake, so she could talk to him before leaving, but after glancing towards the dining room, she noticed that Charlie was no longer there and saw that the a sheet covered the devices. She had plenty of time to get to work, but she wanted to get away from the house as soon as possible because Charlie was beginning to give her the creeps. In that instant, Elena decided that she would only meet Charlie in public, and would never return to his wretched apartment.

However, she thought she should wash up first, especially after sleeping on that dust-coated sofa all night.

Thank gods I brought my backpack with me... Elena told herself.

Luckily, Elena found out that Charlie had indeed scrubbed the bathtub with bleach and Charlie had collected plenty of freshly distilled rainwater to go around. She took one of Charlie's gravity filters hanging on the shower curtain rod and opened the bottle-like container before splashing water on her face. She wanted to wash her entire body but knew that she shouldn't take off her anti- drone cloak.

Suddenly, Elena froze from the sound of shouting. "No, it's not possible! NO!"

Charlie's shouting was seemingly coming form outside the house. Elena almost stopped breathing.

The shouts grew more consistent, Charlie was screaming—

"They're coming! They're coming!"

Elena immediately darted out of the bathroom, headed down the small hall and noticed that the front door was open. There was Charlie, sitting on his stoop quietly and staring out into the street. She was surprised he was out there because the sunlight was beginning to peek out from over the roof of his home. However, he seemed to be oblivious to it because it was still was low in the sky and weak.

Elena vigilantly walked over to him and noticed that Charlie was once again in some sort of self-induced trance. His un-blinking eyes were wide, and saliva hung from the corners of his mouth like bungee ropes. The look on his face caused all the blood to rush to Elena's feet, leaving her face pale and lightheaded.

Elena called out to him through a blocked throat, "Charlie?"

He didn't answer at first. He had the same look on his face that he'd had last night, and he looked right through her when she faced him.

Elena then shook him by the shoulders, but he continued to sit on the stoop, staring blankly ahead.

"Charlie, are you...are you alright?" Elena stammered with a voice pinched with fear.

He still didn't answer. As inured as Elena was to crazy people, this situation with her new friend was something else entirely. The suspense just grew upon her.

It took a whole minute before Charlie began to blink his eyes, and when he came out of his trance, he acted as if he was startled out of a sleep just after a nightmare.

"Charlie, are you okay?"

Charlie looked confused. "I...must have been...daydreaming again...I...I... just have a feeling of impending doom for some reason. I...I...think people are heading over here to get me."

Elena felt the gooseflesh again; her limbs tingled from the fear. Charlie just walked away from her after that, apparently still bothered by the voices he had heard while stuck in his trance. *Run, run Charlie, run from that house and find a new one. They got me, they tortured me, I am sorry. I only gave them your address because they were going to do horrible things to me. And besides, I knew you would have gotten this message beforehand.*

When the voice got louder in his head, Charlie slowly crept back into the living room in disbelief, shaking his head.

"No, it's not real. It's not real," he said over and over. Charlie just continued to pace with Elena hot on his heels.

"Charlie, talk to me!" Elena demanded.

Charlie didn't answer. He continued to pace and even began gesticulating with his arms and hands in disbelief.

The voice in his head grew louder. *Run, run Charlie!*

He realized the voice wasn't his and it wasn't a part of his subconscious either. It was a real voice—it was John's voice.

"What's wrong Charlie?" Elena asked.

Charlie didn't answer. His eyes were ablaze with intense cerebral excitement and Elena felt that the only way to get through to him was to block Charlie's path wherever he paced.

"Charlie what the hell is happening to you?"

With a protective impulse, Charlie clung to her arm fiercely and escorted her into the house. Elena was terrified.

"Charlie, you're hurting me!"

Charlie's rough hands only worsened the awful thrall that was upon her. "They are coming, the police are coming and they want me and my devices!"

"What makes you say that? How do you know they want the devices?" "Elena, please, just trust me! I don't really blame you for thinking that I've gone mad after witnessing my behavior lately, and you have every right to suppose that the abundance of strain on my nerves have at last burned my brain. But please Elena, you must believe me when I tell you this..." Charlie paused, before increasing his voice. "These deep daydreams—these trances—John used to call it remote viewing.

John and I, we can sometimes talk to each other from long distances, but only when intense emotion is involved. I think he's in danger."

Elena couldn't even muster a reply—she was too busy soaking it all in. Elena stared at Charlie's flushed face. His sweaty, long black hair and damp brow told her that he was enduring some sort of torture with in his mind.

Whatever he was hearing, it was real—at least it was to him. Elena wasn't sure if she should pity him, fear him, or most importantly, believe him.

Is he a schizophrenic? Elena asked herself.

As she witnessed his maniacal behavior, all her trust for him began to slip away and his explanation for it didn't exactly help. Even though she was familiar with remote viewing and its hypothetical meanings, she never thought it would be something she would witness happen to a friend right before her eyes. Elena dismissed his disillusionment with an awake-dream he might have had just like he did last night when she saw him talk to the wall. Elena actually hoped that Charlie was insane. At least she would have nothing to fear—no ghosts, no demons, and no police officers too.

"Charlie, just try to stay calm, I think you're overworked and need some rest," Elena said in a careworn voice, but the words went in an out of Charlie's ears. He acted as if he didn't hear her at all. Instead, he scampered over to the front door and peaked out again as the paranoia stole over him completely.

"Charlie, please, you're making me nervous."

Charlie stopped dead in his tracks and jabbed a finger at her before shouting, "No Elena, I heard him! It was John's voice warning me!"

Then, he immediately began lugging his contraptions off his dining room table and towards the middle of the living room one by one, starting with the generator. Charlie's mouth was tight and his squared jaw took a rounded shape, stuck in a permanent frown.

"I won't let them take my work; I'm going to hide these in my secret cellar!"

Charlie tugged an area rug away on his floor and revealed a hatch on the floor. He immediately fumbled in his pocket for a key, which tottered in his trembling hand as he slipped it into a padlock on the floor. He unlocked it and swung the hatch open.

Elena expected to see stairs leading to a basement but there wasn't any.

After Charlie swiped at the spider webs, she saw that it was nothing but a small hole dug down to the foundation of the house. It was a homemade dig up that Charlie had created incase he ever felt compelled to hide anything, including himself.

Elena felt so bad for Charlie that she couldn't help but be of assistance, so she helped him lug the equipment to the hole, as long as it made him happy. It took a minute for them to put most of the devices inside the hole and when Elena set out to lift the final device on the table, Charlie grabbed her wrist and shook his head slightly.

Elena wondered why he didn't want to hide the oblong contraption in her hands. She then noticed that the device had a trigger on it and the front section funneled down into what looked like a tuning fork.

"Not this one," Charlie insisted.

And before Elena could ask why, the sounds of screeching tires were heard coming from outside.

29: Back Against The Wall

"They're here!" Charlie exhaled.

Blue and red strobe lights flashed from outside, and the luminosity penetrated through the openings in the boarded window.

Elena's heart sunk. Both Charlie and Elena impulsively rushed to the window at the same time and turned to each other—each of their eyes meeting in a grave, uneasy glance. Charlie turned sharply away from the window after witnessing armed RAPDA agents and Draconian Ashtar sentries galloping towards both sides of the home. Elena immediately peeked through the window for signs of her father but noticed that her father was not one of them. She couldn't see anyone through all the armor they were wearing. All she saw was three patrol vans and about a dozen men clad in black. Most of them wore full face covering helmets.

One man, a man with a double ducktail haircut approached from the front of the crowd of police and RAPDA agents. He had a cigar in his mouth, and Elena immediately recognized who it was. It was the Overseer.

Part of her was happy to finally have her doubts about Charlie's sanity put to rest. He was sane after all and very gifted as well. However, she had little time to reflect on Charlie's supernatural abilities.

Charlie ran to the hatch on the floor and flung it open again.

"We're trapped!" Charlie shouted before reaching into the hole in the floor.

He took out two queer looking cloaks with mechanical contraptions stitched onto them.

"Here, put this one on—quickly!" Charlie shouted. He handed her one of the cloaks. He then closed the hatch before carefully sliding the area rug back over it, aligning it in accordance with the dust on the floor.

Elena stared at her cloak with squinted eyes. "What in the world are you making me put on?"

Charlie didn't answer her. He then handed her what looked to be nothing more than ordinary winter attire.

"The mask, put on this mask too, and these mittens here."

All of a sudden the front door began to rattle, and a throaty voice was heard behind the door.

"Open up—police! We know you're in there!"

Charlie chuckled madly from delirium. "It's going to take them a while to get through that door. I reinforced the bolts! Those bastards are going to have their hands full getting through unless they shoot their way through."

Elena put on the cloak and the ski mask even though she didn't know why. She figured she had nothing to lose by wearing it, and she had grown to trust Charlie enough to listen to his commands.

A guttural voice shouted from behind the door, *"We're going to break the door down!"*

Elena fidgeted excessively with the cloak, tangling a sleeve around the other sleeve.

"Take off the lead cloak first," Charlie said. "But they'll see..."

"This other cloak here is made from Ferro-magnetic material. It will emit a unique frequency that will not only render you invisible to RAPDA's surveillance methods, but will render you invisible altogether!"

After taking off the lead cloak, Elena finally managed to put on the invisibility cloak, which looked like nothing more than a silver raincoat. She then put on the mittens and the full faced ski mask, and it wasn't long before the back door near the kitchen patio then began to rattle.

Charlie helped Elena with her cloak after he zipped his up. He had to make sure no skin showed anywhere and the sleeves were tugged straight.

"As soon as you zip it up to the very top press that red button near on the inside of the right sleeve—near the wrist.

"What does the red button do?"

"If you press that button, you will transport you outside of your current position in space time to another position in space time."

"English please!" Elena shouted. "It will teleport you!"

Elena shuddered from the thought. "Teleport me where?" "I don't know!"

"You don't know?" Elena asked unnervingly. She jolting nervously with each loud thwack heard on the door.

"Somewhere close—perhaps out in the street, or in the middle of the yard, or even a block away from here. It will warp the space-time around you and dilate time creating a uniform E.M. field with an intense frequency outside the

E.M. spectrum as we know it! The unique frequency should create a temporal anomaly around you that will literally make you hop over and skip over time...or space!"

"Oh I can't believe I'm going to do this!" Elena cried.

"Now don't press the red button until I take out the police," Charlie insisted. "Take out the police?"

"Yes, this cannon here. I'm going to take them out."

Elena just lost her ability to speak for a moment. Her jaw locked in fright. Charlie shook her by the shoulders to make sure his words got through to her dazed and shocked mind.

"Don't worry; I am not going to kill them—remember, do not press the red button and teleport until I take some of them out. For all I know, there could be more of them coming up the street. And I may not know exactly where you'll end up after pressing the button."

Suddenly, they heard a different voice from the outside. Charlie recognized it even though it was muffled. It was the Overseer's voice.

"We're coming in!" Jasso shouted from behind the door. The thwacking sounded differently after each knock because the door was losing some of its density, and it began to splinter in the middle.

"Hurry up with that battering ram!" Jasso shouted.

Charlie proceeded to power up the cannon and Elena was startled after seeing a glowing fizz of electricity move up and down the forked tip of the cannon. He finished putting the final touches on it last night while Elena slept but he never tested it. He was about to for the first time.

Charlie then clasped Elena's wrist and escorted Elena to the dining room wall.

"You stand up against that wall here and press the black button on the inside of the right sleeve. You will camouflage yourself near that flower-patterned wallpaper. It will help reduce the distortion field and you will be harder to see over here. Do it now!"

Elena rolled her sleeve to reveal the electronic box in the sleeve, and she pressed the black button. It initially emitted a faint hum, but only briefly. Elena held out her invisible hand and became astonished by how it mirrored whatever she ran it over. She moved her hand towards the ground, and it appeared as wood. She then placed it flat against the wall, and it literally seemed to blend in and become a part of the wall, taking the design of the patterned wallpaper.

A loud crash sounded at the door. The wood near the area of the lock was chipping off and flaking to the ground. Each thwack of the wood made both Elena and Charlie jump several inches off the floor.

"Charlie, you don't have to fight," Elena said, heaving a sigh. "Come and hide with me!"

After thinking about it for a second, Charlie obliged and joined her. Charlie tucked his cannon tightly beneath his cloak, and then activated it, rendering himself invisible. He took refuge along side Elena near the wallpapered wall, hoping the cannon's sound wouldn't make enough noise to give himself up.

Each time they struck the door, the thud shook the entire floor. Elena cringed every time saw the thick wooden door flexing—threatening to break. The next few whacks on the door caused its iron hinges to loosen, and it would only be a matter of seconds before the front door finally banged open—cracking in half after hitting the wall on its right.

A flood of European RAPDA sentries mixed with local SWAT teams rushed in like running water, pushing and shouldering into each other as they moved through the house in slow, panther-like movements. Several police officers began opening some of the closets first. Some more intimidating RAPDA sentries searched in pairs of two—checking the bathroom, the kitchen, and some made sure to check inside the kitchen cabinets.

Elena and Charlie continued to stand stiffly by the wall, their hearts frozen stiff in trepidation.

"We got the place covered Colonel! You can come inside now!" a scruffy looking cop said.

Colonel Jasso waddled into the house last, with cautious strides. His face was flushed with hypertension and uncertainty. He had an index finger on the small comm. device hooked onto his left ear; he had Brennan on the other line.

"What do you mean they simply disappeared?" Jasso asked with confusion. "We scanned the house just ten minutes ago and detected two life forms in here. Just scan the house again and get back to me as soon as possible. I think that they must be wearing some sort of garment that is making them vanish on your infrared screen."

A sour-faced police officer with frizzy red hair then strolled in from the kitchen.

"Sir, the fridge is operational. However, so far, no signs of the suspect and his cohort," said the officer.

Jasso nodded. "We'll find them, they couldn't have gone too far, we just scanned the place ten minutes ago and found two people in here!"

Elena almost sunk to the floor in an agony of abasement, and she tried hard to stay still as she closed her eyes and prayed. She couldn't see too well through her sheer, ski mask—not well enough to make out everyone's faces. Charlie also had trouble seeing through it, and he relied on his senses to detect the proximity of some of the soldiers. He stood as still as possible as several police came within three feet of him and the wallpapered wall. He held the cannon tightly beneath his invisibility cloak, pressing it on his chest to keep it from moving.

A RAPDA agent with large dark shades came within inches of Elena after one of them noticed the lack of dust on the dining room table.

"Something was moved off of this table recently," the agent shouted as he took off his shade, and wiped a palm on the table to inspect it.

"Check upstairs," Jasso ordered some of his men.

Some of the SWAT team began scuttling up the stairs towards the bedrooms on the second floor. Charlie and Elena stood as still as statues—only twitching slightly when the furniture upstairs was tossed around in the bedrooms.

Suddenly, one of the older European RAPDA agents seemed to become intrigued with the ground beneath him. Charlie's throat tightened after noticing that the agent began to investigate the area rug beneath his feet.

"Colonel, look at this rug here," said the agent. "It doesn't appear to be aligned with the thick layer of dust on the floor."

Damn! They found my hiding spot! Charlie fretted in his mind.

Jasso waddled from one side of the rug to the other side—analyzing the dusty outline on the ground with inquisitive eyes. Judging by the rug's position, Jasso knew that it must have been moved recently and probably for the first time in weeks or months because the rug wasn't aligned properly with the dust on the floor.

Jasso violently tugged the rug away with one arm, sending it flying towards the living room and landing in a folded heap on Charlie's sofa. Jasso's eyes lit up upon discovering the secret hatch on the floor.

"It's a hatch," said the German agent as he removed his dark shades and inspected the padlock.

"Open the damn thing!" Jasso grunted through clenched teeth.

Charlie's heart almost stopped. He no longer felt fear but only an untamed, swelling desire to intervene. In one motion, Charlie hopped away from the wall and unzipped his cloak before pointing his cannon at Jasso.

"Hold it right there you Orion scum!" Charlie growled.

A brief silence came over the room because of the initial surprise, and Jasso's jaw hung so low that his cigar fell out of his mouth. Even the agents and police officers hesitated a few seconds before pointing their rifles, because Charlie had literally appeared out of thin air therefore shocking everyone in the living room stiff.

Nevertheless, after the officers realized what they saw and why, they immediately pointed their rifles at Charlie.

"Hold your fire," Jasso said calmly while putting up a palm.

Several RAPDA sentries came scuttling down the stairs after hearing Charlie's voice and immediately surrounded him with their rifles aimed at his head.

Elena's heart jumped to her throat, and she couldn't help but wonder why Charlie seemed so overconfident despite his predicament.

"Drop your weapons!" Charlie screamed.

"Just tell me when," a police officer yelled out; his trigger finger was twitching.

Jasso put up a flat palm. "Let us have a chat with our friend first," Jasso responded with a half smile across his face. He blinked his eyes clear and cut a look at Charlie.

"What do you say we discuss things first?" Jasso finished sourly.

"I'm not in the mood to talk," Charlie snarled. "Get out of my house before I kill you all!" Elena almost didn't recognize Charlie's voice because his adrenaline made it deepen considerably. His voice scared her.

"I think you should put that thing down before you hurt yourself," Jasso said, and his grin vanished after seeing the demonic fury in Charlie's eyes.

"Drop them—! Now!" Charlie countered in a tone that forbade any negotiation.

Every RAPDA sentry and SWAT cop in the room had his weapon pointed at Charlie, but Charlie didn't seem to care one bit. His chest rose and fell several times, but other than that, Charlie seemed overconfident and had no fear on his face—only anger.

"Tell us when!" an agent said as he stood right in front of Charlie. "You pull that trigger, you die," Charlie sneered.

Jasso's worry meter went up a few points after detecting the confidence in Charlie's words. Jasso exhaled a sharp sigh and put up a submissive palm.

"Just calm down boy," Jasso said coolly. "I know that thing in your hands is a zero point energy weapon, but you must realize that you are surrounded by a dozen men from all sides. You'll never come out of this one alive."

"I'm not going anywhere!" Charlie shouted.

Jasso shook his head. He didn't want to kill Charlie. He wanted him alive.

Jasso fixed his loose hair back into a sloppier shape of its usual double ducktail style. He rubbed the bridge of his hooked nose as he thought about what to do, and he then spoke fatally. "You must pay for what you did Charlie. I am placing you under arrest for assault and battery of seven police officers, as well as four of my personal Draconian Ashtar guards! I also charge you with disseminating malicious doctrine and prophecy that lead to nothing but scandal and angst amongst the undemanding simple citizens of New York City! You only accomplished terror Mr. Beasley, nothing more! You filled their heads with your madness and poisoned their dreams! You are nothing but a public menace— making incessant threats and warnings against me out in public. Your ranting does nothing but dissuade the common people from proceeding with their daily tasks—accusing everyone of failing to see life as it is! And you have incurred much displeasure to not only me but my superiors. We cannot allow you to rebel and pester my people with impunity! So your sermons will end here Mr.

Beasley, and you face charges of heresy against the Overseer, as well as suspicion of harboring a dangerous virus and possession of a weapon of mass destruction!"

"Go to hell," Charlie snapped back as he swiveled around to face all of the police and RAPDA agents that enveloped him.

Jasso sighed deeply and had nothing more to say. He figured Charlie was acting overconfident for the sake of bluffing. Jasso used his calloused hands to rub his face until his cheeks flushed red. He was concerned for Charlie's life because he wanted him alive.

Elena thought that Charlie might have a chance at dispatching several people in front of him, but he was completely at the mercy of the dozen SWAT members behind him. She just couldn't see how Charlie would incapacitate everyone in the room given the circumstances. She wanted to press the red button on her sleeve badly, because she didn't want to die in any crossfire.

However, she wasn't sure if she was more frightened by the idea of being teleported or her current dilemma.

Jasso nestled himself between the armor of three of his RAPDA sentries in the event that Charlie would squeeze the trigger.

"Now come to your senses my dear boy, you are out-matched here," Jasso gritted. "Put that thing down, and let's talk."

Charlie shook his head and spat on the ground. "You, Mr. Overseer, you are the one with your back against the wall."

Jasso exhaled a nervous chuckle. "Don't be a fool! You kill us, and you will spend your entire life in prison!"

"Like I said; I'm not going anywhere!" Charlie replied, and he seemed to grow more pugnacious after each second.

Jasso sighed for the last time. "Fire!" Jasso shouted.

Elena gasped as the whining sounds of disruptor fire rattled the wall she leaned upon. Bright strobes bathed everyone's facial features red, and wisps of smoke filled the room, engulfing Charlie's frame in a thick, gray pall. Elena watched in fright as the dozens of glowing beams shot out from the Draconian disruptor rifles, and she thought that was the last time she would see Charlie alive.

However, she then noticed that some electromagnetic energy bubble was surrounding him and it was absorbing the shots. Apparently, the distorted air around the cannon fizzed as it absorbed every one of the shots, and nothing seemed able to cut through the E.M. bubble that Charlie was wrapped in.

Behind him, loud pops of ballistic ammunition filled the room, and even the solid steel bullets were absorbed by the force field. Whenever the bullets hit the shield, they gave off a deep bass-like sound and fell— tinkling harmlessly on the ground.

"Damn thing can block solid bullets too!" Jasso cracked.

After sensing a disadvantage, Jasso took nervous steps back and sought refuge behind more of his men who still fired continuously in front of him.

"Keep firing!" Jasso ordered while peeking over the shoulder of a SWAT sentry.

Charlie waited for the disruptor rifles to overheat, and he knew they would have to stop firing for at least five seconds because they would need recharging. The men with pistols only had sixteen shot clips, and so Charlie waited for silence that would ensue as the police reloaded.

After the majority of the shots ceased, Charlie set his feet in a wide stance. He turned the weapon on low concentration and pressed the trigger sending an invisible gravity beam stabbing out towards Jasso's RAPDA sentries, throbbing through the entire house.

Jasso was the only one who prepared for it— he had dropped to the floor and rolled away towards the living room wall and away from the gush of gravity.

The German agent in front of Jasso took the brunt of the impact and set off a domino effect when he flew into other men, knocking some into the wall and some into the boarded living room window.

The sound of Charlie's weapon was so gelatinous and unearthly that Elena just shut her eyes and prayed after hearing it. When the walls stopped vibrating, all she could hear were the clacking sound from all of the rifles that fell to the ground, as well as the thudding sound of crumpling armored bodies. All of that tumult had mixed in with Charlie's inhuman growling, as well as all of his curses and oaths of reprisal. Several cops charged Charlie but they were instantly electrocuted after running into the shield that surrounded him.

The remaining SWAT team that stood behind Charlie had begun to fire, but their bullets were no match for the shield. Charlie's cannon let out a scrunching grind and another burst of anti-gravity came out from behind the cannon that time, sending all six of the police officers plummeting into the next room, and into the kitchen cabinets. Some of them flew right through the back door and straight out into the backyard.

Charlie wasn't done. He then stabbed the cannon forward and hit the last remaining guard in front of him, knocking him straight into the wall with a force that knocked all the wind out of his lungs.

Elena's watched Charlie's terrific onslaught with wide eyes, and her face no longer showed anguish and morphed to one of restrained happiness. Elena was suddenly not as nervous because there was only one man remaining in front of Charlie. It was the Overseer himself, who was still on the ground.

Nevertheless, Elena remained cloaked and waited to see what would ensue. Colonel Jasso peered from behind the couch before taking a potshot at Charlie, but the shot was reduced to nothing but a hot facet after it was absorbed by Charlie's shield. Jasso then slipped out his side arm, but before he could point it, something made him stall and hesitate with sheer trepidation.

The most phantasmal thing had occurred, and even a Draconian like Colonel Jasso doubted the reality of what he saw despite being part of such a technological race. When Charlie pointed his cannon to one of his wooden chairs, it floated towards him and then hovered right in front of his cannon's forked tip. The chair continued to hover for a several seconds, just enough time for him to charge the electromagnetic energy in the cannon's kinetic energy recovery capacitor. Before Jasso could muster a shot from his .44 caliber, Charlie propelled the chair forward with a tremendous velocity, hitting Jasso in the face with a bone-jarring force.

Jasso dropped like a ton of bricks, barely maintaining consciousness. The landing made it more painful because his knee twisted, and the force of the wooden chair hitting his face sent waves of pain racing through his head and neck.

Elena couldn't believe how Charlie cleared out the room in less than thirty seconds with the alien looking thing in his hands. She almost felt safe enough to come out of hiding, but she stalled after hearing the buzzing sounds of drones coming from outside.

Jasso writhed in pain on the ground, and Elena thought that he looked as if he wanted to retreat because he began crawling towards the front door. His right knee exploded in pain as he tried to get up, and so he snaked and slithered his body towards the front door and out onto the front porch, instinctively cowering back as he rolled himself down the stoop and onto the sidewalk.

Charlie proceeded to shoulder his cannon and charged towards the front door with his cannon holstered. He sensed more people outside and realized that Jasso had indeed called for backup, because four more police vans screeched to a halt right in front of the house, all equipped with ADS systems.

"Elena hit the button now! The red teleport button!" Charlie shouted from his doorway.

Elena scooted away from the wall and peeked out the front door while still cloaked. Dozens of armored Draconian Ashtar began pouring out of the vehicles, and she immediately took notice of the satellite dishes on the roofs of the vans.

It wasn't long before she began to hear that familiar and terrifying droning sound. Charlie fell to his knees immediately after being hit with the microwave beam. Elena retreated into the kitchen to avoid exposure to the beam. A pang of anxiety almost immobilized her, and she fumbled for that red button on her sleeve. The idea of being teleported made her hesitate when attempting to press the red button on sleeve, but nevertheless she gritted her teeth and pressed it.

Elena screamed before blacking out for just a second.

Before she could blink her eyes, she was outside. Elena was shocked at how seamless the teleporting was, and she never thought the whole thing would be a painless and quiet process. The first thing she did was try to figure out where in the world she was—and she immediately recognized the firehouse on her right, indicating that she was no more than five hundred feet away from Charlie's house.

Before deciding which direction to take, her attention was detained by a cacophony of buzzing noises above her, and Elena couldn't believe how many drones soared in the sky. They were energetic little things, and their propellers made them sound like a swarm of hornets. Some of the smaller dragonfly drones were as low as twenty feet, and some of the larger prowler drones were about two hundred feet in the air.

Elena shielded her gaze from the early morning sun and noticed that one particular drone—no different looking than a small helicopter with a camera— had begun to descend until it was just several dozen feet over her head. Before Elena managed to press the black button on her cloak, the drone cut and dipped at a ninety-degree angle and intercepted her path, meeting her face to face and scanning her iris with a laser.

"Oh damn!" she blathered aloud.

She reached for the black button on her sleeve, but it was too late The drone had scanned her eye had relayed her position to authorities nearby. Before Elena even managed to press the black button, the not too distant roar of an engine was heard coming from behind. In a fit of panic, Elena disregarded the black button and darted in the opposite direction towards an area she was unfamiliar with.

A hulking and fully armored Draconian Ashtar guard hung out of the vehicle's passenger window and screamed, "There she is!"

Elena fought the fear that paralyzed her limbs and headed towards a driveway lined with dead rose bushes. Branches and thorns lashed at her face as she ran. Some of the thorns cut up her cheeks and thighs and even latched onto her t-shirt, tearing it in spots. After a while, Elena slowed to avoid being cut, and in her attempt to turn around, a vine wrapped around her leg and tripped her, causing her to fall on the rock-strewn ground, scraping the side of her hip.

Before she even got the chance to refill her lungs and get up on her feet, she heard an all too familiar sound coming from down the driveway. It was that awful droning sound, and the truck from which it emanated from was the last thing she would see. Just as Elena was about to get up, a nebulous fog took over her sight, and she blacked out.

30: Suspicion

Brennan left Lieutenant Graham snoring in Pandora's chair, deciding to take a ride to Charlie's home in order to see what was going on. The last time he spoke to Jasso was just before the raid—and before they kicked in Charlie's door. In the past hour, everyone from Jasso to local police captains could not be reached. The mystery surrounding the events that took place earlier in the morning led to many questions—questions that Brennan wanted answered—and the only way to get those answers was to head to Charlie's safe-house, despite being ordered to standby in Pandora's room. He figured that only one man was needed to helm Pandora, and Graham would be that person for now. Besides, he was sick of following Jasso's orders, and lost all respect for him during John Lancaster's interrogation.

As he drove towards the new Brooklyn Bridge, he began thinking about his experience in Pandora's room during the raid.

I know something didn't seem right about that raid, even though I saw it all unfold from five hundred feet above in the x-ray spectrum.

Pandora's recon drones picked up two bodies, but for the first time it involved a connected person. Pandora does not display the full identification of the temporary space-faring tourists for the sake of saving hard-drive memory, given the fact that so many tourists visit Earth each week.

The readout said, *Temporary Tourist, Class "A" Orion employer. Detailed*

I.D. pending...

Brennan thought about the connected person he picked up in Charlie's home.

This is all too odd; why would a healthy person want to live with this Beasley fellow?

Brennan wasted no time looking up Charlie Beasley's notorious Youtube video and listened to his entire speech from the rally the other day as he drove.

This man has a following...

After listening to Charlie's speech, Brennan's inferences stirred up from other facts too, and what made him more suspicious was the fact that people on

Earth were developing superpowers, psychically and physically. And for some reason, Brennan thought, they posed a threat to the Overseer, and that is why they were so quick to stick that needle into John's arm.

What if John was right about the serum in those upgrades?

Brennan kept asking himself questions, and more of them piled into his mind earlier in the day after the two life forms he noticed on Pandora's screen showed for just a few minutes, only to disappear just several minutes before Jasso got into the house.

Sure, he figured they must have found a way to shield themselves from Pandora's gaze, but the people in the home kept appearing and disappearing out of thin air, and the connected person magically reappeared five hundred feet away from the home before the person was incapacitated; it was all too confusing for Brennan.

Even though Brennan had plenty to worry about, what worried Brennan the most however, was the fact that so many law enforcement personnel managed to get beat up by the only two people in the house. Brennan knew there must have been a violent outburst of some sort because all the life forms that he detected in the Beasley home became still as stones. At least, all the law enforcement personnel were.

Why isn't Jasso answering?

Angered by Jasso's avoidance, Brennan stepped on the spongy throttle of his company vehicle in frustration, hoping to get to the Charlie Beasley house as soon as possible, but unfortunately, his company minivan had a top speed of only fifty-five mph.

The fog made the streets in Coney Island look much more mysterious, and things got sleazier as Brennan headed further into Brooklyn's red districts. The roads were dissimilar to the way Brennan remembered them, and the innumerable amount of detours he was forced to make made him a bit edgy. As Brennan drove, he adjusted the GPS system to compensate for the detours, but he would regret taking them. He was led to a heavily pined road that forced him to take another detour on Dumont Road. It was a clear road except for the overturned tugboat in the middle of the street, but he managed to slip past it by driving on the sidewalk; little did he know that there be another obstacle standing in his way: the weather.

Rumbles of thunder followed the many flashes in the sky, and within seconds, an abrupt torrent of large raindrops splashed against the windshield, mixing in with the dust he picked up from the dirt roads. The windshield wipers wiped off the initial sludge but failed to keep up with the rain. Brennan could hardly see, so he slowed down to just about thirty mph, depending on nothing but the GPS for guidance. The rain slashed at and pummeled Brennan's company van, and the wind seemed move it into an entirely different lane when it gusted.

"Damn schizophrenic weather patterns!" Brennan said aloud.

As Brennan veered to his right, he turned onto Lamoka Drive and found that there was nothing but empty water-logged flatland ahead. Brennan occasionally saw lumbering silhouettes waddling about on the sidewalks; some mutants were even having sex on the streets.

This is no time to arrest mutants. I'm in a hurry...

Disgusted by what he saw, he jerked his wheel and turned a corner on Douglas Road only to discover that the road would prove to be even more unsettling than the previous one. He came across a few naked corpses sprawled about in the gutter that were being torn apart by a pack of rabid dogs. He had to cover his mouth or be in danger of losing the stomach acid that had almost made it out of his esophagus. The stench of death worsened as he drove deeper and deeper into the red districts, and he knew the smell well—it was the stink of rotten flesh—and that familiar scent haunted him quite often during the radiation induced zombie apocalypse he survived over a decade ago.

His trip would prove to be even more horrific as he drove towards the coast and closer to Charlie's safe house. Parts that had previously been men and women, dangled from the trees, and their fleshless necks were barely held up by the ropes. There were dozens of them hanging from trees along both of the sides of almost two entire avenues. From the looks of the bodies, they were dead for just a few days, but Brennan wasn't sure. All he was sure of was that it was a mass suicide.

"I'm getting too old for this," Brennan muttered as he stepped on the gas, trying hard not to look. However, he couldn't help but look because there were bodies everywhere.

Crows and ravens flapped from body to body, and some were still perched on the skeletal remains, pecking at whatever flesh remained on the bones.

Strands of torn flesh dangled from the belly of one of the corpses, and a coffle of crows were pecking at its innards like hungry snakes. The birds that were feasting on the dead bodies seemed territorial and rambunctious, and when Brennan idled by, some birds began diving into the windshield and began pecking at it as if they wanted to get through and eat him.

Brennan swerved the car left and then to the right in hopes of shedding some of them, but one particular crow was stubborn and continuously pecked at the windshield with its bloody beak and would not let up. Brennan upped the speed on his windshield wipers and the bird flew away.

Brennan did not let up on the throttle until his GPS unit informed him that he was a minute away from his destination. After turning up McDonald Avenue, he saw a dozen ambulances and the entire police force in front of the one house.

Brennan slammed on the brakes, put the car in park, opened the door and turned off the ignition all at the same time. He flung open the car door and approached the house with prepared steps. The crowd of law enforcement personnel spilled from the house's porch onto the sidewalk and into the street. However, he didn't see Colonel Jasso anywhere.

Brennan found it difficult skipping past the platoon of lubberly looking Draconian Ashtar forces because they were so tall and solid and unmindful to the rain that pattered down on their cloaks and military caps.

The scene was chaotic, paramedics were wheeling police officers into ambulances, and more and more police cars were pulling up to the house to replace their injured comrades. Brennan never expected to see so many of them being tended to by medics. Their helmets look cracked! What sort of beating did they take?

Brennan continued to scan the scene as he held a palm over his brow to keep the rain out of his eyes. He didn't see Jasso anywhere. However, he noticed that several RAPDA agents huddled around the umbrella of one particular man who stood near a police van. He was a chubby fellow, clean-shaven, balding, and with two tufts of peppered hair on the sides of his head. The chubby man was apparently speaking on the phone, but Brennan turned away and paid him no mind, even though he seemed to be running the show in the Colonel's absence.

The man was Draconian for sure; his uniform bore the unique Ashtar crest of the Draconian elite forces, which featured a snake wrapped around an apple tree. Charlie figured the man for a southern Draconian that hailed from Alpha Draconis C because he didn't have the aquiline features of those who resided on Draconis B. He had a large gut and a barrel chest but had flimsy, sinewy limbs that seemed not to belong on his body. His noise was a porcine nose, and he had the tiniest pig eyes.

Brennan's approach seemed to catch the chubby man's attention, and the chubby man fixed him with an inhospitable gape.

"Are you Major Brennan?" the chubby Draconian man yelled over the rain. Brennan sensed the man knew who he was.

"Where's the Overseer?" Brennan asked, getting to the point.

The chubby agent then offered Brennan to join him under his umbrella in which Brennan obliged. The chubby man gave Brennan a long searching stare and flashed a brittle smile. He spoke with what seemed to be typical, Draconian English.

"He was here minutes ago, he sustained minor injuries during the raid and might have decided to get to a hospital."

Brennan's brow furrowed. "Was the public enemy apprehended successfully?"

"Yes, yes," the chubby man began with a comforting laugh. "We got him with the microwaves and we're waiting for the paramedics to tell us that Charlie is fit enough to be placed under arrest."

"I'm going to find out if the Overseer is still here," Brennan said before scampering off into the rain.

The chubby man was quick to follow. "Oh, Major..." he called out, causing Brennan to stop on a dime and swivel around to face him again. "The Overseer told me to tell you something."

"Tell me what?" Brennan asked.

"I was just going to call you, but then I saw you wondering in the crowd."

Brennan looked bewildered. "What did he tell you to tell me?" Brennan asked hotly.

"I'm sorry it had to be me to give you your orders, but the Overseer insisted that I tell you because of the minor injury he sustained during the raid. He told me to inform you and your Lieutenant that you can both go home now."

Stunned, Brennan bit his lip sullenly and was all too surprised to learn he had been thrown off the mission at such a critical time. Brennan took a deep breath to recover his nerves before speaking.

"Are...you serious?"

"Yes...I am," the chubby man said through his fake, corporate smile. He then put out his hand, but Brennan took a few seconds to shake it.

"By the way, I'm Corporal Tyburr, and I'm a former Overseer of our European branches. Now, I am simply a part-timer here and acting ambassador of the RAPDA agency in England and Germany. The Overseer has commanded me to inform you and your Lieutenant that he's granted you leave—and you and your Lieutenant must discontinue your association with this mission at once."

Brennan reddened after hearing that. "Injured or not, this is something he should tell me himself, even if it meant waiting a day or two until he recovered from his injury!"

Tyburr shrugged his shoulders; his neck was so stumpy that his shoulders seemed to rise over his head.

"It makes no difference...I'm a Corporal in the Draconian military...and your superior officer."

Brennan perched himself against a nearby police car and rubbed the bridge of his nose to ease the rage that rippled through his bones. For the first time in his life, Brennan felt a sense of duty and responsibility to his home turf and his people. His entire life was all about duty and he dedicated the better part of the last decade to Orion Corp. and its military. However, this time his feelings were different. He cared little about the orders he had gotten, after all, taking an order from a Draconian was no different from an American officer taking an order from a French, German, or Chinese officer during World War I, II, and III for that matter. This time, Brennan was going to do the right thing and do so on his own accord. He didn't care about sucking up to his saviors anymore. Besides, all the conspiracy theories spewed by John Lancaster and Charlie Beasley made Brennan wonder about his employer's overly secretive ways. As he pondered what to say next, Brennan's breath frosted out of his mouth and into the air in large, anxious puffs.

"I thought RAPDA needed me for my familiarity with the city and my drones! And my satellites!" Brennan yelled out with a crooked lock in his eye.

Tyburr's eyes narrowed after hearing Brennan's high tone and a touch of displeasure was heard in Tyburr's typical urbane tone.

"Major I am more than aware of your contribution to this mission and Orion owes you for it. You helped round up all those disconnected people very quickly, and you know your city better than anyone in the RAPDA agency. On the other hand, there is nothing for you to do here anymore Major—nothing at all.

Disconnected people are flocking into the transgenic clinics, and most of them will be upgraded by the weekend at least. Besides, there are only a handful of people left roaming the red districts now. We are expecting even more Ashtar guards coming in tomorrow and we are going to lock down every inch of these red districts. I have enough experience with Pandora to train my men with the satellite grid, as well as all the unmanned recon crafts. It shouldn't take long for them to get used to old American hardware...after all, we've been using the old Chinese system in Europe."

Brennan felt a hot flash run through him again. Even though Tyburr might have made sense, Brennan still thought it was strange to be released from a mission like this. He then began to wonder if it had something to do with the information he heard during John's interrogation. Perhaps he had heard too much, Brennan figured, despite the fact that John's testimony was dismissed as the height of all folly.

Brennan dropped his gaze to the ground and his posture drooped. He took a few steps away from Tyburr and paced a bit. He felt an urge to figure out what exactly was going on regarding Orion and their so-called divine intervention. All of the words John said during the interrogation acted like jet fuel for his curiosity. Brennan could no longer dismiss John's rejoinder as a plain figment of the imagination of a paranoid mind, and Brennan couldn't forget the look on John's eyes after he was injected with the upgrade. Brennan then began to think about all the people who refused to be upgraded, and for the first time, he didn't view them as being deranged for doing so.

The silence that ensued made the rain sound even louder as it pattered Tyburr's umbrella. Tyburr finalized the conversation by speaking through a sly smile.

"After you and your Lieutenant clear out your offices, both of you are to be quartered and fed at your hotel until your shuttle arrives. Then, a car will be appointed to you for delivery to the nearest spaceport."

"What about my paycheck?"

"You will be paid," Tyburr said. "The Overseer told me to inform you and your Lieutenant to check your email accounts. You should find a personal memo there. Perhaps you'll get your closure then."

*Why did I not hear my inbox alarm beep...*Brennan wondered.

Brennan lifted an index finger and pointed it upward to inform Tyburr that he needed a second to himself. Ironically, Brennan heard a chirp go off on his quantum capacitor right then and there, indicating that he had just gotten a new message. Brennan clicked his quantum capacitor on and activated his Eye-Net lenses.

How ironic! I get the message as soon as I'm informed!

The blinking red envelope flashing in the corner of his left contact lens indicated that there was one email in his inbox. Brennan shut his eyes so he could read the text better.

It read—

"Major Brennan, our keenness to finish this mission at once caused the Table of Twelve to call in all of our top military personnel from outer space. Including the Consul of our headquarters in Germany, Corporal Tyburr, who is capable of operating Pandora. Of course, your pay has been wired to your account in full, and now that your services with RAPDA are no longer needed, I'd like to wish you a pleasant return trip to space. It was a pleasure working with you.

Best,

RAPDA Overseer of New York, and Chief Overseer of planet Earth, Colonel Jasso.

Brennan was shocked to get the message and he immediately phoned Lieutenant Graham, tapping his Bluetooth device twice to place the automatic call.

"Hello," Graham answered in his usual cheer.

"Did you get the memo?" Brennan asked him. "Yeah! We're going home baby!" Graham's excitement was tangible through the phone.

Brennan tapped his earpiece twice and hung up on him in frustration.

Graham apparently didn't share the same resentment that Brennan did. He was just happy to be going home, but Brennan was not happy at all. Until now, all Brennan ever wanted in the past week was for the mission to be over with—but not anymore. There was something quaint about the way he was suddenly left out of the loop, and he was almost certain that he was in too deep in this investigation.

When Brennan turned around, he noticed Tyburr's tiny pig eyes crawling all over him.

"Oh and before you get going, I was ordered to have you turn in your RAPDA issue firearms now," Tyburr said in his most deeply flavored Draconian English.

"Right now, in the middle of this mess?" Brennan started reluctantly. "Shouldn't I do that when I get back to headquarters and clear out my office?"

Tyburr shook his head in two stiff motions and stuck out his hand, flat palm up.

"Overseer's orders," Tyburr grinned with conceit.

Brennan didn't like his tone and eyed him crookedly as he handed him his

disruptor-phaser and his .44 snub nose handgun. Tyburr's corporate smile pulled his mouth wider, displaying rows of yellowed teeth, and he then bowed to Brennan before speaking in a very sardonic voice.

"Well Major, if you will excuse me. I have lots of work to do. I do hope we get to work together sometime."

Brennan gave him a wary look and jabbed his finger at him.

"Now look!" Brennan began boldly. "Overseer's orders or not, I'm going to stick around until I figure out what's going on here. I think there are too many conversations taking place behind my back and I don't like it one bit."

Tyburr snickered under his breath as he turned to walk away, but before he took a step, Brennan grabbed him by the shoulder and scooted around to face him again.

"I'm currently the highest ranking officer remaining here on my planet Earth, and I answer to no one. As far as I know, we are still under martial law, and that means that I am the law! I have the rights to occupy or even seize any potential suspects for questioning. I have the right to seize any abandoned estates, along with the titles and deeds to the properties!"

Tyburr was taken aback by the fury in his tone and couldn't find any words. He just narrowed his small pig-like eyes, almost making them disappear inside his pudgy cheeks. Brennan could sense his resentment, and he didn't like it.

"I'm going to resume my duty as Major of the North American Union Army, the last high ranking officer of what remained of that army, and I'll continue to protect my country with or without your say-so!"

And with that, Brennan walked past Tyburr and deliberately brushed shoulders with him as he fixedly headed towards Charlie's house.

31: Reunion

As Brennan headed closer to the house, he still had trouble picking out faces through the large crowd. Even though the steady wash of rain diminished with each step, a gust of wind would blow every few seconds, sending dead leaves into Brennan's face as he wove his way through the swallowing crowd. He could hear the shouting coming from inside the house, mostly mixed voices of police officers boasting loudly about their recent arrest. Brennan could hear the cultured voices of Draconian Ashtar sentries who disputed their claims in a heated manner, telling the local cops that their technology made the arrest possible.

Bomb sniffing dogs were barking and horses were neighing; the rain made it hard to hear anybody within an earshot. Once Brennan got to the porch, he peered into the house through the gaps of bodies guarding the door-less entry. It was then when he finally caught a glimpse of Elena, and his heart skipped a beat or two after noticing her.

I'm tired. I'm seeing things

Brennan exhaled a shameful chuckle and dismissed it as an illusion of an overworked mind. However, Brennan was distracted by his presumption, and he decided to walk closer to the house. He became insensible to all the uproar around him. An exclamation of horror formed on his face as he contemplated whether he was seeing things or not. He squinted so he could see through the crowd, but there were too many bodies. A bluster of rainwater lashed at his face, making it harder to see, and so he continuously wiped away the rivulets of water that streamed down from his balding head and into his eyes. The guards in front of the front door were all seven footers and superbly muscled, and they made it difficult for Brennan to see.

That girl inside...looks just like my daughter...

Brennan bobbed and weaved his way around a pair of paramedics who were hauling a body down the front stoop with their stretcher. Brennan jostled his way up the last of the wooden stairs and snaked around several police officers before getting to the doorway. Brennan fixed his eyes towards the area in the house where the girl he presumed to be his daughter was last seen. After locking eyes with her again, he made no mistake in confirming that it was indeed his daughter in there or someone who looked exactly like her.

Elena?

He almost went into a state of shock, and at first, he thought the rain played tricks with his eyes, but there she was, sitting on a chair in the dining room, having her blood pressure taken by a medic.

I always knew she would return and take to activism. But...not like this...

Brennan told himself.

A new energy rose in him after seeing her, and not only because he made a most unexpected revelation but because he saw Colonel Jasso inside there as well, who was seen limping inside house. Jasso held an ice pack to his head and several strands of his silver hair stuck out from bandages that were wrapped around his head. All of the questions Brennan had piled up in his mind meant nothing. He could ask him later, Brennan thought.

Brennan wasted no time heading for his daughter, and he was in such a state of shock that he walked with slow, dreamy steps. Jasso took notice of Brennan and immediately cut him off in the living room before he had the chance to approach his daughter.

"You Earth people are always full of surprises! Did you know that your daughter was friends with our beloved pariah! Your daughter just told me to summon you! I almost had a heart attack after she told me she was your daughter!"

Brennan tuned Jasso out. He couldn't hear anything because he was in shock. All he did was take slow, dazed steps towards the couch where Elena sat and conversed with a medic, completely unaware of her dad's presence. There were so many people wriggling in and out of the house that they only made Brennan more obscure in the thick of it all. Jasso flung questions at him, but Brennan didn't have time for his nonsense.

"Did you know she was here when you scanned the place?" Jasso began briskly, pointing over to Charlie, who was sprawled on the couch in a semi- conscious state. He was bombarded by a higher frequency than Elena had and he was still out of it, almost unaware of the medics who plugged an IV into his arm.

"Well...was she connected or no?" Jasso then asked.

"Connected yes, but no name, no I.D.," Brennan said dreamily, never once taking his eyes off his daughter as he hopped over the bloodied bodies of several unconscious police officers on the floor.

Jasso punched his palm in frustration. "Yeah I should have known," Jasso grunted. "Pandora doesn't record the personal data of space faring tourists, only their titles and job positions...just for the sake of hard-drive space. Anyways, we have to take her in you know; she's going to have to face a judge—"

"Not now Colonel," Brennan interrupted.

Jasso stalled after noticing Brennan walk away from him and head straight for his daughter, who was cuffed to a chair. After noticing him, Elena sprang up to her feet so quickly that she took her chair with her because her left wrist was handcuffed to it. She wasn't as shocked as Brennan was because she expected to see him. Jasso told her that he would call him for her, but oddly enough, he never did.

"Dad!" she cried out towards Brennan who immediately hugged her. "Un-cuff her," Brennan growled over to any nearby police officers that would hear him. One freckled female police officer nearby heard it and looked at Jasso for the order, and Jasso regrettably nodded his head once.

"Keep her chained, but not to the chair," Jasso said, rolling his eyes.

The freckled police officer un-cuffed her from the chair and then cuffed her in a traditional manner—with both wrists at the small of her back.

Brennan and Elena were speechless for almost a minute; and only Brennan hugged her because she was cuffed. For the first time, all that built up negativity towards her dad was just gone instantly, and she felt safe. Brennan pushed aside his desire for inquiry and was simply glad to see her unharmed for the most part, except for a few abrasions on her cheeks and limbs from the thorn bush she got caught in when she tried escaping the police van. He hugged her and kissed her repeatedly on the forehead. She looked paler to him, much paler than usual, every line of her face was stamped with fear and her hair was an uncontrived tumble of wavy blonde locks.

"I knew you would sneak back down here someday, as soon as an opportunity presented itself."

Elena exhaled an un-lively chuckle and stared up at her dad with her doe-like eyes, which blinked slowly.

"Are you okay? Are you hurt?" Brennan asked while cupping his hand under her jaw, turning her face so he could examine it. Elena just shook her head; she managed to stare at her dad in quick glances, hastily dropping her eyes all the time from the guilt that hit her.

"Just a few scrapes here and there, but I'm fine."

"Oh honey, I know that you always sought to come back here, but I must ask..." Brennan paused before glancing over at Charlie's semi-conscious body and smiling mirthlessly from disbelief. "What...what led you to befriend this man?"

"He's not what you think," Elena replied meekly. "Was it those speeches of his that enamored you?" "Did you even hear the speeches?" Elena asked.

Brennan didn't care to answer but did so in an impassive way.

"Yes, some of it," Brennan began inquisitively, "but regardless of his speech, he did attack innocent police officers who were just following the Overseer's orders. This will not sit well with a judge."

"You should hear his entire speech," Elena insisted.

Brennan was becoming curious after realizing that his daughter put a lot of stock in the man. Charlie must have said the same things Lancaster said back at the precinct, and Brennan no longer thought them to be rage-induced potshots from another poverty-stricken have-not who was mad at the world instead of being mad at himself. Brennan had an idea of what fueled Charlie's anger—they were the very same things that fueled his friend John's anger—and now fueling Brennan's anger for that matter.

Brennan looked at Charlie over on the sofa as he was being tended to by a paramedic. Charlie was moving more and more after each minute that passed, but the microwave bombardment suppressed so much of his adrenaline that his adrenal glands couldn't muster up enough of it to make him walk.

Brennan exhaled a sigh. "I don't know how you managed to get caught up with this guy honey, but after they book you, prepare to see a judge. Not even I can help prevent that. Luckily your census records indicate that your stay here on Earth wasn't extensive, and you obviously just met the man."

Elena's eyes lit up, and she almost wanted to cry.

"Don't worry though," Brennan said in a consoling voice, "you couldn't possibly be linked to the building of the weapons. However, they're going to ask you if you agree with any of Charlie's malicious doctrine and his so-called heretical ideals."

"Dad, he's no heretic," Elena shot back. "This isn't 1450 A.D.!" Brennan's lips pressed white. "Elena, don't you see what's going on here?

This isn't Earth anymore, this is not our planet anymore. And after this is over and done with, you're going to come back to the ship and get away from this hell," Brennan insisted.

"I'm not going back to the ship," Elena said firmly. "I originally snuck down here on the space elevator car so I could avoid a trail and avoid being registered on the census registry—just so I could give myself time to establish myself here without you butting into my life and controlling it all the time! I have a new job and a new apartment here. I'm also getting a car on Monday. Oh Dad, I hate the ship, and I'm never going back, and for the first time in my life, I won't listen to anything you have to say about the matter!"

"That's a discussion for another time," Brennan sighed deeply. "All I know is that I want you away from this man because the Overseer doesn't like him too much. And from I've seen so far, you don't want these Draconians on your bad side!" Brennan quivered a bit when he spoke, because his blood boiled.

"Charlie is not a threat!" Elena snapped. "And according to him, you Dad— you are the threat!" she shouted.

Brennan's eyes widened, and he never expected to hear such a radical thing come out of his daughter's mouth. His daughter's outlandish claim only seemed to fuel his curious inquiries towards the Overseer's agenda.

"He said that?" Brennan said in a cracked voice. Elena nodded slowly.

All sorts of negative fancies began piling up at the forefront of Brennan's mind, and he then began to wonder if he was even more of a thorn in Jasso's side now that his daughter was involved with his enemies.

Suddenly, Jasso came limping through the muddled heap of a living room, and he had the sleaziest look on his lacerated face. Brennan had no idea that he was listening to their conversation the entire time, picking the perfect time to interrupt them.

"Umm...Major..." Jasso started critically, fighting the blaze of pain in his cheek that became worse when speaking. "I know there is a lot on your mind, so I'll be as succinct as possible. We must take your daughter and her boyfriend—"

"He's not her boyfriend," Brennan snapped.

Jasso smirked and nodded slowly. "Her friend then," he corrected himself with a most sardonic tone. "Elena and Charlie must be taken to the precinct now, just for some questioning."

"And then what?" Brennan asked rather nervously.

"She might have to stay behind bars for a few days at best, just until we get things sorted out and get her a lawyer. She just needs to be questioned further, and we must make sure that she had nothing to do with the weapons found here; and of course, we need to know what she thinks of the terrorist's intentions towards us," Jasso said sleazily, and the bleakness of his tenor spoke volumes.

Brennan swallowed a lump. "Very well Colonel. I'll meet you at the precinct. But before I go, I'd like to know why you decided to terminate my employment..."

"We'll discuss it later," Jasso said boldly. And without further word, Jasso nodded and began to walk away.

Brennan felt his pulse race. He surely didn't like the idea of his daughter being locked up, especially after remembering what happened to John Lancaster's eyes right after they upgraded him. Brennan only hoped Elena would claim ignorance to it all so they could let her go, and before Brennan could say another word to his daughter, a brawny cop with crooked teeth and a spotty face grasped Elena's arm and escorted her away from him.

"Take her boyfriend too," Jasso ordered the cop with crooked teeth.

The policeman looked puzzled. "The male can't walk and is not cleared for transport yet," the cop said mechanically.

"I don't care! Cuff him to the stretcher and deliver him to the cell that way," Jasso said under a fiery gaze.

The cop with crooked teeth informed a nearby medic of the impending transfer, and then forcibly escorted Elena towards the front door as the medic prepped Charlie for the gurney. Elena gazed at Brennan over her shoulder with glassy eyes.

"Easy with her officer!" Brennan barked at the cop, but the cop didn't pay him any mind as he tugged Elena along roughly out of the house.

Brennan followed and watched her intently from the doorway. Outside, lighting cracked and the rain picked up as it pounded the awning that was perched above the front door. Brennan stood shuddering with his hands half- clenched as he began making his way out of the house; the rain ran down his thin hair and cheeks, and it almost steamed off his hot, flushed face.

Brennan scrutinized the cop and his daughter as they made their way through the coffle of police officers and paramedics alike, and eventually across the street and towards a police car. He and Elena stared at each other the entire time as she was escorted to the squad car. He never took his eyes off her, even after the car door was closed. And when the car drove away, Brennan cringed after seeing his daughter's frightened face stare back at him through the car's back window.

Shortly afterwards, Jasso hobbled past him on the porch with a cane. A police officer held an umbrella over his head so his bandages wouldn't get wet. Brennan's eyes crawled all over Jasso, careful not to lose him in the crowd, and Jasso felt eyes upon his back so he turned around and gaped at him in a forbidden manner. Brennan never stopped staring at him, and Jasso never stopped glaring back—not until he walked up to his new right hand man, Corporal Tyburr.

He and Tyburr then became engaged in what seemed to be a lengthy and surreptitious conversation, and Brennan noticed that their mouths were close in proximity to their ears. Even though they were not facing Brennan directly, Brennan knew they were talking about him. Both of them had their eyes rolled to the side, eyeing Brennan down as they whispered to each other.

*This doesn't look good...*Brennan thought. He didn't have to hear what they were saying to form such a cynical conjecture.

32: Clarkson's Arrival

Back at the precinct, Brennan was surprised to receive an email from Jasso after everything that transpired. The email was written in large letters and it read

—*Head to the briefing room here at HQ, we're having a meeting in an hour with the General himself, and he specifically asked for you to attend*

-Colonel Jasso, Chief Overseer of planet Earth

Brennan pumped a fist. "Now I can finally speak to him about Jasso!"

He would have jumped for joy after hearing the news, but his daughter's arrest still dampened his spirits. Brennan reassured Elena as much as he could to help her stop crying, but the minute she landed in her holding cell, all of her resolve had dripped away with her tears.

Before leaving, he made sure to call Lieutenant Graham in order to ask him if he could keep an eye on Elena, and Graham happily obliged even though he was a bit miffed that he wasn't invited to the meeting himself. Brennan was happy it turned out that way; having Graham at the precinct helped alleviate some of the anxiety in his body so he calmed down a bit.

Brennan had some time to spare before the meeting and figured he would use it to listen to Charlie's speech from the rally the other day. He listened to bits and pieces of it all morning long, and the more he listened to the speech the more Brennan began to feel as if Charlie's wild claims held water. One thing that really irked Brennan was the fact that he couldn't interrogate Charlie Beasley, and no one was allowed anywhere near him because he was still unfit for questioning.

However, Brennan didn't buy it. He had also learned that John Lancaster was nowhere to be found at the police precinct either. Earlier in the day, Brennan spoke to a police captain and inquired about him, but the police captain said that he was transferred out to a courthouse for his hearing.

When Brennan arrived at RAPDA headquarters, he was surprised to see the parking garage absolutely jam packed with black RAPDA-issue vehicles. Every single RAPDA agent from the European branches in England and Germany had arrived to help with the crisis occurring in New York.

When Brennan finally managed to get to the briefing room, he hoped to see General Clarkson already there, but he had not arrived yet. It was Jasso himself who sat at the head of the table, with Baal ensconced to his right. Both were drinking iced coffee in long swigs, and after staring at their concrete slabs for faces, Brennan knew they were not happy to see him at the meeting. Brennan made little eye contact with both of them and headed straight to the back of the room only to find another unwelcome face.

Colonel Tyburr was waddling around the water cooler, and he was gorging on several muffins near the coffee cart. Brennan matched the crooked look he gave him as he helped himself to a coffee. There was a bottle of Frangelico coffee-liqueur next to the hazelnut milk, and Brennan put more than the standard amount in his coffee in hopes of stilting his nerves.

"Should I stay?" Tyburr shouted across the room. Jasso shook his head with closed eyes.

"No, you are needed in Pandora's room," Jasso announced in his usually calm, low, but commanding urbane voice. "Go and finish training our European agents."

"Yes sir," Tyburr said, lifting his sausage-like digits ahead of his chest for the Draconian salute. Before leaving, he gave Brennan another crooked stare, and Brennan matched it. Tyburr smirked, turned on his heels, and dragged his thick, ungainly limbs out of the room.

What's he smirking about? Brennan asked himself. He didn't like it one bit.

Jasso and Baal never once stared at Brennan as he served himself near the coffee cart. They both stared straight ahead, drumming their fingers on the long oak table, rattling the ice cubes in their iced coffee glasses, undoubtedly annoyed by both Brennan and Clarkson's arrival. Jasso seemed more impatient then Baal. He twiddled his fingers, he squirmed frequently in his seat and his cigar remained unlit in his mouth as he gnawed at it.

After pouring his coffee, Brennan inspected the coffee cart and noticed a dozen powdered donuts lined up on a tray, as well as some banana nut muffins. Before leaving the coffee cart, Brennan thought he should find out just how much Baal and Jasso detested him—so he put two extra muffins on his plate and then offered the two men a muffin before sitting down.

"Banana nut or corn?" Brennan asked as he placed the paper plate on the table. Baal shook his head and pushed away the plate. Jasso never even acknowledged the muffins to begin with.

Sensing their aggravation, Brennan chose to sit as far from Baal and Jasso as possible, near the middle of the table. Brennan and Baal regularly exchanged glances as they waited, and seemed to speak to each other in silence. This exacerbated Brennan's already frayed nerves, and Brennan quickly turned away from Baal after noticing the flash of hunger in those sly eyes of his. However, they would only get worse because Clarkson then strode into the room, and his presence seemed to make Baal's eyes grow darker.

Clarkson entered with a most vigorous trot, and his walk had nobleness to it.

He walked with sauntered steps, and never before had Brennan seen someone walk with such gallant strides. His military uniform was the same one Jasso and Brennan wore except that Brennan didn't have a cape. Clarkson's suit was a typical scarlet colored Orion Corp. military suit but much more garmented. It was also double breasted, and Clarkson wore a vest underneath it. The short cape that hung from his shoulders was much longer than Jasso's cape, and it drooped to the middle of the back. The only other distinction from Jasso's uniform was the long skirted coat, the scarlet-colored kepis, a silk sash, and a fringed epaulette. Clarkson also had a plethora of medals and ribbons on his lapel, and his beautifully wrought jewelry really made him seem like a daunting man. He sat down without saying a word and he only acknowledged Baal and Jasso with a short nod of the head.

Brennan looked up at Clarkson with interest, and it has been many years since Brennan saw General Clarkson face to face. Of course, he had aged considerably in the past ten years, given the short Draconian physical life, but

Brennan recognized the same old lively looking blue eyes of his. Clarkson's hair was always long, but it had grown even longer with age— and whiter too. It hung like a mane, lessening near his hunched, broad shoulders in idle ringlets.

His facial features were pure Draconian. His Olympian brow shadowed his deep-set eyes, and he had the broadest of cheekbones, indented cheeks and a V- shaped jaw. He was clean-shaven, like most Draconians, and he had what

seemed to be a thousand freckles dappled on his face, sprayed on and around his aquiline nose and thin tinny lips.

Despite the length of the table, Clarkson sat down at the far head of it, just about sixty feet away and opposite of Colonel Jasso. Clarkson tugged the swathe of his cape before sitting down and wasted no time with small talk.

"I'd love to catch up with you all, but I rather get down to business right this very minute," he began in his debonair voice, and he sounded bothered. "We have much to discuss," he resentfully finished.

Jasso was ready to answer and spoke quickly. "General, I share your exasperation, since you had to set aside your primary duties to meddle with the situation here on Earth, but I can assure you that everything is going as planned."

"That's nonsense Colonel," Clarkson began gruffly, "I decided to make the trip from the Alpha Draconis system after reading the local tabloids here on the galactic web. I wish to speak of certain matters regarding the mutants and the fringe events taking place here. Not to mention the confiscation of several weapons of mass destruction that I was not made aware of until ten minutes ago!"

Jasso replied with strained civility. "Like I said General, most of the mutants have been detained, and I didn't think there was reason to let you know. The sorcerer who attacked our military personnel has been arrested. We upgraded him and he is ready to face his trial. Also, the inventor who invented the W.M.D.'s was also arrested."

Clarkson stared at Jasso with wide eyes, before cocking his large, round, blue eyes to the ceiling in frustration. "I'm concerned about the fact that you never got in touch with me and—"

"But General..." Jasso interrupted.

"And don't tell me anything about the ionic interference with you interstellar communications,' Clarkson snarled, speaking over Jasso. "You mean to say that you couldn't put one of your agents on an EMP-proof shuttle and send it over to the Niagra, which has been in orbit for almost five days now?"

Jasso sighed deeply. "If I knew that you held a great interest in this campaign, I would have gone to great lengths to attempt to contact you. I just thought you had more important things on your plate,' Jasso said in an obsequious manner.

"Of course I'm concerned Colonel! I almost lost an entire platoon of my soldiers. Half of them were attacked in a malicious manner, and they will never see with their own eyes ever again. And I, the General and leader of these men, never heard a thing about it until this morning. If I didn't browse the Earth internet this morning, then I would have never found out!" Clarkson wailed.

"I apologize for not confiding with you earlier, but I sustained an injury this morning—"

"Enough with the excuses Colonel!" Clarkson snapped "Your incompetence has been an issue from the start and it is becoming expected of you."

Jasso and Baal turned to each other and shrugged their shoulders. Baal rattled the ice in his mug and stared into it, remaining speechless.

Clarkson then pulled out a shiny transparent crystal tablet, and a ticker scrolled across the screen. "Our corporation stock is down a whole lot as you can see here, and our stock depends on the stabilization of this civilization here on Earth," Clarkson said to Jasso directly, before turning to Doctor Baal on his right, and then staring at him with hard eyes. "And to you Doctor Baal, I hope you know that the table of twelve did not take it lightly after learning that your seat was empty during our latest meeting in regards to our status as a corporation."

Baal gave out an ignobly smile. "I am deeply sorry I could not attend that meeting," Baal replied with unnatural civility. Brennan couldn't believe how phony he sounded; it was as if Baal was mocking the General. Baal continued with his vilest tone yet. "You military people have no idea how hard I've been working to fix this situation! I had to make sure my neuroscientists produced enough nanobots for the upgrade campaign and time has been rather short for me," Baal sniggered, and a smile of amusement then softened his rugged features.

Clarkson did not share the merriment of his men, and his eyes grew colder. "Let's get to the meat and forget the potatoes for a minute," Clarkson then replied with grand harshness. "It appears that one of our most precious of planets, planet Earth, was recently downgraded, and is officially now a class D planet."

"Class D? I had no idea!" Jasso was quick to reply.

Baal didn't seem to look surprised at all, instead, he showed less concern then Jasso did.

"That's right Colonel, this planet is now a class D planet, and our stock in the galactic market of celestial bodies dropped twenty percent overnight and here's why: beside the increasing civil unrest and rumors of the mental and physical degradation of the Earth masses, there is also a decline in harvested minerals."

"We have a lack of workers," Baal chimed in quickly, "it's going to take more than ten years to get the population back up!"

Clarkson put up a palm and waved him off. "No, that's not it—that's not it at all, in fact. Strangely enough, the only thing coming out of this planet is crude oil and natural gas. Too much of it in fact."

"We mine Iridium here too," Jasso said.

Clarkson put two palms on the table and lurched over it, speaking in his angriest voice thus far. "Yes, but not as much as we should be harvesting," he growled. "Iridium was our highest priority on this planet, and without it, we could never produce anti-protons! Yet, you waste our resources on your hydrofracking, which does nothing but contaminate water sources even further! And not to mention all that oil you drill for! I mean, I see the numbers Colonel! I see them! Most of the workers are too busy drilling for fossil fuels and natural gas. Do you know what carbon emissions are doing to Earth's atmosphere? You continue to melt ice in the artic with HAARP generated x-rays just so you can find un-tapped reservoirs, and that only leads to more global heating because there is no ice to reflect solar heat away from the oceans! And as for natural gas, well, sure natural gas is clean, but the method for acquiring it is too high risk, and this planet cannot afford to be polluted any further!" Clarkson paused to take a breath and he sank back in his chair. "Oh, and mining aside, the planet itself is in shambles. Besides the rising crime rates, Earth's space programs remain in an abortive state and they have been that way since the natural disasters killed off eighty percent of the population. There is more space junk in orbit than most postindustrial planets have, and four out of the six remaining colonies on Earth are hardly even powered with electricity. I mean—this is just strange! Nothing is being invented that would help get the planet spinning again!"

Brennan squirmed in his seat as he listened to the aliens discuss their business. He badly wanted to get things off his chest, but he figured he'd wait for Clarkson to stop talking first.

"This planet contains a civilization that is no different than what you would find on any other primitive pre-industrial class E planet. And by the looks of it, Earth isn't too far from becoming a class E planet either!"

Jasso rose from his seat. "General, please realize that even though Earth is no longer a class C planet, the loss in Earth stock is short term. Once we get everyone healthy again, the population will begin to rise, and hopefully more people will increase our production and mineral output."

Clarkson laughed so hard he began to cough. "Since when did you become the analyst?" he cackled.

Baal then unexpectedly rose from his chair and spoke brightly. "I believe the successful and consistent mining going on worldwide would ensure long term profit, and here is why: additional Iridium grottoes have been found all over the planet, and the only reason why we're focusing on crude oil is because we need to find a safe and sure way to move our automobiles, planes, and ships so we can rebuild this planet again. I have formed extensive tunneling operations out here in the American west and far out in the East, all the way down to Europe, to Asia, and down to Australia. I have discussed the singularity of the local geological formations with several former Earth geologists currently employed at our lunar colony, and they now counsel with me. They reviewed and taught me the extent and potential output of the Iridium grottoes, and I estimate the future of our mining enterprise will be titanic!"

"So exactly how much time do you need to get this planet spinning again?" Clarkson scorned.

"We just need more time—that's all. We need more time," Jasso said, hoping his demand would be enough to satisfy Clarkson but it was not.

"I'm sorry to say Colonel, but you had ten years and things are getting worse, not better. I think that this planet is being run irresponsibly and to be quite frank, I am beginning to think that I lost you to that bottle of whiskey!" Clarkson shouted, his cheeks flushed and his brow permanently puckered.

Jasso's face drooped from dejection; he sighed deeply and sat back in his seat. From that moment on, Jasso only spoke in answer, and rarely lifted his gaze from his commanding officer who continued to growl at them in frustration.

"So little has changed in ten years! Radioactive pollution is higher than it was a decade ago; Earth's oceans are the most acidic of all habitable planets, dipping under the eight-point-zero mark on the PH scale. The soil is irradiated, and not one significant piece of technology has been invented in the last ten years since our arrival other than fancy electronic phones and toys. Tell me, Mr. Overseer, how much time does it take to train some able-minded workers in the factories in hopes of rebuilding a few electrical transformers? I can't believe that in ten years, the major cities of Earth are still operating without electricity for sixty percent of the year!"

Jasso didn't reply, he just glared into his coffee mug and rattled the ice cubes. Baal did not answer either, and his expression was nothing like it should have been. While Jasso showed a defeated look, Baal showed the opposite. In fact, he seemed to have a smirk on his face.

Baal put both elbows on the table, and then pointed to Clarkson before speaking. "General, you are not a man of science, and I'm afraid it will be impossible to explain to you how complex this mission is," Baal said bluntly.

Brennan watched Clarkson's face shift into stone from the pent up anger he held inside him. "Doctor, may I be frank with you?" Clarkson asked sourly.

"Please do," Baal answered amiably.

"Doctor, most of us on the Table of Twelve all know that you always had a reputation for blunt speech, and you are notorious for being a bitter man with a great a sense of your own worth. However, you seem to be unaware that you are outmatched here."

"Outmatched?" Baal replied contemptuously.

"Yes, outmatched!" Clarkson snapped. "You doctor—are unbloodied. You are book-smart but inexperienced. And did you forget about my experience in leading the terra-forming missions after the great Sirus B wars? I worked with plenty of terra-formers and scientists before, and I know enough to realize that ten years is more than enough time to get a planet back to habitable conditions!"

Baal raised an eyebrow, and even though he knew Clarkson spoke the truth, he showed a body language that spoke digression. Baal did not reply with words but only showed an underhanded grin that further disturbed the General. Neither Baal nor Jasso cared to reply to such criticism; they simply sat in their leather chairs, divided by the big table and a sea of personal differences.

After receiving no retort from either Jasso or Baal, Clarkson wrathfully broke the silence.

"You have all become bloated, lazy, and swollen of mind and ego!" Clarkson began fiercely. "And I don't know if you realize it or not Colonel, but several of us on the Table of Twelve are thinking about replacing you with someone that will do a better job at protecting our investment that is Earth!"

Jasso did not reply, and Brennan noticed that he kept giving Baal a few side- glances every now and then as if he relied on him to save him from his fall from glory. However, Baal seemed more interested in wiping away the lint off his jacket and tie.

Another heart-freezing silence came over the room, and Brennan once again began to wonder why he was invited to the meeting in the first place.

Am I to be the Overseer's replacement? Brennan asked himself.

Brennan thought this was the best time to speak his mind and so he slowly got up from his chair and then cleared his throat.

"General, I'd like to offer some input if I may," Brennan said.

"Of course Major!" Clarkson was eager to say. "It's why I invited you to the meeting in the first place. I wanted to know—what have you learned about the mutants?"

"I have much to say, but first; in regards to the weapons confiscated during the raid this morning...well...they weren't all weapons," Brennan said.

Jasso immediately sprung up from his seat to object, but Clarkson put up a flat palm.

"Let him finish," Clarkson said in a voice that rang with authority.

Brennan felt a weight come off his shoulders after realizing that Clarkson backed him up.

"The men that created them initially sought to build generators based on electromagnetism and bio-fuel. They started to construct them after their requests to rebuild the city's electrical transformers went unreciprocated by the Overseer."

Clarkson's face turned to stone as he stared down Jasso.

"And why was that request to help build the transformers unrequited?" Clarkson asked.

"It was two men, only two men," Jasso snapped nauseatingly. "What could two electronic engineers do? Rebuilding electrical transformer stations were always arduous tasks—even before the catastrophes and before the population became squeezed of scientists and engineers..."

"With all due to respect Colonel, that's because Orion took most of the scientists and engineers that survived in the first place," Brennan said. Brennan felt a lump form in his throat after seeing Jasso's lips quiver in anger.

"Oh and you suppose that it's my fault that no one on this planet has managed to obtain a doctorate in the last ten years?" Jasso disputed hotly.

Clarkson sat back in his chair after hearing that and rubbed his hand through his silver mane. He had no words to say for the first time. Baal continued to smirk as he checked and smoothed his fingernails, seemingly uninterested at what he believed to be wasted banter.

Brennan jutted his chin and broke the silence. "Colonel, those two men proved they could do a whole lot. Before the catastrophes, free energy was on the rise, yet there is nothing on the internet that gives people an opportunity to learn the ins and outs of magnetic engineering, solar harnessing, geothermal energy, biofuel production, wind farming, and so forth. And so, I beg—please, reopen the universities and revise the curriculums in accordance with the fundamentals of Charlie Beasley's pioneering work. It will teach people how to live off free, sustainable energy, and you won't even have to bring in any extraterrestrial resources to help educate the masses because Charlie's work could be reverse engineered."

"Fair point," Clarkson agreed.

There was a silence in the room after Clarkson endorsed Brennan's claim. All Jasso managed to do was exchange glances with Baal and light his cigar.

Baal had a sly look to him, as if the whole conversation meant nothing to him, and he already knew the outcome of the debate.

Brennan then gritted his teeth and decided to unleash what was heavy on his mind.

"Oh and one more thing," Brennan said tentatively, pausing a bit after he felt his throat tighten with fear. "There might be another reason why no one graduated with a doctorate in the past decade. And why there haven't been any scientific breakthroughs in a long time. I heard one of Charlie's speeches on the internet and learned a few things..." Brennan trailed off a bit after realizing how

crazy his next words might sound to uninformed ears. "Charlie Beasley spoke about the nanobots and...their true purpose."

"True purpose?" Dr. Clarkson said, regarding Doctor Baal suspiciously.

Brennan nodded vigorously. "Well, according to Mr. Beasley, the upgrades given to the masses have a deeper purpose. Perhaps, it's more like a side effect." Brennan stalled his speech after witnessing the steely gaze from Doctor Baal.

Jasso unconsciously rammed his lit cigar into an ashtray, until the last fiery bit of tobacco had died out. The air seemed to thicken around them all as they waited for Brennan's words to seep out of his tightened throat.

"Charlie Beasley said that you were supposed to bioengineer people to withstand radiation levels in order to prevent mutation, but you furthered the purpose of the nanobots and used them to control the synapses and cognitive ability of the human brain instead. According to Charlie Beasley, you did all this in order to manipulate the allegiances and emotions of man, and most of all, you did it to put an end to the new industrial age that was beginning to bloom just over fifteen years ago!"

"This is blasphemy!" Baal growled. Jasso forced a chuckle.

Clarkson lurched forward in his chair. "Now what would make him say such a thing?" Clarkson added. He too was in disbelief.

Baal once again sprang up from his seat and pumped an index finger towards the ceiling as he shouted. "I absolutely repudiate Beasley's theory, and his accusation is a prudent measure to entice anarchy amongst the masses! This is a prime example of how deluded Beasley is and how his radiation sickness has consumed his thought processes!"

Brennan noticed several physiological reactions on Baal's face that suggested he might be lying, and there was a change in the stress levels of Baal's voice. Brennan wanted to get closer to see if there were any telltale contractions in his pupils, but he couldn't tell from where he sat. Brennan did know one thing however: that Baal looked as anxious as ever and even Jasso's expressions changed. It seemed as if Jasso's poise had completely evaporated.

All sorts of questions played over in Brennan's head. Did he know? Was he covering it up? Was he to blame? Or perhaps it was all a failed science experiment with unknown side effects?

Brennan pondered all those things, and if Baal knew, he surely did a great job at acting insulted and waxing over accusations that he knew to be true.

"This is absurd, I won't bother talking about this; that Mr. Beasley is a paranoid mess," Baal snickered.

After hearing such a bold claim for the first time, Clarkson then had difficulties suppressing his battle ready attitude and decided to make his presence felt.

"I'm sorry Doctor, but the Major didn't exactly accuse anyone here of anything did he?" Clarkson asked in a tone that suggested he was demanding the Doctor to argue with him.

Baal just looked at him with eyes wide, but didn't reply right away— in fact, he seemed to be groping for words.

"These accusations are absurd!" Baal flared, slamming a hand on the wooden table. "My nanobots are the same as those given to all Orion personnel that are scattered throughout the galaxy. Even the ones that are in me and you!"

Clarkson and Brennan wrestled with that fact for a moment, and the room went silent. Brennan smelled lies for a living, and knew very well what lies smelled like after interrogating so many prisoners of war in his lifetime. He could sniff out defiance and fear like a dog picks up stress from a human, and it wasn't long until he realized how lame Baal's last defensive remark really was.

"We should at least test them to make sure they are the same," Brennan began fiercely. "I think we should initiate a full investigation to find out if your nano medicine has unwanted side effects!"

"You mean to tell me that you really believe that madman's theories are enough to warrant an investigation?" Baal laughed, and then put his feet up on the table. "Tell me Major, does this Charlie Beasley fellow have any evidence to back his claims?"

"No, he doesn't seem to have evidence but—"

"End of discussion!" Jasso interrupted.

Brennan overrode his voice. "But he has plenty of indirect evidence," Brennan answered keenly. "Perhaps after you learn of my discoveries, you will no longer scoff at Charlie Beasley's theory or mock my endeavor to investigate the nanobot shipments as well as all of your labs "

"So what is this indirect evidence you speak of?" Baal asked with high interest. A thin sheen of sweat covered Doctor Baal's brow, and Colonel Jasso formed a wanly smile as he waited to hear what Brennan knew.

"Please edify me!" Clarkson chimed in enthusiastically.

Brennan spoke with swift words. "I point to the murders that took place last week. Isn't it strange that crime was non-existent for ten years? There hasn't been one single murder on the entire planet in over a decade. Not one single act of theft, or an act of assault, and not even a case of road rage reported. Ever since the Earth survivors were implanted with your nanobot medicine, crime ceased all together. Also, let's put aside the crime stats for a moment and focus on another piece of indirect evidence, which involves the mutants themselves, especially the ones with powers. It seems as if most of these mutants began to develop these superpowers after their implants disconnected!"

Baal and Jasso attempted to discredit the claim by displaying their amusement.

"This is incongruous talk!" Baal chortled mirthlessly. "The damn crime went down because we gave everyone jobs and good health! And so everyone was happy until people started mutating into rabid animals!"

"Relax, Doctor!" Clarkson barked at him before turning to Brennan and nodding at him with an outstretched arm. "Continue Major."

Brennan took a deep breath. "Gentlemen, look," Brennan began tenderly. "I'm simply looking at all this from a third party perspective; like I said—I'm not accusing you of knowing this beforehand General, why do you shout as if I'm accusing you of something?"

"Because a man of your caliber considering Charlie's outlandish conspiracy theories should not be considering a raving lunatic's theories; that's why I'm shouting!" Baal shouted.

Brennan paced the room and thought about what to say next. He studied both Baal and Jasso's expressions and he was sure they were nervous. Jasso ruffled the few tufts of silver hair that poked out of his bandaged head. Baal continued to sit, red-faced, never deviating his gaze away from Brennan.

Brennan then scratched his head, and cleared his throat before speaking inquisitively. "Now, I wanted to bring up a fact—something to think about," Brennan began as he paced around the long table. "I was informed a while back that the nanobots given to the Earth humans were catered to them and them only. I believe that they were programmed to reduce the people's sex drives in order to prevent people with Chernobyl AIDS from spreading the disease."

Baal's tone changed into a concise one, speaking quickly and innocently. "Yes, Chernobyl AIDS was something that occurred back in Russia during the notorious meltdown in the mid-1980s. Many people with radiation sickness had gotten AIDS from the radiation poisoning, which damaged their lymphatic systems, henceforth, giving them a disease similar to AIDS and making them prone to opportunistic retroviruses."

Clarkson cocked his head to the side, furrowing his brow. "Therefore, there is a bit of hormone control involved here," he said with a brisk nod.

"Hormone control is a huge step away from mind control General," Baal countered. "The simplest of drugs can control hormones, but controlling a person's mind..." he paused for a more dramatic effect. "...outlandish!"

Clarkson didn't bother with any rejoinder of his own anymore and acted as if he had made his decision already. Clarkson rose from his chair, tugged the wrinkles out of his blazer and walked over to one of the large glass panes that bordered the entire room. He stared out towards the cityscape so he could think better, and when his worried face caught the sunlight, Brennan knew he had gotten Clarkson's attention. After several seconds, Clarkson turned from the window, faced the men on the table and spoke with his most authoritative tone yet. "I've decided that we will pay civilians to volunteer for a brain study in order to find out if the nanobots stimulate, alter, or interfere with the brain's deeper electrochemical functions."

"You can't be serious?" Jasso snorted as he stopped his coffee mug halfway to his mouth.

Baal chuckled. "General, look—"

"It's a Goddamn order!" Clarkson snapped back.

Baal and Jasso looked defeated. Their gazes hit the ground, and Jasso subtly shook his head.

"Now Doctor, I don't expect your neuroscientists to have intentionally warranted this—after all, science is fallible. All I ask is if I can see the data regarding your neuroscience company's work on molecular medicine and its effect on trans-cranial current stimulation. Before we initiate any brain studies, I'd like to collect the data in order to present it to my personal science team right this minute."

Suddenly, Baal's facial muscles seemed more relaxed. He sipped his coffee and hoisted a comforting smile on his face. He and Jasso whispered something into each other's ear, and a rapacious expression stole over their faces. Brennan could have sworn he saw Baal nod every so slightly. His eyelids seemed to droop. His lower lip sagged. Brennan thought they were planning something— not planning what to say, but what to do.

Baal stuck out a flat palm, "Can I see your tablets gentlemen?" Baal said as inoffensively as possible.

"Our tablets?" Brennan and Clarkson asked in unison.

"Yes gentlemen, your tablets. I can upload some of my blueprint files onto your tablets right this minute."

Both Brennan and Clarkson felt a logical sense of relief come over them as they fumbled through their pockets for their tablets and then slid the tablets on the table towards where Baal was sitting. Baal scooped up both of the tablets and put them into his pocket before showing a wide grin, but he showed no teeth. After tucking the tablets away, Baal got up and shot towards the door with

Jasso on his heels. Before walking out of the room, Baal turned around in a jerky movement, lowered his chin, and spoke with his gravest tone yet.

"Science..." Baal began with an energetic nod, "has no place on Earth." With that, both Baal and Jasso quickly scampered out of the conference room and closed the door, leaving Brennan and Clarkson staring at each other with uncertainty. By the time they realized what happened, it was too late. Clarkson lurched out of his seat and sprang ahead towards the door with a frenzied gasp, but it was too late. The door lock clicked, and both men were locked in the room.

33: The Truth

Clarkson drew his firearm, and pointed it at the door lazily, as if he already knew that his gun wasn't the solution. He then proceeded to fire a passionless shot. The beam never hit the door, and instead, it was reduced to a facet on the security force field that enveloped the entire room.

"Don't bother," Brennan said hopelessly. "You won't short out the shield with that thing. Every room in this damn building can be shielded this way in the event of an intrusion." Brennan then walked over to the coffee cart in the corner of the room. He was so stressed that he began to take swigs from the bottle of coffee liqueur.

"I should have known—I knew they were up to no good down here!" Clarkson scowled. "This is why I wanted you to keep in touch with me, and now I know that Jasso cut off communication on purpose in order to prevent me from sticking my nose in this mission!"

"It seemed so suspect," Brennan shook his head. "Five straight days of communication outages do not happen because of solar flares unless the flares were constant, and they weren't! Now, they took our tablets so we have no way of calling for help!" Brennan flared.

Clarkson then rubbed his squared chin and spoke cunningly, "We on the Table of Twelve found Baal suspicious after he began spending lots of time on Earth, and he never gave us any reasons for his trips here except for his usual need to monitor the people's health. It was as if he was expecting the people to mutate again at any day, or any month, or any year."

Brennan poured himself a second glass of liqueur and sat on a plush lounge chair that stood near one of the many windows. Brennan stared at the sun, wondering if it was the last time he'd see it. The slanted rays of the morning light easily pierced through the large panes of glass, bathing the room in its richness, but it didn't do anything to inspire him. He felt like a rat in a cage— useless and hopeless. He almost cried at the thought of never seeing his daughter again and that she'd be left to rot in a cell somewhere, or killed for that matter.

However, after sipping a glass of coffee liqueur, a curiosity then emerged which helped brighten his eyes a little bit. Brennan realized that Baal didn't want him dead or Jasso would have shot him and Clarkson on the spot.

"I'm not sure they even want to kill us, or they would have done so with two quick shots."

"I'm not sure, but it may still happen," Clarkson replied. Then, his words seemed to slow down in pace, and he hushed them down to a whisper. "Now Major listen up—I didn't want to say anything incase Baal was listening, but I'll whisper it to you to give you a heads up because I don't want to see you worry yourself to death," Clarkson said as he huddled closer to him. "I expect my personal guard should arrive here shortly to attempt to rescue us."

"You have men here?" Brennan asked, surprised.

"Yes Major, I do. They are fixed with an order to initiate a rescue mission in the event that I am killed. And it goes into effect whenever I travel from planet to planet, and moon to moon. If I don't reply within a given parameter, they automatically initiate a rescue mission."

"How long until you're declared overdue?"

"Usually no more than five hours, but in this case, it's three. They arrived on Earth days ago under the guise of atmospheric density testers. They should be gearing up as we speak right about now," Clarkson paused while staring at his watch.

"But there are so many floors in this building and so many rooms!" Brennan fretted.

"Oh don't worry about that Major," Clarkson waved him off. "My men will know of my location from the homing beacon I activated several minutes ago."

Clarkson pulled out a small little electronic device that looked like a typical audio tracking bug. It was so small no one could ever find it inside a pocket.

"Let's hope Baal doesn't kill us first," Brennan said grimly. "We could only pray..."All of a sudden, the crystal pane monitor near the comm. station in the corner of the room began to flicker to life all by itself, and within seconds, the image of Doctor Baal's face appeared on it, seemingly coming to them live from a security camera feed, which was near a prison cell. Baal spoke into his handheld and the speakers on the comm. station crackled to life.

"Long time, no speak gentlemen," Baal chuckled.

Clarkson tugged his blazer straight and marched towards the comm. station with disgust in his eyes. He pressed the communication button to activate audio input and barked into the speaker.

"Doctor Baal, what in the hell is the meaning of this?"

"Relax my liege..." Baal began, stretching his voice. "I'll start off by saying this—I'm not going to kill you or the Earthman. At least not yet."

Clarkson reddened, "What the hell—"

"I have decided that it is better to mind-wipe you both. I will erase all your memories of our misdoings—and only then will I set you both free on this wretched planet so you can live the rest of your lives wallowing about the common herd without knowing a thing about what I've done here on Earth."

Clarkson's icy blue eyes swelled. "Let us out of here Doctor and we'll talk it out!"

"Not yet friend," Baal answered quickly. "I prefer to talk it out this way; after all, I'm a doctor and you are both military men. I felt I was at a disadvantage back in the conference room before. However, lets focus on the future gentlemen...I have something to tell you both, and I do hope that you will change your mind after hearing what I have to say about these mutants."

"You want to win my consent?" Clarkson asked, stunned.

"I am sure I will win your consent once this conversation is over. I am almost sure of it" Baal bragged. "I believe that your ears are worthy of the words I'm about to say, and I believe in graciousness amongst seasoned warriors."

"You trap your superior officer in a room, and you expect me to forget about it later?"

"I beg you General, please—I would hate to do this to one of my own. The last thing I want to see is a mind-wiped Draconian General that was chastised for leaking forbidden data."

"You son of a bitch.."

"Please General, once you hear me out, you will no longer militate against my cause, and having you on my side will help me sleep better at night," Baal said jovially.

Clarkson exhaled his displeasure and chuckled mirthlessly in disbelief.

Brennan then decided it was a good time to chastise the man and so he edged forward from the back of the room. "If you can sleep at night knowing that you created a society full of mindless slaves, then you should be able to sleep after mind-wiping us," Brennan started hotly. "And by the way...where's my daughter?"

"Relax, she's still in her own cell," Baal answered feebly. "I'm keeping her quartered and well fed. However, if I don't win your consent, then I will immediately proceed to wipe her memories too. But don't worry, I'm not a monster," Baal then paused, softening his tone. "She'll retain all of her childhood memories, including those that will let her know that you are her dad."

All of a sudden, Baal turned on his heels and started walking towards the prison cell behind him, completely away from the camera. The camera zoomed in on him to compensate for the distance. Brennan stared at the background and noticed that there was a prisoner behind those prison bars. It was hard to tell who it was from the poor vantage point and poor video quality, but Brennan immediately figured it was Charlie after noticing his clothes, the same clothes that he wore during the time of his arrest.

Baal slid a lock on the cell's door and walked into the cell, and towards the prisoner. Charlie was curled up in a ball in one of the cell's corners. There was nothing in there but a toilet bowl and what looked like a tray full of food. Baal crouched beside the seemingly unconscious Charlie Beasley and grabbed a handful of his hair.

"General look...look at this man before you," Baal began pitifully. "He is a prime example of why I had to resort to controlling the mind of Earth folk. Look at Charlie here: his genetic structure is failing and it is beyond repair! My actions...' Baal paused for a more dramatic effect, "are justifiable actions and you will soon know why," he continued boldly.

"What could possibly justify your actions!" Brennan lashed out.

"Although it may sound a bit rough on the ears at first, I assure you that it's all for the common good of Earth men and women "

"You won't convince me Doctor!" Clarkson spat out quickly.

"Oh but I will," Baal said confidently. He then sprang up and out of the cell, approaching the camera again. "After I explain everything to you, you will understand."

"Nothing you say will convince me," Brennan lashed out. "Yeah, you're out of your mind!" Clarkson then shouted.

"General, once I'm done explaining, you will be so convinced that you'll even go as far as proving your loyalty by inoculating the people yourself. Then, in doing so, you will have gained my trust. Once you have a hand in all this, then I won't worry about you double crossing me."

"You are mad Doctor, I won't be a part in this crazy agenda of yours," Clarkson said in a softer voice, his spirit dampened by hopelessness.

"Once I tell you, you will align with my agenda, I'm sure of it," Baal smirked.

Brennan suddenly approached the screen and decided to let out the words he had held in. "You are taking away their souls Doctor! Is it because of the super powers?" Brennan asked

Baal's smile was gone as quickly as it washed over his face, and he spoke stiffer than usual. "As a matter of fact...yes...that is one of the reasons," Baal said before walking into the prison cell again. Doctor Baal kneeled down and held Charlie's limp and semi-conscious head straight up by his hair so he could face the security camera.

"I'm afraid of what these powers will do to the body. You see, these powers of his, they are too strong for his body and brain to handle. That is what I am afraid of Major. I'm afraid for him and anyone else who develops these powers. This is why I am inoculating the masses—they must remain barren, spiritless

souls or their bodies would burn out! Especially now, since the sun is cooking everyone as it is," Baal said pitiably. "When we set out to cure the mutants that survived the catastrophes over a decade ago, we realized that there were other dangers that needed to be addressed...not just the radiation. The radiation poisoning was the least of our concern, and it is only partially responsible for the DNA mutations."

"Partially responsible?" Brennan asked.

"Yes, partially," Baal began gravely before folding his arms behind his back and pacing a bit. "You see, the radiation only facilitated the mutation process but didn't cause the DNA to mutate in the first place. It all started over twenty years ago we believe, when new waves of energy began to affect the people of Earth and their DNA entirely. A unique planetary alignment in Earth's solar system was and still is responsible for this unique energy signature that is affecting Earth and its people, henceforth, becoming the culprit of the mutations. And when it started, mankind on Earth was on the 'doorstep of a new cycle' and in some cases, a new age of enlightenment. Mankind on Earth was being released from its ignorant slumber and was about to embark on a new spiritual renaissance. However, as you all know, if the brain changes, so does the body.

And DNA plays by its own rules once the strands get moved around. Charlie was one of the rarer ones to have a strong enough body that allows him to make use of his new powers without the full effects of the DNA shape-shift. You know what they used to say on Alpha Draconis General…that enlightenment always comes with a price!"

"I was a never a spiritual man," Clarkson said. "Edify us if you will," Clarkson demanded.

"When this rare solar planetary alignment began to affect the Earth's aura over a decade ago, it affected the bioelectric auras of humans as well. This new energy allowed for the physical and spirit realms to merge within the consciousness of man, essentially rewiring not only people's minds, but mutating the DNA as well. Like I said, DNA plays by its own rules; a couple of strands move around and people can either evolve or de-evolve."

"Looks like a lot of people are evolving and not de-evolving," Brennan chimed in.

Baal waved an index finger no. "No, don't let the superpowers mislead you Major. You see, these DNA mutations are causing dormant genetic material to awaken, including viruses contained within the dormant junk DNA. Unfortunately, some genetic material harbors ancient viruses, viruses that humankind has since adapted to and evolved from; they are called retroviruses, and these retroviruses bring about old human traits and attributes that were once necessary to survive in raw nature. In a sense, these mutants are being infected from within, and many of them mutate too quickly for the body to adapt to the retroviruses. Charlie here, he was lucky. His DNA is changing slowly, giving his flesh much more time to acclimate to the new blood coursing through his veins. However, in most cases, a mutant begins to awaken dormant traits but fails to rewire completely. And so, the mutations cause complete, utter brain burnout and all sorts of cancers. Of course, the radiation in the atmosphere only adds fuel to the flame, and it's not the radiation that is responsible for deactivating my nanobots. It is the retroviruses; they are responsible for overriding my DNA stabilizing nanobots. The retroviruses are overriding and shutting down my nanobots in many people, and making them susceptible to radiation poisoning in the process."

Brennan was intrigued by the info coming out of Baal's mouth, but like Clarkson, he was too preoccupied with searching the streets below for signs of Clarkson's rescue team. Clarkson hoped to prolong the conversation in order to buy time for his rescue unit.

"Okay, so you say that these retroviruses are not affecting everyone in the same manner, yet, you still seek to inoculate everyone in equal fashion," Clarkson said.

Baal cleared his throat and thought it would be best to get into the details, hoping it would change the mind of his fellow Draconian. "Some get sicker than others, but eventually even the mutants with superpowers will get sick. Bestial regression is bestial regression, and soon enough all of these mutants will begin to degrade into rabid zombies."

"Tell me about more about the unlocking of junk DNA," Clarkson said, prolonging the conversation as long as possible.

"The old genetic material brings about many primal instincts in almost everyone. Animal instincts if you will, similar to the attributes that Earth Neanderthals used to have. In a sense, our junk DNA is like a toolbox with old tools that are never used."

"Your being prejudiced Doctor!" Brennan yelled from the back of the room. Baal hardly bothered to reply directly. "You see... some people, like Charlie,

begin to feel more in touch with their inherent psychic senses after they rewire into more animal-like beings, developing primal psychic abilities in the process

—and like most animals, they will be able to sense other dimensions and energies. They will develop what is called *animal magnetism,* and mutants can essentially displace neural energy and move it from person to person like some sort of telepathic virus. A man like Charlie can easily manipulate others and can bend people to his will. Why—mutants such as Charlie might even develop the ability to summon thought forms, which are non-physical entities that can do his bidding. As people like Charlie Beasley and John Lancaster begin to shift into this new consciousness, their relationship with everything from time, to gravity, and to nature, will change. Their symbiotic relationship with nature will be redefined all together! The world that Charlie knew as an ordinary human was just a small slice compared to what he is aware of now. And therefore, like Charlie, some of those canyon dwellers that resisted arrest are embracing their new lives despite the weaknesses that come along with it…such as light sensitivity and the need for lots of nutrients in order to feed their new, powerful cells forming in their bodies."

After Baal said that, the usual, precise rhetoric in his tone was gone, and Brennan began to wonder if Baal really did find these beastly humans fascinating. Baal went on and on, speaking as if he spoke to himself.

"The lucky ones, like Charlie and John, will develop a feline-like ability to manipulate prey or animals in general by using complex pheromones. They might even become empathic like wolves! Some develop the super-hearing, super-scent, and super-strength from the new ape-like adrenaline being made in their adrenals."

"Doesn't sound so primitive," Brennan muttered.

"Yes, you can say that Major, but believe it not, cats and dogs have superpowers that you Earth humans wished you ever had. As humankind on Earth became more technologically advanced, those Neanderthal-like supernatural powers were not needed as much, and so if you don't use it, you lose it. I ask myself often enough: why do we even need to be strong?

Technology such as power tools do it all for us now. Why do you need to be empathic like a wolf? There is no need to sense the emotions of your fellow humans because we have developed complex verbal languages. And who needs telepathic abilities when you have telephones? My point is that man is better off without these powers for their own sake. These animal traits are not needed and the mutations required for obtaining them pose huge health risks!"

Brennan finally found the urge to speak. "Doctor, it sounds as if you care nothing about the health of my fellow Earth people. I've seen the look on the Overseer's face whenever he spotted a mutant with the satellites. He seemed hell-bent on capturing every single mutant, and you can't stand there and tell me it was because he was concerned for their health!"

Baal nodded his head violently. "You are right Major," Baal said. "There are other concerns here rather then the health of your people. You see, people like Charlie here before me will only lead to the destruction of Earth."

"Destruction of Earth?" Brennan whined.

Clarkson marched up to the monitor and shouted, "Doctor, these mutants aren't exactly developing the ability of fly, or shooting lasers out of their eyes! What is so dangerous about a guy like Charlie?"

"Major Brennan, my agony does not stem from the thought of Charlie's physical superpowers but from all of his mental superpowers that will emerge,"

Baal answered quickly. "Mutants like Charlie will begin to develop the ability to recall genetic memories from past lives, better known as retro-cognition."

"Retro-cognition?" Brennan asked.

Clarkson turned away from the window and answered for Baal. "Yes, it is the ability to recall memories from past lives—we Draconians have this ability. It makes up for our short, physical lifespans."

"That's right!" Baal growled; his voice vibrated the speakers on the comm. station. "Many lower mammals and other animals have this ability as well. This is how a baby goat knows it should run when it sees a fox even though it never saw one before in its life—or a bird, who is skilled at building nests without any teaching for example. Before humankind developed a complex language, or began writing books, humans had the ability to access their genetic memories, which are all stored and recorded within the coils of our DNA. You see, our DNA acts as an antenna for the celestial frequencies that make up human consciousness. Now that these mutants are unlocking junk DNA, they are forming new strands of DNA that makes it possible to tap into the new ethereal forces affecting Earth right now, henceforth making it possible for them to tap into their genetic memories from past lives—lives lived on other planets and even lives lived on Earth. This new consciousness shift affecting certain people on Earth gives them access to all knowledge of human experience and the history of the cosmos. In turn, people have their own library book, as it is called, as well as a database, which contains a record of all the lifetimes a person has led. Each person's brain is finely tuned to tap into this collective hive-like mind."

"Earth humans have experienced this in the past. People like Einstein and Tesla for example; everything that they called progress was simply a matter of remembering what once was. Many Earth native Indians linked these psychic phenomena to their spirit guides, and Hindu teachings refer to these records as the *akashic records*. However, this retro-cognitive ability is not something humans on Earth should experience." Baal paused, switching his tone and expression into one that showed bemusement. "A lot of people do not use this ability to elevate themselves in a spiritual manner. Most use this retro-cognitive ability for personal gain in order to move about the Earth as Gods!"

"Are you saying that Einstein and Nikola Tesla had retro-cognitive ability?" Brennan then asked.

"Most likely," Baal said with alacrity. "Men such as Einstein, Newton, and Tesla pioneered their respected fields of science, and in my opinion, they never could have pioneered their work without this supernatural ability. This is the case with Charlie's inventions. Geomagnetic technology is far too advanced beyond what is already proved and tested amongst the scientific community! No university in the world has ever delved into such sophisticated sciences, and this man couldn't have learned this knowledge in any other way except through retro-cognition! Like Einstein, Charlie is a college dropout! It is my conclusion that Charlie can see history through the eyes of another. In his case, a past life."

"So they learned how to build those contraptions by remembering them?" Brennan asked.

"Yes, basically," Baal began enthusiastically. "However, it is possible to tap into the memories of a future life too, and this super-ability is why mutants such as Charlie will be responsible for the destruction of what remains of Earth civilization."

Clarkson turned his gaze away from the window and headed towards the monitor again. "How so?" Clarkson snapped.

Baal began pacing the prison cell after placing Charlie's limp head back on his pillow. "General, I belong to a secret Draconian society known as the Society of the Snake. We have been hunting witches, sorcerers, and even scientists on this planet for years—centuries even. Anyone who showed signs of retro-cognitive ability, or any psychic ability in general was automatically considered a threat. From the witches and wizards who used to roam the Earth, to the sorcerers of modern times, like Nikola Tesla for example. Many people, including he, had slipped through our fingers through the ages—as did Einstein

—and look what happened! His work led to atom bombs. And if we didn't shut down Tesla, his work would have caused some mad dictator to split the Earth in half."

"You mean to tell me that you've been halting mankind's evolution on Earth for hundreds of years because you think we're unfit to handle advanced technology?" Brennan lashed out, parting the sweaty hair off his brow.

"Yes, Major, that is right," Baal scowled in disgust.

"My goodness…" Clarkson began dazedly, "you created a scientific dictatorship…it is you who perverted science when you decided to shackle the mind of mankind on Earth!"

"It had to be done for the greater good," Baal said with gusto. "There was a time when we allowed the people of Earth to evolve. We stepped back and let the humans on Earth go on their own without our guidance. This occurred many years ago during the renaissance era. At first, we thought it was a good idea, and we thought humankind had passed its test after we saw what resulted—such as all the great art and sciences that led to a new industrial revolution. However, it all ended after Leonardo da Vinci began his career as a military engineer, henceforth creating a power struggle in Italy, a country which had been at peace for many years before. After da Vinci, crusades and wars followed, and we learned that the mind of man was not in line with their hearts! So, we began hunting sorcerers to prevent wars on Earth, but over time, the population grew and many witches, wizards, and sorcerers began slipping through our fingers. By the turn of the twentieth century, we at the Society of the Snake began to lose control all together—especially during the early 1900s. That is when we knew man's mind was expanding too rapidly, and so in order to keep advanced technology suppressed, we manipulated Earth's economy into blooming into an oil-based economy. And in order to stilt the mind of man, we tried drugs and fluoride and genetically modified foods, but it was not sufficient. It was our nanobots that saved your race, and our nano-medicine made it easier to shackle the mind all together."

After hearing that, Brennan's jaw remained slack, his heart jumped to his throat, and blocked the pile of vile words pent up in him.

"You have plunged your hand a bit too far into the mud Doctor!" Clarkson shouted.

Brennan spit towards the monitor. He would kill Baal if he were next to him.

Baal then emitted a jovial smile, but it was actually a smile of contempt. "Please General, spare me your reproaches! You are one ignorant Draconian

and are obviously emotionally compromised here, and you're failing to see the logic! We all know you are a less reputable member of our Draconian nation. You carry the last name of an Earth human after all. I know of your ancestry, you know! You hail from a line that first seeded the Earth, and I know about the Earth blood you carry in your veins, why...your voice drips with the ignorance of your Earthly influence!"

Clarkson reddened and walked so close to the monitor that his nose almost touched the screen.

"My family history has nothing to do with my siding with these people!" Clarkson barked out.

Baal chuckled. "You have no idea what some of these people are turning into!"

"I'm not aligning with this crazy transgenic program of yours!" Clarkson lashed out.

Baal only laughed.

On the other side of the room, Brennan poured himself another drink. He was having a nervous breakdown.

Baal was then seen turning his gaze towards Charlie in the prison cell. "You will be very afraid soon General, very afraid if I don't stop these dormant genes from awakening! You have no idea what will happen once humans begin making contact with the forbidden zones of the brain, the parts of the brain I have worked so hard to keep locked. The hearts and minds of Earth humans are not in accord! And so...the gates to these genetic memories must remain locked!"

"The gates?" Clarkson asked.

"Yes, the gates in the mind, the gates of perception, the specific neural pathways that lead to the forbidden zones of the humans brain where the crystals are located...that's how retro-cognition works, and that's how higher brain functions come about, like most psychic ability in general."

"Forbidden zones? Crystals?" Clarkson asked.

"The forbidden zones are the parts of the brain that contain certain crystals.

Just like computer processors contain quartz. These are areas in the brain responsible for receiving celestial frequencies linked to the collective mind, and these areas of the brain are responsible for all higher spiritual activity in general. New Ageists know it as the other side, and I call it the *forbidden zones* of the brain. Many retroviruses in your junk DNA allow the brain to rewire itself to the point of expanding into these previously dormant zones."

"This is all too much," Brennan said through his hands, covering his face as he stood slumped on the lounge chair.

Baal lapsed into a mad chuckle. "It appears that this knowledge of this particular brain science was known by some Earth men in the past...perhaps only kept within secret convents or families, but I do believe that both of you men are familiar with the Superman comic books right?"

Brennan's eyes fluttered as he tilted his head to the side. "What? Why bring this up now? What...are you talking about?"

"Superman?" Clarkson yelped, chuckling from hysteria. "What do you mean?"

Baal just ignored him and kept speaking. "Do you recall when Jor-el told his son Kal-el—"

"Enough of this incongruous talk," Clarkson interrupted and continued towards the window, hoping to see his convoy pull up to the building any minute now.

Baal disregarded Clarkson and put up an index finger of protest. "Do you recall when Jor-el told Superman that he has access to all those crystals which contained all of the education and knowledge from all the human civilizations that ever existed since the dawn of the universe?"

"Oh right, I do remember that," Brennan said, and nodded in rapid succession from a sudden onset of excitement.

"Well those crystals Superman used were all metaphors for the crystals in the cells of the human brain, the area of the brain responsible for retro-cognition and all psychic ability."

"So Superman spoke to dead people?" Brennan asked.

"He spoke to his dead father mostly," Baal nodded viciously. "In a sense, his father Jor-El was a representation of his genetic bloodline, and his consciousness was stored in that green crystal..." Baal trailed off again, rubbing his chin. "I was always fascinated by that story, and so the answer is yes: Superman spoke to dead people. That is what is in the crystals of the forbidden zones of the brain; they are reservoirs for the pool of souls that make up the human knowledge base. This can be described as an archive of sorts, a zero-point subspace nexus that is parenthetic to all of the knowledge humankind has amassed throughout history on Earth, or human history elsewhere, such as on other celestial bodies and/or other parallel universes. There are other reasons why this ability is dangerous, and I haven't even begun to cover them all. Some other problems that I have with this unique ability are that humans do not fare well after crossing over to the forbidden zone of the mind—A.K.A. the other side."

"Depending on a psychic's state of consciousness, or brain wave frequency, one may tap into not only their genetic memories but also other timelines as well as past and future ones, resulting in schizophrenic behavior. Psychic mutants would essentially live on the cusp of many worlds, realms, and dimensions. The veils between these realms are thin curtains of quantum noise and can be intervened with by a means of quieting this noise through mediation. However, the gross human body would not adjust in time to undergo the needed adjustments between ethereal life and terrestrial life. Why do you think the name of Superman's race is Kryptonian?" Baal began, challenging the men to answer but there was no retort offered by neither Brennan nor Clarkson. Clarkson and Brennan awaited the answer with bright eyes. "He was called a Kryptonian because he had access to the crypt in his mind—a crypt of old souls and ancient secrets. Of course, Kryptonite as you all may know is Superman's biggest weakness and you must all know what Kryptonite is."

"A fragment of his home planet, which exploded," Brennan chimed in, suddenly becoming interested in what he first perceived as non-essential banter.

"Very good Major," Baal squealed. "In a sense, the crystals in the forbidden zones of the brain contain fragments of alien worlds...the human genetic memories if you will. Of course, as I said before, enlightenment comes with a price because as you all know, Kryptonite is radioactive...and when these crystals in the brain become activated, the ethereal frequencies then allow the brain to tap into some dangerous radiation levels to the surrounding brain cells. Once the neural connections are made, they begin emitting radiation and essentially results in cellular necrosis in surrounding brain cells—sometimes even leading to brain hemorrhages. Therefore, by now, you must see the parallels in the Superman story with what is going on right now, and in a sense, the Superman story embodies the real-world crisis we are facing today. This is why I have to stop these Supermen from roaming the Earth once again for their own sake, and for everyone's sake for that matter."

"Spare me the history lesson Doctor," Brennan lashed out ever so suddenly. "Yeah, I'm not convinced," Clarkson then said.

Doctor Baal exhaled deeply and walked out of the camera's range of view in a fit of anger. Then, the screen went black.

34: Last Chance

"Where'd he go?" Clarkson said in a slurred voice, regretful of the fact that Baal was gone, and his plan to prolong the conversation to buy time for his rescue team went down the drain. Clarkson occasionally peered down to the city streets below, hoping to spot his team's black cars. However, there were no cars, no helicopters, and no rescue team. General Clarkson chafed the tension out of his head by massaging his temples. Brennan sweated through his thick, cotton suit and decided to haul himself out of his chair for another visit to the coffee cart. He paced the room with his glass of sweet coffee liqueur in his hand, waiting for Baal and his troops to pop in through the door at any second.

Suddenly, the console's monitor flicked to life again, and this time the camera angle on the monitor changed. The view came from a higher perspective inside the prison cell where Charlie sat against the wall with slumped shoulders and his head hanging to his chest, and he seemed to be shivering too.

Baal then stepped into the frame and into the prison cell heading straight for Charlie's half-dead body. Baal grabbed him by the armpits and wrestled him towards the small cot nestled in the corner of the prison cell. After laying him down, a man in a white coat stepped in and began waving a device over Charlie's semiconscious body. Even Baal began prying into Charlie's mouth with his fingers, opening Charlie's lips and parting them so he could inspect him. He then turned his gaze towards the camera and spoke.

"I grew tired of this unremitting conversation gentlemen, and so I figured I give you two some time to decide what will become of your lives."

Clarkson routinely checked his wristwatch, and his gaze never deviated from the streets even as Baal spoke.

Baal then raised the tempo of his voice, caught in a self-absorbed tirade. "So you see my friends—I want nothing but empty vessels walking my planet, sterile of spirit and divination! I must close the forbidden zones of the mind, forever locking the doors that lead to the crystals in their parietal lobes in order to protect the people from ancient wisdom, ancient technology, and most importantly to protect people from themselves!"

Brennan almost threw his coffee mug at the monitor, but Clarkson cleared his throat to get his attention. Brennan knew what Clarkson meant after he saw Clarkson point to his watch, and so Brennan took a deep breath and decided to prolong the conversation in hopes of buying more time for Clarkson's rescue team.

"Doctor, you say the Society of the Snake's primary reason for halting humankind's evolution on Earth was not to protect them from health problems, but in order to protect them from destroying the Earth with their newfound powers. However, you can't assume people will follow the footsteps of their effete ancestors! After all, Charlie was forced to weaponize his geomagnetic technology, and it is my belief that future generations will have proper hearts— hearts that are in alignment with their powerful minds!"

Baal immediate began to laugh. "Oh no, that's unlikely! Take it from me, I know! I have seen the same thing happen on Earth over and over again whenever we allow super-humans to walk the Earth. These mutants must be stopped at all costs! We Draconians used to have a name for mutants like Charlie. We used to call them *older models*." Baal paused after witnessing the phobic look of horror on Clarkson face.

Brennan was taken aback by it, and he wondered why Clarkson grew so worried after hearing the term *older model*.

Baal laughed. "And General..." Baal stopped talking so he could grin devilishly. "I'm sure you know what an older model is," Baal ended gravely, his debonair voice made him sound creepier.

Clarkson dipped his eyes to the ground, put his fingers to his chin, and seemed to get lost in his thoughts. Brennan confronted Clarkson with narrowed eyes and faced him.

"What is an older model?" Brennan asked. He wondered if it had something to do with Neanderthals, but wanted to hear it from Clarkson's mouth.

"You rather not know," Clarkson said with trepidation.

Baal thought he had finally gotten through to his fellow Draconian, and he spoke through his widest smile yet. "One of the most terrible legends on Earth is coming back to life," Baal said, "and out of the unknown past. Major, I bet you also know what an older model is."

"No Doctor, I don't."

"Major, an older model is most infamously known to you Earthlings as the Nephilim; one of the first forms of modern human, a human that is closely related to the Neanderthal. This form of human has a notorious past that stems all the way to Atlantis, a great world that was tarnished by the misuse of occult forces—and the misuse of science!"

Brennan's tongue suddenly thickened in his mouth. "But Doctor, my daughter told me Charlie was one of the nicest men she had ever met!"

Baal turned to Charlie's sedated body. "Until his mind goes," Baal began eagerly, before sitting beside Charlie and inspecting his teeth, as well as the excessive hair growing out of his nostrils. "In order for an older model to overcome their evil nature they must do so with great effort—through long periods of meditation and study. Their new consciousness will bring a new reality that no dream can conjure. It will bring about a terror in a person's heart that will stun their minds, and the spirits they will communicate with will tell them things they are better off not knowing! The land of the dead is a dangerous place for you Earth mortals to linger, and besides, people like Charlie are too passionate for science and too passionate for knowledge anyway. These things should be left to the frigid and the impersonal because they would offer Charlie nothing but tragic alternatives to the solutions of his problems, mostly fueled by his emotional baggage. Even worse, the ominous connotations of his newly developed powers would often lead to catalepsy and the worse depression of any kind. All of Charlie's constitution will be weakened! The shadowy dread from the negative demonic entities he will face will gnaw at his vitals every day and every night, and it will never leave him. These new humans, or shall I say, these older model humans, will never sleep calmly again when they think of the interminable terrors that lurk behind time and space. People like Charlie will

feel alienated and separate from connected humans, and people like Charlie will wind up suicidal—or wind up becoming drug addicts!

"If fear doesn't get them, then anger will! People like Charlie will only wind up with megalomaniacal ideals. They will conjure up things to serve their personal agendas," Baal paused, his tone then turned to a squeal. "What will it take to convince you to support my venture? Another nuclear holocaust?

Another sinking of a continent such as Atlantis? I have made some genealogical discoveries that my own maternal ancestry had possessed for many years, and you may look at me as a monster but please know this...I am doing everything in my power to prevent another Atlantis! Your Earth history never recorded the times where humans had destroyed themselves with technology—it's happened before!"

"But doctor," Clarkson interrupted, "the Earth is already in ruins, what else do people have to lose?"

Baal's eyes seemed to vibrate as he growled into the camera. "My planet Earth is what I'll lose! At least the Earth is still spinning and is still rich in resources!"

"You've got to let nature take its course," Brennan cried out hopelessly.

Baal laughed madly. "No way, no how should these Earth humans experience the occult! Unguarded intellects are in great danger when crossing over to the other side. The healthier mutants would undoubtedly take advantage of their power, and they would begin to develop god-complexes, leading to megalomaniacal delusions of grandeur. Their ingenuity will intermingle with their primal nature, and before we know it, we will have a bunch of rabid megalomaniacal psychopaths running around my planet with advanced weaponry at their disposal! You must trust me! You must! Our secret Society of the Snake has documented all of the proof of the Nephilim's savage whims. The terror and mystery that will arise from their new minds will become a stressful union, creating an ever-darkening terror. They will indisputably time travel to the times of Atlantis, a consciousness time travel, fueled by their immortal minds and retro-cognitive abilities, bringing them to recall memories during a time when these older models ruled the Earth and destroyed it! Believe me when I tell you, that uneasy lies the head that wears the crown—and I wish I could find a way to give people access to one hundred percent of their brains.

However, the only way to stop tyranny for thriving on this planet once again is to control DNA entirely to prevent the endogenous retroviruses from awakening in the first place!"

The men were awestruck by Baal's information and needed a moment to soak it all in. For the first time since being locked in the room, both Clarkson and Brennan were no longer occupied with coaxing Baal on and on with questions just so they could buy time for Clarkson's rescue squad to arrive. This time, they wanted to ask more questions because they were curious and scared— scared of the man curled up in the prison cell depicted on the monitor, and scared of what would happen to Earth civilization if more of these older human sorcerers began to walk the Earth again.

Clarkson and Brennan exchanged wide-eyed glances and knew that Baal must have been telling the truth. Brennan saw no reason to dissent from his dictum, after all, Baal's information was far too detailed and he told it with passion. Clarkson joined Brennan by the coffee cart, and he was so wrung up that he poured himself a drink of super-sweet coffee liqueur. The two men brooded in silence for almost a minute before huddling up for a discussion. Both had trouble finding words, and after hearing Doctor Baal's testimony, a huge portion of Brennan's anger had evaporated. In some degree, Brennan felt as if he was beginning to share

Baal's spirit. There was a reassuring honesty in his expression that made Brennan share his dread. After all, he did not know Charlie well enough to have him figured out to be purely righteous in his heart. And he figured Elena didn't either. The thought of humanity being replaced with beings he thought were no different from vampires was a horrifying idea.

After a good thirty seconds of heart-freezing silence, Baal's voice shook the speakers on the comm. station. "What will it be gentlemen—your memories or your minds? Will you do the right thing and help me rid the world of these vampiric monsters?"

Brennan tried to keep his face impassive, but he couldn't muster up a word.

Clarkson however, had a tougher time keeping his emotions suppressed. He parted several loose strands of silver hair that stirred along his forehead, wiped his brow, and flicked the oily sweat to the ground in frustration. After downing another drink in one gulp, Clarkson's jaw set stubbornly, and he approached the monitor.

"Oh Doctor..." he called out to Baal. "I assume that you are familiar with Earth religion—am I correct?"

"Yes, as a matter of fact I am," Baal said.

Clarkson gave him a long doubtful look. "Then perhaps you recall the teachings of the Christian faith and how the Nephilim and the archangels tie into it?"

Baal laughed. "The Nephilim are the offspring of the archangels, and like the archangels, they all have fallen."

"What about the archangel Michael—wasn't he too an angel that had fathered Nephilim?"

"No one knows for sure, but if so, then I can assure you that no Nephilim took after Michael— but instead, taking the traits of Lucifer."

"What about Christ?" Brennan chimed in from the couch.

"Oh come on," Baal smirked. "Who knows if these people even existed?

We're basically talking about comic book characters here!"

Brennan marched up to the manner and jabbed his finger at it. "It's okay; there is great truth in myth. You said it yourself before, with your dissection of the Superman character!" Brennan shot back.

Baal waved him off. "Christ was never officially considered a Nephilim." "The Mormons believe Christ and Satan are spirit brothers," Brennan

replied.

"Christ is a one in a million my friends, and he was just a poster boy for a Nephilim with a proper spirit. You see, Christ's dying on the cross represents the death and rebirth process when crossing over to the other side where the forbidden zones of the brain are located. When a person emerges through the gateway in the mind, they basically die on the cross—on the crossover that is— and the crypt of souls they unleash upon their carnal shells morph them into a new person, and they are reborn into an immortal more or less. A human with the knowledge and experience of many lives."

"And did this happen to Charlie?" Clarkson said with a suspicious squint. "Yes, but he is a phony…he is a leper messiah!" Baal spat back. "He is a false, scabrous prophet with a deranged mind."

Brennan fired back in a beseeching tone. "You seem to be supercilious in your method of thinking Doctor! You're being too conservative, and if haven't figured it out by now, Earth has no chance if you play it safe and hold back its progression for the sake of your fearful prejudices. Perhaps there will be more like Christ out there, strong and able to combat the dark forces that haunt their minds. Perhaps this celestial force and new energy that is affecting Earth could not have come at a better time. And just as you said—junk DNA is a toolbox with old tools. Perhaps the humans on Earth need their primal instincts again so they can survive in the raw nature of new Earth, and tap into their retro-cognitive powers so they can remember the times when our ancestors traveled the stars. The time is now when people must heal the Earth by moving away from polluting energy and move onto clean, green energy!

Perhaps humankind needs to be more in tune with nature instead of destroying it all the time!

Humankind is after all on a precipice, and these retroviruses have awakened at the right time if you ask me!"

Clarkson nodded boldly. "The stars have aligned this way for a reason, and man is evolving right now for a reason."

Baal was about to speak, but Brennan rode over him. "I truly believe that the future generations will use the knowledge and technologies to heal more than destroy. And if some mutate into rabid zombies along the way, then consider it a part of nature's course of trial and error."

Clarkson nodded at Brennan. "Well said!"

Baal did not reply right away; instead, he turned from the camera and doubled over as he put a forearm on the prison bars. He shook his head several times before turning back to the camera. Baal's eyes seemed to fluster, and his lip quivered before he spoke.

"A Christ, a Noah, a Tesla, a Mohammed, an Abraham, a Charlie Beasley— they're one in a trillion," Baal squeaked, punctuated by a nervous giggle. "Have you thought what would happen if some idiot gets a hold on Charlie Beasley's technology? It happened before with Nikola Tesla. Tesla only sought to bring free energy to the masses—just like Charlie—and before you knew it, people were using his principles to create artificial earthquakes! Thanks to Einstein, your planet became irradiated way before the poles shifted and caused your magnetosphere to weaken. You people couldn't build a single nuclear power planet without causing a string of meltdowns—meltdowns that your media never reported. And not to mention all the weaponry! I can't begin to tell you how many times we had to step in and meddle with Earthly conflicts just to disable ICBM's whenever some mad dictator chose to start a nuclear Armageddon!"

No one seemed to speak after hearing Baal's tirade. Brennan didn't receive Baal's data with the same amount of astonishment felt by Clarkson. Unlike Brennan, Clarkson had no idea that a Draconian secret society had pulled strings on Earth for so long. Brennan knew of the aliens within his government, and he knew of the theories that stemmed as far back as ancient astronaut theory.

Brennan read plenty of yellow journalism in his day and remembered the accounts of many witnesses, mostly air force pilots, talking of UFO's hovering over missile silos and disengaging them for no reason.

Or was there a reason? Brennan thought.

Brennan just sat limpidly on the lounge sofa, his face buried in his hands.

Clarkson was already on his fifth drink. Both of them wanted to speak, but their hearts were stuck in their mouths.

Over on the monitor, Baal's features seemed to have shifted, and he was clearly growing impatient with such unremitting speech. His lips were drawn back as he continued to speak, hoping to convince Clarkson to side with him because he desperately needed the General on his side.

"General...look..." Baal began, his voice low and urgent, "you may be wearing many ribbons on your lapel, but believe me when I tell you that you are a baby soldier fighting in a very, very old war. If I could only show you the map to the older model's failures...you would surely side with me. You must help me save our planet from these monsters for fear that they will not only wind up destroying it but even worse; they might develop space craft and begin infecting other planets."

Brennan lost it after hearing that. "General, if a civilization is capable enough of growing into the heavens, then how could they be considered infectious? Any human race that develops advanced space travel deserves to get there!"

Baal waved him off. "Oh spare me the lecture, you babies! The very thought of seeing you monkeys reach the heavens is enough to turn my stomach upside down! Keeping Earth humans out of space is my society's primary goal. This is why we used the Church to hunt down witches and sorcerers in the past, and it is the reason why we mind control them today! This is the reason why we suppressed technology and kept Earth running with oil-based economies for all these years! This is why we tinkered with Earth's magnetosphere and allowed for your North and

South poles to shift causing the tectonic plates to move around—causing the Earthquakes, the floods—it was us! We reduced your population with our geoengineering and weather manipulation. We were the ones who created a deluge of biblical proportions in the process. Why…we flooded Atlantis back then and flooded Earth all over again a decade ago! We did this to keep the population limited so we can control you more efficiently.

We had to stop mankind on Earth from ushering in a new industrial age so we can continue to keep you unstable savages quarantined from the stars!"

After hearing Baal's last words, Brennan's nerves became so raw his chin could not stop quivering. The true horror of the situation sank into his mind, and it suddenly became clear that he was staring into the eyes of the man responsible for killing so many of his relatives, friends, and billions of fellow Earthlings.

Brennan ran up to the monitor and began wrestling it off its brackets before staring at the screen and shouting, "You devil, you devil!"

Clarkson tried to restrain Brennan, and he grabbed him from behind, but Brennan shrugged off the grip of the stronger Draconian rather easily due to his immense rage. As Brennan wrestled the monitor off its screws and brackets, he stared into Baal's face and kept cursing him out. Baal was seen throwing his head back, and he let out a sinister laugh—fueling Brennan's ferocity. When Brennan finally tugged the monitor off the brackets, he was about to haul the monitor and smash it against the wall, but Clarkson clasped onto his arms and stopped him.

"Please, we must prolong the conversation," Clarkson whispered in his ear as he cradled the large monitor in his hands and proceeded to stick it back to the wall, tightening each screw with his hands just tight enough to keep the screen from falling.

Brennan put both palms on his face in order to hide the tears that welled up in his eyes. His cheeks reddened more and more as he gazed at Baal's poisonous face, who in turn continued to emit the most menacing cackles.

Clarkson wanted to continue to talk to Baal but it would be impossible to say anything more after hearing Baal's admission. He knew that it didn't pay to continue on with that madman on the screen, and he grew tired of asking profitless questions.

Clarkson escorted Brennan away from the monitor and towards the other corner of the conference room so he could calm down. He too needed a break from seeing Baal's face and was smitten from the info he just received. It is not everyday that someone comes face to face with a murderer of billions. Both he and Brennan were hypnotized with horror, mingled with rage.

It took a minute before Clarkson managed to say something to Baal in a voice drained from antipathy. "You mistook me for a madman Doctor, if you thought I would align with your plan. You give us Draconians a bad name, and I choose to be erased along with Major Brennan. However, be advised; there are others who are aware of your suspicious behavior and the nature of the scientific dictatorship that you established here on Earth. And in time, they will move in on you and put an end to your deceits!"

Baal let out an obnoxious laugh, but strangely enough, he suddenly stopped laughing after his portable comm. device chirped.

"What is it?" Baal was heard saying after tapping the comm. piece in his ear.

In just several seconds, all the look of triumph on his face had morphed into a look of worry.

"I'll be right there!" Baal shouted and instantly darted away from the camera's range.

That was the last thing Brennan and Clarkson heard from him before the screen went black.

Before Clarkson and Brennan could find the time to reflect on Baal's sporadic behavior, a loud thud made them jump, and the faint sounds heard from afar were identified as disruptor blasts.

35: Infiltration

"Just in time!" Clarkson boomed after hearing the fusillade of gunfire. He was sure his rescue unit had arrived. A muffled sound of smashing glass was heard in the distance, swallowed by the roar of a hundred shouts all at once.

Brennan briskly marched towards the comm. station in the corner of the room and began gliding his fingers on the old-fashioned keyboard that operated the PA system, as well as the security camera feeds. After punching in a command, the crystal pane monitor that dangled on the wall had flicked to life. After a few minutes of fiddling through menus, a collage of small squares appeared on monitor. Each square depicted a different view from an assortment of security cameras, cameras stationed near the PA system's speakers throughout every floor in the entire building. Each square showed a different part of the building, all the way from the lobby, to the parking garage, and down to each of the hallways of every floor.

"There!" Brennan blurted out, alerting Clarkson to the screen and specifically to a small square in the upper left hand corner of the monitor.

"Camera number one-twenty-three," Brennan pointed. "Jasso is walking towards the elevators in the main lobby!"

Both of them focused their attention to the block that showed the camera view near the lobby elevators and sure enough, there was Colonel Jasso ordering several of his black suited European RAPDA agents to point their guns towards the elevator doors. As soon as the elevator doors opened, a dozen or more soldiers in steel exo-skeletal body armor poured out of it with guns drawn.

"Those are my men," Clarkson asserted, his face shook with excitement. The camera feed showed about six men in view. All of them had their rifles drawn and looked like more like cyborgs than humans. They were sheathed in the most sophisticated exo-skeletal armor that Brennan had ever seen, complete with full faced helmets and built in zoom visors that allowed them to see in a wide-ranging array of spectrums.

"The lobby cam, enlarge the frame and keep it steady," Clarkson demanded as he continued to follow the action with mute appeal.

After Brennan enlarged the view, they saw the faces on the screen with more detail. The situation looked grim. Clarkson's six hired guns were being surrounded by scores of RAPDA agents as well as Jasso's Ashtar guards who looked like they were about to fire any second. The camera feed showed about a dozen of them in the picture, but there could have been more, because more and more started walking into the frame.

Suddenly a familiar looking man walked into the frame and stood in a shooting position. Brennan could spot his Neanderthal of a friend from anywhere—it was Lieutenant Graham—and he was taking part in the standoff with his phaser drawn.

Why isn't he guarding Elena at the precinct? Brennan thought. "Is that your Lieutenant?" Clarkson asked.

Brennan nodded. Part of him was glad to see his friend, but a part of him was worried that he would be killed. However, what bothered him the most was the fact that the Lieutenant was supposed to keeping an eye on Elena, and Brennan began to fear that something must have happened to her that caused Graham to leave her.

"How did he wind up with my men?" Clarkson wondered.

"I don't know but I wouldn't want any part of this if I were him. Your men seem outnumbered," Brennan sulked.

Nevertheless, Clarkson seemed confident in his soldiers and spoke through a smile.

"Oh don't count them out of this one!" Clarkson beamed. "And I believe that there are more than six men; they must have split into groups."

Then, the discussion in the lobby seemed to get heated. Brennan immediately looked for Graham, but he had since walked out of the frame and could not be located. All of a sudden, Clarkson's mercenaries seemed to pull out what looked like old-fashioned .44 Magnums and began firing rapidly, using their free palms to continuously swipe at the pistol's hammers like old-fashioned gunslingers used to do throughout the western American frontier. The shots were precise, hitting everyone in vital and exposed areas between all bulletproof vests and body armor. All of the Ashtar guards crumpled to the ground in bloody heaps, as well as some RAPDA agents and even some local police officers. Jasso also seemed to catch a few slugs because he had dropped to the ground like a ton of bricks.

The fact that there was no audio made it even more eerie to see such carnage occur so quick and quietly. Clarkson's mercenaries made headway after the last of Jasso's men were down, scampering away and disappearing off the frame.

Only the bodies of Ashtar guards and RAPDA agents alike were seen lying silently on the ground. Almost none of them moved, including the body of Colonel Jasso, who was only identifiable by the cigar that was still tucked in his mouth.

Brennan turned to Clarkson and noticed that he looked sadder than he should have looked, considering what just occurred. However, Brennan knew that all of the Draconian Ashtar guards that were shot seconds ago had served under the General for many years.

"So many of these men were once part of my army, and they are now dying for these monsters—blindly taking the Colonel's orders without any knowledge that my team is working for me!"

"There's a lot more of Jasso's men in the sublevels," Brennan said fearfully. "Mostly all of Tyburr's European field agents."

"Don't worry," Clarkson smiled. "My guys know what they're doing, and they know the layout of the building. They will be looking to come here first, which is the location of my beacon's broadcast."

Despite Clarkson's professional cool, Brennan sensed he was still a bit worried. Suddenly, the tumult of obvious pursuit was heard from outside the door. The rushed footsteps were muffled but seemed heavy and could only be made by armored boots. The pleas of dying men drowned out some of the sounds of crumbling sheet rock, and the sporadic flashes of bright light made for an eerie strobe effect underneath the crack of door—each flash of light was synced to every shot that was heard being fired.

Clarkson and Brennan were two of the most battle-tested men in the world, and yet even they shuddered at the thought of what would happen to them if Clarkson's team did not make it.

"Scan through the camera feeds for this floor!" Clarkson demanded as his gaze stood fixed on the dangling monitor in the corner of the room.

Brennan immediately flipped his nervous fingers around the antiquated keyboard, and after several seconds, Brennan located the camera feeds that came from their floor.

The scene outside the briefing room was so grim that Brennan didn't know whether to shout for joy or cringe from the horror. The feeds came from three separate cameras outside the briefing room, mostly perched on each side of the long hallway that stretched from the briefing room to the elevators. A fourth video feed came from the opposite side of the elevator doors, where a procession of cubicles stood. There seemed to be a feast of corpses out there, mostly RAPDA agents as well as the bodies of Draconian Ashtars that had guarded the conference room. Even though the images on the monitor were in black and white, all of the men looked bloodied and savagely slaughtered.

Brennan was astonished after witnessing such a terrific onslaught. "I can't believe how your men are just barreling through everybody."

"My men are capable Major," Clarkson conceited.

Suddenly, the tumultuous sounds of what seemed like thudding footsteps became louder and louder from just beyond the briefing room door. Both Brennan and Clarkson turned to the monitor, which showed a man in exo- skeletal body armor making his way down the hall. When the man got to the door, he knocked.

"General Clarkson?" a sharp, tinny voice said from behind the door.

"I'm in here!" Clarkson shouted, and he felt a huge sense of relief after being assured that his men made it.

"Hold on, we detected that security E.M. barrier inside and some of my men are heading to the security station down in the sublevels to disable it," the tinny voice said.

Brennan felt his blood pressure drop fifty points, yet some anxiety remained.

The voice from behind the door was not human; it sounded electronic, and sounded as if someone were speaking from behind a breathing apparatus.

"This is Red Leader, override alpha, alpha one alpha! I have confirmed the location of the General. I need this shield down!" the man known as Red Leader shouted.

Brennan glanced at the monitor and watched Red Leader from the perspective of a nearby security camera. Brennan noticed that the mercenary's armored suit was tarred with blood and soot.

Clarkson placed his mouth dangerously close to the shielded door and shouted, "The shootout in the lobby...is the Overseer..."

"Dead—most likely dead," Red Leader answered. "Where is Doctor Baal?" Clarkson asked.

"Doctor Baal is still unaccounted for. He was last seen at the thirty-second precinct according to an agent we interrogated on the way here. Some of my men are going over surveillance evidence of Baal's escape route as we speak, but so far, my men haven't radioed anything to me," Red Leader said.

"Are you alone?" Clarkson then asked.

"Yes. After we cleared the floor, my team went down to back up a few of my men way down in the sublevels," Red Leader said. "Once I get you two out of this room, I'll arm you both, and we should have no problem rejoining the team. We got almost everyone, save for a few RAPDA agents in the sublevels."

Before Brennan could ask about the whereabouts of Lieutenant Graham, the security E.M. field fizzed away with a strident zap. The door unlocked and then opened, and a plume of smoke entered the room, obscuring Red Leader. All that could be seen were myriads of neon colored blips that snaked along the mercenary's body armor, and only its luminescence cut through the smoke.

Before long, the smoke had finally cleared and Red Leader appeared in the doorway. The mercenary's ocular visors then slid up with a hiss, revealing Red Leader's ordinary face, notable only for his fierce, battle-tested eyes.

"I'm here to escort you out of the building General," Red Leader said robotically; his ocular scopes showed a HUD display through the lenses. What made the suit marvelous to the eyes wasn't so much the design, but that dim halo of energy that surrounded the suit. The halo looked similar to the E.M. shield that trapped the men in the briefing room—sort of appearing like a distortion of the surrounding air.

Clarkson then waved an arm towards Brennan. "This here is Major Brennan of Earth."

"Yes, I expected you," Red Leader said. "We met your Lieutenant Graham outside on the street. He was trying to get into the building but several RAPDA guards denied him. Of course, until we showed up. He told me that you should still be in the building with the General."

"Where is Lieutenant Graham now?" Brennan asked.

"He's with my Alpha team down in the sublevels inside Pandora's room, and he's helping them gather surveillance evidence in and around the police precinct where Baal was last seen."

"There must be dozens of RAPDA agents down there!" Brennan shouted.

Red Leader's helmet clanked against his chest as he nodded. "They better side with us then," Red Leader began with good posture. "Some never gave us the chance to explain the situation to them, and so we had to kill them. I hope that they are not engaging in any unnecessary firefights, but many men are angry that we killed the Overseer—and they are shooting first and asking questions last. Unfortunately, they are forcing our hand into killing them."

"I feel so useless without my weapons!" Brennan flushed

Red Leader snickered and pointed down the hall. "Oh there are plenty of weapons scattered on this floor. We took out two Ashtar guards and two RAPDA agents that were guarding your conference room."

Brennan peeked down the hall but could not see through the thick haze of smoke that filled the long hallway.

"Got anything powerful for the Major here?" Clarkson asked.

Red Leader reached into his satchel and rummaged through it before taking out a solid rectangular object that looked like a very thin TV remote control.

"This here is almost identical in power to most of your basic type-1 phasers," Red Leader said. "The jog dial there sets the base phaser pattern and the button fires. It's simple as that."

"What do you call this thing?" Brennan asked.

"We call it a pulse wand you can also choose which type of fire you want to expel, and it is currently set to shoot out black hole lasers."

"Let's get moving then," Clarkson demanded.

"Allow me to lead," Red Leader shouted, and his visor slid back down to cover his face.

In an instant, Red Leader shot down the hall, and the hydraulics in his armored suit's joints hissed with each step. Brennan fought the pain in his hip as he tried to match Red Leader's speed, but Brennan's steps became smaller after taking the time to gaze at his surroundings. Several of the European RAPDA agents that guarded the floor were sprawled on the ground, some half burned from phaser shots, and the congealed blood that covered their wounds looked black and charred even on their black suits.

An orange glow came from the cubicle area near the water cooler and some smoke had collected into the corners of the ceiling. Suddenly, the sprinkler system activated and the water pattered on the men's heads and shoulders as they passed the cubicles. Small fires were scattered, partially subdued by the sprinkler system to some degree, but some flames still leapt up the walls. Flames pawed at their legs as the men scampered across the cubicle section and towards the elevators where the wisps of smoke grew thicker. Each breath sucked hot air into their lungs and the men all coughed violently except for Red Leader who had the front of his helmet flipped down with its built-in breathing mask. The smoke got thicker and thicker as they progressed, so Brennan and Clarkson tucked their noses in their shirts. Brennan had to look hard to see past the thick smoke and he slowed his steps in order not to bump into something.

All of a sudden, the elevator doors dinged open, revealing two well-muscled RAPDA agents in black suits and armored vests. The RAPDA agents fired instantly; some shots whizzed past Brennan's head, chewing up some of the wall behind him. Brennan and Clarkson hit the ground, rolled their bodies backwards and took refuge behind one of the intersecting corridors that stood perpendicular to the main hallway. Both of them tightened their grip on their pulse wands and peeked around the edge of the wall.

Cold shivers played along Brennan's spine and even the thin hairs on his head stiffened after witnessing Red Leader's actions. Red Leader just stood calmly as he loaded a capacitor into his rifle in a most nonchalant manner given the circumstances. The two RAPDA agents swiftly moved behind a set of cubicles for cover, and began shooting from behind them. Whatever shots they managed to land on Red Leader dissolved into facets after hitting the electromagnetic field surrounding Red Leader's asymmetrical defense layer system, which provided additional shielding to his full body armor. The scene was rushing, and the entire corridor became illuminated by the red glare of disruptor fire. In just seconds, dozens of beams whizzed past Brennan and Clarkson, emitting a rich, red radiance that lit up everything and everyone.

While Brennan waited for Red Leader to finish them off, Clarkson riotously fired from behind the wall. His aiming was raucously crude, but provided for some decent suppression fire for Red Leader, who began growling as he stabbed his rifle forward. He fired shot after shot towards the two agents that cowered behind the cubicles, and after a few seconds, the carpeting around the walled areas of the cubicles caught fire causing the two agents to make the fatal mistake of withdrawing from their cover. Red Leader only needed to take two more shots after that.

Red Leader's incandescent beams hit the two men square in the middle of their backs, cutting through their bulletproof vests and burning their organs. The agents hardly shrieked after being shot and lay torn and bleeding on the ground from their cruel wounds.

Before Brennan could form a cunning smile of triumph, a cruel and mocking laugh was heard coming from the his left, seemingly coming from a body near the water cooler on the other side of the room. Red Leader curiously followed the piteous sniveling sound and found a wounded European RAPDA agent emerging from a cubicle, dragging himself painfully across the bloodied carpet.

The men loosened their grips on their weapons, including Brennan, who noticed that the agent posed no threat as he struggled to move. When Brennan walked up to him, he immediately recognized the man's sausage like fingers—it was Corporal Tyburr.

"Where is Doctor Baal?" Clarkson growled towards Tyburr as he pressed the tip of his pulse wand to his forehead.

Tyburr could hardly speak, blood bubbled on his lower lip, and he just continued crawling towards the elevators very slowly, moaning out what sounded like, "You can't stop us."

Just as Tyburr reached out and upwards with his phaser, Red Leader let out a scream of bestial rage and fired a shot at the center of Tyburr's spine. A whisper of smoke emerged from the gunshot wound, charring the fabric black. Tyburr's eyes fluttered after being hit, but he did not die right away as Brennan expected him to. His bloodstained fingers reached upwards, and squeezed his hand as if he wanted to choke everyone. He let out a rattling gasp before giving Clarkson a final stare through his pain-glazed eyes, but he struggled to find enough oxygen in his lungs that would allow him to speak. A thin film of blood bubbled on Tyburr's lips, his mouth quivered before his last breath, and then his head plopped inertly to the floor. He was dead.

Red Leader lowered his rifle and flipped his visor up, revealing a mingled expression of vexation and alarm. Brennan pumped a gleeful fist, but Clarkson regrettably shut his eyes due to the regret he felt for killing his own.

He bit his lower lip and said, "Two down and one to go."

36: Finding Baal

After a three-hour-long manhunt, Brennan began to feel his old war-torn body beginning to break down. His hip flexor stung, his joints throbbed, and his feet were killing him. He barely kept up with Red Leader's hasty pace as they carefully picked their way through the building's many floors, from up on the roof, to the sublevels. Few of Baal's men remained, and those who did immediately expressed their fealty towards Clarkson after learning that the Overseer committed mutiny. Some gladly gave up their weapons, and were taken to the thirty-second precinct where they would undergo some questioning.

After finding no other opposition to detain or kill, Brennan, Clarkson, and Red Leader set out to meet the rest of Clarkson's men, as well as Lieutenant Graham, who waited in the main lobby. Apparently, he had bad news to tell the General, and everyone including Brennan knew it had something to do with the surveillance evidence that was gathered from the precinct and outlying streets surrounding it.

Brennan fought the pain in his bad hip as the elevator jerked downwards, and before the elevator reached the lobby floor, Brennan began to hear what sounded like roaring voices coming from beyond the elevator-shaft wall. The doors dinged open to reveal the rest of Clarkson's mercenaries, who were perched against the lobby's double row of tall marble pillars. There were at least a dozen of them or more. Brennan couldn't tell because the men stretched out into the smoky distance.

The lobby was a complete war zone. The surrounding marble walls were cracked and blackened in many spots. Water from the sprinkler system mixed in with the pooling blood that streamed from the dozens of dead bodies scattered about; some of them completely buried under slabs of marble and sheetrock.

Clarkson's team stood at attention upon noticing the General's presence. Water from the sprinkler system streamed down their armor, and it made them look shinier in the light. Brennan wondered where Graham was and just as he

was about to start shouting his name, Graham's washed out face was seen through an aperture between several helmeted men.

"Lieutenant!" Brennan called to him. Graham's head immediately snapped up towards his direction, and he let out the widest smile Brennan had ever seen on his square face. "I thought your old saggy ass finally weighed you down and you got yourself killed!" Graham boomed as he wriggled his way through the crowd of armored mercenaries. They both exchanged a brief hug.

"I'm okay...but why aren't you guarding Elena?" Brennan was quick to ask. "She's fine," Graham assured him. "After Baal stormed out of the precinct,

he mentioned the shootout that took place here and almost all of the police officers left the place so they could partake in the firefight. Before I left, I talked one of the officers into giving me the key to her cell, and he obliged. After all, I was in charge of guarding her and delivering her food and all. So, after the place cleared out, I freed her from the cell and told her to take refuge in my car until I get back."

Brennan felt a hundred pounds lighter after hearing that. He squeezed Graham's arm from the sudden onset of emotional relief that overcame him. "Thanks," Brennan nodded.

Brennan and Graham had no time to share their more recent war story because General Clarkson hovered above them expecting a briefing.

"What have you found Lieutenant?" Clarkson asked.

Graham gave him a millimeter of a smile and was about to offer a handshake but quickly changed his mind after seeing Clarkson's stern expression. "General, the recent power outage made it impossible for us to resort to the footage from street cameras, but luckily, the thirty-second precinct runs on a different grid, and so we got some footage of Doctor Baal's escape from the main entrance cam. Apparently, Baal took off in a black limousine, which picked him up just outside the precinct."

"And?" Clarkson asked stiffly, hoping there was more to it.

"I asked dozens of police captains and none seemed to know where Baal was going. Baal was very secretive and told no one about where he was headed

or which hotel he was staying in. When I got to Pandora's room, I then tried running a scan, but Baal seemed to have disconnected from the galactic grid entirely. He's a damn ghost!"

"I figured that," Clarkson groaned. "Baal would never connect himself to Earth's census registry."

"Perhaps only the Overseer would know, but Red Leader said he was dead," Brennan chimed in.

"I shot him myself," Red Leader nodded before pointing towards an area near the main security desk.

Then, a mercenary in blue armor stepped forward and his visor hissed upwards. "While you were rescuing the General, we bombarded this place with our grenade launchers in order to take out several Ashtar back-up units. A whole hunk of marble from the pillars fell on the Overseer's body," the mercenary said, pointing towards a heap of rubble next to where the granite security desk used to be.

Clarkson let out a breath before speaking in an unyielding voice. "Then it is imperative that we find the Overseer's body so we gain access to his office for intel. We must gather as much evidence as we can that will lead us to this secret society of Draconian Overseers that have meddled too far here," Clarkson's words rang against Brennan's ears. 'In the meantime…" Clarkson paused, before turning his gaze towards Red Leader, who was perched against a marble wall with several other mercenaries. "Continue to perform a few rounds; there might be more survivors in the building."

Red Leader acknowledged his order with a swift salute. He then relayed the message to his men that were scattered around the lobby, and they all hurried to the elevators in unison.

Clarkson then barked out another order from across the lobby. "If you find any survivors and non-hostiles, remember that they are to be informed that they were fighting alongside traitors. Let them know that they still must face trial in order to get to the bottom of where their ties to Baal and his secret society begins and ends."

Red Leader gave a curtly nod, and he and his men vanished into the elevators.

Clarkson then turned to both Brennan and Graham and only stared at them as he formulated a plan. The look on Clarkson's face woke the dread in their hearts. Water continued to patter against his wool blazer and dripped from the medals on his lapel. His long, salty white and wet hair was dangling over the hard lines of his face, and he chewed his lip before speaking. "Major, I'm going to head to the thirty-second precinct and inform the police of the situation at hand. I'm going to tell them that I'm taking control of the police department effective immediately and will tell them that your daughter is to be released from prison and adequately fed until our mission is done here."

Brennan waned back into a gently simmering quiescence. "Thank you for taking the time to think about my personal matter General, but I believe she's safe. My Lieutenant found a way to get her to safety."

"Okay good," Clarkson said, faintly surprised. "Because we are going to have to cut through a lot of red tape, and there are going to be a lot of people asking questions as to who gets the right to hold the scissors. I'm going to tell them everything about the Overseer and Doctor Baal, and will tell them why I'm linking them to a terrorist organization. All law enforcement—from local police to the National Guard—as well as every single one of our RAPDA agents in Europe and Asia, are to be told of the mutiny and conspiracy as briefly as possible. Then, the first thing we're going to have to do is send some properly trained medical doctors down here to implant the proper nanobots inside everyone."

"Of course General," Brennan said in a level voice before continuing with a doubtful tone. "I guess it wouldn't hurt to protect people from the radiation even though Doctor Baal said that the solar radiation wasn't the main cause of the mutations."

"Well..." Clarkson started doubtfully. "If Doctor Baal is right about these new celestial energies that are affecting people's DNA, then I'm not sure the standard radiation protection bots would stay connected long enough anyway.

However, it couldn't hurt to administer them to the populace. Perhaps the bots will help keep DNA from mutating too quickly. After all, fast mutation is what's killing the mutants."

"What about Baal's bots; how do we flush those out?" Brennan asked. "Oh we have ways to destroy nanobots with simple solutions made of

ammonium nitrate," Clarkson said confidently. He then turned to look at Graham. "Lieutenant Graham, you will continue to take care of Brennan's daughter. I want you to summon a shuttle and get her back to her ship. Tell Captain Bailey about everything that went down here."

Graham answered with a nod.

Clarkson turned to Brennan and gave him a hard stare. He placed a hand on his shoulder and spoke with words that stung, "I'm heading towards the precinct now, I want you to find that bastard!"

Brennan exhaled a sigh as he looked around the shattered lobby. ' It may take days to find Jasso's body in this mess."

Clarkson shook his head. "Then do what you can to get into Jasso's office and gather as many notes possible. We'll need evidence that proved what went on here on Earth," Clarkson paused, and continued to speak apprehensively. "We are going to need everything we can find."

37: Finding Jasso

The lobby was a mess. Slabs of sheetrock and marble lay atop most of the dead bodies, and some were buried in the rubble all together. Luckily, a couple of young and rough-hewn paramedics helped Brennan move all the broken wood and marble off most of the bodies. There were no signs of Jasso's body anywhere. And to make matters worse, the threat of spreading fire could force Brennan out of the building sooner than later, and hopes of retrieving evidence would go down in flames, literally.

Brennan curiously inched his way through the lobby with unhurried steps and wide eyes, occasionally hopping over corpses and puddles of congealed blood. He could not avoid some of the blood because it had mixed in with the water from the sprinkler system.

Fire department helicopters were heard humming outside, and they continuously sprayed the top floors in order to control the fires. Every now and then, a firefighter would inform Brennan whether or not the fires were being contained enough to prevent an evacuation. That was the last thing Brennan wanted. The few fires that still breathed throughout the lobby were small, but large enough to bathe the place with a smoky orange light. There was only one firefighter in the lobby. He was a brawny and long armed man, wide of shoulder and with tree-trunks for legs. He only needed a fire extinguisher for the job since the fires were so small.

The smell of charred flesh and sooty water made Brennan sick to his stomach, and Brennan thought about calling off the search until the place was cleaned up a bit more; however, after the fireman doused a small fire, Brennan thought he should check under the pile of charred wood which was previously inaccessible before the fire was put out. Brennan threaded his way through some shattered flowerpots and some black, smoking hunks of wood. Then, to his surprise—a cigar floated in a pool of watery blood on the ground near the area Jasso was thought to have fallen. The cigar stood just a few inches away from a bloodied hand that protruded out of the pile of marble and glass.

That must be him!

Piled on top of the body were large shards of glass, splintered wood, as well as a few hunks of marble that had toppled from the surrounding pillars. There was a familiar looking symbol on the sleeve of the protruding arm too, and Brennan knew it was a Draconian uniform because of the serpent patch.

Brennan moved ahead with high anticipation and began removing each piece of glass carefully. The removal of a piece of plywood verified Jasso's presence, and even though his face was partially burned and covered in congealed blood, Brennan recognized him, and his pulsating carotid artery indicated to Brennan that he was alive indeed.

A shaft of daylight happened to shine directly on Jasso's black and sooty face, showing his facial injuries better. Blood bubbled from the sides of his mouth and absorbed into his beard. Cerebral spinal fluid gushed from his ears, all the way down his neck and collar. He had charred clothes around a particular wound on his spleen area, but there was little blood.

The wound must have been cauterized, Brennan thought. In a sense, Jasso was lucky to be hit with an energy beam and not a bullet, or he probably would have bled to death despite the fact that he was shot in the gut and away from any vital organs.

Brennan knelt down and reached into Jasso's coat pockets, careful not to place his knees on all the shards of glass on the floor

"What...what are you doing?" Jasso mumbled in a hoarse voice.

Brennan never bothered to answer. He continued to rummage into his pockets, hoping to find his security override card that would grant him access to his office.

"Relax, conserve your energy, medics are on the way," Brennan said, carefully digging into Jasso's pockets. A wince and moan caused Brennan to pull his hand away from Jasso's coat pocket. His cracked ribs grated when he shifted over a bit, and Brennan actually felt bad causing a dying man more pain in spite of Jasso's degree of villainy.

"I'm going to need your override keycard Colonel."

Jasso took a while to realize it was Brennan in front of him, but then his vision came into focus. The sight of his enemy almost proved to invigorate Jasso somewhat, sparking him to life. "What...are you...doing?" Jasso slurred through a loose mouth.

Brennan ignored him of course and continued to dig through the inside of his coat pocket carefully. However, Brennan forgot to take into account how sharp Draconian reflexes were, and failed to notice the fact that Jasso had reached into his boot with his left hand for a knife. It wasn't until Brennan heard the ping of hard steel scraping against the leather scabbard that he became aware of Jasso's sneaky endeavor. Even in near death, Jasso mustered up a bit of adrenaline and pushed the blade towards Brennan's belly. Luckily, Brennan had seen it in time and sucked his stomach in, and the blade whooshed past.

"You're not getting into my office," Jasso said with a mouthful of blood; his tongue was thick, making his voice hoarse and low. Jasso kept swiping the blade as he lay on his back, but his arms were rubbery, and his swiping was without much force. Brennan still took a few steps back though, and his eyes never deviated from the tip of his blade.

How terrible would it be to be killed now, Brennan thought, after all he went through in life. *How terrible it would be to be killed by a man who would not make it through the hour...or the minute, judging by his severe wounds.*

"Give me that override card," Brennan demanded.

Jasso managed to let a sly grin form on his bloodied mouth. "Come and get it if you want it," Jasso said defensively, continuing to swipe with the knife in order to prevent Brennan from getting into his pockets.

Jasso then attempted to get up and used what was left of a nearby table to help spring him up on his feet. Brennan grabbed his pulse wand and set it for incapacitation in the event that Jasso gained enough strength to rally up a hostile attack. He even thought about knocking Jasso out, but something told him that it would be an unjust thing to do because even a low energy shot would probably kill him, given his condition.

Should I kill him? It would put him out of his misery! But what if he could be saved? Brennan didn't want murder on his hands.

Jasso let out a papery dry chuckle, and he slashed his knife through the air. "I'm going to kill you!"

Brennan took the threat lightly because the man could hardly move. His knees buckled with each step, and Brennan figured he couldn't possible pose a threat. Nevertheless, Brennan treaded back carefully and kept his pulse wand aimed at Jasso's chest. He figured that if he was healthy enough to stand, then he was strong enough to stab him. Brennan saw no honor in shooting an unarmed man, even though he was responsible for killing billions.

Brennan decided to disarm him and in an instant, he lunged for the Jasso's wrist. The water from the sprinkler system made Jasso's bloody skin even greasier, and so Brennan didn't get a good grip on him. Jasso jerked his knife back and was surprisingly still strong enough to pull his hand away from Brennan's grip. Jasso swung the knife again, but was far too slow to get it anywhere near Brennan, who carefully jerked backwards.

"You won't get near my office!" Jasso said with poise, but Brennan shook his head. Brennan thought he was a bit too confident given his condition. Jasso could not muster up an intimidating charge at all; he waddled forward with wobbly legs, thrusting his dagger forward, desperately swinging his blade with stubborn determination. Apparently, some blood dripped down the entire right side of his torso, and down his leg, and it trickled out of the cuff of his pant leg. It was a miracle that he lived through his wounds, and Brennan could not help but admire the strength of a Draconian human.

Jasso then pulled the knife back to prepare for another attack. He stabbed his arm forward and the blade lurched towards Brennan's Adam's apple. Brennan sidestepped the first lunge with ease, but decided to use a different maneuver on the second attempt. Brennan yanked his body sideways to get a better angle on his assailant, and after Jasso missed, Brennan reeled at his arm again, grabbing it tightly and turning it around so that the knife's tip faced backwards, pointing it at Jasso's own chest.

Jasso stared at the blade and stubbornly resisted as he latched onto Brennan's wrists. If Jasso were healthy, Brennan would be dead by now, and even though a Draconian of his age had the strength of three Earthmen, he could not match Brennan's strength in his condition. Jasso spit blood right into Brennan's face, which helped him gain some momentum from the distraction it posed, but that was all the advantage he would gather. Brennan wrestled the tip of the blade closer to Jasso's throat, and Jasso's eyes crossed inwards as he gazed at the shimmering blade inching closer. Jasso stared at the tip of the blade with fear, and every ounce of energy contained within his body was diverted to his one arm—knowing that one push from Brennan would plunge the knife through his neck and end his miserable life.

"Give it up Jasso and live long enough to see yourself tended to by medics," Brennan snapped.

Jasso only showed his bloody teeth after hearing that and continued to struggle with him, but couldn't get his arm free. Brennan shuddered from so much anger that he thought about stabbing him at that moment. He looked around the lobby to make sure that there weren't any firefighters around that would see him do so, and lucky for him, there weren't any. Brennan thought of all the friends he lost because of this man before him; memories of the horrors he experienced because of Jasso and his cohorts began to flicker through his mind. Jasso was the man responsible for the manipulation of Earth's magnetosphere, and he let the sun cook everyone. He caused the earthquakes and floods, the damage to his house, the death of his parents, the imprisonment of his daughter, and the intrusion into the minds of the people of Earth. Brennan just wanted to plunge that knife through him right then and there. However, he dismissed the idea after realizing that Jasso wouldn't last long. His ribs grated and his breathing was torturously painful for him, so he figured he would leave him be and make him die slowly.

With determination, Brennan snapped Jasso's arm in half using a jujitsu move, and the loud snap from the cracked bone echoed through the entire lobby.

Jasso shrieked in pain. His knife fell instantly, and Brennan kicked it away into a heap of broken plant pots. With a surge of anger, Brennan grabbed Jasso by his bloodied jacket and slammed him back into a marble pillar, knocking all the wind from his lungs. Jasso slid down the pillar in agony, leaving a streaky and bloody handprint on the white marble as his body slowly sunk down to the floor. Jasso's mouth was wide open as if stuck in the middle of a scream, his wounds reopened as the clotted blood on his clothes separated from his flesh.

Just then, a stooped looking female police officer with pebbled skin scampered through the main rotating doors and into the lobby.

"Major, I heard a scream. Is everything—"

"Fine," Brennan quickly replied, putting up a palm. "This one's still alive, tried stabbing me."

The police officer took her side arm out and approached, but Brennan waved her off.

"Its under control, he won't make it through the hour. Nothing the paramedics can't handle," Brennan said plaintively.

The stubby officer took a deep breath and holstered her firearm. "Holler if you need me, I'll be right outside the door here…where it's dry," the cop jested and headed back.

Brennan fell to his knees and immediately began to frisk Jasso for anymore potential weapons he might be harboring and of course, the key card. Jasso winced and groaned; his breathing sounded raspy. After finally finding his wallet, Brennan rummaged through it in hopes of finding his keycard, but there was nothing in there but credit sticks. The breaths coming out of Jasso's mouth grew fainter and fainter with each minute that passed. His eyes fluttered open every now and then, and his eyes became pain glazed and blood shot. By the time Brennan checked all of his back pockets Jasso's breaths came in largely spaced intervals, and sometimes seemed to stop all together.

Did he pass out from the pain?

Brennan felt for a carotid pulse. He had one, but it was thready.

What a strong son of a bitch! Where is that card damn it!

Brennan shifted Jasso around, pausing instinctively whenever Jasso croaked from the pain.

In one last faltering breath, Jasso said, "You are fighting a very old war; it will never end." His mouth formed a thin and tortured smile.

Brennan paid him no mind; even though Jasso was right, the least Brennan could do is blow the whistle on the entire operation to ensure that Jasso would be the last Overseer to operate behind the curtains on Earth.

Trapped in the thought, Brennan continued to grope frantically for the card in the other back pocket of Jasso's pants until he finally came across that thin piece of plastic he was looking for. Sure enough, it was the security override card.

Jasso's throat moved convulsively. "You can't win, we are everywhere," he said lethargically and with half-shut eyes. "We are everywhere…"

After that, his eyes turned to glass, his head went limp, and his breathing stopped.

Jasso was dead.

38: The Evidence

After Brennan strolled into Jasso's office, he was surprised to see the room so tidy, and it seemed to combine the attributes of office and bedroom because a bed stood nestled in one of the small room's corners. Brennan never thought he would stay there for more than a few hours, but he was wrong. After he courted himself on Jasso's plush leather recliner, he flicked on his PC, kicked his legs back on his polished oak desk and sat there all day long after stumbling across much more intel than expected.

His scavenger hunt would keep him on Earth for a lot longer then he planned on staying. What stalled him at first was the fact that the information had to be backed up. He didn't feel secure enough to simply confiscate Jasso's hard drives. After all, they could be subjected to damage, and every bit of the prospective evidence stored inside them could be wiped clean—especially if he lugged them up through the soupy, ionic atmosphere that separated him and the Niagra, which was waiting for him up in orbit.

There were countless emails and documents to be discovered within Jasso's personal computer that would surely help Brennan blow the whistle on the Society of the Snake, and so Brennan took his time dissecting each bit of information in unremitting fashion. Brennan was so overwhelmed from the scores of Intel he had gathered that his inquisitive glances at the screen locked his facial muscles as rigid as a mask. Brennan first made sure to find all the detailed blueprints of Baal's nanobots, and it took a while to find a way into Jasso's private email inbox due despite his hacking ability.

After the hack, Brennan came across a detailed email that explained how the nanobots were nothing more than designer viruses that were designed to eliminate enlightened people from planet Earth. The data was so extensive that Brennan had gone through almost all of his crystal flash-drives in just one afternoon.

Brennan slept in Jasso's office the first night and on the second day, Brennan had more crystal drives delivered to him, including several yottabyte sticks, which were capable of handling heaps of data. Brennan learned about the so- called mutant genocide after coming across another PDF filed titled "The Protocol." He learned that Baal and the secret society sought to not only alter the minds of the Earthlings but also planned on creating personalized bioweapons for any humans that displayed any spiritual behavior, regardless of whether or not their DNA had mutated or not. The protocol would go into effect so they could genetically target anyone that would not conform to their new world order.

Brennan learned that the secret society kept a DNA bank on all Earth citizens from as far back as the 1940s. Perhaps even longer, he thought. He scanned through hundreds of folders into the wee hours of the second night, studying the detailed files that explained how live cells were collected from each and every person born in a hospital in order to create a molecular profile on everyone. This way, the Society of the Snake could easily create a genetic blueprint necessary for creating gene specific pathogens. That way, if the society wanted to rub someone out, they could genetically assassinate someone by tailoring gene- specific cancers to anyone they chose.

Brennan learned that the Society of the Snake preferred certain races for their experiments too. Apparently, their plans were to genetically target anyone who had a higher percentage of Neanderthal DNA, and it became evident after Brennan discovered a recorded video chat on Jasso's computer. After discovering dozens of recorded conversations on the matter, Brennan concluded that people with higher percentages of Neanderthal DNA were more susceptible to shape shifting, and their dormant genetic material tended to awaken more than it did in other humans.

Brennan learned that Baal's gene-specific, nanobot viruses would detect a mutant's atavistic traits, as well as detect all their rearrangement breakpoints in a person's genome sequences. The nanobot viruses were so smart that they would determine whether or not they would serve to cure a person or deem them as "too broke to fix." Those that shape-shifted into older models would have been easily wiped out by Baal's latest upgrade, which supposedly consisted of next- gen nanobots that were stable enough to have a twenty-year lifespan. The programmed bots were so intelligent that they could detect whether a person was shape-shifting or not. If a person mutated and gained access to the forbidden zones of the brain, the nanobots would disregard their primary duty as cognitive stabilizers and transform into cancer causing genotypes.

Perhaps the most frightening thing of all of Brennan's discoveries, was the fact that the Society of the Snake planned to distribute the upgrades and gene specific viruses by aerosolizing them and germinating them in clouds. The rainfall would become infectious after that, and no mutant could escape the reach of the Society of the Snake. Luckily, Brennan stifled Baal and Jasso before they could initiate such a hardhearted and inescapable attack. Earth would have become uninhabitable if the designer nanobot upgrades ever went airborne.

Brennan would further become disturbed by not only Jasso's computer files, but several penciled doodles he found scribed into the hard wooden desk of his

—surely carved by Jasso himself, Brennan figured. The scribbles on the desk read: *After I get rid of these last members of the paternal race, my last reminders of hell will be expunged forever*

On the third day after Jasso's death, Clarkson joined in on the scavenger hunt after receiving a phone call from Brennan. Brennan told him that his scavenger hunt might take longer than he planned and suggested that Clarkson come help him read the hundreds of newly discovered emails he had dug up.

Neither Brennan nor Clarkson would have thought they would ever discover anymore evidence after all that Baal told him. Brennan figured he heard it all— but he was wrong. It was not until Brennan came across a rather long and descriptive email from Doctor Baal himself that would blow the lid off everything; the data in that particular email helped them uncover the Society of the Snake's true motives. Brennan trembled from each word that he read, and by the time he got to the last paragraph, he thought his heart would crack his sternum from its hard beating.

Brennan read on and on about the Society of the Snake's initial endeavor, which was completely the opposite of what they tried to do in recent times.

Apparently the society invaded Earth many thousands of years ago, and the Society of the Snake wanted to help propel Earth into a class C civilization more quickly for the sake of boosting Orion Corp. stocks. The only way to quicken Earth's status was to enlighten the humans that lived on it, and so the secret society used Draconian DNA to create Earth human/Draconian hybrids, and they helped introduce technology into Earth civilization just to speed things along. It seemed as if the secret society of Draconian Overseers were not patient enough for evolution to take its course so they initiated a eugenics program to help speed up the minds of man, which happened to be the complete opposite of what they tried to do in recent times.

Brennan dedicated a whole crystal flash-drive just for that particular email alone. It was something he would want to keep for himself and take to his grave. After reading for three days straight with little sleep or food, Brennan almost decided to put an end to the scavenger hunt after realizing he had enough evidence to present to the galactic court. Until of course, he made another discovery on the fourth day.

Brennan discovered some alarming information after stumbling across not only digital evidence, but also several leather-bound books piled up on Jasso's dusty bookcase. Brennan dissected each of Jasso's old books feverishly and intently. As Brennan read aloud, Clarkson took industrious notes, writing everything down in a digital medium so he could easily present everything to the galactic court. The books would be presented as well of course, but it would take too long to flip through each of the chapters.

There was too much information scattered in the books, so Clarkson wrote down the important things. The books were a mystery even to Clarkson, and Clarkson claimed that no such books ever existed in even the most prestigious Draconian universities. If any other copies existed, then the books were surely kept isolated within the halls of undisclosed lodges. Brennan spent the entire day flipping through each of their pages with zealous fingers, barely finding time to eat or drink.

However, nothing would prepare Brennan and Clarkson for what they were about to read in a book titled *Adam's Apple*. Brennan and Clarkson read the book in just six hours, and it led them to references from the bible. After reading it, Brennan had learned the details regarding the Draconian eugenics program.

Clarkson had brought up the universal symbol of medicine, called the caduceus.

The caduceus was modeled after the "Sumerian seal," which Brennan was very much familiar with. The Sumerian seal featured two dragons intertwined around the tree of life, and it surely represented the integration of Draconian DNA into Earth's prehistoric man. After all, Brennan knew that the "Tree of Life" was a nickname used by the scientific community to represent the DNA double helix. Of course, another piece of information would come to Brennan's mind, only adding to help complete the giant puzzle that made the big picture. Brennan told Clarkson that the most notable difference between modern man and the Neanderthal was the voice box. The information led Brennan straight to the Bible's Genesis, and he immediately thought about Adam. He then thought about the nickname for the human voice box—A.K.A. the *Adam's Apple*. Adam is the biblical version of the first man on Earth, and after reading it all, both Brennan and Clarkson speculated whether Adam was probably not only one of the Earth's first humans, but instead, the first modern human/alien hybrid.

Clarkson was familiar with much of Earth's literature, not only its religious texts but also its sciences. Clarkson brought up an interesting debate when he claimed that the very same apple fell on Isaac Newton's head. "A metaphor," Clarkson said, which of course represented "knowledge." This very apple led to Newton's epiphanies. The knowledge that the apple brought was made possible by the apple seed, the seed of the Draconian, which made it possible for the Earthman to have an immortal soul—all due to the mind's ability of retro- cognition. The insight gained from this form of immortality was not only responsible for all the great things that Newton created, but it also led to more intelligence, therefore more fear, and in addition, more evil.

It was not long until Brennan stumbled across another set of doodles written in ink on the very last page of the book called *Adam's Apple*—*We must clean up our mess,* was written on the book's sleeve.

Jasso also scribbled the name "Leonardo da Vinci" on the last page, and it wasn't long until Brennan realized why. Right under the name were the words "O, Draconian Devil." Brennan and Clarkson checked the name three times and realized that Leonardo da Vinci was indeed an anagram for the words O Draconian Devil. Every single letter matched perfectly, and Clarkson had come up with a notion that Brennan could only agree with. Leonardo da Vinci probably never existed, and his name represented a composite character. He represented one single personage that represented all of the technological marvels contrived by the immortal man. Clarkson reminded Brennan that the Draconian genes weren't inscribed for the physical, but spiritual. Older Model Nephilim type humans could be Asian, Latin, Black, White and so-forth and the Nephilim soul isn't tied to one specific group.

Brennan found several notes written in an email from Doctor Baal himself. They read— *If our children here on Earth let down their parents, we'll have no choice but to cause a deluge that would wipe out a huge portion of the population in order to make it easier for us to DNA control the survivors. We will cast them aside with the deluge, a flood of hellish proportions. Just like the first deluge. With it will come electromagnetic pulses from the natural solar flares that will rock the earth, after we put huge holes in the magnetosphere, leaving the Earth defenseless against the flares. Large waves swept the lands back then and they will again!*

Brennan copy and pasted it all and backed up that specific information on three separate flash drives just in case of damage.

On the fifth day after Jasso's death, Brennan and Clarkson thought they had read enough and decided to call it a mission. Clarkson left RAPDA headquarters to oversee the delivery of the ammonium nitrate serum that would disable everyone's poisonous nanobots. Only after the mandatory blood cleanse would one be allowed to be upgraded with the standard radiation-proof bots that all space faring persons carried in their blood. Unfortunately, the Earth was still sick, and Earth folk still needed to fuse with cybernetic technology until Clarkson found the time to de-irradiate the Earth and strengthen the magnetosphere again—if that was even possible at all.

In order to play it safe, Clarkson made sure that each vaccine's contents underwent a crystallography test right before being injected into a person. The testing of the bots would reveal all of the natural cellular functions that they would replace that way, no one could ever sabotage nano-medicine ever again. The whole process of "the cleansing" would take a week or two at the most, and Clarkson assured that every single person on Earth would be cleansed of their designer viruses and cured of radiation sickness in no time. At least, Brennan thought, the new bots would help potential shape-shifters regain their immune systems for a short while, and if the new bots would ever disconnect again, then perhaps it wouldn't matter. After all, Clarkson's top priority was to strengthen the magnetosphere so that the solar radiation would no longer hinder the mutation process that a person must go through in order to revert to an older model humanoid.

39: Denouement

The first year after the Earth was freed from alien control was a fruitful year.

Cancer rates dropped after the magnetosphere was strengthened, but mutating civilians still had it rough. Evolution didn't come easy, and a lot of people had a tough time adapting to their new, expanded minds. However, at least their physical problems slowed. Without the solar radiation many people handled their evolution well, including Charlie, who headed a major campaign to get society plugged in again—wirelessly and cleanly. More was accomplished in that one year than in the previous decade. Yet, in all that time, Baal was never found. Brennan had no idea where he was—no one did. For all he knew, Baal was still on Earth, disguised and surreptitiously tucked away in the outskirts of town like the canyon dwellers used to do. Brennan wondered if he was on some other planet, plotting a similar agenda with that secret society of his. Like Jasso had said, "they were everywhere," and Baal would probably never be found.

Brennan figured that the Society of the Snake would probably never be revealed from behind the curtain that they concealed themselves with, but he would look for him until his last dying breath.

Brennan and Clarkson presented their evidence, and investigations commenced for many months, shifting over to every pre-industrial and postindustrial civilization known to the galactic council of twelve. Surely, Baal and his secret society must have infiltrated the political, economic, and social infrastructures of many planets and not just Earth. However, after many months of galactic wide investigations, Brennan learned that most planets with type-2 space faring civilizations maintained very clean eugenics programs, and there was no evidence of any more prison planets controlled by the Society of the Snake. In a sense, Brennan didn't care. He was just glad that Earth was no longer being self-sabotaged by its rulers.

On the first anniversary of Jasso's death, Brennan realized that he would never return to the Niagra because Elena wound up coming back down to Earth that day, and she made it just in time for a special ceremony held at the old City Hall where she would see her dad crowned by Clarkson himself.

Clarkson tasked him with the title of temporary Overseer of planet Earth, and it was his responsibility to get his home planet up and spinning again.

Brennan gladly accepted his new position as chief Overseer of Earth but was well aware that it would be a position he would give up once governments were established in the six remaining colonies on the planet. Brennan vowed to give the job up as soon as possible, and he promised to the citizens of New York that he would be the Earth's last Overseer.

When news spread throughout the galaxy about the injustices placed on Earth and its people, every single one of the so-called Earth VIPs that were initially recruited by Orion Corp. returned to Earth in order to contribute to Earth's rebuilding process. The timing was perfect, and their skilled positions were badly needed. In less than a year, the young men and women of Earth soon began learning about free energy, and most of all, agriculture. Agriculture was the most lucrative field in the post-apocalyptic city, and the food grew flawlessly right after a few simple nitrates were added to the soils of Earth's tainted farms. Many of the younger, healthier, mutated citizens shunned the idea of living in any of the remaining Earth cities, given the fact that so much real estate was at hand. Many older models had a simple way of thinking and cared little for materialism. Many people lived alone with their families, miles away from the hubs of Earth's six remaining major cities, choosing to live in peace with their own farms to sustain them. So many people got used to living without electricity that they began to embrace it. Mall parking lots were turned into community farms, and no one had to work for food anymore. It wasn't long until four different factories opened up within the city that were dedicated to manufacturing Charlie's generators as well as his solar trees. Charlie had the honor of naming the products and decided to officially name them Bumblebee generators because of the sound they made. Over the course of the year, the scientific community used Charlie's invention as a foundation for creating an anti-gravitational drive for spacecraft—all in hopes of finally getting Earthlings into far space for the first time in history.

Brennan remained mostly happy at the fact that his planet was safer today then it has ever been in the last few hundred years or more.

But was it safer than it was when the aliens controlled it? Brennan often asked himself this.

Even though the alien grip on Earth had been released, Brennan could not go a week without a restless night or two. Brennan would walk the streets of New York City at night, worried about whether or not he opened up Pandora's Box to the world. Baal's words rang in his ears every day and every night, and Brennan maintained a memory of every detail of the conversation with Baal he had on that awful day in the conference room. Maybe, Brennan thought, the fact that humanity finally had access to one hundred percent of their brains would lead to the utopia Brennan and Charlie hoped for. Brennan only hoped he would not be forced to watch it head towards the path foreseen by Baal—but only time would tell.

Baal's words niggled at his mind every minute of his days. Often, he thought that perhaps the technology Charlie rediscovered is a two-edged sword. Like the sun that gives life and kills life. Perhaps one man's tool is another man's weapon; Brennan wondered if the Church's endeavor to suppress knowledge and keep humankind ignorant was the right thing to do. Brennan also wondered if the alien-controlled Church was right to arrest Galileo for inventing the telescope. Of course, the Church did so not because they claimed Galileo's theory was wrong but because he was right.

Brennan would often think about the more recent times, mostly about Morgan Stanley, and whether he was right to take away Nikola Tesla's funding, therefore destroying Tesla's dream of providing free, wireless energy to the masses.

What if some average Joe decided to cook his neighbor with a device such as Charlie's generator—a device can be revised into a direct energy weapon? Brennan asked these questions each day, and he could only wait for an answer. The ancient world of Atlantis was forming again on Earth, and only time would tell if it would destroy itself like in the past.

Brennan had often wondered how the newly evolved humans or better yet, older humans, would be remembered in a century from now. Would Charlie's name and legacy hold? Alternatively, would the new generations of super- humans further lead to doom?

Brennan sure had faith though, and he knew the universe had called for humanity to evolve on Earth, at such a specific time when humanity faced a precipice. Brennan knew that in such a time like now, humans would need an animal body to survive in the raw nature of post-apocalyptic Earth. Besides that, the humans would need their old psychic faculties to help bring on conscious time travel to times in the past and future where they would envision more scientific attainments necessary for rebuilding the world in a cleaner way, without the man-made pollution and global warming from the safer but older, oil-based energy systems.

Almost every single person on Earth was evolving into beings with a notorious past, including Brennan himself who continued to live without DNA protection and remained cancer free. Even though Brennan found himself a bit more sensitive to the sun, he began to feel more "awakened" more and more each day. Of course, the more drastic consciousness shifts happened in younger people, and at times, Brennan wished to keep RAPDA's electronic surveillance program running until he made sure that none of these new humans would take advantage of nature's hidden forces, just as Doctor Baal had originally feared.

Brennan often hoped that the mutant older models would no longer desecrate the occult knowledge for selfish ends just like their effete ancestors did all those years ago. However, electronic surveillance was something he wasn't going near. Despite all the power in his hands, Brennan pulled the plug on Pandora, and therefore decided to put an end to the ability to survey the masses from a digital medium. He even went as far as decommissioning every single one of his spy drones.

Nevertheless, in order to help him sleep better at night, Brennan found himself barging in on his daughter's dates with Charlie during their Friday night excursions at the La Candela restaurant. Brennan routinely sought reassurance and looked at Charlie as a sort of poster boy for mutant-kind.

Brennan always sought to make sure that Charlie kept his head on right, maintaining a righteous countenance, and Brennan always looked to chat with him over a drink or two whenever the opportunity presented itself. As much as he trusted the young man, he couldn't help but become paranoid every now and then. Brennan feared that Charlie might one day grow tired of some of the older, less evolved humans he was surrounded with, and perhaps he would decide to take advantage someway and somehow.

So one warm winter night during a dinner of steamed king crabs, Brennan joined Elena and Charlie for a night cap at La Candela restaurant and spent most of it asking Charlie questions about his experiences with occult knowledge and his release from ignorance.

Charlie always grew serious when talking about such topics, and he told Brennan that it was a scary thing, that there were many dark and hideous beings that lurked amidst the sands of time. Brennan never forgot what he said one night. Charlie often said that the angels that travel through the currents of time were always benevolent, and it was a person's emotional baggage that made angelic knowledge demonic. The angels always arrive during times of struggle, whether in the form of a genetic memory or a message picked up through time. The planets knew exactly when to align in the most specific patterns that would bring about essential celestial energies—energies that would transform the physical mind and the very fabric of the cosmos itself. "But always for purposes of expansion and growth as a species," Charlie would often say. It was up to the people to use science and knowledge to heal and not to destroy.

If nature decided that the older models should once again walk the Earth, then perhaps they would stray from the misdoings of their notorious past when they destroyed Atlantis, causing the Overseers to slam humankind's celestial portals right in their faces.

"Not all history repeats itself," Charlie would often say. "No one is strong unless he or she was once weak. No one becomes fearless unless he or she was previously afraid—and no civilization could reassemble itself unless it had already been shattered."

Charlie would often tell Brennan that there was one thing he was sure of: that the providence of destiny was always resolute, forever lying in the coils of everyone's genes, as well as the swirls of every galaxy in the universe. Once again, a human renaissance would take place on Earth, full of fresh hopes, new challenges, new wonders, and new fears.

- THE END

About the Author-

Anton Troia was a former Emergency Medical Technician, and studied electronic engineering at DeVry University. He was born and raised in New York City, where he still lives with his two audacious dogs. Anton always found NYC to be a strange place, but he hopes that will change someday.

Anton's stories warn about the dangers of technological progress. His stories take place in future societies that are plagued by technological induced traumas, which affect the ecological, political, social, psychological and physical contours of modern society. Anton's novels are usually dominated by monopolistic corporations, authoritarian governments, and scientific dictatorships and Anton will always delve into the ongoing tug of war between science and ethics.

Anton's themes veer into the paranormal elements as well and he has a knack for seamlessly weaving historical fact and mythology. His thematic focus strongly reflects his personal interest in the paranormal, metaphysics, para-psychology, theology, philosophy, and social commentary--always wrapped in a tapestry of fiction of course. Anton's prose, with his lingering use of adjectives, has a very pleasing 'pulp' style that is evocative of classical golden-age Sci-Fi mixed with Victorian horror literature.

For the official websites of Anton Troia and for The Last Overseer, click-www.antontroia.com. Or you can say hello on the official facebook page at www.facebook.com/AntonTroia. If you enjoyed this novel, please remember to leave a review on Amazon.com! Nothing would make Anton happier. And it would only motivate Anton to continue writing!